Now This

Also by Nancy Star

Up Next

Now This

Nancy Star

POCKET BOOKS
NEW YORK LONDON TORONTO SYDNEY TOKYO SINGAPORE

This book is a work of fiction. Names, characters, places and incidents are products of the author's imagination or are used fictitiously. Any resemblance to actual events or locales or persons, living or dead, is entirely coincidental.

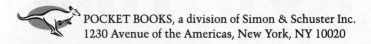

POCKET BOOKS, a division of Simon & Schuster Inc.
1230 Avenue of the Americas, New York, NY 10020

ISBN: 0-671-00895-1

First Pocket Books hardcover printing June 1999

10 9 8 7 6 5 4 3 2 1

Printed in the U.S.A.

To my kind and loving husband, Larry,
and my daughters, Isabelle and Elisabeth

Acknowledgments

My grateful thanks to all my ever-supportive friends and family. A special thank-you to Jessica Keefe for her entertaining, sometimes hilarious, stories of true-life talk show escapades; to Chief Thomas J. Russo who kindly offered his law-enforcement expertise; to Kate Collins for her steady advocacy and careful reading; to Nancy Yost for her consistently sage advice and constant encouragement; to my first and trusted reader, Larry. Finally, to the Oprah producer who years ago called to invite me on, and then off, the Oprah show, thank you for igniting my imagination.

One

IT WAS TOO NOISY. Intolerable. She looked up from her desk to search out the culprits.

There they were. Children—two of them. Her eyes drilled into theirs with a well-practiced look of reproach. They stared back but didn't stop.

It was the little one who was worse, making noises with his nose. He'd probably say he was just breathing, but those weren't breathing noises—at least not any she'd ever heard before. The big one, well it was hard to tell for sure, but it seemed to her as if that awful slurping sound came because he was sucking his own tongue. Unbearable.

The thought flew in: *Why aren't any of the other people who are browsing the shelves bothered? How is it possible to hear the noise of a child sucking his tongue from all the way across the room?* Just as quickly the thought was gone and all she knew was this: she was the one in charge of the children's room of the library and it wasn't going to run amok on her shift.

Who are these ill-behaved monsters? she wanted to know. *Who left them here?*

She banged her blue pen down on the desk. The noise of it resounded in her ears like a cannonball. She burst out laughing.

Eyes looked up out of books with a mixture of surprise and fear. There was absolutely nothing funny going on, especially not to her. But on she laughed, an unstoppable girlish laugh. She stood, thinking, *Maybe fresh air would help,* but before she could get her feet to move, she was back in the wooden chair, looking to the world as if she'd meant to sit down.

When a child's nervous giggle joined her own, her laughter stopped, like that. The room became silent, too silent, even for a library. No pages turned, no spines were pulled off crowded shelves, no keys clacked on the computers' card catalogue.

The small boy started crying, bawling, sobbing so loud it made her shake. She clutched her arms, rubbing goose bumps that weren't there.

"Don't you know how to read?" she heard herself bark. She watched her own arm stretch out, saw it tremble as she pointed to the sign on her desk, its antique font spelling the words QUIET, PLEASE.

The mother appeared before her out of nowhere, as if she'd flown across the room. She was shouting, too, so loud her words were garbled, unintelligible.

". . . three years old," the shrill voice broke through. "Just a child," she continued.

Me? the librarian thought. *I'm just a child?* Rage began percolating in the pit of her stomach. That mother looked awfully familiar. She'd been coming every day, sitting, watching, waiting for an opportunity to disrupt the place. Why? What was she after, anyway?

The child coughed with a force that rattled the windows as well as her brain.

"He's doing it on purpose. You came on purpose," the librarian shouted. Now her teeth were chattering, too.

She didn't notice that all around her people stood gathering their bags, abandoning Eric Carle picture books; skinny chapter books about Amelia Earhart, Michael Jordan, Lenni Lenape Indians, well-worn copies of *Your Big Backyard* magazine.

"I know about you," she yelled, because suddenly it seemed there'd been warning signs she'd been ignoring for days.

"Don't stare at me," she shouted, but she was talking to people's backs now as they scurried out.

Within minutes, she was alone. It was quiet. Finally she could work. She stood up, slowly.

There. This was better. She would shelve books. That was always relaxing. And it needed doing. They were starting to pile up again. It was so easy to get behind.

She was considering why it took so long for her to walk over to the cart today, why her legs were so uncooperative, as if they were on strike, when Mr. James, the manager, came downstairs to see her. He looked sad, as if someone had died.

Later, walking home, she reviewed what he had said. She was scaring people, especially the children. She didn't look well. She should see a doctor, right away. He offered to make the call.

That's when the warning light clicked on. Call whom?

As she walked, half stumbling, the short distance home, her head began to clear. Was it because of the heat? Was she having a relapse of the flu? The thought made her laugh again, but this time she managed to stop before the trilling sound got under her skin.

Already the afternoon's events were becoming hazy, like a dream. Had it been a dream? Was she that unwell? Had Mr. James actually told her she'd scared away a room full of people? But how could he know when he wasn't even there?

It must have been the woman with the boy who told him. Something was wrong with that woman, coming every day to watch her. Something was terribly wrong. Again, she laughed.

When the laugh passed, she considered what to do next. Should she go back and warn Mr. James? But then he hadn't seemed all that concerned about her to begin with. He'd made no move to stop her when she hurried out. Could he have wanted her to go all along? Had he been trying to get rid of her for some time? Had he sent that woman to spy on her?

Yet he'd always seemed so kind. Was she wrong about that, too? What else was she wrong about?

She pondered the dilemma, oblivious to everything else around her.

The account in the newspaper said the engineer saw her crossing the tracks even as the gates were lowering. As soon as he saw her lie down, he blew his whistle and engaged his brakes. She lifted her head, looked right at him and smiled. But she didn't move. By the time the train had stopped, he knew she'd been split into pieces. The only reason he was able to sleep that night was because it seemed so clear to him: she wanted to die.

There were reports that earlier in the day she'd been behaving oddly. She lived alone and had never before exhibited any signs of depression, though witnesses interviewed at the library said that lately she'd appeared unusually agitated.

A relative flew in from out of town to handle the arrangements.

Mr. James told the new librarian that if anyone asked what had happened, she should simply say, "I'm afraid I don't know," and then offer help in locating a book. And that was exactly what she did.

Two

MAY WOKE WITH A START, sat bolt upright in bed, then swung around to see the clock. The numbers seemed to glow brighter than usual, as if to underline the bad news: 5:45, the clock silently announced. She had slept late again.

Untangling her feet from the twisted sheets, she sped to the bathroom and plunged into a not-quite-hot-yet shower. Ignoring the urge to stand still and let the water pound on her as it heated up, she grabbed the shampoo, squirted some on top of her hair, and spread it without bothering to work up a lather. She added two sloppy palmfuls of conditioner on top, then speed-rinsed it all out at once. The faucet handle was pushed in as abruptly as it had been pulled out and the shower, an assault on her body, was over.

It worked. She was wide awake now.

She struggled into black jeans and a black sweatshirt, her day-off clothes, the fabric resisting her still-damp body. A quick comb-through of her hair, a high-velocity brushing of her teeth, and done.

She could do this. She could make the girls their school lunches while simultaneously eating a piece of toast and guzzling coffee, leaving at least one full hour to go through six show folders and a bulging accordion file stuffed with mail. It was 6 A.M. and she was already an hour behind. *Not bad*, she thought, *for a Wednesday.*

She added napkins and stay-fresh freezer packs to one pink and one green lunchbox, then zipped them shut and stuck them inside their matching backpacks.

"Next," she said out loud, grabbing the pile of folders she'd carefully laid out on the kitchen table the night before. She sat down, finished the last of her coffee—cup one—and opened the folder at the top of the stack.

She let out a long sigh. For weeks she'd been pitching this show to her boss, talk-show host Paula Wind, for whom May produced Emmy-quality eye-welling human-interest stories. But neither Paula nor their executive producer, Colleen, liked it. And most annoying of all, neither could articulate why.

Then yesterday word came through the grapevine that Montel was pursuing it, too. It was the usual routine and she shouldn't have been surprised or annoyed that suddenly the show went from iceberg cold to must-have-it hot. But when she called to finally book the guest, he balked, complaining she'd been stringing him along.

May started a familiar list of stage-one things to do to win back his allegiance. *One,* she scribbled. *Send giant gift basket of snack food.* She'd bet anything the way to this guy's heart was through his enormous gut.

"I said, can I wear shorts?" Delia shouted.

May looked up, surprised to find herself eyeball to nose with an exasperated seven-year-old. "Why are you shouting?"

"Sorr-ee," Delia apologized. "The first time I asked, you didn't hear me."

From experience, May knew the first try was probably a quiet utterance from at least two rooms away. But this wasn't the time to lecture on Effective Ways to Be Heard. May checked her watch. "What are you doing up?"

"Mom. It's the first day of school. I always wake up early on the first day of school." She spoke as if she'd been going to school for decades. "Don't worry. I won't bother you. Just tell me, can I wear shorts?"

May had no idea what the outside weather was, but inside, it was humid and hot. "Sure." She put her arms around her daughter's narrow frame, but Delia squirmed out of her hold.

"I have no time for hugs," she said seriously, and headed back to her room to study her wardrobe.

May turned back to her folder.

"Mommy," another voice called out a moment later. "Hurry. Quick. Come here."

She left the folder open on the table as if that would ensure she'd get back to it and jogged upstairs to see what calamity had befallen her five-year-old now. Nothing subtle or mild ever happened to Susie.

"It worked," her younger daughter announced brightly when May arrived in her room. Tousled and sleepy-eyed, she sat up in her bed and gestured toward the pile of stuffed animals that half covered her quilt. She had given the menagerie, a floppy lion, a cougar with one ear sticking up, and a bean-filled jaguar, specific nighttime instructions to protect her from bad dreams.

It didn't take an advanced degree in psychology to figure out why Susie was plagued by nightmares. Ever since returning from her summertime visit to her father's Malibu beach house, she'd been waking herself and everyone else, screaming in the night. But even May couldn't solely blame this on the changes of the past year—her ex-husband Todd moving out to California, then quickly marrying his Barbie-doll–body cutie pie, Chloe. Begrudgingly, even May had to give some credit to last winter's unfortunate "episode" in her office.

That's how everyone referred to it at work—on the rare occasion they referred to it at all—the "episode," as if it were some rerun of classic TV. They never said, "when Wendy, a secretary on *Paula Live,* turned out to be a maniacal killer, stalking producers like May all over town."

Wendy was locked up now for life, but May and Susie were still concocting ever-changing rituals to keep the nightmares at bay. The jungle animal theme had been Susie's idea.

"No bad dreams?" May asked, happy to hear it.

"I don't think so," Susie said, not quite ready to commit to a cure. "At least none that woke me up."

"That means it worked. Your animals scared the bad dreams away."

"Delia, it worked!" Susie called to her sister.

"Now it's my turn to work," May said tentatively. "Just for a few more minutes. And you know what? You girls got up so early, you have plenty of time to play together before you have to get ready for school." She kissed Susie on the top of her sweet shampoo-smelling head and hurried back downstairs, figuring that if she moved fast and stayed focused she could still squeeze in half an hour of catching up.

"You just said you forgot what the dream was," Delia called out to her sister as she pulled on her shorts. "It will probably come back to you later," she continued, loud enough so May could hear without straining. "Tonight. When you're alone. Trying to fall asleep. In the dark."

A moment later, Susie was standing in the kitchen doorway, her arms filled with all the stuffed animals she could carry. She sat down at the table across from May. "I won't bother you," she said. "I just want to be with you."

"Okay," May replied gently and, dubious, turned back to the folder.

"Don't worry. I won't talk to you," Susie told her.

May smiled but kept her eyes on the sheet of paper she was determined to read.

"Do you want me to pour you some more coffee?" Susie offered.

May looked up. "No thank you, sweetie. I'm fine. I just need to finish reading this."

"Okay." There was a millisecond of silence and then: "Is it fun doing work?"

Before May could answer, Delia, dressed in matching purple T-shirt, shorts, and socks, stomped in and sat between them. "If you want some advice," she offered her sister, "kindergarten is very different from pre-K. Very different."

May struggled to ignore them, silently repeating the words she'd so far read over four times.

"What do you mean?" Susie asked.

"Shh," Delia said. "Can't you see Mom's working?"

"I'm being quiet," she insisted. "How is it different?"

"Well," Delia said in an exaggerated half whisper that was harder to ignore than a yell. "They hardly ever let you play with toys. They'll try to convince you the counting bears are toys but they're not."

"Mom," Susie whined. "Delia's scaring me on purpose."

"Delia," May's voice rose in warning.

"What?" Delia wanted to know. "I'm just saying it so she knows. When I went to kindergarten, you and Dad never said."

"Well, I'm not going to kindergarten," Susie announced, and stomped upstairs.

May knew when it was time to give up. She closed the folder and put it on top of the tall "to do" pile, which instantly collapsed, a mountain of papers sliding on to the floor.

"Don't worry, Mom," Delia said. "I'll help you work."

May thought about all the articles she'd ever read about moms working at home. They always seemed to be illustrated with the same photograph: one child—never more than one—quietly playing in a toy-strewn corner while the mom sits at her laptop, the phone at ear, smiling lovingly as she looks on.

Maybe they aren't actually photographs at all, she thought now. *Maybe they're holograms.* Tilt the picture one way and see the mom happily working the phone while alongside her, the young child builds an architecturally stunning Lego cathedral; tilt it another way and see the child screaming for attention, pulling at the mom's sleeve while she desperately struggles to keep her hand over the mouthpiece of the phone so the caller doesn't hear the noise.

"Just tell me what part of your work you want me to do first," Delia said, in her best all-business voice.

"Actually, I'm done," May told her. Then, loud enough so that even someone sitting at the top of the stairs sulking could hear, she called, "Anyone want first-day-of-school chocolate-chip pancakes?"

"I do," Delia yelled over the sound of Susie clomping downstairs.

Without prompting, Susie washed her hands and got out the eggs. It was her turn to crack.

Three

THE BUS STOP was even more chaotic than usual. Even though on days to come the older children would wander down on their own, on this, the first day, they all indulged mothers who tagged along with the open agenda of catching up on a summer's worth of news. Who was moving out of town? Who went back to work full time? Whose homesick kid came home early from camp? Whose teenager was pulled in again for underage drinking?

They didn't see each other much in the summer. Between work, vacations, and weekends spent hiding out in air-conditioning, there wasn't much opportunity. It wasn't like in the winter, when at least there was snow shoveling to bring people together.

The children formed their own chat groups, comparing their brand of vital statistics: who got what notoriously nasty teacher, who made what traveling team, who got to stay up how late the night before, who had what hidden body part pierced?

When the buses finally came, late because the routes had been changed and were once again new, there was a last-minute sorting of children so that no teenagers ended up in the pre-K center, no second-graders got carted off to the middle school by mistake.

May waved as her girls settled into their seats, one of her hands fluttering for each. Delia, at the window, returned the wave with a broad smile. She was the picture of a happy child—a back-to-school Gap ad. Next to her, leaning forward in her seat so she could be sure her mother saw every inch of her mournful gaze, was Susie. The only product she could have advertised was Prozac. Waving sadly, as if the bus was headed toward the penitentiary instead of kindergarten, she clutched the stuffed lion she'd sneaked on board and sniffed it, the scent of its fur, her talisman, working to ward off bad things.

Which bad things? May wondered, and as she continued to wave, she thought about how sad it was that the question was multiple choice.

Stacey nudged her. "You can stop waving now."

May came out of her thoughts and saw the buses were gone. She dropped her arms and joined in the friendly laughter.

"My house at twelve o'clock," Stacey announced. A congenital planner who loved nothing better than organizing people, today Stacey was hosting the First Annual First Day at the Bus Stop Luncheon.

"I still don't know why you couldn't do a breakfast," groused Audrey, a nurse on the pediatric floor of the nearby hospital.

There were murmurings of assent from the other mothers who couldn't make it. But they'd already been through this in June. It was clear then, when Stacey first suggested the idea, that between full–time, part-time, and volunteer work schedules, there was no time that was right for everyone.

"Well, I'm coming," Emily promised. A dedicated mother to five boys, Emily served as the unofficial emergency mom and resource center for the entire bus-stop population. Listed first on everyone's school emergency contact card, she was also the one to call for anything from last-minute bus-stop pickup favors to the phone numbers of the best plumber, pruner, or gutter guy in town.

Marlene would come, too. She had only one child, Jordan, but he required more maintenance than Emily's five put together. Between playground bloody noses, bullying, back talk to the teacher, forgotten homework, failed tests, and bouts of spontaneous crying, Marlene was called into school so often that this year she decided to take a job volunteering for the undesirable job of lunch aide just to save commuting time when the assistant principal made his daily request for her to come in to talk.

She'd make it to Stacey's party, though, because in the volunteer lunch aide lottery, Marlene drew the early shift, the 11:07 meal that school administrators insisted on calling lunch even though all the kids knew it was no more than a midmorning snack. May suspected that even if her shift had conflicted with Stacey's lunch, she'd have found a way to come. Marlene collected gossip like a hungry squirrel going after nuts and she couldn't bear to miss an opportunity like this.

May could attend because months ago she'd promised her children she'd take the first day of school off from work. This meant telling her office she was going out on research.

She didn't like to lie. There was a time when she wouldn't have, no matter what. But self-preservation took precedence now. Colleen, recently promoted to executive producer after May turned down the spot—disinterested in the opportunity to increase her work hours from twenty to thirty a day—had two grown children of her own. But any memory of their dependent youth had either faded or been surgically removed. With equal treatment of both sexes, Colleen greeted all intrusions of family life with stinging disapproval.

The result was that no one working on the show ever had a sick child, a school play to attend, a parent–teacher conference, a hospitalized spouse, or a kindergartner's first day of school. Instead, there were only incidents Colleen could relate to: toothaches and sinus infections—statistically improbable numbers of them—with an occasional bladder infection, varicose vein removal, or dermabrasion thrown in.

At first, May had mistakenly assumed Colleen's notorious antifamily philosophy wouldn't be a problem for her. After all, shortly before their former boss, Gil, decided to take a sabbatical and become a cattle rancher in Montana, he had worked out a solution for May's time-crunch problem: a schedule of three extended days in the office and two days working from home.

What May didn't anticipate—she couldn't have—was the impact this would have on Gil's successor. Having never approved the plan and unable to undo it, Colleen did all that was left. She loathed it, loudly and at a high and constant pitch.

And somehow, consistently, school events—plays, conferences, class parties, class trips, this first and abbreviated day of school—as well as cases of strep throat, stomach flu, and pinkeye, all seemed to fall on one of May's scheduled long days in the office.

Of course there was Sabrieke to cover for her with the kids. With her easygoing nature and her nurse's degree, the Belgian baby-sitter was more than well qualified for surrogate motherhood. But ever since the "episode," ever since Wendy showed up at the house for a visit—the perfect guest except for the cord she fondled in her pocket, the one she planned on wrapping around May's neck—May felt a compelling need to be more present herself.

Her current compromise was occasional fictional fact-finding missions and made-up meetings when necessary. She tried not to feel too guilty about it. After all, she always caught up, staying well into the night whenever she felt she was falling behind. Unfortunately, that was more often than she'd like to admit. Keeping track of every human-interest story that might make a good show for Paula meant playing catch-up was a way of life. There it was: work was May's personal undertow, ready at all times to suck her in and drag her down.

The buses long gone, the women hastily concluded their summer news catch-up and dispersed. May hurried back to the files that sat still undone on her kitchen table.

Settling in front of them, she poured increasingly bitter cups of coffee and, finally free of interruptions, chugged through the work. Her personal goal was always to construct at least a two-hankie show, and her track record was good. She reviewed next week's offerings, getting stuck on the one featuring the girl who raised her twelve siblings while keeping her parents' abandonment a secret from the neighbors. It was still too soft. It needed something else. It needed one of the runaway parents as a guest. She made a note to have her assistant, Charlotte, try tracking them down. Then, temporarily satisfied, she moved on to the accordion folder stuffed with mail.

On top were over two dozen press releases that Charlotte had attempted to prioritize, with mixed results. Quickly, May annotated them further, scribbling *more* across the top of the page if she was intrigued, slashing through the text if the press release didn't appeal at all.

Slash, slash, slash, she sped through the first ten sheets before finally marking one *more.* On that one, Charlotte would call the press contact to ferret out additional details, in this case about the girl who wanted to donate one of her kidneys to save her mother, against her mother's will.

At first May didn't see the note sandwiched between the pile of slick press releases and the bulging stack of viewer mail, people writing in from around the country because they were convinced their story was compelling enough to make the rest of America tune in. But as she lifted up the letters, glancing at the top one—about an autistic boy who learned to talk with the aid of his family's immigrant housekeeper—the typewritten ivory sheet fluttered to the floor. She lifted it and read.

Dear Ms. Morrison,

I need your help.

My aunt Margaret recently died, and when I went through her apartment I found a note on her bedside table. The note had your name and the *Paula Live* show number on it.

Aunt Margaret and I were very close, but because she lived in Boynton, Pennsylvania, and I live in Rochester, New York, I don't know much about her private life. I do know the police are wrong about her death. They've told me it was suicide. This cannot be true. Aunt Margaret was happy and content, not someone who would ever harm herself.

What I want to know from you is why she was coming on your show. I am currently locked in a fight with the insurance company over the cause of her death and if she had some secret she was planning on sharing with the world, I need to know it now.

I also have not ruled out the possibility that her death was caused by foul play.

Can you help me?

Yours,
Matthew Harris

May read the letter twice, wishing that in the second reading it would morph into a request for Paula's head shot or a pair of tickets to the show. It looked innocent enough, but to May's practiced eyes, it was trouble. These kinds of things, letters from upset relatives, were always trouble.

She considered forwarding the letter directly to the legal department but decided to have Charlotte check the pending files first. The name *Margaret Harris* was unfamiliar, but then May chased dozens of show leads a day. She had an entire drawer of pending Pendaflex folders on shows in various stages of development, some thick and nearly ready to go, some with nothing more than a ripped-out newspaper item or a business card with a name scribbled on it that might—but more often would not—pan out to be an idea worth pursuing.

She glanced at the clock, then checked her watch. It didn't seem possible, but half the morning had already vanished. She called into her voice mail and listened to twenty-two messages, then transferred over to Charlotte to have her follow up on the dozen that were important.

She was done and signing off when Charlotte added that a Matthew Harris had just called, for the second time. May stared at his letter, still at the top of the pile. She knew it. Trouble.

"Start checking the files," she told her diligent assistant, and explained about the letter. "Put him off if he calls again. Tell him I'm out of the office. Tell him I'm out of the country. I don't want to talk to him until we find out why we were talking to his aunt."

She got off the phone, dragged her black leather carryall into the living room, and dumped out the ten annotated magazines and three nonfiction books that were on her agenda to peruse this morning for possible show ideas. She finished the magazines and checked her watch before breaking open the first book.

How did it happen? The morning was gone.

She stopped in the bathroom and ran a brush through her hair. *Good enough,* she told her reflection.

She'd promised Stacey she'd get there early to help set up. As usual, she was late.

Four

Stacey's husband Scott swung open the door. He was dressed in the same chinos and polo shirt combo he always wore, but the bag swung over his shoulder let May know that today he was headed out for the golf course. *Right,* May thought. *It's Wednesday; doctors' day off.*

"Maysie!" he greeted her, and she stiffened. It was a habit Scott shared with Stacey, anointing everyone with a nickname. When Stacey did it, it was endearing. Scott just made her want to gag.

"Neem leaf extract," he said, staring at the flush of May's transparent skin. "Not only will your complexion improve but"—he leaned closer and winked—"insects absolutely hate the stuff. Next summer, we're going to market a line of neem soft-gels as a mosquito repellent. Brilliant idea, right? An antimosquito pill? We're brilliant, right?" he shouted toward the street.

May turned and saw Nick Ellman, the junior partner in Scott's complementary medicine practice, a nineties mix of doling out herbs and antibiotics. He got out of his pale blue Isuzu trooper, slammed the door, and waved.

May moved her hand spastically in reply. She always

felt awkward around Nick, at least ever since Stacey had insisted on setting them up.

The blind double date happened shortly after Stacey moved onto the block, shortly after the "episode," shortly after May had begun dating Paul O'Donnell, the New York City police detective whose case she'd solved.

At the time, she hadn't yet realized how serious her feelings for Paul had become. But sitting across from Nick, struggling to find anything he said even mildly interesting, she realized her heart was no longer open for business.

It wasn't that Nick wasn't nice or smart or good looking, either. He was, even if his dark brown hair was always a little too long and his shirt collar stood away from his neck as if it didn't exactly fit. He had the distracted look of someone perennially preoccupied, a quality May found attractive—one she shared. She just found it more attractive in Paul O'Donnell.

She'd 'fessed up that night when Nick walked her to the door, explaining she was more involved than she'd realized and apologizing for wasting his time.

"It was an enjoyable waste," he told her kindly, and asked, "Any point in trying to compete with NYPD Blue?"

"I don't think so," she'd answered plainly.

They'd been awkward acquaintances ever since.

"Still engaged?" Nick teased her now.

"Congratulations," Scott boomed, extending his hand. "Stacey didn't tell me you were engaged."

"I'm not," May protested as Stacey, her damp hair admitting she'd snuck in a late-morning swim, came out of the house. Rosie, her athletic yellow Lab, stopped alongside her and shook hard, spraying them all with water.

"Haven't you taught Rosie to towel off yet?" Nick asked as he wiped his glasses dry.

"I've been trying. *Rosie, towel,*" Stacey commanded. The dog obediently sat beside her and looked up with adoring eyes. "Come on, girl. If you don't learn how to towel off, you can't go swimming with me anymore." She squatted next to the dog and gave her a vigorous rubdown, unintentionally showing off her swimmer's body, her broad shoulders, muscular arms, her well-defined thighs and calves.

The pool—the only one on the street—was the reason Stacey decided to buy their house. The move was her decision, born the day she woke up in a hotel room with no idea what city she was in, what day it was, which of her accounting firm clients she was servicing, or why. She'd shut the door on her hotel room minibar, zipped up her Hartmann carry-on, and flown home to announce her decision that she was hopping off the partner track to become a telecommuter.

It wasn't a crowd-pleasing moment at work, where her boss had been grooming her for partner for years, or at home, where downsizing was the inevitable consequence.

Things will work out for the best, she promised her family as they packed up and moved out of their brick Tudor mansion on the other side of town to what she described as a real family block. It wasn't long after they met that May discovered the central truth of Stacey's life: things really did work out for the best for her.

The two women met at the bus stop the day after the Blums moved in. It didn't take them long to discover they were both workaholics in recovery. The chemistry was instant. They became fast friends.

"Stace," Scott said now, turning to his wife. "You didn't tell me Maysie was engaged."

"I'm not engaged," May repeated. "I'm involved."

"Involved is okay," Nick said, smiling. "Involved means there's hope."

"Forget it, Nickster. There's no hope," Stacey told him as if May weren't there. "We've been out with them. They're much too well behaved to actually maul each other in public, but honest to god, they give off heat."

May laughed. She couldn't vouch for the ambient temperature when she and Paul were together, but being with him almost always made her feel as if she were running a temperature. And because she had paper-thin skin, her body temperature was announced by flushed cheeks that were as clear to the world as a pair of billboards.

"Let's see if we can give off steam, too," Scott said and grabbed Stacey to plant a long, hard kiss on her lips.

Nick and May stood awkwardly, waiting for their friends to pull apart.

"Did we do it?" Scott asked, with his usual gosh-darn eagerness.

"My glasses are fogged up," Nick told him, and after giving him a what-a-man pat on the back, climbed into his Trooper. Scott hopped in on the passenger side and they drove off, laughing.

"What a couple of characters," Stacey said as she led May inside.

May refrained from commenting. Scott's boyish charm was lost on her, a fact she knew enough to keep to herself.

They settled themselves on the living-room couch, before a coffee table spread with platters of smoked fish, rolls, cheeses, and carefully cut up fruit. Rosie lay on the floor beside them, panting.

"You have the only dog in America who can be trusted not to steal food off the table."

Stacey laughed and glanced at Rosie. The dog was shivering. "The pool wasn't that cold, was it, girl?" Then she shook off a chill herself. Rosie got up and moved closer, stretching her neck across Stacey's leg.

"The perfect dog," May said admiringly, stating the fact without envy, "to go with the perfect life. The nearly perfect life," she corrected herself. "This is for you." She handed over the book she'd been holding, *Girl Power: How to Raise Them with Respect.*

"I hear it's good," May said, even though she hadn't read it herself. She usually skimmed only a fraction of the dozens of books she received each week from publishers eager to have their authors appear on *Paula Live*. She knew, though—through osmosis, it sometimes seemed—which ones were good, which ones would climb the best-seller lists even though they weren't good, and which ones would appeal to which friends.

She knew, for example, that Stacey's fourteen-year-old daughter was going through a rough bout of hormonal rage. Sophie, who did occasional weekend baby-sitting when Sabrieke was off with her boyfriend Manu, was always polite and well mannered with May, but things were different at home. It had hit bottom over the summer when one morning Sophie woke up and announced to her father that she wished her mother would drop dead. Hours of tears and slammed doors later, the emotional barometer was registering improved, but wounds remained sore, if not oozing.

"You can never have too many books about living with teenage girls," Stacey observed now, reaching for May's offering, which somehow she missed and dropped on top of May's foot. "Sorry, I've been the queen of the klutzes all day," she said, and quickly picked up the book and laid it on the table. Then she lifted the carton that sat at her feet and steadied the box on her lap. "Let's see if there's anything in here for clumsiness." She lifted out one bottle after another, studying the labels. "These are the new ones," she said referring to Scott's most recent business venture, a line of his own herbal remedies that he and Nick were selling on the internet. "Is there anything you need? You want to try some of that neem leaf extract?"

The doorbell saved May from answering. She wasn't much of a believer in this stuff. She was more a one-multivitamin-and-a-calcium-pill-when-she-thought-of-it kind of person. But to be polite, she accepted the gifts Stacey offered, the bottles turning into dust collectors on her dresser top.

"What do you have there?" Marlene asked as she strode into the room, drawn by the sound of jiggling pills. She was an actual patient of Scott's and a bonafide believer in the alternative road to health.

"It's the *new* product line Scotto's selling," Stacey explained. This was their second outing distributing on the internet. Their first was a disaster, their supplier unreliable. They'd lost a lot of money. A lawsuit had been threatened, the old merchandise boxed up and stored in the garage while they awaited resolution.

"Is Scott going to offer that melatonin stuff?" Emily asked, wandering in last. "Carter's going to Japan next month and I told him if he can find some melatonin and take it, maybe he won't be so jet-lagged when he gets back."

"Listen up, Donna Reed," Marlene said to her hopelessly out-of-touch neighbor. "Melatonin is about as new as green tea. You can get it at any drugstore. You can get it at the supermarket, for god's sake. Anyway, what's Carter going to Japan for?" But before Emily could answer, Marlene thought of another question and turned to May. "What's the update on the show?"

May knew it would come up, but she'd thought it would take at least a full minute to weave it into the conversation.

It had been Emily Cooper, May's next-door neighbor, who first suggested the idea for the show. That in itself was nothing new. The Coopers made dozens of suggestions a month. Carter left ideas on her voice mail, sent clippings to her office by legal courier, stuffed printouts of obscure internet stories through her front-door mail slot—all for the chance to boast to fellow lawyers and clients that he'd found a hot idea for his hotshot producer neighbor, May Morrison.

May acknowledged each idea, no matter the heat, with the same mild thank-you, and then proceeded to put it out of her mind. Other people's experience had taught her that seductive though it was, doing a show about or even suggested by a friend or relative was nothing but trouble. She'd told Carter more than once that Paula had a strict policy against producers accepting ideas from friends. But to Carter, who believed giving up was one of the seven warning signs of impotence, that was nothing more than a dare.

Then Stacey went away for a return trip to a longevity spa in Arizona, run by some of Scott's friends. The spa promised to put its clients on the path to extended—which Stacey explained was the next best thing to eternal—youth. Several months after she was back, Emily marveled aloud that Stacey looked noticeably younger.

"You should do a show on that place," she'd told May. "You should put Stacey on it."

May had uttered her usual mild thank-you and then tried to put it out of her head. But the idea stuck, hovering at the edge of her consciousness for weeks. When a month later Stacey confided that several other friends who'd been to the spa with her over the course of the past few years had experienced changes that were even more dramatic, May gave up her resistance and the show was born. Hector, her favorite cameraman, was booked to shoot his second video for the story, closeups of Stacey's face, in a few weeks.

It had been a hard sell to Colleen, the former health and self-help producer who remained possessive of the beat. But Paula loved it. Barely a whisper past thirty, she was already convinced she was at the precipice of a steep decline. Every day, she came to work with a list of new, hip, young talk-show hosts who were chipping away at the cracks in some of her smaller markets. A spa offering not only shiatsu massages, underwater seaweed soaks, magnetic power boosts, and plastic surgery but also a large staff of physicians armed with hormone cocktails that they guaranteed would extend or restore energy and vigor spoke directly to her current fear—that her biological clock was ticking so loudly her at-home audience could hear it.

Emily eagerly jumped in, dragging May out of her thoughts. "Oh, May, I promised Carter I'd ask you when the show is going to tape. He wants to take the day off and be an audience member. He can do that, right? The kids want to come, too. We told them they can skip school that day. That's okay with you, right?"

"You can't let Carter come," Stacey protested. "Or your kids. If I see anyone in the audience I know, I'll get totally tongue-tied."

May knew it. She shouldn't have done it. Putting a friend on the show was verboten, combustible, suicidal, a plain old bad idea. But it was too far along to back out now—now that Paula loved it.

"You'll be fine," May assured Stacey, and hoped she was speaking the truth.

Marlene leaned over to check out the box of pills on the floor. She pulled out a bottle and examined the label. "What's this? Scott never mentioned this."

Stacey took a look. "That's gotu kola. From the new line. They've got all the latest Asian remedies now. Kukicha tea, ginseng, gotu kola."

"But what is it?" Marlene sounded miffed that she didn't know.

"It's for better concentration. Do you want some? We got an enormous shipment. The warehouse renovations aren't done yet, so now Scott's started storing boxes in our bedroom. I told him, 'If you bring home one more box, I'm going to start giving this stuff away.' And he did, so I am. What would you like? Licorice root? Milk thistle? Vitex? Scotto says vitex is great for PMS."

"I cannot wait for this show," Emily enthused. "You are going to be great."

Stacey moaned, then handed another bottle to May. "Here. Take this for stress. Two in the morning before you eat."

"See?" Emily said. "You're an expert. You could open your own practice. Maybe they'll spin you off into a show of your own."

"I think you're spinning off into a world of your own," Marlene muttered and opened her palm. "I have stress. I'll take that."

Stacey handed over a bottle and Rosie gallumphed over and stuck her snout in Marlene's hand.

"My God," Marlene said. "Even Rosie wants something for stress."

"It's licorice root she's looking for," Stacey explained. "She loves the smell. You know, we could all learn a lot from animals. Her body needs something that's in the licorice root, so, plain and simple, it smells good to her. They're so smart that way. Unlike us, they listen to their instincts."

"See what I mean?" Emily said. "You explained that so well."

"If I listened to *my* instincts," Stacey went on, "I would not do this show."

"Come on. You have to," Emily said. "For the block."

"How about this," May interjected, to end the public discussion. "Don't commit to it yet. I'll call Hector and beg him to come over this week to finish up the video." Convincing a potential guest to come aboard came as easily as breathing to May. "Then we'll take it one stage at a time, baby steps, and see how it goes. Once we groove it up a little more, we can decide. You'll decide."

"If you don't want to do it, I'll do it," Marlene offered. "I didn't go to your spa, but I take all those herbs every day."

"No. Stacey will do it," Emily said firmly. "It will be so much fun."

"Having someone come over to the house to take close-ups of my wrinkles doesn't sound like much fun to me."

"You want to talk about wrinkles?" Marlene asked.

While Marlene took them on an unsolicited tour of her own, May excused herself to call in to work. From Stacey's kitchen phone she checked her voice mail—nineteen messages—left a to-do list on Charlotte's machine, and then called over to Hector, who said he was overcommitted and solidly booked but for her he'd find room on Friday.

She smiled as she hung up. It had been totally unnecessary for her to feel guilty for lying to Colleen about how she was going to spend her day. When would she accept that there was no distinction between her work life and her home life anymore?

She returned to her friends and they all got down to the business of eating lunch. When it was time to leave, Stacey followed her to the door and stuffed the bottle of valerian, which May had left on the coffee table by accident on purpose, in May's purse.

"Two a day. You really should start supplementing. I promise you'll feel better."

Even though she was a natural skeptic, in the face of Stacey's ever-growing vigor May paused to wonder if maybe she should rethink this. Maybe she should start taking exactly whatever it was Stacey was taking. Her friend was a convincing argument for the stuff.

"I'll go on your program if you'll come on mine," May tried.

"We'll see," Stacey said.

"I hate *we'll see. We'll see* always turns out to be *no.*"

"Maybe, then," Stacey said. "That's my best offer."

"Okay, I'll take the *maybe.*" And she hurried home before her friend could change her mind again.

Five

SHE WAS HALFWAY THROUGH listening to her twelve voice-mail messages—up to the one from fellow *Paula Live* producer Margery Riegle warning her that Colleen was on the warpath looking for her—when she glanced up at the clock.

"Damn," she shot out as she slammed down the phone. She bolted out of the house and ran all the way around the block, getting to the corner just as the first bus groaned to a stop.

No time for mother gossip now. The girls poured off, chanting a chorus of first-day-of-school traumas and triumphs.

"The principal even made an announcement over the loudspeaker," Delia explained in her tale of how her lunch-box went missing and then mysteriously turned up in her backpack again.

"I was the only one in my kindergarten class who could tie my own shoes," Susie boasted.

"That's because they're Velcro," Delia reminded her.

"Where's Sabrieke?" Susie asked quickly. Her anxiety was generalizing so that now, even a pleasant change in routine, such as May's being at the bus stop to greet her, made her feel uncomfortable and worried that something was wrong.

"Sabrieke has the day off," May explained, "because I'm home. She'll put you on the bus tomorrow morning."

"Oh." The day-off explanation never satisfied Susie, who still believed Sabrieke took care of her because she loved her, not because it was a job. "Did Sabrieke explain that you're supposed to get us a special snack because it's the first day of school? That's what she did last year."

May instantly adjusted her plans for the afternoon—calling Colleen would have to wait a bit longer. "How did you know I was planning to take you out for ice cream?"

First stop was for three orders of triple scoops that threatened to roll off their cones but never did. Next came school-supply shopping. Delia's teacher asked for only one spiral notebook and a pencil case, but somehow they ended up leaving the store with four trappers, a ream of tracing paper, and two sets of scented markers.

By the time they got home, there were an additional dozen voice-mail messages on May's machine, including three from Colleen.

"Can I save them for you?" Delia offered.

"You saved them last time," Susie complained. "I never get to save them." She got close to May and tried to whisper so that her sister wouldn't hear. "Will you show me what to do?"

"If you're not old enough to remember Mommy's code, then you're not old enough to save her voice mail," Delia explained like a crabby schoolteacher, and then, after glancing at her mother's scowling face, sent herself to her room. To show solidarity with the oppressed, Susie stomped off after her.

May knew they'd be back within a phone call, so first she dialed the unfamiliar number that Paul had left.

"O'Donnell," he answered on the first ring.

"Hi. Where are you?"

"Sitting in front of this big ugly metal thing—I think it's called a desk—that's covered with flat white things that have little black marks all over them—I think they're called paper."

"So you finally got a desk job."

"Yup. Once a year I like to stop by to find out who's been spending their afternoons snoozing in their seats while I'm out risking my limbs. How's everything over there? The girls make it through the first day of reform school?"

"Far as I know, nobody got paddled," she told him. "How about the boys? Did they do okay?"

May was careful not to kid around too much about Paul's three sons. It was just a little over two years since his wife passed away, which was also when he found out how tough a job it was to raise the boys. It was one of his few regrets, that he hadn't realized it until Eileen was gone. He admitted it without shame: he wasn't much of a Mr. Mom. The only reason his life wasn't a total disaster was that his sister Bridget, who lived just down the street, volunteered to take on the care of the boys while he was out getting bad guys off the street. An emergency room nurse, she changed her hours to work the graveyard shift and slept while the boys were in school.

If it weren't for her, he'd have probably married the first attractive woman to come his way. According to Bridget, the line was a long one; neighborhood women had started fighting over veal roasts at the supermarket meat department the day after the funeral, to see who would bring over the first meal.

"When am I going to see you?" he asked May.

"Now is good," she replied.

"Now is a foot and a half of paperwork I was supposed to do the last three times I saw you."

"Later is good."

"Later is the boys. I have to be home for dinner so I can hear what bad teachers they got. What about tomorrow? Can we have breakfast?"

A call-waiting click on May's line interrupted them.

"Got to get that?" Paul asked. He hated call waiting and she knew it.

"No," she said and reminded herself there was no urgent need to answer; the girls were safely home, so it wasn't going to be the school nurse calling in with a head-lice report.

"What time are you getting in to work?" he asked.

A second click sounded in her ear, and this time a host of crises flooded her mind: Sabrieke with a flat tire, her mother in a prone position on the floor, Stacey's kids locked out of the house and needing her spare key.

"I promise I'll be right back," she told Paul, then depressed the receiver. "Hello?"

"May I speak to May Morrison, please?" The husky voice was polite but unfamiliar.

"Who is this?" she asked.

"Is this Mrs. Morrison?"

"Is this a sales call?"

"No. Goodness, no. My name is Matthew Harris." And then, because she didn't respond, he added, "I wrote you a letter about my Aunt Margaret. I hope you don't mind that I called you at home."

It wasn't the first time she'd ever felt the tiny hairs on her arm stand up—as if she needed them to warn her. "Mr. Harris," she forced herself to say even though her throat felt tight and her teeth seemed determined to keep her mouth clenched shut. "How did you get this number?" Charlotte knew better than to give out her home number and May wasn't in the book.

"I really am sorry to bother you," he went on, ignoring her question. "I tried you at your office several times, but your secretary wouldn't put me through. I need your help."

"If you want my help," she told him stiffly, "call me at work. I am not available now." She slammed down the phone.

It rang a moment later. She yanked the receiver to her ear. "Listen carefully, because this will be your only warning. If you ever call me at home again, I will immediately call the police and file a report that you are harassing me. Do you understand?"

"This *is* the police and who the hell is harassing you?"

"Oh," May said, and after she let her shoulders fall away from her ears, where they had risen, she told Paul about Matthew Harris and his letter.

"What are you going to do about it?"

She laughed because he was so transparent. "Why don't you just say what you mean?" She lowered her voice and did her best Detective O'Donnell imitation. "'Don't go looking for trouble, May. Leave that to the professionals.'"

Paul raised his voice an octave in reply, "'Don't worry, dear. I'm done with all that snooping around. From now on, I'm leaving the getting rid of the bad guys to you.'" His voice dropped back to its normal register as he snapped at someone, "What the hell are you looking at?"

May laughed again.

"I've got to go," Paul said. "If I stay on the phone with you any more, I'm going to end up sent down to the nut case in Counseling. That's the big thing this week. Another wacko cop killed himself and now they've got a quota to fill of cops going to Counseling."

"Now that would be terrible," she kidded him.

"It would be," he told her. "I might get cured of my obsession with you. What time can I see you tomorrow?"

"Now," she tried a second time.

He was silent, thinking. Then he said, "I wish I could come over after the boys go to bed. But most nights, Brad goes to sleep later than me. How late will you be up?"

"At least until eight-thirty," she told him, and it wasn't much of an exaggeration. "Come anyway," she said. "Pick the lock and come on in."

She meant it as a joke. Their relationship wasn't at that point yet, the point where he'd let himself in, come up the stairs, crawl into bed to join her. In fact, they hadn't yet managed to spend a single night together. The last time they'd planned for it, when the girls were visiting Todd in Malibu, Bridget took the boys to her house for a sleepover. But then Sean—or was it Brad?—had hit his head against the sharp corner of Bridget's TV table and Paul ended up fleeing to the emergency room where he stayed until dawn.

"Put your alarm on, May," he told her now, his voice devoid of humor. "Think of Matthew Harris and put your alarm on."

"I'll lock up tight" was her best offer. Ever since May had installed her alarm, Sabrieke had kept setting it off, shocking May out of the pleasant middle-of-the-night-coma stage of sleep. The last time it screamed on and woke her up, it was just before 3 A.M. and it had taken her over two hours to fall back. That was two hours of reliving the horror of Wendy's pursuit and the pain of Todd's declaration of Chloe-love, which she hated to admit still hurt. That's when she decided she'd prefer to take her chances with the alarm system off. After all, it wasn't like she didn't lock the doors.

Of course Sabrieke, who couldn't seem to remember the alarm code, was also iffy about locking doors. She claimed it was because in her small home town in Belgium, only thieves locked their doors, to keep the police out. She'd promised, though—after May threatened a curfew—to remember to lock it from then on.

"How did that guy get your number anyway?" Paul asked, not ready to let it go.

"Charlotte gave it to him," she said, so he wouldn't worry. She thought because he couldn't see the hairs on her arms rising up at the question that he didn't know how much the call had unnerved her.

She was wrong. He heard the tension in her answer as clear as if she'd shouted it out. He jotted down the name *Matthew Harris* on a piece of paper. He'd check into the guy later. May might not like it, but then again, there was no reason she even had to know.

Six

STANDING AT THE KITCHEN DOOR, Stacey flicked on the backyard lights and watched the inch of fog that sat like a cloud, skimming the pool surface. The pool heater had been on all day, bringing the temperature up one degree an hour. She set it like that this time of year because once the sun went down, the autumn chill returned full force. Sometimes the result was this, a heavy mist, worthy of a Broadway production of *Brigadoon.*

"Cool," Sophie said, coming up behind her. It was her ultimate compliment.

Not for the first time, Stacey considered inviting her daughter to join her for a swim. It was one of the few activities they could do side by side without fighting. Sophie had tried to argue in the pool only once but had found it too frustrating. Water went in her mouth and her mother couldn't hear, so what was the point?

But when Sophie wandered off, Morgan came into the kitchen to fix herself a cup of tea and Stacey thought, no, she wouldn't ask Sophie to swim. Not with Morgan hovering about, shadowing her as usual. If Sophie swam, she'd have to invite Morgan, too, or else endure hours of hurt and martyrdom.

Again, she thought about broaching the subject of letting Morgan go. It was definitely time. Sophie hadn't needed a baby-sitter for years. In fact—when did this happen?—she was now old enough to take care of her brother on those afternoons when Stacey had to go into New York.

If only Mikey wasn't so attached to Morgan; if only at the beginning they hadn't treated her quite so much like a family member. Mikey was going to have a hard time of it when Stacey explained that his second big sister—Morgan's words—had been fired.

Scotto, too, she thought suddenly. *When did he get so attached to Morgan?* she wondered.

She put the problem out of her mind and let Rosie follow her outside. The dog sat obediently, watching her as she dropped her terry robe onto the iron lawn chair, then dove in. Rosie followed, paddling alongside for two laps before struggling out and lying down at the edge of the far end of the pool to watch her swim the rest.

She enjoyed Rosie's company, especially on a night like this, with mist hovering over the water and the backyard cloaked in darkness. It wasn't that she was afraid. It was more that she was aware of how oblivious she was when she swam, oblivious to everything around her. She wasn't like May, anticipating lunatics lurking in the bushes. But she knew that if there ever was a stranger in the shadows, if there ever was someone watching, she would never hear it, she would never know. In the pool, she was cocooned, deaf, blind.

It was exactly why swimming relaxed her so, why it freed her mind. She figured things out in the pool. Concentrating on nothing more than the pressure of the water on her face and the sensation of her arms stretching up, around, and back, hearing no noise but the sound of her own steady breathing, she could sort and solve.

From an early age, the children knew—never bother Mommy when she's swimming. When Sophie was little, she would sit right at the very edge—it was in their old backyard, the pool with the Italian cerulean tiles and the deep end with a diving board—until one day Stacey forbade her, worried that she was so enveloped by the silence of the water she'd even be oblivious to that, the sound of her daughter slipping in.

Bleeding only, she instructed them when they were older. *Disturb me for nothing less than blood.*

Morgan never got it. As if responding to some unexpressed disapproval for the entire idea of a swimming pool, she managed to find constant cause to interrupt Stacey's daily exercise. That's why lately Stacey had taken to slipping out when she figured Morgan was most likely to be otherwise engaged. This evening, for example, she'd waited until Morgan prepared her tea and got on the phone with Sabrieke.

Stroke, stroke, breathe. Stroke, stroke, breathe. Flip under the water and back.

Tonight, she thought, it would be Morgan on her mind. It would be Morgan's future in the family that she'd worked out.

Stroke, stroke, breathe. Stroke, stroke, breathe.

She was wrong. Another—an unexpected—thought came, and it was this: May's show didn't sit right.

Stroke, stroke, breathe. Stroke, stroke, breathe.

No one would understand, least of all May. To Maysie, appearing on *Paula Live* seemed as natural as a milk run to the store. To their friends, it was a prize, like winning the lottery.

Stroke, stroke, breathe. Stroke, stroke, breathe.

It was clear now, clear as water. She didn't want to do it. There was no upside, except that her kids thought it was cool. And then there was Scotto. Was that the problem?

Stroke, stroke, breathe. Stroke, stroke, breathe.

He couldn't wait for her to do it. The timing was terrific for him. All she had to do was mention the new line of herbal remedies and his business would reverberate with the aftershock.

Stroke, stroke, breathe. Stroke, stroke, breathe.

That was it. That was it exactly. They had spent hours discussing the plug—rehearsing what she would say, strategizing when she should say it. She didn't have the heart at the time to admit to him that she didn't want to do it. She didn't want to be worrying, *Is it time? Should I mention his products now or will there be a better opening in a minute? Will May get in trouble if I do it? Will Scott be disappointed if I don't?*

Stroke. Stroke. Breathe. Stroke. Stroke. Breathe.

No. She didn't want to. It was simple as that. *Be honest,* she told herself and then thought, *It's not so simple. Scott will be more than disappointed. He'll be mad.*

Bam. She reared up out of the pool, her pounding head breaking through the water. Her hand reached for the concrete wall, grabbing the spot where, at her fast swimmer's speed, she'd just rammed her head.

Why did she do that? She knew this pool. She knew its length. She knew when the wall was coming. She swam with her goggles on, with her eyes wide open. But even if her eyes had been closed, she could always sense the wall. She'd been swimming laps for so long she boasted, and truly believed, she could swim in her sleep.

Rosie barked as Stacey touched her own head. It was aching, a dull throbbing pain. She found her scalp, felt for blood, checked her fingertips. There was none. She dunked under, let the water wash over her hair, hoping it would help stay the pain, but it didn't. She lifted herself out onto the small concrete deck, toweling off quickly.

Her body shook with a chill as she hurried into the house, Rosie following her. *Damn, I feel dizzy.* Had she been this dizzy before? Had she banged her head because she was dizzy and hadn't noticed it or was she dizzy because she banged her head?

She found Morgan in the kitchen, standing in front of the open refrigerator now, staring inside, waiting for the right food to announce itself. Stacey opened the freezer, took out an ice tray, dumped its contents in the sink, and threw several stuck-together cubes into a plastic bag. Gingerly, she held the bag to the tender spot, all under Morgan's watchful eyes.

"You all right?" the baby-sitter asked, her interest mild.

Stacey settled into a chair. "I'm fine." She had to be fine. There was still too much left of the evening for her not to be fine. "I just banged my head."

"How did you manage that?"

"I'm not sure. One minute I was swimming and then, bam. I hit the side of the pool."

"Must have been lost in thought again. And what were you daydreaming about this time?" Morgan had a small-town nose for the scent of gossip.

Stacey knew this and threw her a crumb. "Going on *Paula Live.*"

"Right. That. It's so American, isn't it? A rejuvenation spa. I mean, at home we'd rather live for a short while but enjoy it. Smoke lots of cigarettes, drink ourselves silly, and take as much sun as our holiday permits. Here, you're all so completely concerned about living longer, you don't even notice you're thoroughly miserable all the time. I was discussing this with my friend the other day. We were trying to figure out—maybe you can tell me—exactly how do they make fat-free cheese? I mean, what do they put in it?"

Stacey watched her baby-sitter take a leftover baked potato out of the fridge, slice it open, and ladle several tablespoons of mayonnaise on top. The sight of the gelatinous spread made her queasy.

"I'm going upstairs to lie down for a minute," she said, leaving the cheese mystery unsolved. "Where's Sophie?"

"With Michael," Morgan said. "On the computer. Again."

Stacey didn't bother pursuing why Morgan thought this was a bad thing. She just trudged upstairs to her room. If the children were engaged with the computer and Scott wouldn't be home for another hour, she could sneak in a nap and no one would even notice. For no reason she understood, the thought struck her as funny. She fell asleep with a smile still stuck on her face.

When she woke, she was groggy, confused. She shot out of bed, didn't realize one leg was completely asleep, and fell hard on the waxed oak floor.

"You all right?" It was Scott running up the stairs.

She quickly stood, shook her leg awake, glanced at the clock, saw she'd been sleeping for over three hours. "When did you get home?" she asked when her husband arrived at her bedside.

He looked at her, a funny, unfamiliar expression in his eyes. "Don't you remember? I woke you up. We had an entire conversation about it."

She could read the worry etched on his forehead. "I do," she assured him, because now that he mentioned it, she did remember, sort of.

"I checked your bump. You said you felt warm. Remember?"

"Yes," she said as it came back to her, the pain as Scott pressed on her head, the cool slightly alcohol taste of the thermometer in her mouth. "I told you I wasn't sick," she reported. "I said I was just tired." Her body, her legs, felt heavy as stone. She lay back down on the covers.

"Rest," Scott told her.

"I'm fine," she protested without conviction.

"Stay there," he said. He hurried downstairs to retrieve his large brown bag of medicinal tricks.

By the time he was back, she had fallen asleep again, but he woke her, as he did every hour through the night, shining his small penlight into her eyes to make sure she hadn't suffered a concussion. Each time he did, she came fully alert, answering all his questions in a plain, lucid manner. But in the morning, she remembered none of it, didn't understand why she woke feeling drowsy, stumbling as she got out of bed.

When the children left for school, she sat on the bottom step of the hall staircase and wept. *What's wrong with me?* she asked the air once the surge of sorrow passed.

Her hand trembled as she dialed May's number, but it was too late. Her friend had already left for work.

It's probably just some flu, she told herself. The flu could make you feel weepy and dazed. Shaking off a chill, she climbed back upstairs and into bed to sleep off whatever it was she had.

Seven

THE EARLY-MORNING SUN reflecting off the limestone building across the street cast May's office in a rosy glow that matched her overheated cheeks. The TV, tuned to a morning talk show, droned in the background. As usual, May clutched the remote in her hand, periodically clicking from one show to another, one tenth of her attention fixed on who had what guest, what guest was good, what story stunk.

"You checked everywhere?" she asked Charlotte, now that her breathing was back to normal. Her assistant had knocked the wind completely out of her when she popped up like a jack-in-the-box from behind May's desk. Charlotte wasn't getting paid well enough for this, she thought, for coming in at 7 A.M. to rifle through her folders and scare her out of her shoes.

"I went through everything on my desk, everything on top of your desk, and I'm almost through with your drawers," Charlotte reported. "If Aunt Margaret is not in 'W through Z,' I give up. Personally I think this Matthew Harris is a nut case."

May clicked the remote and they both glanced at the screen.

"Oh my God. Look at their guest," Charlotte screamed, and then started laughing. "Is that who I think it is?"

They both listened, then began laughing together. "Yes indeed," May said. "That's our own Betty LeMieux. One of my personal hall-of-famers." The woman had been on *Paula Live* several weeks before for a show on binge eating. No one had expected or escaped the bounty of her projectile vomiting.

"I had to throw away the shoes I wore that day," Charlotte recalled. "They were my favorite shoes. Taupe suede. Unwashable."

"Don't feel bad," May said. "She had to throw hers away, too. And I had to lend her mine, remember?"

"How could I forget? I'm the one who had to go to Bergdorf's to buy you a new pair after she wore yours home."

"Well, I couldn't very well shop at Bergdorf's barefoot." May raised both her feet, showing off her black square-heeled pumps. "Nice choice, Charlotte." She looked back at the screen. "Betty looks like she's going to keep her breakfast down today. Boring segment. Next." She switched to another show. Nothing great. She refocused on the problem at hand.

"Matthew Harris is definitely a nut case. Unfortunately, he's *my* nut case. How do you think he got my home number?"

"Not from me, I can tell you that."

"Probably Henry," May said. She was convinced her former assistant, now the show's most junior producer, had majored in *All About Eve* at whatever pseudocollege he'd bought his way into and talked his way out of. She'd fallen for his "teach me everything; you're so smart" routine in a big way. Only later did she realize that her Rolodex was now his Rolodex, her contacts permanently implanted on his hard drive.

She could deal with that. In her profession, ambition was a given, something to be respected. What irked her about Henry, aside from that over half of what he stole he deleted from her files, was that he took himself so seriously.

"I bet anything some of our folders are in his drawers," Charlotte said, echoing her thoughts. "Or in Hun's filing cabinet."

It was May who'd dubbed Henry's ambitious young assistant, Dawn, Hun because that's what Dawn, though half her age, insisted on calling May.

"You cannot go through Hun's filing cabinet," May told her, "even though we know she wouldn't hesitate to go through ours. We won't sink that low."

Charlotte, disappointed, slumped.

"Especially because at last week's bookers' meeting Henry complained that unauthorized persons have been going through his things."

"I have not," Charlotte defended herself.

"I know that," May reassured her. "But Henry's convinced someone is. After the meeting was over, I saw him in his office setting traps like a Hardy boy, tying loops of thread between his desk drawer knobs."

As if on cue, Henry knocked and poked his head in, Dawn at his side.

"If Colleen's looking for us, can you tell her we went shopping. To dress a guest," he added before May could make a snide remark.

"What guest?" May asked.

"The homeless man who turned out to be a cellist," Henry said.

"Don't waste your time," May told him. "I called the guy—Bernard—last week. He talked gibberish for ten minutes and then told me God wants him to do only one show and someone else got to him first."

"I got to him first. He's doing Paula. For me."

May stared, her cheeks coloring. "Henry, I'm the human-interest producer. If that guy comes on, he's mine."

"Colleen says no one can own a beat," he said defensively. "Besides, Bernie's old-fashioned. He doesn't believe girls should work. His words," he added quickly, and he fled, Dawn behind him.

May smiled at Charlotte. "Let's rethink this."

She slid open her bottom drawer, looking through emergency pantyhose, spare lipstick, Band-Aids, tea bags, nail polish to stop runs. Finally she found what she was looking for: a stash of hotel matchbook-size sewing kits. She held one up to show Charlotte.

"He used black thread," she said. "While you're glancing—which is allowed—at the top of Henry's desk, I will carefully be replacing Miss Muffet's black thread with this." She pointed to a tiny skein of burgundy-colored thread. "If accused, I will gladly take a lie detector test and swear under oath the truth, that I never opened any of his drawers."

While May carefully replaced Henry's thread with her own, Charlotte perused—but didn't touch—his desk. It was futile. Anticipating roving eyes, he'd put all papers away under lock and key.

Carefully pocketing the evidence—scissors, black thread, red thread snips—May returned to her office. She glanced at the TV, at the photogenic man talking to Montel. "I've seen him on five shows this week," she muttered. "Another professional guest."

As if she were wired to a switch, she flicked back on her focus, turning it toward a last-minute review of her show, up next, on children who'd rescued their parents.

Almost immediately, Charlotte buzzed, interrupting. "It's Matthew Harris on the phone. He insists he needs to meet with you."

This was really starting to bug May. It was interfering with her focus, threatening the carefully constructed balancing act she used to keep all parts of her life running smoothly. And today, like every other day, she had no spare time. Her guests would be arriving within the hour. She dug around her leather satchel until she came out with the letter she'd stuck in the zipper compartment. *Good,* she thought as she reread it. He'd mentioned his aunt's hometown—Boynton, Pennsylvania.

"I'm not here," she told Charlotte. "Get rid of him. Then call the local paper in Boynton, Pennsylvania, and have them send us a copy of the issue with Margaret Harris's obituary."

She disconnected Charlotte, flicked the remote to quickly check in on five other shows, and then phoned the Boynton, Pennsylvania, police.

"I'd like to speak to someone about the death of Margaret Harris," she explained to one, then another, then a third disinterested voice.

Finally, she reached someone who wanted to know why she was asking. She rushed through the relevant details, the letter from the nephew, the unproductive search through the *Paula Live* pending files, the nephew's persistent calls.

"I can't find any record that she was going to be coming on the show, but I thought maybe I could at least offer him some fresh information about his aunt's death. He's quite upset," she explained.

"I can't tell you a thing about the deceased, ma'am," the policeman reported. "But I can tell you this. I've met the nephew on multiple occasions. And I believe him to be a seriously disturbed individual."

"Oh," she said.

Margery, her long-legged colleague, walked into her office, sat across from her desk, and passed her a piece of paper, which May glanced at—it was Charlotte's handwriting—but didn't read.

"My advice to you," the cop said, "is to put as much distance between this guy and yourself as you can manage. He's a persistent son of a bitch. I got him out of Boynton, but it wasn't easy."

May hung up the phone and her friend observed in her sugary drawl, "Lordy, lord, you look whiter than a Klansman. What's the matter, sugar? Did you just find out your detective has another wife and a second set of kids squirreled away somewhere?"

May shook her head, then quickly scanned the note Margery had handed her.

"Now you've gone downright green. Sugar, what's wrong?"

"Not much," May said as she stood. "Other than that I've just been warned that the gentleman currently sitting in reception"—she held up Charlotte's note, exhibit A—"who says he won't leave until I see him, is a dangerous individual, at least according to the policeman who ran him out of town."

"Phew," Margery said. "For a second, I thought it was something serious."

Eight

HE WAS BUSHY; that was her first impression. He was like a thriving bush that needed an acute seasonal cutting back. Everything was overgrown: his wavy hair, his thick eyebrows, his coal-black beard. He was a hairy bush holding on to a briefcase as if it contained his life's savings in cash.

On the way to reception, May had gathered a small army around her. Margery, Charlotte, Carl from the mailroom because he was big, and at the last minute, Colleen. Colleen wasn't big, but she was mean—plus, she carried Mace in her purse. Margery had a gun, which would have been better, but she had left it at home.

Fanatic guests and overzealous fans were an irritation for everyone in their business, so once she filled them in, her colleagues were happy to help her out, relieved that this time they weren't the ones being pursued.

By the time they burst through the double glass doors, they had their story straight. They let Linda introduce Matthew Harris, as if there was any doubt who were May's guests, the young children and the parents whom they'd rescued, and who, sitting off by himself with his briefcase on his lap, was the lunatic they were going to get rid of fast.

They led him to the canning room, a small office right off the lobby so named not only because it was where the popular soda machine was housed but because it was the infamous site of one of Paula's mass firings. It was also the place where show crashers—viewers desperate to be guests, imposing fans, unwanted job applicants, and about-to-be-dumped boyfriends—were taken before getting kicked out.

Matthew followed them into the small windowless room. No one sat down. Matthew put his briefcase on one of the folding chairs.

May extended her hand. "How nice to finally meet you," she said.

He looked taken aback. He'd come to fight his way in. He didn't expect this.

"Nice to meet you, too," he said, his dark eyes widening from a nervous squint into a tick-prone stare.

"I am so terribly sorry to hear about the passing of your aunt," Margery said. She stretched out her hand and gave him one of her most forceful shakes, the kind she reserved for violent criminal guests. "I had a favorite aunt once who passed. My friends were surprised at how hard I took it. Everyone kept saying, 'She was only your aunt. It's not like your father died.' What the hell did they know? When my father died, I opened six bottles of champagne to celebrate."

"She doesn't get along very well with men," Colleen explained.

Matthew's eyes darted about as he addressed the crowd. "I appreciate your taking the time to see me. I'm just trying to find out why my aunt was coming on your show." He turned to May and said defensively, "That's all," as if she'd been accusing him of something else.

"What did your aunt do for a living anyway?" Carl asked. May had carefully prepped him on exactly what she wanted him to say. She'd gone over it several times but you never knew, with Carl.

"A librarian," Matthew said quietly. "A children's—"

"Librarian," May said over his voice, as if she knew all along what his aunt did for a living. As if she knew exactly why Margaret Harris had been scheduled for the show. "Matthew, I'm so sorry to tell you this, but the show your aunt was going to come on—it's been canceled."

"What was it?" Matthew asked. "What is it about? What was wrong with her?"

"Heavens, Lordy, sugar," Margery said, moving closer to the doorway. "Nothing was wrong with her."

"No." May forced out a laugh. "It's just that Paula Wind, our host, her mother was a librarian. So she wanted to do a show about librarians and others like them, in the helping professions."

"Like nurses," Margery added.

"And postmen," Carl offered, digressing from his script. The three women glared at him and he closed his mouth.

Colleen lurched forward and grabbed Matthew's hand. "Thank you for coming by. Your aunt must have been swell."

"We're terribly sorry about what happened," May said, taking hold of his arm to guide him toward the door. "I wish we could have been some help."

Confused, Matthew Harris let himself be led to the elevators, where the women and Carl all waved good-bye. Then they ducked back inside the canning room and collapsed in a laughing, knee-slapping huddle.

Colleen was the first to stop. Then Carl noticed. Within a moment, they were all silent, staring at the figure of Matthew Harris standing, glaring, in the doorway.

"I left my briefcase," Matthew said, pointing to the chair. "Care to share the joke?" His eyes were back to their original narrow slits.

"Here you go, sugar," Margery said picking up his briefcase and carrying it as she strode back through the reception area to the elevators. "Now don't go thinking we were laughing about you. It's got nothing to do with you."

"It was something I said," Carl jumped in. "About the mail. A postal joke. You know. Going postal."

"I don't think so," Matthew said, challenging him.

The elevator bell rang, a light came on, a set of doors opened.

"Good luck," May said quietly. Her colleagues close together now, slowly moved as one in a horseshoe shape around Matthew Harris so that he had no choice but to board the empty elevator.

He muttered something. The doors closed. The elevator went down.

"What did he say?" May asked no one in particular.

The youngest of May's guests, a redheaded, freckle-faced parent rescuer who sat at the end of the couch, closest to the elevator, quietly answered. "He'll be back. He said he'll be back. Is the man coming on the show, too?"

"Hush now," her mother said, slapping her hard on the wrist. "You sit and wait. I'm sure they'll be calling for us soon." The woman smiled pleasantly and then, engaging no smiles in return, went back to flipping through the pages of a month-old *People* magazine.

Nine

MAY CHECKED IN with Sabrieke, heard that the girls got off to school fine, not counting Delia's complaint that her elbow hurt and Susie's that her tongue felt itchy, and then raced off to the green room to meet with her young guests so they could go over the bullet-point questions Paula would use if conversation began to flag.

Charlotte had done her homework. The green room was stocked with rock-candy lollipops, Pez, sheets of candy buttons, and a large bowl of Hershey's Kisses. More important were the caffeine-rich liters of Jolt and Mountain Dew. Sugar and caffeine were must-haves for kid guests, who had the potential to turn mute in front of the camera if not sufficiently stimulated.

That wasn't a problem this time. While the grown-ups were getting their skin tone smoothed out in Makeup, the three kid guests were quickly ripping the foil off of two pounds of chocolate Kisses and scarfing them down. Unfortunately, neither Charlotte nor May knew that the little blond boy who dragged his mother out of the river was allergic to chocolate.

His lips swelled up in the middle of the first segment. When his mother noticed she let out an audible "oh my God." Paula immediately turned to the camera, donned her most brilliant smile, and segued into "What does a seven-year-old do to save her mother from carbon monoxide poisoning? Find out when we come back," and the show cut to break. Twenty minutes of ice and antihistamine later, the swelling receded. After a forty-minute delay, most of it spent feeding the boy tall glasses of Jolt to perk him up, the show went on.

"At least he didn't die," May pointed out during the cranky postmortem Paula quickly convened in her dressing room. "And otherwise the show went well. That freckle-cheeked little girl will be fielding offers to do commercials by the end of the day."

Begrudgingly Paula conceded the girl was cute. "But what does that do for me other than make me look old in comparison? And speaking of old," she went on, the meeting derailing further, "how the hell is that rejuvenation story coming along?"

It was noon when May got back to her office, condolences offered along the way by production staff members who had heard the news of Paula's latest tantrum. She put it out of her head—no time for wallowing—and moved on. She caught Hector the cameraman just as he was leaving for a shoot.

"You are so lucky," Hector told her and she didn't bother to correct him. "My afternoon appointment just canceled. I can meet you in New Jersey at three."

This time she did feel lucky. She phoned Stacey and caught her on the way out. "I can get the cameraman at your house at three."

Stacey hesitated. "I don't know."

"Let him come. You can always back out later."

A few more nudges and Stacey agreed. The afternoon shoot was set; the morning show was done. May relaxed into perusing her three-page morning call sheet and was deciding whom to call next when Linda, their dark-haired fashion-plate receptionist, knocked on the door.

"Charlotte's relieving me at the desk for a second. And there's a gentleman waiting for you in reception."

She buzzed Charlotte at the front desk, and her assistant whispered, "You'd better get out here now."

On the way, May picked up Margery, who suggested taking Frank along this time. Frank, Paula's giant personal bodyguard, agreed to come, since any threat to an employee could become a threat to Paula. At the last minute, they snagged Carl again as he went on his hourly rounds to pick up the mail. The human wall, Frank and Carl, burst through the double doors first, Margery and May invisible behind them.

"Who's the guy who's here for Ms. Morrison?" Frank bellowed.

"That would me," said a voice May recognized.

"What's your business with her?" Frank barked, his jowls inflating as if he were a threatened blowfish.

May struggled to squeeze past him. "Frank," she said. "You remember Detective O'Donnell, don't you?"

Frank blinked as he struggled to think.

Paul stretched out his hand. "Haven't seen you for a while, Frank. How's the personal-protection business going?"

"Fine," Frank muttered, and May couldn't decide if his green pallor came because he'd been caught off guard or because he was disappointed that another melee had been averted. It wasn't a mystery that Frank thought Paula needed a bodyguard the way a lion needed a pocketknife.

"You got some trouble here?" Paul asked after her loyal troops had slunk off and they were alone, not counting Linda, who was back at her post, refreshing her makeup.

But May didn't want to get into it here. She didn't want to get into it at all. "How about lunch?"

They ducked down to the coffee shop across the street.

"Quiet morning?" she asked him as they settled into a booth.

"You going to make me guess what was going on up there, or you going to tell me straight out?"

"We had a little problem with a visitor. Nothing we couldn't handle." More than that would make him worry. It was hard enough a struggle keeping her own worries at bay. She didn't need to compound it with his. She picked up the menu and hoped his line of questioning was over.

"So Matthew Harris showed up after all."

His gut was so good it sometimes scared her.

"I got rid of him," she said, skipping to the end of the incident. "He's gone. It's over."

"He's trouble," Paul warned.

"Why do you say that? Just because he got run out of town by some cops?"

His eyes softened and she knew—they might have different sources, but they'd both ended up with the same information.

"Are you sure you got rid of him? Sometimes guys like that stick around like gum on a shoe. Are you really sure?"

She nodded but didn't speak. If she spoke, he would have heard the slight tremor in her voice. It wouldn't have been something Todd would have ever picked up on, but Paul would have heard it as surely as if she had screamed it out loud, that no, she wasn't sure at all.

"Promise me, if he drops by again, you'll call me, not the Mod Squad upstairs. Will you?"

She looked at him, at his deep-set gray eyes that were drilling into her, at his long fingers that gripped the edge of the Formica table as if he already had his fingers around Matthew Harris's neck.

"Yes," she said, and then, because he was too good at his job for her to resist, "Don't you want to know what really happened to his aunt?"

"No. It doesn't concern me. So long as it doesn't concern you. And if Mr. Harris is truly gone for good, it doesn't concern you. Does it?"

"No. Of course not. I'm just curious," she said, and then regretted it when she saw that her curiosity translated instantly into three deep lines that spread across Paul's brow.

"You want me to look into it for you?" He released one hand from the table and stretched it out toward her. She put her hand into his, let him close his long fingers around it. It shocked her still, how even this, holding hands, sent heat whipping up her legs.

"No," she told him. "I'm putting Matthew and Margaret Harris out of my head." But she didn't meet his eyes, because then he would see it wasn't as simple as that. Matthew and his aunt were ignoring her cerebral eviction notice. Even now she couldn't completely stop ruminating about them, wondering exactly how best to find out more.

It was like a riddle, something Susie would come home with from school. *Why did the dead woman write down my name?*

I don't know. Why? was always the answer to Susie's riddles, and the same response came to her now. *I don't know. Why?*

"You feel okay?" Paul asked.

"I'm fine." She touched her cheek with her free hand. It felt warm. Paul reached across the small table and touched the other side of her face. His fingers felt even warmer on her skin. They both smiled, nervous, like teenagers.

The waitress stopped by to take their orders, tuna on pita for May. Cheeseburger deluxe, extra cheese, for Paul.

"Bridget asked me again if you're coming to the barbecue," he said once the waitress was gone.

"What did you tell her?" She'd managed to avoid committing to his family barbecue so far, but soon she'd have to give him an answer. And how could she tell him the truth? It wasn't that she didn't want to meet his relatives. It was that she didn't want them to meet her. As far as she could tell, everyone in his family over the age of eighteen was either a cop, a firefighter, a nursery-school teacher, or an emergency room nurse. What would they make of her?

"Bridget told me not to ask you anymore. She said I'm pushing you too hard. 'Don't go so fast' she told me." He opened his palms as if to ask, *Is she right? Should I be going slower?*

May leaned forward in her seat. "I agree," she whispered. "We have to stop meeting this way. It's not decent."

He joined her in a tentative laugh. Between their combined five kids, May's job, and Paul's beeper, their time together—intimate time—plain didn't exist. As if they were a pair of hormonally charged teenagers, they'd been reduced to kissing on the couch, then jumping apart at the sound of descending footsteps. If her memory served her, at least when she was a teenager her parents had the good sense to go up to bed early when a boy came calling and to stay there until the front door slammed shut. Delia, on the other hand, descended at regular intervals to ask them what they were doing, why they were sitting so close, why Paul's hair looked so messy. May wondered if this was why she felt overheated when she was with him, why her cheeks felt hot enough to smolder.

The waitress slid their plates before them, but it was too late. Paul was already checking his beeper, reaching for his wallet, slipping the waitress a twenty.

"I'm sorry," he told May, standing up. "Seems as though some bad guy decided I'm not hungry."

She stood, too, and they came together in the aisle for a quick peck good-bye, which turned into a long, hard kiss that neither of them wanted to end. Even when his gun pressed against her rib cage like an oversize belt buckle, hurting her, she didn't pull away.

"Hot soup," the waitress called out because they were blocking her way.

Reluctantly, they pulled apart.

"When will you be home?" Paul asked her quietly as they walked to the street. He stroked her hair, gathering it tightly in his hand as if that would satisfy him.

"I'll be at Stacey's with a cameraman at three, so I should be home early."

"I'll call you later," he said, and then added, "Be careful." He didn't bother to laugh at the absurdity, the wishful thinking of it when she replied, "I always am."

Ten

SCOTT OPENED THE DOOR just as Hector and May concluded their last-minute consultation on exactly what they would shoot.

"I have it," Scott said, pointing at the straining buttons on the cameraman's extra-large shirt. "The perfect solution for you."

"I didn't even know I had a problem," Hector said.

"You're right. You have no problem. Not anymore. Not if you start now. Soy. It's a totally natural weight-loss miracle. Why anyone ever took fen-phen is beyond me. Soy. Twice a day. I promise you, the weight will ask to come off."

"Really?" Hector's dark eyes shined brighter. Those who knew him well could always tell when Hector was feigning sincerity because his barely discernible Spanish accent became suddenly exaggerated. "Only twice a day?" His English turned as thick as Mexican coffee.

May was about to intercede, but Stacey arrived at the doorway just in time.

"You don't need soy," she said, offering Hector her hand, drawing him into the house. Rosie circled them, walking between their legs as if she were a cat. "My husband loves to tease. You're perfect as you are."

Hector took her small hand in his and kissed it. "A pleasure to see you again," he said. "And you, too," he said with a slight bow to the dog.

Stacey smiled, showing off her dimples. Hector instinctively turned to Scott, who wore the baffled look of a man unused to people's taking offense.

"Don't worry," the cameraman said, his accent once again turning to sludge. "Kissing the hand of a beautiful woman is the custom of my country."

"What country is he from?" Scott whispered to May as soon as Hector turned his attention back to Stacey.

"The Bronx," she reported, then quickly took control before the situation completely deteriorated. "Hector, how about setting up in here this time?" She led him into the living room.

"Definitely. This room is my favorite. It's beautiful," he said, admiring the mix of antiques, folk art, and unassuming furniture Stacey had purchased in department store sweeps. "Of course, it's not as beautiful as you are," Hector continued, still pouring it on.

"She has wonderful style, my wife does," Scott said, and although the words were complimentary, his tone spoke of ownership, with a hint of warning.

May glanced over at Stacey. Her friend's smile was tight and forced. Had she just walked in on a fight? Something was wrong.

"Exactly where in the Bronx did you grow up?" Scott asked Hector.

"I'll tell you, amigo, if you help me move this furniture so I can set up my lights."

Taking advantage of the men's forced camaraderie, May led Stacey into the kitchen. "You look like crap," she told her friend, once they were alone.

"Good. I think people should look how they feel."

"What's wrong?"

"I was in bed all day yesterday with the flu."

That explained the dark circles under her eyes and her sallow complexion. May took a step back, away from the bubble of their commingled air. She didn't have an opening for the flu this year.

"But it's not that."

May's antennas stood up, on full alert. Again, she silently cursed herself for buying into the idea of this show. But it was too late now. Now Paula was married to it, on her back about it every day. Now Colleen, who didn't even like it, had started to badger her. Now the task was simply this: get it done fast and make it the best it could be.

"I don't want to back out," Stacey told her quietly. "I know you've invested a lot of time in this. But I think it's a bad idea for me to do it." She glanced through the doorway, and for a moment they remained silent, listening to the rumble of men's voices tinged with stiff jocularity. "I mean, I think you should do it. Just not with me."

And May thought, *That's it. That's perfect. We'll take the show out of the friendship. I'll regroove the spin, round up new guests. Perfect.*

"There's only one problem," Stacey went on.

May looked at her and waited to hear it.

"I'm having some trouble with my friends—the ones we talked about bringing on the show."

"No problem," May said. "I can find other guests." And she thought, with relief, *That would be better.*

"No. They were all really excited about coming on the show. I want you to talk to them." She sat down at her kitchen table and gazed out through the window to her backyard. She looked completely defeated.

"Then what's the problem?"

"I'm not sure," Stacey admitted. "I tried calling everyone last night and again this morning, but I got nowhere. Risa's sick," she explained. "Greta doesn't answer her phone, and Toni hung up on me—I can't even tell you why."

"Then forget about them. I can find other guests. These things happen all the time. I'm actually very good at rescuing shows that fall apart."

"I don't understand why Toni is so mad at me. And I don't know why Greta's machine doesn't pick up."

"These things happen. Don't worry about it. Are you sure you're okay?" Stacey was not herself. Other people might worry—May worried all the time—but it wasn't Stacey's style. "Do you want me to send Hector away?"

"Why would you do that?" Scott asked, his voice startling her. She hadn't heard him come into the room.

"I don't feel well," Stacey explained. "I'm not a hundred percent myself yet. I think we should reschedule."

Okay, May thought. *She hasn't told Scott she doesn't want to do* Paula Live *yet.* This show was quickly losing its groove. "I think that's a good idea," she said, going along with her friend. "We'll reschedule."

"Come on, Stace," Scott protested. "Hect came all this way. It's a shame to waste the opportunity just because you're a little under the weather." He directed the next to May. "This won't take long, will it?" Before she could answer, he turned back to his wife. "When it's done, you can go right up to bed. I'll be your slave for the rest of the day. Dinner in bed, whatever you want. But Hect's here. He's ready. What do you say?"

May tried to like Scott, but he grated on her. Even his doting seemed self-serving to her.

"I've got a blazing headache," Stacey told him, and she began to wring her hands. Her agitation was infectious. Now May felt anxious, too.

Scott tried again. "Come on. You can do this. Let's just get it over with." He took her by the elbow and led her into the living room, where Hector had just finished rearranging his white reflective umbrellas.

"We don't have to do this today," May protested.

"Nonsense," Scott said. "Hector didn't come all the way out here to admire the furnishings. Did you, Hect?"

"It's Hect*or,*" the cameraman said, and then glanced at May to gauge the problem. "Everything copacetic here or what?"

"She doesn't feel well," May explained. "I think we should reschedule."

"Hold on," Scott insisted. "Hect. Hect*or,*" he said, correcting himself. "Can you shoot fast?"

"Is ten minutes fast?" He glanced at May, not sure if this was the right answer.

There was no right answer, other than that she wanted to get this over with without a confrontation.

"Let's do it, then," Scott said, taking over the shoot. "Let's go for it."

Stacey glanced at May to see if she was going to give away their conversation. But May said nothing. She'd let this happen, let Hector shoot, then toss the film in the garbage later. It wouldn't be the first time she'd done that.

"Okay," Hector said. "Any chance I can get your dog at your feet? She's a nice-looking dog."

"Rosie," Scott called, eager to please.

Stacey stopped him. "Leave her alone, honey. She doesn't feel well today, either." She went on, as if someone had asked her to. "I called the vet this morning. She said dogs don't catch the flu from humans. But I guess no one told Rosie that." The idea of it cracked her up. Hector laughed along agreeably.

"Come on, Stace. Rosie's not too sick to lie at your feet."

Hector interjected, "Don't bother. It's okay. It's fine without the dog."

They settled into an uneasy silence. Hector quickly adjusted his lights until he was satisfied and then he started filming, first a long shot of Stacey in the chair, then close-ups of her eyes, her mouth, her profile.

In less than ten minutes, they were done.

"Beautiful," Hector announced. "How do you feel?"

"Happy I didn't throw up," Stacey managed to say.

Hector laughed at what he thought was a joke, then silently began collapsing his tripod, loading his video equipment into his camera bags.

Scott cornered May in the hallway. "This is going to be a totally friendly piece, right?"

"Of course." There was no point telling him the discussion was academic. She'd let Stacey break the news to him later, when they were alone.

"Because I'm not letting Stacey get involved in some negative story about complementary medicine."

"He doesn't mean 'letting,'" Stacey interrupted, and then, realizing an opening had presented itself, she grabbed it. "But you know what, honey? I kind of agree with you. I think it would be better if I didn't do the show."

"What do you mean?" he asked, his voice panicky.

"Sweetheart," Hector interrupted, swinging his heavy bags over his shoulders. "To my great dismay and disappointment, we are completely done." He took Stacey's hand, and kissed it again. Looking at Scott, he asked, "Soybeans, right, amigo?"

Scott nodded, even though he was no longer interested in Hector's health.

"I've got to talk to Greta," Stacey said as soon as Hector disappeared down her front path.

Scott swung around. "What you've got to do is go upstairs and get some well-deserved rest."

"I've got to talk to Greta," Stacey said to May, as if May could make it happen. "I've got to call back Toni."

"She's got to go to bed now," Scott insisted.

"Feel better," May told her friend as she headed for the door.

"She will," Scott answered for his wife.

As soon as May walked out into the September night, she began breathing deeply, as if she'd been holding her breath the whole time she was inside, holding her breath against bad air. Something was gnawing at her, making her gut do somersaults. *What?*

She pushed the nagging worry out of her mind and hurried home.

Eleven

THE SUN SAT LOW IN THE SKY. The street was deserted. A cool wind whipped down May's shirt, raising goose bumps on her arms. She hurried to her house, key in hand, but she didn't need it. The door wasn't locked.

Damn. Sabrieke forgot again.

May stormed into the dark house calling, "Sabrieke? Sabrieke, you left the door unlocked."

Silence answered.

Why are all the lights off? she wondered, flicking them on as she walked. She put down her oversize bag on the hardwood floor and called again.

"Hello?" Her voice echoed through the underfurnished rooms, to no reply.

She checked her watch. It was 5:30. Everyone should be home. Delia should be at the kitchen table doing her homework. Susie, with no work to do, should be finding creative ways to annoy her. Sabrieke should be getting dinner started, mediating arguments. Where were they?

A rush of adrenaline flooded through her. She flashed on an image of Wendy, twirling a phone cord in her hand, backing her up against the wall.

"No," May shouted out, squeezing her eyes shut as if

that would make the picture go away. The sound of her voice startled her.

"Girls?" She quickly climbed the stairs. "Delia? Susie? Sabrieke?" No reply.

She hurried through the second-floor bedrooms, through Delia's, Susie's, hers, then into the bathroom, then up the stairs to Sabrieke's room. Panic was hitting now, bringing with it the sensation that she wasn't really here, that she was watching this happen to someone else.

"Sabrieke?" Her voice brought her back, back to the doorway of her au pair's empty room, where she stared at an unmade bed, at clothes piled on the floor as if Sabrieke had dressed and left, in a hurry.

A note, she thought. *Maybe there's a note.* She raced down to the kitchen and checked the cluttered table—none there—then strode across the room to the small kitchen desk where the answering machine was flashing on and off, two messages. She pressed the playback button and waited, with clenched teeth.

"Ms. Morrison," came the polite male voice. "It's Matthew Harris here. You can reach me at the following number—"

She fast-forwarded to the next.

"It's me," came Stacey's voice. "I need to speak to you. There's something. . ."

May didn't stop to listen. Only the basement was left. She swung open the door and climbed slowly down.

Why hadn't she moved the switch to the top of the stairs like her contractor, Pete, had recommended? At the time, she was so tired of pouring money into the house, she'd just said no, drawing the line there, at moving the light switch to the top of the stairs. *How dumb,* she thought now as she walked down in the dark into the cool, damp basement.

"Surprise," shouted a pile of voices, and the light switched on in the small semifinished area Pete had renovated for her as a playroom.

Delia and Susie popped out from behind the old wicker couch. Paul's sons, Brad, Sean, and John, tumbled out of the nook that Pete had reclaimed from an old utility closet.

"Did it work?" Sean asked. "Did we scare her?"

"Yup," Susie said, proud of herself. "I think so."

"Hello," Sabrieke greeted her, emerging from the laundry room with a full basket of newly washed and neatly folded clothes. "I didn't hear you come in."

The children were in a jumble on the floor, laughing at their success.

"You didn't lock the door," May snapped. "Anyone could have walked in and you wouldn't have even known."

"Dinner has arrived," Paul called from the top of the stairs, the scent of Chinese food wafting down.

"Uh oh," Delia said. "I think she's mad. Mom, are you mad?"

"If you have a problem with the door, you should speak to your boyfriend," an affronted Sabrieke advised as she slipped past May to bring the laundry upstairs.

"Why are you mad?" Susie wanted to know. "We were just surprising you."

May couldn't explain it to them, how her mind always zipped to the worst now, how the nightmares that plagued Susie while she slept came to May while she was wide awake.

"Come on," Paul called down. "Am I supposed to eat all these spareribs myself, or am I going to get some help?"

A stampede of children crushed up the narrow staircase.

"I am going to go out now with Manu," Sabrieke told May in the kitchen. Then her voice softened. She wasn't wired to stay mad for long. "You are all right?"

"Yes," May said. "I'm sorry for getting mad at you." She didn't bother describing what fears the unlocked door had unleashed. Even after the events of the past year, Sabrieke still believed the world was safe.

Paul picked up on her mood right away. He didn't yet know what, but he knew something was wrong.

"You feeling all right?" he asked quietly as they stood side by side pulling bowls, plates, and serving spoons out of cupboards.

"I'm fine," she said, too quickly.

"What's wrong?" He wouldn't give up now. Not when he could practically smell her discomfort. "Are you mad that I just dropped by?"

The phone rang and she grabbed it.

"It's me," Stacey's voice came on in a hurry. "Didn't you get my message?"

"I have to call you back," she told her friend. "I'm in the middle of something here."

"Oh," Stacey said, disappointed. "Okay. But don't forget. It's important." She giggled, then added, "I don't mean to laugh. There's nothing funny about it at all."

"I'll call you back," May said again, and hung up the phone.

"I thought I would surprise you," Paul went on to explain. "I figured you didn't expect to see me again today. I thought it would be a good surprise."

"It was."

"How am I supposed to tell?"

She took a breath and blurted it out, how when she came home the door was unlocked. How she thought something awful had happened. How she yelled at Sabrieke, who told her Paul had been the one to leave the door open. "That's all," she said when she was done.

"Damn," he said. "I told Brad to lock up behind me. Brad O'Donnell," he called out.

"Never mind. It's okay," May said. She didn't want this, fighting with his kids.

Brad came into the room, knowing by the tone of his dad's voice it wasn't going to be about an allowance increase. He looked scared.

May stiffened. She'd never seen how Paul, the cop, handled such situations.

"Did you forget to lock the front door when I went out to pick up dinner?"

Brad hung his head, thinking about it, then looked up and met his father's eyes. "I guess . . . maybe . . . probably . . . yeah."

"You guess, maybe, probably, yeah," his father echoed his words.

He changed his story. "I did. Yes. But I didn't mean to," came the rest of the confession. "I just forgot."

"Don't you think an apology is in order?"

The boy turned to May. Even in the short time since she'd met him, he'd sprouted like a beanpole. He would be tall, like his father, with the same gray eyes and lanky frame. He would be breaking hearts soon, this boy.

"I'm sorry Mrs. Morrison," Brad said politely.

"Please call me May," she asked gently, not for the first time.

Brad checked with a glance to his father to be sure he wouldn't be showing any disrespect. His father nodded, and he began again. "I'm sorry, May. Sometimes I forget that stuff. I won't let it happen here again."

"See that it doesn't, son," Paul said, then tousled his boy's hair and knocked twice on his head as if to make extra sure the promise would stick. "Now go tell everyone that dinner is on the table."

"Okay, Pop," Brad said and fled the room.

Paul looked at May and smiled. He knew she'd been watching him carefully. "So. How did I do?"

"A plus," she told him, and put down the egg rolls. Paul moved closer and they melted into each other's arms. May wished the layers of their clothes, of their lives, would melt away as well.

Delia, racing to the dinner table ready to eat, stopped when she saw the embrace. "Yuck," she proclaimed.

May and Paul sprung apart, laughing—and hot.

Twelve

SHE WOKE WITH THE THOUGHT *Will Paul and I ever be alone?* The question stayed with her, percolating in the background noise of her mind, as she rode the bus into work.

In the spring, she had thought the summer would be the time. The girls would be away for a few weeks and *Paula Live* would be on hiatus. But it didn't work out that way. First, there was the night Paul's son went to the emergency room, and almost immediately after that, there was the tall blonde discovered in Central Park with her throat cut. It was the second of what would turn out to be six stalking-slashings that dominated the tabloids to the end of August, when Paul finally caught the bastard.

But now she was wondering. Maybe it wasn't as simple as that their children and their work stole all their time. Maybe between the sweet memory of Paul's late wife, Eileen, and the shadow of Todd's bad behavior, even when their children and jobs deserted them, they weren't alone.

Not now, she told herself, feeling the cumulative weight of a pile of out-of-town papers on her lap. She turned her focus back to them, scanning the *Miami Herald,* tearing out two graphs from their metro section and then moving on to the *Atlanta Constitution.*

When she got into the office, it was still early enough that the reception area was deserted. Flicking on the lights, she stuck her security card in the slot next to the double glass doors, just as she'd done hundreds of times before. Except lately she felt uncomfortable being the only one in. She preferred when some other early bird was there, too, someone who didn't crave commiserating over coffee but who would hear if something happened.

What? What is going to happen? She shook off the irritating fear as if she were shooing away a fly. That was last year. That was over.

She sat down at her desk and flicked on the TV, scanning the early-morning talk shows, stopping to pay attention to the one about the babies switched at birth. She scribbled a note for Charlotte to follow up on that, then turned on the overnight viewer calls. The end-of-show placard had asked, *Do you still love your high-school sweetheart? Would you like to be reunited?* Thirty-eight people had called in to say yes. *That's me. Pick me.*

May listened, eager viewers' voices babbling on endlessly, as she opened the mail she'd never gotten to the day before. Occasionally she'd jot down the name of someone whose story sounded like it might be worth a look-see. With an occasional glance at the TV and her ears softly listening to the long-winded call-in sagas, she plowed through the piles of paperwork mounted on her desk. When her phone began trilling, despite the early morning hour, she turned the ringer off and let her voice mail handle that.

It was some time later—two hours later, she saw after glancing at her watch—when an angry voice outside her office broke her concentration.

"Someone has been going through my things."

She got to the hall in time to see Henry racing past her doorway.

He heard her, stopped, and backtracked. "Look at this," he said as he held up a strand of red thread.

"Is that dental floss?" she asked. "My god, are you bleeding?"

"It's thread," he said, glowering.

"Did something rip?"

He shook his head, very slowly.

"So what's wrong?"

"It's red thread," he said meaningfully. "Not black thread." Then he continued on, hustling down the hall calling, "Colleen! Colleen! Look at this."

Stifling a laugh, May returned to her office, Charlotte right behind her.

"Is this going to be a problem?" her assistant asked.

"Henry's booby trap? It doesn't even register on the problem meter." May handed over a stack of annotated correspondence. Before she could feel the swell of pride that came with a clear desk, Charlotte gave her back an even larger pile; fresh mail, first of the day. Audience laughter called them to look at the TV screen. Nothing good.

May let her paperwork fall to her desk with a thump. "Let's talk problems. First crisis of the day is rejuvenating my rejuvenation story."

"Did it die?"

"It fainted. To revive it, I need the names of the spa's medical director and PR person. And let's keep this little setback to ourselves. We don't need Colleen and Paula knowing we're back to nowhere on this one."

"Did I hear my name?" Colleen asked, breezing in, smelling like a lemon grove. It was her latest obsession, aromatherapy as a form of business management. She had bottles of oils lined up on her credenza, poised for a dozen scent changes a day. Lemon was the sorbet smell, to clear the nasal palate. Henry stood at her side, his face collapsed into a scowl, the lemon smell making his mouth pucker.

"What's up?" May asked as Charlotte quickly slipped out, back to her desk.

"Don't change the subject," Henry barked.

"What is the subject?"

"Are you the one who's going through my things?"

"No," May answered quickly. "But a little girl with golden locks carrying a bowl of porridge just raced by. Why don't you try her?"

Henry was halfway out the door to find the culprit when he realized what May had said. He retreated to his den in a frustrated huff.

Colleen made a mild attempt to conceal her amusement, then shook it off as she returned to her office to refresh herself with the power scent of vanilla, which she needed in preparation for a phone call with a network honcho.

That crisis over, May moved on to her first appointment, with a publicist from a women's magazine she rarely had time to read, who wanted to tip her off to a possible show idea. May liked it—a teenage runaway reunion story—but had to cut the meeting short. She'd promised Margery moral support during her morning taping. Her guest had been acting up and Margery was worried the show might implode.

As May hustled to the elevator, Charlotte started shouting out the newest names on her call sheet.

"If it's not about my kids, it can wait," May told her as the elevator doors closed. She hit the lobby and raced across the street arriving in the studio, breathless.

She looked at the monitor, the live feed from the studio.

"I thought he was a godamn scumbag," a man in a sheriff's uniform was saying.

Colleen sidled up next to May. "Welcome to *Tales from the Crypt,*" she muttered. "We're dead."

Together they watched the monitor as Paula plowed on, trying to get enough coverage so that the show could be saved in the editing room. "Did you ever think maybe he's just a troubled kid?" she asked the foster father of five juvenile delinquents.

"Troubled? He's a basic bastard goddamn scumbag is what the hell he is."

"Does he have Tourette's?" May asked Colleen.

"Maybe. He's cursed fourteen times in five minutes," Colleen reported. "Which would be fine if he would keep it to the allowable curse words. But he's going for the big boys. The censors will be drooling."

"You just missed F-word number fifteen," Moosey, the sound man, announced.

"So I said," the sheriff continued, "'If you think you can live in my house and be an asshole and be a scumbag and be a shit-eating bastard son of a bitch—'"

"That's it!" Paula screamed, shooting up out of her seat. "Colleen? Where are you?"

"Eau de Death, anyone?" Colleen muttered and went through the door to the studio set.

May watched on the live feed as a rumbling grew in the audience. Then the feed went dead.

"So," May asked Danny, the cameraman. "What's new?"

He shook his head and looked away. His day was bad and he didn't think it was going to get any better.

It didn't. Not for him or for anyone else. Margery gave the sheriff a strong talking-to and he managed to regain enough control so that the show went on to completion with only one additional *damn* and nothing any worse. Except for Paula's mood. That was worse. The postmortem was painful.

"If I have one more foul-mouthed ignorant trashcan guest," Paula began, "heads will roll. Do you hear me? Heads will roll out this goddamn door."

They let her rant. There was no way to stop her other than to let her rant until she ran out of steam. Afterward, May took Margery to the steak house on the corner, where they ordered lunch so they'd have something to help wash down the wine.

"You know it's her own fault, sugar. She just won't let me do any more bad-news shows. Do you know how hard it is to cover the crime beat with nice shows? It's impossible. If only I could go back to perverts and pedophiles, I could get some interesting people. It's Wendy's fault. If she wasn't in jail, I'd kill her."

"It won't last," May counseled her and it was the truth. None of Paula's edicts lasted for long. But that fact held little power to console.

May got back to her desk at three o'clock and found a neatly typed list of the names of the managers of Stacey's Nirvana Spa. There was no public relations person, Charlotte reported. The director, Dr. Lichtman, personally handled all publicity inquiries. May dialed the number of the Arizona spa, but before the call connected Linda buzzed in to interrupt her.

"Emergency on line two," she said.

May switched to the incoming call.

It was Charlotte, phoning from the St. Regis Hotel, where May had sent her to help the "Twins Separated at Birth" get settled in their rooms without running into each other. Tomorrow, Paula was going to bring them together for the first time in ninety-one years.

"Clara doesn't feel well," Charlotte reported, referring to one of the elderly twins. "She's got terrible stomach cramps."

"I'll be right there." May hung up the phone and raced out her door, hoping her ninety-year-old guest wasn't planning on croaking before she came on the show.

By the time she got to the hotel, Clara had been sent to St. Clare's Hospital. May followed in a cab, camped out at Clara's hallway bedside, and three hours later, pleaded with the emergency room attending physician to let Clara out so she could fulfill her lifelong dream of meeting her long-lost sibling. Convinced Clara was no longer dehydrated, the doctor agreed. Her guest was back in her hotel room by midnight. May got home just after one.

I've gone to sleep, Sabrieke's note said. *The girls are fine.*

May fell into bed without seeing the other note, the one that sat by the phone on her night table, the one that said, *Call Stacey, urgent, anytime.*

Thirteen

"Look at this," Clara said, and handed over her wedding photograph, which Paula held next to Ruthie's so the camera could get a shot of both at once.

The audience, watching the monitor, gasped, then applauded at the sight of two seventy-year-old wedding photographs of women in nearly identical gowns.

May, standing just offstage, applauded, too. She was swept right along in the sentiment of the moment, the friendship between these long-lost sisters blooming before her eyes, just as she'd planned.

For a moment, her thoughts drifted to her own friend, to Stacey, who'd been trying to reach her for days. But then the show pulled her back, the audience roaring with laughter at some coy comment Clara had just made.

There was no postmortem necessary for this one.

"Beautiful," Paula said as she breezed across the street, back to the office, flanked by Colleen and May. "Moving, touching—I loved it." She stopped in the middle of the street and shouted it out. "I loved it."

A half-dozen taxis screeched to a halt, their drivers pressing their horns. "Screw you," Paula yelled to them and holding her ground in the middle of the street, turned back to May. "Thank you, thank you, thank you."

"You're welcome," May said and hurried her host across the street and back into their building.

"You know," Colleen said as the elevator rose. "In a way, they were almost too good to be true. Where did you find them?"

With dismay, May heard the implication of the question. Unscrupulous producers had been long known to create fictional guests, to bend or rewrite reality to make a better story. But not someone like her. It was unthinkable. "What are you suggesting?"

"Don't worry. I know you would never intentionally do anything untoward. All I'm asking is, are you sure they are who they say they are?"

"Of course I am." Any producer of May's stature knew enough to carefully vet her guests. It was as bad for the producer as it was for the show if a guest turned out to be a fraud. What bothered May now was why Colleen was asking at this point, after the show was over. It wasn't uncommon for someone to raise the question during a pitch meeting, or at a booking session. But now, after it aired, and aired well? It was becoming clearer to her by the day. She had drastically underestimated the depth to which she'd fallen into Colleen's disfavor.

"I'll be curious to see what the numbers have to say," Colleen continued.

"Well, I don't care. I loved those women," Paula said, walking between them. "And you know what, May? We're going to celebrate over an early lunch. I'm in the mood for Jean Georges. Or should we go downtown to Balthazar?"

Ask Colleen along, May screamed in her head, as if wishing it could make it happen. It wasn't worth it to leave Colleen out. It would only make May's life more miserable later on. But Paula's communication skills didn't include reading minds.

"How about if we let Colleen pick?" May tried, hoping that was neither too subtle for Paula nor too obvious for Colleen.

"Oh," Paula said, momentarily confused, and then again, "Oh. Are you coming?"

"Are you asking?" Colleen dryly replied.

"She's asking," May told Colleen. "She's coming," she reported to Paula. Then she left them to sort out where to go while she ducked back to her desk to get her bag and check her messages.

"May?" she heard Paula call. "Are you ready to go?"

"One second," she answered and lifted up the phone receiver. It would only take a second to call Stacey and see if everything was okay. Her friend had been drifting in and out of her mind all morning and she needed to touch base.

"May?" Paula called again, her voice tinged with irritation.

And no one was picking up at Stacey's. By the fourth ring, Paula's patience had run out.

"We're going," her hungry host screamed. "Good-bye."

May hung up and left for lunch.

Fourteen

People teased him about it, but he didn't care. He liked to whistle while he worked, especially on hot and sunny September days. In fact, on a day like this, he couldn't imagine why everyone else wasn't whistling, too.

The weather was a perfect seventy-seven degrees—he knew because he kept a thermometer attached to his belt. The air was dry, the sky cloudless. The trees, their leaves a deep early autumn green, formed a heavy blanket that undulated in the gentle breeze. Sure, in February he might dream of earning a living as an office drone, but on days like today, he couldn't imagine a better gig than this: delivering packages from his dark chocolate brown truck.

He was thirsty. He usually kept two thermoses beneath the passenger seat, juice in summer, hot cocoa in winter, but today his wife had forgotten. Hey, that was okay. A little thing like thirst wasn't going to ruin a day like this.

Balancing the small square box on his shoulder, he rang the bell and waited even though he didn't have to. This package didn't require a signature. But it wasn't his way to dump a delivery on the front steps and leave it there. He didn't want any of his customers calling to complain that their Lands' End beach towels, their L.L. Bean backpacks, their Dr. Curewell's Herbal Remedies were ruined in a sudden rain. That's why he enjoyed a special relationship with the families on his route. That's why his arm got sore from returning waves as he traveled along these same winding roads every day. He took extra care with his customers and they appreciated it.

He'd try around back.

"Rosie," he called as he walked, but the dog wasn't out.

He sure was thirsty. Mrs. Blum would give him a glass of water. She was the kind who wouldn't mind. Most of his families were.

Still whistling, he strode down the driveway, feeling like the lucky guy he was. He enjoyed the military feel of his starched brown uniform, the orderliness of his truck in the morning when it was stuffed full of stock, the sense of satisfaction as he emptied it.

He put the package on the slate patio steps and glanced through the conifers at the narrow lap pool that practically took up the whole backyard. Mrs. Blum was doing laps, again. It was no accident, how great she looked in a swimsuit, a woman her age. He knew his customers like they were members of his own family. And he knew this: so long as there was no lightning, most days at lunchtime Mrs. Blum could be found swimming laps in her heated pool. She'd swim in the rain, but not lightning.

"Hey, Mrs. Blum," he called to her.

At first he thought she didn't hear him. It took a second for him to realize she wasn't moving. There was that tree in his way, was how he explained it to the cops. That tree partially blocking his view.

Once he realized what he was looking at, he screamed. He'd never actually screamed out loud before—just screamed, no words—not since he was a kid. Maybe that was why for a moment he thought the howling sound was coming from somewhere else.

Within minutes, and without intending to, he drew a crowd of neighbors to the edge of the pool. Someone summoned the police. Someone else jumped in and dragged her out. Despite heroic efforts, it was clearly too late for a rescue.

"A swimmer like that . . ." he said, holding his clipboard in front of his chest like a shield, his voice trailing off.

Two cops arrived a second later. What seemed like the entire force soon followed. The backyard became dense with bodies, neighbors corralled to one side, detectives questioning them one by one. But because he was the first to find the body, he was kept off by himself, questioned by no less than three different detectives even though he didn't have much to say to begin with. In between the questioning, he watched. A pair of uniformed officers was guarding the prone body. A lone photographer, his white shirt glued to his back with sweat, was snapping pictures. Men with rolled-up shirtsleeves were picking at the ground, studying, gathering things he couldn't see. Then the ambulance arrrived, and several more men raced onto the scene to busy themselves.

The final insult came when the cops told him he had to turn over his electronic clipboard. *Fine,* he told them. *Here.* It didn't matter now. The only place he was going now was to the dispatch office to punch out. After this, there was no way he was going back to work. Not after this.

Fifteen

"HER BODY WAS JUST LYING there on the concrete," Emily began, and May interrupted immediately.

"Whose body?" Candidates, none of them good, raced through her mind.

"Water leaked out from her bathing suit all around her. All around her the concrete was dark, like she was lying on her own shadow. But her face . . ." Emily stopped. She couldn't say the rest.

So now May knew who. But not what. Not what for sure. "Is Stacey okay?"

There was silence on the phone, dead silence.

"Is she all right?" May whispered, but already she knew the answer.

"She hit her head," Emily said, her voice quivering. "She drowned. She's dead."

After May got off the phone, she went through the motions of a functioning person. She told Charlotte to cancel all her meetings and she told Colleen's assistant why she was leaving early. She even packed her bag with the afternoon out-of-town papers, as if later she'd be able to work.

When Paul called in the middle of it all, her voice

betrayed no emotion as she efficiently transmitted the news.

He immediately knew she was in shock. It was something he saw often, people stunned by death.

Paradiso, his youngster partner, was still a sucker for a pretty woman wailing in grief, but Paul knew the people who suffered the worst pain did it quietly, like statues, going numb, like May was now.

He told her—didn't bother asking—that he'd pick her up in fifteen minutes. She said okay. She had neither the strength to argue nor the energy to figure out what to do.

"What's with her?" Paradiso asked as he dropped his partner off at his car. "Is she attracted to people who are about to turn up dead or something? I'm telling you, Paul, I got girls, normal girls, coming at me all day long. Let me fix you up with someone normal."

O'Donnell slammed the door, no comment necessary. May and Paradiso had zero patience for each other, and on a good day, they both knew enough to keep it to themselves.

He cursed the traffic as he snaked his way up to her street. He found her waiting outside her building. It was a seventy-degree September day and she was holding herself, rubbing her arms, like she was cold.

He helped her into the car as if she were an old lady, unsteady on her feet. She said nothing, just buckled her seat belt on automatic pilot and stared out the window. He didn't push it, he just turned on the car, left the radio off, and drove.

As he inched the car around the winding entrance to the Lincoln Tunnel, he crept to a stop beside a guy selling roasted peanuts and bought a small bag.

"Here," he said, handing it to May.

"I'm not hungry."

"You've got to eat."

She accepted the bag, put a nut in her mouth, and sucked on it as if it were a Life Saver.

"Chew it," he reminded her, and she began, rhythmically, as if she were doing it in her sleep. It didn't make sense that it made him feel better to see her eat, but it did, as if her eating proved she'd be okay.

They didn't speak for the rest of the ride. He wanted to know the details of what happened, but he didn't want to push it. He knew she'd tell him eventually, when she could. When he got to her street, he pulled up in front of her house.

"No," she said quietly. "Up the block. Where the cars are."

He followed her directions and pulled the tan Buick behind a long line of parked cars. At least, he noted, there was no squad car, no ambulance, no news trucks, not now. Suddenly he felt grateful for the traffic. "You okay?"

She nodded, glad for his company even if she couldn't tell him.

"You sure you don't want to go home first?"

"I can't," she admitted. "Not yet." As bad as this, facing Scott, was going to be, facing her children would be worse.

They sat in silence in the locked car for several minutes. Then Paul put his hand on her shoulder. "If we're going in, we should go in" was all he said.

She tried to say okay, but it came out like a sob. She hunched over, collapsing into herself, as if she'd been socked in the stomach.

Finally, he thought.

The sobs came and came some more, and Paul did nothing to stop the flow. He just moved her hair away from her wet eyes and off of her sticky cheek. Only when it seemed she was finally coming to an end of it did he reach across to his glove compartment and take out a pile of unused McDonald's napkins, which he placed gently in her lap.

He knew she wouldn't cry herself out completely, not now. He knew her crying jags would come and go for weeks, maybe months. It was something he discovered after his wife died, that there was no scheduling grief. Lucky for him he wasn't one to cry, so neither his old partner Bingo nor the youngster Paradiso, whom he acquired right after the event, ever knew. To them, he was a quiet guy who sometimes got a little quieter—and if they ever noticed, at least they had the good sense not to say.

After a moment, May let out a shaky sigh, wiped her eyes, blew her nose in one of the napkins, and took a couple of deep breaths.

"It stinks," Paul said. "I'm sorry."

"Me, too." When she turned to face him, she looked remarkably composed, as if the cry had washed her clean and calm. "Let's go."

He followed her up the front path and waited for her to ring the bell. "We'll get through this," he said, putting his hand on the back of her neck, under her hair where her skin felt hot and moist.

She leaned against him for a moment as if stealing his resolve. Then she stood up straight and pressed the bell.

"Thanks," she told him.

He felt a rush of love but kept it to himself. It wasn't the time.

The door swung open. They walked inside.

Sixteen

THE WOMAN AT THE DOOR looked familiar, but May couldn't place her. The woman couldn't place May, either, and she wasn't shy about it. "Who are you?"

"I'm a neighbor. My name is May Morrison." She didn't know when to stop, and the woman wasn't giving her any help. "I'm a friend of Stacey's."

"And you are?" Paul asked, stepping forward.

The question carried a tone of authority that caught Nick's ear all the way at the end of the hall, where he stood with a portable phone to his ear. He quickly disengaged from the call and strode over.

"Come on in," he said, and brushed by the doorkeeper with a clipped "They're okay."

"That's Lydia, Stacey's sister," he explained once they'd moved out of earshot. "She's not a bad sort—it's just we've had a lot of gawkers and she's taken it upon herself to stand guard." He stopped at the entrance to the living room, extended his hand to Paul.

"I'm Nick Ellman. You must be the New York City Police Department."

"You can call me Paul," the detective replied, returning the firm shake.

As May started into the room, Nick rested a hand on her shoulder. "Scott will be glad to see you," he said, and then disappeared, back to his post, manning the phone.

It took her a moment to locate Scott, who sat in the middle of the sofa, surrounded by a crowd of people she didn't know. Rosie, chin on her paws, lay at his feet. *Stacey must be upstairs,* May thought, and then caught herself.

A woman was telling him a story and his eyes were closed. May studied him to see if he was awake or asleep, but it was impossible to tell.

"Scott?"

His eyes flashed open at the sound of her voice and he mouthed her name, *Maysie.* Then a flicker of pain crossed over his face, as if seeing her alive only underlined that his wife was not.

He rose, very slowly, and leaned toward her to accept her hug. She felt him turn stiff in her arms, staving himself for her tears. But her crying jag was over. She wasn't going to fall apart here.

There were hardback chairs set all around the coffee table, few of them empty. She sat down in the nearest one. Paul took the seat beside her. Her eyes scanned the platters on the table, the same plates and trays that had been set out earlier in the week, only this time the food, pieces of ham, Swiss cheese, pickles, had been haphazardly scattered, not carefully arranged as Stacey would have done.

The group remained silent, as if waiting for the newcomers to do their share. May felt uncharacteristically tongue-tied. Paul stepped in to fill the void.

"If there's anything I can do," he offered, "you let me know. Anything at all."

May knew he wasn't one for small talk. She held back an appreciative smile.

"Thanks," Scott said. "I will."

The silence returned.

"Where are the children?" May broke it at last.

"Upstairs with Morgan," Scott said. "Sophie is taking it hard."

"It's a tough age to lose your mom," she said quietly.

"What's a good age?" Scott asked.

She decided to ignore the hard edge to the question. "What about Michael?"

"He's trying to be strong. He feels bad for me, of all things. I think he's making up for his sister, who says it's all my fault."

"Why is that?" Paul spoke up. It was a casual question, one that any of them might have asked, but coming from him, it sounded like the beginning of an interrogation.

Scott must have felt that way, too, because she could see him stiffen, protecting himself from a potential assault. "It goes like this." He kept his eyes averted, looking at his feet. "If I hadn't made her life so stressful, she wouldn't have had to swim every day. If she didn't swim every day, she wouldn't have swum yesterday. If she hadn't swum yesterday, she wouldn't have bumped her head." He looked back up. "And drowned."

"It's ironic, isn't it?" It was the woman who'd been telling the story when May first walked in the room. Her eyes were thick with makeup, a lack of smudging indicating she hadn't shed a tear. "I mean, she was so dedicated to her daily swim. Who could have guessed that's how she would go?"

"Marcy," someone hissed, shushing her.

Scott's nurse, May silently said, and a slew of memories raced through her mind. When Stacey had first mentioned Marcy, she had described her as a woman pathologically dedicated to her job. Her use of the word *pathological* had struck May as surprisingly extreme, but Stacey insisted she meant it as a compliment, that it was a good thing for Scott to have a nurse who was intent on protecting him from all distractions and annoyances. Months later, Stacey lightheartedly let drop that the doting nurse had turned into a bit of a lovestruck stuck-on-her-boss nudge. She insisted it didn't bother her though. She was happy Scott's needs were being catered to at work. She found it amusing, entertaining. She never worried that Marcy's feelings were returned in kind. Big hair, long blue nails, and a bubble-gum addiction weren't her husband's style.

May's eyes went to Marcy's nails. They weren't long or blue now; they were clipped short and manicured with clear polish, the way Stacey wore hers. And she wasn't chewing any gum. She was leaning in to Scott, asking if there was anything else he needed, a drink, something to eat, a pillow for his back.

He declined, but his gentleness in answering her suggested he appreciated the attention. And May wondered whether maybe Stacey had gotten it wrong. Maybe Marcy's feelings were reciprocated after all.

"Can I ask you something?"

At the sound of Scott's voice, May came back to the present. She followed his gaze to where it rested, on Paul's face.

"Sure." The tendons in the detective's neck flexed as he spoke but his easy tone belied any tension.

"The police want to do an autopsy," Scott said, "but I don't want it done. It's against my religion. If you're Jewish, you're supposed to be buried as you were born, in one piece. What do you think I should do?"

May studied Paul, waiting for his reaction. She knew he had plenty of experience with people whose religions prohibited autopsies. She knew he always did his best to accommodate grieving families whenever he could. It was a judgment call. If it appeared to him to be beyond all doubt that the victim died from natural causes, he was happy to respect the family's beliefs, whatever they were. But if he smelled, even faintly, the slightest odor of foul play, if even one small thing didn't look right—or if it all looked right but his gut was in spasms—religious beliefs went out the window along with the dead person's soul.

She watched him struggle to find the right answer now,

when all he knew so far, all he might ever know, was that the woman who died in her own pool was an expert swimmer. *And what kind of accident is that supposed to be?*

When he spoke, she was reminded that Paul was a seasoned detective, mindful that this wasn't his case. He asked Scott, "Has a detective been by to talk to you?"

Scott nodded and Paul asked, "What did he say?"

Nick walked in the room, Morgan at his side, in time to hear the question, in time to see his friend struggling to answer. Scott didn't have to say it was painful to talk about this. Nick could sense it. And he stepped right in and relieved him.

"The detective told Scott it seemed fairly straightforward. That Stacey was doing a fast backstroke and hit her head against the wall. That she went unconsious and drowned." He checked with Scott, as if needing his approval to go on. Scott nodded, a slight gesture.

"It wasn't the first time she hit her head," Nick said quietly. "She did it a couple of days ago." His voice dropped even more. "Just not as hard." His eyes moved to Morgan. He gestured toward her. "She was there."

The baby-sitter, her red cheeks even ruddier than normal, looked up, uncomfortable with the attention. "It happened just the end of last week," she explained because all eyes were on her, waiting. "One minute she was swimming along and then suddenly she's in the house making an ice pack. 'What happened?' I asked her. She said she was daydreaming while she was swimming and that she hit her head on the side of the pool. Got a nasty bump. She went right upstairs to lie down. She told me she was fine. She *was* fine," she insisted as if someone were arguing the point.

"No one's accusing you of anything," Scott said, although May detected blame in his voice.

Morgan heard it, too, and bristled. "I came to tell you the children don't want to come down to eat. They've asked me if they can eat in my room. What do you want me to tell them?"

"Whatever they want," Scott said, as if details such as this weren't worth the time to discuss.

"I'll get them some food, then," she said, and left the room.

"When I was a kid, I came this close to slamming my head on the wall of a pool," nurse Marcy said, showing the width of a few strands of her hair. "Some man I didn't even know kneeled down and stuck his hand out to cushion my head. He saved my life. Which is why," she went on, "I don't think it's very smart to swim if no one else is around."

"Marcy." Nick shot her a look that asked her to shut up.

"What?"

He discretely put a finger to his lips so she would understand, but she didn't.

"What am I saying?" She was annoyed, the warmth she felt for Scott clearly not extended to his partner. She moved closer to Scott, rested her hand tentatively on his shoulder.

He ignored the touch. "Detective," he said, and the crowd around him came alert with his use of the title.

"Call me Paul."

"Paul. What do you think I should do? About the autopsy."

Paul didn't answer right away. Unlike May and most people she knew, he wasn't afraid of silence. He didn't assume that if he stopped to ponder a question, he would lose his audience. He told her once that was probably because his audience was either handcuffed and under arrest or dead.

"I don't see that you have much choice. I guess the main question is . . ." and he looked around, surveying the crowd to determine if this was the right place—or the right time—to ask this.

Scott understood the pause. "I'd like to speak to the detective alone, please."

The crowd, disappointed to have to leave the room now

that the conversation was getting interesting, stood up slowly and even more slowly, dispersed. May was half out of her chair when Paul said, "Stay."

Whether or not Scott would have liked her to, he kept his feelings to himself. May sat back down.

The three of them alone now, the detective started again, his voice intimate and soft. "My opinion is, the police will order an autopsy whether you want one or not. They have to in a case like this."

Scott squinted as if he was trying to peer into Paul's brain. "Why? If she died because she hit her head on the side of the pool, if the detective has no doubt that's what happened, then why?"

"The point is, *why not?*"

May turned to see a woman standing behind her, the woman who answered the door, Stacey's sister, Lydia. How could she have missed the resemblance? Though she was two years younger, Lydia looked like Stacey's dark-haired twin.

"Personally, I'm all for an autopsy because frankly, I don't believe my sister hit her head and drowned."

"I don't care what you believe," Scott said, exasperated with her. "That's what the police believe. That's what I believe. That's what happened."

"If the police believed it, we wouldn't be having this discussion, would we? Would we?" she asked Paul.

"I'm sure it's a matter of policy," he told Scott quietly. "Even if they are completely convinced it's an accident, they have to follow procedure."

Lydia glanced at May. "Who are you again?"

May quickly introduced herself once more.

"Right," Lydia said briskly. "I remember. Stacey talked about you—you're the producer."

May nodded. She tried to resurrect all the things Stacey had told her about her sister. She was a banker. Single. Unhappy about being childless. Driven. Without tact.

"Look, Scott," Lydia tried again. "Accident or not, something was going on with Stacey. She was worried about something. I want to know what it was."

"Please," Scott moaned. "I don't want to go through this with you again."

"Too bad. You've got to tell me. Why did Stacey leave—"

"I know," he interrupted. "She left three messages for you yesterday. And every one of them said 'Important. Call me right away.'"

May felt a chill traverse her spine.

"Right," Lydia said. "And goddamn it, I was in meetings all day and never got a chance to get back to her."

"Same with me," May blurted out. For several seconds there was silence. Then May went on. "She called me at home, at work. She was trying to reach me for days. She said it was urgent that we speak." Her voice got quiet. "But we never did."

"You see?" Lydia said.

"See what?" Scott barked. "That you both feel guilty as shit that you never called her back? Well, guess what? It's too late now. So deal with it."

"I will, brother-in-law. I will deal with it forever. Which is why I need to know: what was wrong with her?" She turned to May and Paul and explained, "We weren't close."

And May remembered a few other things. That there was jealousy. That Lydia sent absurdly extravagant gifts to the kids at the slightest opportunity. That Stacey begged her to stop but she refused.

"If we spoke once a week, it was a lot," Lydia was explaining. To Scott she said, "Something was wrong."

"I'm sorry. I don't know. I can't help you. She's dead. And she didn't leave a note. She wasn't planning on dying."

"How do you even know that for sure?" Lydia asked him.

Scott groaned. "Right. She swam into the wall as hard as she could because she was committing suicide. Is that what you're hoping?"

"I'm not hoping anything. I just want to know whatever there is to know. Is that so strange?" Lydia turned and asked May. "Don't you want to know?"

"Yes," May admitted. "If there is something to know."

"Why don't you want to know?" Lydia asked Scott.

He hung his head. "I don't want her cut up. I don't want her mutilated for no reason."

"But it would be good to know for sure," May said. "For closure. So when you bury her, it's done. You can go ahead and grieve. And after, you can begin to heal."

Paul spoke up, conscious that his words might not be received well. "Actually, just so you're aware of procedure, you won't know anything by the time you bury her. Toxicology takes twelve to fifteen weeks to get results."

"What the hell are they going to do a toxicology workup for?"

"Procedure," Paul said. "They'll look for drugs, alcohol."

Scott didn't want to hear any more. "Enough. First I hear suicide. Now you're telling me Stacey drowned because of an overdose? You people are out of your mind," Scott snapped. "It was an accident."

"I'm sorry," Paul said, backing off. "I'm sure you're right."

Scott nodded, as if that was all he needed to hear.

"What was so urgent?" May wasn't ready to back down. "What did Stacey want us to know?"

Lydia watched carefully for Scott's reply.

"You don't give up, do you? Everything is a drama; everything is material for your goddamn show."

"This has nothing to do with my show—" she protested, but Scott cut her off.

"Well, this is no show. This is my life."

May felt as though she'd been slapped. She was stuck and couldn't mobilize her feet for the necessary retreat.

Paul read the situation and stood up, quickly reaching

out a hand to help her rise. "We have to be going. You call me if you need anything, all right?"

Scott's eyes were closed again, but he nodded to let Paul know he'd heard.

Once they were outside, May asked, "What the hell happened in there?"

"It's not often I say this," Paul admitted, "but I haven't a clue."

Seventeen

SHE STOOD AT THE PAY PHONE at the Charlie Brown's in town, the strong stink of air freshener wafting out of the adjacent restrooms like a sigh every time someone opened the door. When Sabrieke answered the phone, May could hear the relief in her voice.

"I tried to reach you at the office," Sabrieke explained in a rush, "after Morgan called me with the news. But you had already left. I didn't know how to get in touch with you." She dropped her voice. "We've been watching videos and having a popcorn party. I hope this is okay."

May assured her that given the circumstances, it was okay to break the no-TV-on-school-nights rule. As for how the children were, Sabrieke reported that so far they had no clue of the tragedy up the block. She was leaving the task of telling them for May to do when she got home.

But May couldn't go home yet. She wasn't ready to face them. The children needed to be told in a way that would assure them they were safe. They needed to be told in measured tones, by someone who was calm and in control. That wasn't her, not yet.

So she agreed to Paul's suggestion of dinner first. That

way she could gather her resources, plan her approach. Instead, she found she was ravenous, starved. All she wanted to do was to eat. After placing her order for steak, French fries, onion rings, and garlic bread, she filled up her plate at the salad bar twice, devouring it fast, as if food, quickly eaten, would fill the void. She was halfway through her steak and a few petals into her onion ring flower when she finally petered out.

Paul smiled at her appetite, then picked at the remains on her plate while she filled him in on what was on her mind.

"How can Scott be a hundred percent sure Stacey's death was an accident? If you were a cop who showed up at that scene, would you buy that story so fast?"

Paul reached into his pocket and pulled out a crushed box of Zantac. "It's not an unbelievable story." There was only one pill left. He swallowed it dry, depositing the crumpled cardboard on his empty plate.

Then he reached over and stabbed another piece of May's steak with his fork. When he was done, he used a hunk of garlic bread to mop up some of the bloody gravy on her plate. It still surprised her that the enormous quantities of food he ate never settled on his lanky frame. "I'd say so far—and I'm just guessing now—the police have no physical evidence to indicate her death was a homicide. And they have circumstantial evidence to suggest it was an accident."

"What makes you so confident in a bunch of local police you don't even know?"

"I have no reason not to be confident in them. From what Scott says, it sounds like they're doing everything right. Unless you know something I don't. Do you?"

"I know that Stacey was a healthy woman and a great swimmer."

"Who had hit her head on the side of the pool once before, just last week. Which doesn't make her death any less senseless. Fatal accidents are always senseless. That's what makes them so hard to accept."

"I don't accept it."

"I know. Because you're right. It shouldn't have happened. You think if only she'd been swimming slower, if only you had dropped by and she got out of the pool, if only you'd called and she stopped swimming to answer the phone, it never would have happened. But that's how it went down. Things happen. Bad things happen."

"But something was wrong," May whispered as if this was a secret from the elderly man eating alone at the next table. "Something was wrong and she wanted to tell me about it. She wasn't feeling well, remember? Maybe she was calling to tell me she was sicker than I thought. Isn't that possible? Wouldn't it be worth finding out if she was sicker than we knew?"

He stared hard. "And if she was sick, then what? Say she found out she was sick with something bad. Say the autopsy confirmed it. She's not any less dead."

"But why doesn't Scott want to find out? If it were you, I'd want to know."

"In this case, you don't get a vote."

"If it were me dead, wouldn't you try to find out?"

"What do you think there is to find out?"

"What really happened. I don't know," May admitted. "Maybe Stacey hit her head while she was swimming or maybe someone pushed her in and that's why she hit her head. Or maybe she had a heart attack or blacked out and hit her head. Anyway, how do we even know for sure she died because she hit her head?"

"There was a contusion," he offered, quietly stating the obvious.

"Well, maybe it was last week's contusion, from when she hit her head before."

"That's why there's going to be an autopsy. To make sure." His voice was soft; he didn't want to argue this.

"Anyway, what about Stacey? Doesn't she get a vote? She swam every single day. She wouldn't have . . ." Her voice trailed off.

He finished the sentence for her. "She wouldn't have chosen to die that way. You're absolutely right."

May said nothing. She was thinking again about the calls Stacey made, to her house, to her office, on her voice mail. The calls she didn't return. She laughed at the pathetic absurdity of it. "I was too goddamn busy to answer a lousy phone call. Can you believe that?"

"Don't beat yourself up about this, May. You couldn't have saved her. And you'll give yourself an ulcer trying to guess what she wanted to tell you. Maybe she wanted you to pick her kids up from school tomorrow. Maybe she wanted to have her dry cleaning delivered to your house. It could be nothing. It was nothing."

"How do you know?"

"My gut."

"What about my gut? My gut says your gut's wrong."

He let out a laugh and she had no choice but to join him. But her laugh was short-lived.

"I'm going to find out what was wrong. What about Morgan? Do you think she knows something? I've got this feeling Morgan knows something."

"May, let it go. Let the police finish their investigation. There's nothing in this for you."

"She was my best friend," she told him. "If it was your best friend, you wouldn't just let it go."

"You two lovebirds ready for dessert?" Their waitress stood waiting, her hair piled high atop her head, her short skirt showing off the opaque section of her pantyhose.

"How about a doggy bag of chocolate cake, for the girls," Paul suggested. "Bad news always tastes better over cake."

May nodded. It was a good—a sweet—idea.

"You want some company when you tell them?" he asked when they pulled up in front of her house.

"No," she said. She had to do this alone.

He waited until she was in her house, until he heard the happy shrieks of Delia and Susie greeting her. Then he started up his car and drove off, fast, home to his kids.

Eighteen

HER PLAN WAS TO GIVE THEM the cake first, then get them ready for bed before she told them. But Delia detected something off in her mood right away.

"Why did you just sigh?" she asked as soon as May walked in the door.

"I don't know," May answered. "I didn't notice I sighed."

"You did," Delia reported, and then added, "Why are you looking like this?" She imitated her mother's face, a tight, worried gaze.

May tousled Delia's silken hair, then sneaked in a quick tickle under her armpit. "Why are you looking like this?" she countered, crossing her eyes and stretching her tongue up toward her nose.

Delia collapsed on the floor, laughing, and Susie quickly joined in on the game. Soon they were imitating each other, their teachers, their friends, even their friends' pets.

Ignoring the lump in her throat, May egged them on to eat their cake, drink their milk, and then pushed them through their nightly chores, brushing teeth, brushing hair, changing into pajamas.

When they were done, she said, "I have something serious to talk to you about," and led them to her room. They arranged themselves, with some negotiating, on her bed. Delia got the left side, Susie took the right, and May, sandwiched, got the sliver in the middle.

When they were finally snuggled together, Delia asked, "Are you getting married?" Her voice was blank, giving no clue as to whether this would be good or bad news.

"No," May said.

"Phew," Delia said with a sigh. "You know, it's really boring to have to just sit and do nothing while someone gets married."

May nodded. Susie scowled. "So what is it? Is it something disgusting? Is it about poop?"

"Susie," Delia shouted in the way that meant *You are being such a pest.*

Insulted, Susie climbed out of the bed and, shoulders slumping, marched to her room and slammed the door.

May sat up, quickly rethinking her approach. Nothing, not even this, was going as planned.

"Ignore her," Delia advised, the voice of experience, "and she'll come back."

But May couldn't ignore her, because this couldn't wait. Her own grief was building, slowly. If she didn't get this done soon, she wouldn't be able to do it tonight at all. She got up, knocked on Susie's door, found her daughter sitting in a corner sniffling, and said, "We have to talk about something not so happy."

Something in the tone of her mother's voice made Susie let go of her sour mood without a battle. Taking May's proferred hand, she let herself be led back into the cozy master bedroom. The bedrooms were the only rooms to which May had taken the time to add the finishing touches—coordinated curtains, wallpaper, carpets, decorative pillows—absent from the rest of the house.

"Something sad happened today," May began, once they were back lined up in bed. She tried to be brief, vague, skimpy on details. She knew from the show she'd produced on child mourners that she was supposed to let them lead her; she wasn't to tell them any more than they wanted to know.

Susie was the first to speak up when she was done. "Mommy, promise you won't ever go swimming?"

"It's okay to swim," May said. "People swim all the time and nothing bad happens."

"You just have to know how to do it, right?" Susie was getting practical, which May took as a good sign. "You know how to do it, don't you?"

May nodded. They were sorting it out. They would be okay.

"But Mrs. Blum knew how to swim," Delia pointed out. "She got medals for swimming when she was a kid. They were in the basement. She showed me, remember?"

"She never let *me* see them," Susie complained.

"Well, it's too late now," Delia said, and slipped into a sulk.

"Look, accidents happen," May told them. "But the good news is, they don't happen very often. So we don't have to waste our time worrying about them. Because usually, almost always, things go right."

"Can you tell us a story about something that goes right?" Susie asked, desperate to feel the world was safe.

"How about one of those stories where we each add a sentence?" Delia asked. "Please?"

"Sure," May agreed, grateful that they hadn't asked for a pony, a boat, a move to California. There was little she wouldn't have agreed to. "You start," she told her older daughter.

"Once upon a time," Delia began, "there was a girl who wanted a cat more than anything in the world . . ." She passed the story on to May.

"So she saved up her allowance, and one day when her mother wasn't watching . . ." May tapped Susie on the arm.

"She snuck fifteen kittens in the house."

"That's too many," Delia advised.

"Okay," Susie agreed easily. "Fourteen kittens and a dog."

"You can't mix up cats and dogs," Delia said decisively.

"Let her tell it however she wants," May insisted, but her tone was mild and forgiving. She was delighted, envious even, at the girls' resilience.

They continued for half an hour more, until the girls got tired and the story became overridden with nonsense words and giggles. When May gently suggested it was time to stop, no one even bothered to complain. But before May could feel too smug at how well she'd gotten them through the night, Delia asked, "Can we sleep with you?"

The request took her by surprise. Although the girls occasionally crawled into her bed on weekend mornings when they woke up early, they weren't a family who snuggled in bed together at night.

Susie seconded the idea. "Can we?" Before May could say no, Susie added, "I'm scared."

Of course, May agreed. It was 9:30 when she turned out the lights. Several minutes passed, and then Susie, perched at the doorway to her dreams, quietly asked, "What if it wasn't an accident? What if a bad man killed Stacey and he's still outside?"

May was quickly trying to formulate the age-appropriate answer when Susie proceeded to her next worry. "What if a robber came?" Running out of concrete ideas, she went to the generic: "What if?"

May held her and, keeping her voice steady and calm, said, "The police say it was an accident, sweetie, so you don't have to worry. None of those other things happened."

"I'm scared," Susie admitted.

Though Delia didn't want to admit it, May could feel by the stiff tension in her body that she was scared, too.

Concrete cause and results, that's what they would have liked: a bad man came and now was gone. That's what would make them sleep easier. Not this, the discomforting knowledge that there were random accidents lurking in the universe, waiting to happen, even to nice people like Stacey, like them.

"Mommy?" Delia's voice came out of the dark. "The police could be wrong, couldn't they?"

May said, "The police aren't wrong."

"But they could be. I mean, anyone could be wrong."

"That's true," May said, giving in, "but this time they're not. They've checked everything just to be sure. Double-checked and triple-checked." She felt a tear seep from the outside corners of her eyes and swiftly wiped it away. Then she pictured herself explaining to Paul that the other reason she had to get to the bottom of Stacey's death was so that her children could sleep without fear.

It seemed to her only seconds later that Delia's and Susie's breathing changed and they were both asleep. She lay beside them for an hour, wide awake, planning in the dark, thinking of how she would go about doing right by her friend, and make her children feel safe.

It was sometime after one when she gave up trying to sleep. She got up, warmed a glass of milk, and paced the house. It was two when she called her office, checking her voice mail, busywork to pass the time.

The automated voice announced that there were twenty-two messages in her mail box. She never made it past the ninth one. The ninth one had come in at 11:30 in the morning. The ninth one was from Stacey.

"I'm in trouble, May," said her friend's trembling voice. "I just found something out and I'm scared."

"What is it?" May whispered as if Stacey were alive on the other end of the phone. "What—"

Her dead friend's voice interrupted her. "I need your help."

May saved the message and replayed it several times before hanging up. But even after she did, as she sat perfectly still, she continued to hear it in her mind. And behind the words were other words, left unsaid.

Why aren't you calling me back? Why are you letting me down?

Nineteen

IT WAS SOMETIME BEFORE 5:00 that Susie woke screaming. May tried to soothe her by reminding her it was only a nightmare, just a dream, nothing real. But Susie remained stuck, half asleep in a place where words held no meaning.

Only when her sobs had exhausted her did she succumb to her mother's arms, and burrowing into May like a puppy, she fell back to sleep. Somehow, the noise didn't rouse Delia. Despite the quiet afterward, May stayed wide awake.

When the alarm finally went off, Susie sat up, perky and rested, and jumped out of bed to make sure she was the one who got to turn off the radio. When May asked about her dreams, she insisted she'd had none.

Did I *dream it?* May wondered. She was so tired now, she couldn't be sure. Then her arm brushed the front of her nightgown and she felt the damp residue of her daughter's tears. *It was real,* she told herself, and then remembered the rest—Stacey's call—and thought, sadly, *That was real, too.*

She reached across the bed, over Delia, for the phone to hear the message again.

Delia opened a sleepy eye. "What are you doing?" She was alert with suspicion. "What happened?"

"Nothing happened." May quickly dialed into her voice mail. "I just remembered I forgot to clean out my old messages. It's something you have to do when your voice mail box is full or else you can't get new ones."

"I'll do it," Susie offered, hopping out of bed again, this time to get to the phone first.

"You don't know how," Delia reminded her, then turned to her mother. "Why don't you let it stay full so no one else can bother you?"

May didn't answer, didn't hear when Susie defended her desire to keep her mailbox neat. She was riveted, listening once again to Stacey's plea. She didn't see the small hand approach the phone. By the time she noticed the little finger pressing her code it was too late.

"There," Susie said, proud of herself. "You only had to show me one time and now I can do it all by myself."

"Thank you," the automated voice announced in May's ear. "Your mailbox is empty."

"Why did you do that?" May snapped.

"Sorry," Susie whispered. "You said you wanted to clean it out."

Delia came to her sister's aid. "She didn't know, that's all."

May, too weary to be mad, fell back into bed.

"Remember the girl with the cats?" Delia asked, trying to recapture the hilarity of the night before. When no one seemed interested, she tried again—"You can't catch me"—and bolted from the bed.

That worked. Susie was after her in an instant.

Without regard for the prone body that was their mother, the girls chased each other around the room, rambunctious and lighthearted.

How do they do it? May wanted to know and stumbled out of bed, clinging to her sleepiness as if it were a blanket she wasn't ready to relinquish. She shut the bathroom door, shutting out her children's giggles, and turned on the shower. Stepping inside, she let the hot water pound down on her.

As her head began to clear, the events of the previous day settled on her, heavy as weights. Her shoulders sagged under the power of her loss and no amount of water could rinse the feelings away.

When she was done, toweled off, in her robe, she came out of the bathroom and found, impossibly, the girls already dressed, sitting at the edge of her bed, hands clasped in their laps, waiting for her.

"We're being good," Susie reported, her feet dangling, her smile wide to show she'd just finished brushing.

Above her, May could hear the rattling noises of Sabrieke rising to begin her day, but here, in her room, at 6:25 in the morning, with absolutely no prompting, her children were dressed and ready for school. And May thought, *They haven't forgotten what happened at all. They're trying to be good so that nothing bad happens to them.* More than anything, that realization broke her heart.

She sent Sabrieke back to sleep and broke another cardinal rule, no television in the morning, telling the girls they were free to watch until 8:00. While they did, she dressed, then sat at the kitchen table with a blank pad, to make her list, to plan her attack on the truth.

Stacey, she headed it. *People to talk to.* Underneath that she scribbled names as she thought of them: Lydia, Morgan, Stacey's boss, Nick, Marcy, Emily, Marlene, Sophie, Scott. She looked at the last two names, then drew a line through them. Scott didn't want to talk to her right now and Sophie needed to be left alone.

Who else? Who were Stacey's other friends? She must have had work friends, or rivals, but she never mentioned them. Who were they and would they know what was on her mind?

In a flash, she remembered the folder that sat on her bedroom dresser, the folder for the spa show. She ran up and retrieved it, quickly finding the piece of paper Stacey had given her, the one with the names of all her spa friends on it. She added the names to the list—she'd have to find a way to get their numbers—Risa, Greta, Toni. When she was done, she looked up and found the girls standing in the doorway, waiting for her to notice them.

"It's eight o'clock," they announced in unison.

They had never turned the TV off on their own before, not without threats—never once.

"Can we go out to breakfast?" Susie asked, sweetly.

"If there's time?" Delia added.

May opened her arms and the girls entered her embrace. She held them close for several moments. They didn't have to tell her they were scared. She could feel it in their hard, urgent hugs. "I love you both," she whispered and they squeezed her harder, as if to break her. And she made herself a promise: *I will make them safe.*

As she walked out of the house May didn't notice the car coming down the street, but the man inside noticed her. She didn't see him pull over and park at the curb. She didn't see him get out and stare. She didn't see him at all until she looked in her rearview mirror as she was backing out of the driveway. Then, like an apparition, he was there.

"I'll be right back." she told the girls. "Stay in here." She turned off her car, got out, and locked them in. She didn't want this. She didn't want her children frightened.

"Hello, Ms. Morrison."

"What the hell do you want?" she barked. Her mind was racing, trying to retrieve his name. She got it. "I don't appreciate your showing up at my home, Mr. Harris." Her voice trembled with anger.

"Why do I scare you so?" he asked, but he backed off several steps to let her know he meant no harm. "What exactly are you afraid of?"

"You're harassing me and I won't have it. I won't have you frightening . . ." Her voice drifted off. She didn't want to mention her children, not to him.

He followed her glance to her car, but the children were no longer visible. They were huddled on the floor, either playing hide and seek or hiding from their fear.

"Guess what?" he said, almost cheerfully. "I didn't come here looking for you. I didn't even know you lived here. What a coincidence, right?"

"I don't believe that," May told him.

"I don't blame you. I don't believe in coincidences, either. But here's the thing. I found my aunt's address book." He held up a narrow, weathered leather book. "I've been tracking down her friends." His words were friendly but his voice was cold. "Here's coincidence number one. One of her friends is your neighbor."

"Who?" May asked.

"Great," Matthew said. "Keep pretending you don't know anything. Here's the next coincidence. Your neighbor is dead."

"Stacey."

"At least you admit that."

"Stacey Blum was friends with your aunt?"

"You're good," he said. "You're very good."

"What's your aunt's name?"

"Forgot already, did you? It's Margaret," Matthew reminded her, enunciating carefully. "Margaret Harris."

May struggled to think if Stacey had ever mentioned anyone by the name Margaret. She searched her mind and came up blank. She would have remembered the name if it was someone important, she was sure of it.

Matthew waited, the smirk on his face a silent I-told-you-so.

"You're wasting your time," May told him. "If Stacey and your aunt were good friends, I would have heard of her."

"Mommy," Susie called.

May turned to see Susie getting out of the car.

"Honey, get back in there now," she snapped, and then, sensing a change in the atmosphere, she turned to see Matthew striding purposefully toward her, his bushy hair looking wilder than ever.

She pulled her cell phone out of her purse and brandished it before him like a gun. "Stay away from me or I'll call the police.

"I just want—" he got out, but she wouldn't let him go any further.

"I'm pressing nine," she told him.

"I just want to show you—"

"Not here. Not at my house." When he still didn't back away, she told him, "I just pressed one. Okay? I pressed nine-one. If I press one again, the police will be here within a minute."

Matthew Harris let out a long, frustrated sigh, turned away, and retreated to his car.

"Mommy," Susie called again, and clambered back out of the car.

May ran over quickly, willing her body to stop trembling as she bent down and listened to Susie's complaints, that she was hungry, that Delia was teasing her, that she forgot to take her stuffed lion along.

She answered all her daughter's worries in order, and when she swung her head around, she saw Matthew Harris was gone, vanished as suddenly as he'd first appeared.

"Let's go," May said, pulled a reluctant Susie back into the car, and drove off.

Twenty

OVER FRUIT CUPS, PANCAKES, and a side order of bacon to share, May struggled to keep her mind from wandering, but it was hard. Matthew and his Aunt Margaret were pulling at her more than ever.

Margaret and Stacey, she silently repeated over and over, searching her memory for a connection, but she came up blank.

Delia determined to engage her mother, asked, "Did Grandma let you watch TV after school every single day?"

"Mostly," May answered, and forced herself back to where she was, in the diner with her children, drinking pulpy orange juice, watching Susie gobble silver-dollar pancakes as if she were storing up food for the winter.

"Was your favorite show *Rug Rats?*" Susie asked.

"They didn't have *Rug Rats* in the Stone Age," May explained. "They had *Magilla Gorilla.*" She continued, distractedly giving up as many details as she could pull from her mind's musty filing cabinet. The girls squealed with delight as she described the exact components of the Swanson's salisbury steak TV dinner compartments, how she always unrolled her Yodels before eating them, and that once when her mother sprained her ankle, her father let her have a Scooter Pie on a hamburger roll for dinner, and then made her promise not to tell.

When she saw that the stories had the power to divert her children from their worries, she delved deeper to come up with more. She tried favorite toys of the past: Chatty Cathy, Video Village: The Game, Miss Cookie's Kitchen Colorforms.

"They had colorforms when you were alive?" Susie wanted to know.

Then Delia asked, "What did that man want?" and suddenly the spell was broken.

With the power of a fierce undertow, May's childhood memories were swept back into the underground of her unconsciousness.

"It was a mix-up," she explained, quickly paying the bill and ushering them out to the car.

"You sounded mad at him," Susie told her.

"I was a little mad," May admitted. "But it was just a mix-up."

The discussion ended. They traveled to school in silence. As soon as May pulled the car to the curb and turned off the engine, the girls spilled out, anxious to escape the stifling mood. She watched them race to the playground swings, where they hopped on, light as air, and pumped with so much energy it looked as if they were trying to pick up speed and fly away.

May glanced around. She didn't recognize these parents, the ones who drove their children to school every day. But by their easy banter, she could tell that news of Stacey's drowning hadn't yet begun to circulate. It would, soon. She was sure of that. And once it hit, it would spread fast from parent to child to child to parent like a bad cold.

Someone should alert the school counselor, she thought. Children, not just her own, were going to be upset. She nominated herself. Who else was there? Certainly not the two young women who stopped alongside her, who didn't bother to look her way before jumping into their morning gossip.

"She's acting strange," one began, her Irish accent grabbing May's attention even before she saw the green-tipped spiky hair. "She won't go out. She says she can't go out, because he doesn't want her to go out. 'He won't let me,' she says."

May recognized the tone immediately. She'd heard her own au pairs speak to their friends on the phone in that tone, dismissive disgust with their hopelessly thick host families.

Spiky Hair's friend, tall and skinny, confided next. "She told me he went into a rage the last time she went out. Even though all she did was talk to her friends and dance a bit with some of the other girls."

"And the children love her so, don't they? I feel so bad for the children, losing their mum like that."

May shivered involuntarily, and the motion caused Spiky Hair and Tall Girl to glance her way. Seeing nothing that interested them, they went on talking.

"Do you know what I think happened?" Spiky Hair said, and then her voice dropped so low May couldn't hear her.

Very slowly, she inched closer to them, concentrating, straining to listen, holding her breath to cut down on noise. But the girls were ear to mouth now, and she couldn't hear a thing.

She reminded herself that she had absolutely no proof she'd just eavesdropped on a conversation about Morgan and Scott, nothing more than an offhand comment about some children whose mother had died. But how many children had mothers who just died?

"Excuse me," she said, and the girls jumped up like Pop-Tarts. "I'm a friend of Stacey Blum's," she told them. "I hope you don't mind my asking, but were you talking about Morgan a moment ago? I couldn't help but overhear. I wasn't trying to listen."

The girls looked stunned. Tall Girl looked to Spiky Hair to answer, but then the bell rang and children came rushing from all over the playground toward the red opened door of the school. By the time May spotted Delia and Susie, by the time they ran over to her, their backpacks slapping behind them like heavy wings, the au pairs were gone.

"Who are you looking for?" Delia asked, as she watched her mother turn in a circle, searching the crowd.

"No one, sweetie," she said, giving up the search, making a mental note to try to track them down later.

Delia wanted to walk to her classroom unescorted. Susie asked for the same privilege, but May refused.

"You're in kindergarten. Can't you be seen with your mother when you're in kindergarten?"

"Okay," Susie relented. "But no kissing."

After dropping Susie off—no kissing—May went directly to the office of the student assistant counselor, Mrs. Lazar. Luckily she was in and alone.

According to Delia and Susie, Mrs. Lazar was approximately 200 years old. To May's eye, she might be even older. But despite her ancient years, or perhaps because of them, the children regarded her as their special friend, the one to whom they could tell anything. Famously kind, the generous distributor of Jolly Ranchers, lollipops, and, in real emergencies, Kit Kat bars, she had a sign-up sheet outside her door that was always filled with names, or in the case of the youngest children who couldn't write yet, pictograms.

"Yes, I heard," Mrs. Lazar told May, after May had explained why she was there. "Mr. Blum called to say Michael wouldn't be in for a few days. It's just tragic."

May nodded her agreement.

"And so hard for the children. Are your children having a tough time with it?"

"Yes," May admitted. "But you might not know it. They're on their best behavior."

Mrs. Lazar sighed. "Isn't that how it always is? We want them to be good little angels and when they finally are, it's for some awful reason, like they're scared out of their little wits. I'll talk to them." She scribbled something in the black-and-white composition notebook that lay open on her desk. Then she touched her bony fingers to her mouth and looked off into the distance.

"Is something wrong?" May called her back.

"I was just wondering. Do you think they'll go ahead and move or do you think their plans will change? Silly of me to ask. I suppose Mr. Blum doesn't even know yet himself."

"Probably not," May said. She didn't want to admit she didn't have a clue what the counselor was referring to.

"I haven't had a chance to pull all their records together yet. Mrs. Blum didn't give me much notice. When she called, she said she had to come by and pick the records up today, and when I told her it would take some time to gather all the papers, she said she didn't have any time. She was so upset," the counselor recalled.

"When did she call?" May tried to keep her voice casual.

"Yesterday. Yesterday morning," Mrs. Lazar said, remembering. "Oh, my. Do you think I was her last call?" She stared at the opened notebook on her desk.

May struggled to read it upside down, and as she looked, she saw a single tear fall on the page.

Mrs. Lazar snapped the book shut. "Don't worry. I never cry in front of the children."

"I'm not worried." May rested a hand on Mrs. Lazar's liver-spotted arm. "Do you want a Kit Kat bar?"

The counselor laughed quietly, then wiped away the wet on her cheeks. "I hope Dr. Blum doesn't do anything too hasty."

"I'm sure he won't," May said, though she knew nothing for sure, nothing but this: something was very wrong. If Stacey had been mulling over moving, if the thought had even vaguely crossed her mind, she would have mentioned it to May. Yet she hadn't. *Why?* Something had happened. *What?*

"I'll speak with your children," Mrs. Lazar said. "I'm sure they'll be fine. They just have to grieve for a while, same as you. Same as me."

But May didn't hear her. She was thinking, searching her mind for answers, coming up blank.

"Is there something else you'd like to talk about? Mrs. Morrison, are you all right?"

May brought her attention back. "Yes. There is one thing. I need to get in touch with an au pair I saw outside the school today. She's from Ireland, I think, or England. She has blond spiky hair that's green at the ends. Do you know who I mean?"

Mrs. Lazar laughed. "Oh, no. I'd remember someone who looked like that. But then I don't have too much to do with au pairs."

The counselor went on talking, but May drifted off again, planning her next move. When Mrs. Lazar's voice finally cut into her consciousness, it was filled with worry. "You should talk to someone," she advised. "I'd be happy to give you a referral."

"No. That's all right."

"Then you must promise me you'll find someone on your own."

May smiled and stood up. "Thank you for your help" was all she said because she hated making promises she knew she wouldn't keep.

Back in her car, she sped through town quickly, calling in to the office on her way to let Charlotte know she'd be in a little late. She gave herself an hour. An hour would be enough for now.

As she turned the car onto her block, she struggled to remember Stacey's maiden name. It came in handy as a producer, having a good memory for names. It took a minute, but she got it. Steiner. Stacey's sister was Lydia Steiner.

She pulled her car around the back and flew inside. She took the stairs two at a time up to her small third-floor office. Through Sabrieke's closed door, she could hear the sound of morning television.

"Hi. I'm working home this morning for a little while," she called from the hall.

"All right. Hello," Sabrieke answered. May could hear tears in her au pair's voice. Stacey's death was hard on her, too. But May didn't have time right now to probe and console.

She closed her office door, closing out extraneous thoughts, and logged on to the internet. Once she was on, she ordered her search engine to find all listings for Lydia Steiner.

After a moment's hesitation, it answered with a list of eighty-nine *Steiners,* first initial *L.* She scrolled down, ten choices at a time.

Two were in New York City, three were in New Jersey, one was in Westchester County and the last was in Connecticut. She dialed them all, spoke to Laurence, Lainie, Laura, and Lynn. Then she listened to the voices on three different machines, none of them Lydia. Dead end.

Okay, she thought. *Next try.* Lydia worked for a bank, a large well-known bank—but May didn't know which one. Back at her computer, she pulled up a page of all the large commercial banks in New York City. Dialing Bank of America first, and then on down through the alphabet, she was routed through one maze after another of lengthy voice mails. Each time she reached a human, the answer was always the same. "We have no record of a Lydia Steiner working here. Are you sure she is an employee of *this* bank?"

It was way down the list at Marine Midland when the automated receptionist said, "Thank you," and she was connected.

A voice came on the line, hard and quick: "Lydia Steiner."

May scrambled to think of how to begin. "I'm sorry to bother you—" she started to say.

"Who am I speaking to?" Lydia snapped.

"I'm May Morrison. Your sister's friend. We met at her house yesterday. Do you remember me?"

"Of course I remember you. It was yesterday."

May caught on fast; there would be no small talk. "I'm trying to find out what happened to Stacey."

There was silence, then Lydia said, "Good. Someone should."

"I wanted to ask you a few questions."

"Like what?" Lydia's grief had changed quickly into something else, something hard, hard to penetrate.

"Did Stacey ever mention a friend named Margaret to you?"

"Did she work with her? The only friend she ever mentioned was some woman she worked with whose name I forget, so don't ask. And you. Which says a lot about that woman and you."

May scribbled a note on the pad on her desk. *Friend from work?* Then she pushed on. "Did your sister mention recently that she wanted to move?"

"No. But it wasn't the kind of thing she would have mentioned. Last time she moved, she only told me after the fact. Probably so that I'd know where to send the girls birthday gifts."

"What about Morgan? Did Stacey ever say anything to you about Morgan?" She wrote *Morgan* on the pad and waited for the answer.

"The nanny? Not much. All I know is she's Irish, she smokes on the sly, and she doesn't drink or do drugs. What are you getting at?"

"Did she ever say anything about Morgan and Scott?"

"As an item?"

May wrote *Morgan and Scott?* on her list and said, "Yes."

"No," Lydia answered. "But it wouldn't surprise me. Look, I never cared for Scott, and Stacey knew it. So she made her choice and shut me out. Those two were like a private corporation, a secret society. Gates were closed. No one else allowed in. Who needs to be around that? If it weren't for my niece and nephew, I would have written them both off long ago. But I didn't. I showed up, an aunt bearing gifts, theater tickets, a night at the circus, dinner at the Hard Rock Cafe. I guess that's over now," she said quietly. Then she went on, "I won't be any help to you. Not that I don't want to, but believe me, you know more about my sister than I do. Hell, maybe you should be the one to go through all her things."

May's senses went on alert. "I'd be happy to do that if you think Scott would let me. It's going to be such a painful job for him."

"It's going to be such a painful job for me. He asked me last night if I'd take care of it for him. It's the longest sentence he's ever said directly to my face. Of course, I said yes. What I want to do," she lowered her voice to confide, "is to get those children out of that house for a while. Until we know for sure what happened."

"What do you mean?"

"You know it as well as I do. One night you're watching a news story about a grieving widower, the next night they're carting him off to jail. They're always so convincingly innocent at first, aren't they?"

"You think Scott killed Stacey?" May asked.

"I think there's more than a good chance of it. Don't you?"

"I don't really know," she said, because she wasn't sure, not of that. "What I do know is I'd like to help you with Stacey's things."

Lydia thought about it, then said, "Scott wouldn't be very happy about that, which I wouldn't give a damn about, except that I really want to keep him happy so I can get hold of those kids."

"He wouldn't have to know," May said quietly.

Lydia thought some more. "Our secret?"

"Absolutely."

"Okay. If he wants to be out of the house when I go over there to go through her things, I'll give you a call and you can join me."

"Thank you," May said and rushed off the phone before Lydia could change her mind. She checked her watch. She had one more stop to make and then she had to get to work.

Twenty-One

"I'M LEAVING," SHE YELLED through Sabrieke's door.

"Okay," a sad voice came back.

I'd better talk to her later, May told herself, and raced downstairs. When she got to the front hall, she stopped, then trudged back up.

She knocked, heard a quiet "Come on in," and opened the door.

Sabrieke was dressed and lying on her bed watching the small TV that sat on her white wicker dresser, half a foot away from her. Regis and Kathie Lee were bantering about men who had sweat marks on their T-shirts.

May noticed the wastebasket, a short throw away, filled with damp balls of tissue. "Are you okay?" she asked.

Sabrieke shrugged, then sniffled. "Just sad."

"Me, too," May said, and sat alongside her.

That was enough to get Sabrieke crying all over again, her body shivering as she tried to control herself.

"Crying is not something I like to do," Sabrieke explained as she wiped her face with the back of her hand. She took a deep breath, regained her composure, then went to the small oval mirror that hung above her dresser. "Oh, lah lah," she said as she examined herself. "Manu is coming and I can barely see my eyes, they are so puffy." She began gathering small jars and sponges neatly arranged on a shelf of cosmetics. "I need to go fix this. Do you mind?"

"Of course not," May said, but didn't leave. She felt like she should say something, do something more, but she could come up with no better than "Are you sure you're okay?"

"I will be," Sabrieke reassured her employer, "if I can find my eyes before Manu shows up." And she disappeared down the hall into the bathroom to make repairs.

May hurried out to her car, calling Charlotte on her cell phone on the way.

"You got something in the mail about a Margaret Harris," her assistant reported. "An obituary."

"Great," May said, and then listened to the rest of Charlotte's report on the morning's crises and comedies, none of which needed her urgent attention.

It was just before ten when she pulled up in front of the redbrick building that was her local police department. Although she drove by it every day—it was only a few blocks from her home—she had never before been inside.

She stopped at the front desk, where a woman sat working the phones. She was carefully dressed in a starched white shirt. Her long red nails curved under slightly on top and lightly tapped her desk as she spoke. "Can I help you?" she asked May, as she hung up from a call. She smiled pleasantly.

"Yes. I'd like to talk to someone about filming a show." She hadn't planned on this approach, using the show as her cover. In fact, she hadn't planned at all. But there it was, a reflex that came as naturally as blinking.

"What kind of show?"

"A TV show. A talk show."

"Permits are at town hall. Twenty-one Oxford Place." Her phone rang and she picked up the receiver. "Police department."

When she finished the call, she looked up at May with eyes that said, *Are you still here?*

"I'm a producer for the talk show *Paula Live,*" she began again. "I live in town, four blocks up, on Willow Street. My name is May Morrison."

The woman had a beautiful smile, with perfectly straight white teeth so small they looked like baby teeth. "How do you do. Nice to meet you. Permits are at town hall. Twenty-one Oxford Place."

"I'm not looking for a permit. I'm looking to talk to someone about producing a show here, about crime in America. I want to use our local police officers as the centerpiece of the show." For a moment she considered dropping the pretense, saying to the woman, *Look, that's not it at all. I'm just trying to find out what happened to my friend. I'm going fishing for details. Tell me what you know.*

The woman said, "You want Chief Smargiassi," and before May could say another word, she picked up her phone and said, "Joanie, I've got a woman here who wants to see the chief." She listened, then hung up the phone. "Someone will be down to see you in a moment."

As she waited May thought, *I should have called first.* What was she thinking? She wasn't thinking, that was the problem. Professionally, she knew better. You don't just drop in on a chief of police. She'd spoken to many over the years, in small towns across the country. The big municipalities like New York, Chicago, Denver, could afford a press officer, a public relations person, a community liaison to talk to someone like her. But in a town like this, if a story broke and she needed information, it was usually the chief of police who handled the press.

A friendly-faced woman came through a door and stretched out her hand. It was ice cold. "Joanie Bart. Assistant to the chief. What can I do for you?"

May went through the whole story again.

"You should have called," Joanie said gently. "The

chief is having a bad day today. Why don't you call and we can set up an appointment."

It was a good idea. Seeing the chief on a bad day without an appointment wasn't going to be productive. But before she could agree, the chief appeared, news of her arrival drawing him out of his office. The truth was, he enjoyed getting out of his office.

"Hello, I'm Chief Smargiassi," he said, extending his huge hand. He was an enormous man, probably once a star on his high-school football team. The pictures in the local paper—the chief at the town fair, the chief alongside the mayor at the Memorial Day parade—never captured his bulk.

She returned the handshake firmly, then apologized for stopping by without calling. "I'll call Joanie and make an appointment," she said, suddenly wanting to delay this visit. "I'll come back when you have the time."

"I have the time. You're here. I'm here. You know," he moved closer to confide, "I've been dealing with headaches all morning long. You'll do me a favor if you insist on seeing me right now."

Joanie pointed up the wide stairs.

"Can you see me right now?" May said, struggling to sound like she meant it.

"After you," the chief said, and she walked in front of him, climbing up past dingy walls to the second floor, where a vacant lobby awaited her. The chief brushed past her, pushed open a door, and escorted her several feet down the hall into his office.

It was a good-size office and could have belonged to any executive. Framed photographs hung on the walls behind a desk cluttered with papers. A couch in a brown nubby fabric sat at the far end of the room. A wing chair was arranged next to it, the old leather seat permanently depressed.

Chief Smargiassi pointed her toward a chair in front of his desk. Then he took his seat. It could barely contain him. The phone rang instantly.

"Smargiassi," he said into the receiver. "I know," he said, and then a moment later he said, "I know that, too. I know," he said for the third and last time. "And I don't care. I don't have to say this, do I? I want it fixed. You got that? Good." He slammed down the phone, looked at May, and smiled. His thick hair had been carefully arranged and sprayed. He wore cologne. He cared how he looked.

He wants to be on TV, May decided in a flash.

"So what's this I hear. You really want to do a TV show about me?"

Uh oh, May thought. She said, "We want to do a show on neighborhood policing."

"Who are 'we'?"

"Sorry. 'We' are *Paula Live.* Do you know the show?"

"No, but that doesn't mean anything. I watch *Law & Order* and *ER.* That's it."

"*Paula Live* is a daytime talk show. It's on here at ten o'clock—" She stopped midsentence because the chief had turned back to his phone and started dialing. He smiled again as he waited for someone to pick up.

"Hi," he said a moment later. "You ever watch a TV show called *Paula Live*? Any good? Yeah? I got a woman sitting here who works for them. Yeah? Okay. I'll tell her." He hung up and said, "My wife says she thinks your show is good. Next to *Oprah* she likes it the best. She hates that Springer guy."

"Our show is very different from—"

He interrupted. "Did you know I almost went on *Oprah* once? But then a hostage situation happened, of all things, so I couldn't go. It was a show about what it takes to run a police department. They really wanted me. They were very disappointed."

"What our show will be about is real policework, the kind that goes on every day in real places, not the stuff made up by TV cop show writers."

"Because you know they don't get it right," he said. "They get the big-city cops right, but when it comes to a town like us, they never get us right. They make us dumb, racist, or corrupt. They don't show the hard work, the dedication. Not in the movies, either. I once almost got a job consulting on a TV show. They wanted my opinion to make it more real. But we'd just had a double homicide that was still burning hot and they couldn't wait, so I had to say no."

May pushed on. "So we thought, wouldn't it be great if we took Paula out with a cop on a typical day to show people what it's really like."

"I'd be happy to take her out in a car. When does she want to come?"

Time to backslide. "We're not quite ready yet," she explained. "I have to do some research first, background for Paula so we can give the show a good shape."

"Shape?"

"It needs a point of view. A tight spin."

"A spin?" He was looking at her sideways now, like he wasn't sure if this was good or not.

"For starters I'd like to get an idea of what we're dealing with," she said. "I want to find out what kinds of activities your police officers encounter on a typical day."

"First off, there's no such thing as a typical day."

"That's what I need to know. You know what I think would be a big help? If I could go through the records, the public records, of what's gone on, say in the past week. Just to see what a typical week is like. Could I do that?"

"That's a lot of paperwork you're talking about," the chief said. "It's a lot of paperwork."

"I've got time," she said. "I'm getting paid for this."

"That's some job you got," he said. "You know, I have a niece who's just graduating college. She's very interested in a job like yours. She majored in TV or something like that."

"Have her call me," May said, handing over one of her cards. "I'd be delighted to talk to her."

He leaned over and picked up the phone. "Joanie, get me copies of this week's arrest reports, incident reports, and investigation reports. This week. Right. Right. Right." He hung up. "She'll be a few minutes with that. You know, I met Dennis Franz once. When I watch *NYPD Blue,* I occasionally see something he picked up from me. Some of the words, you know?" He began to list the phrases Dennis Franz had borrowed from him, and May listened politely until Joanie came in with the stack of papers. She handed them to the chief, who shuffled quickly through them to make sure there was nothing included she couldn't see. He handed the whole stack over to her.

"I don't want to be in your way. Is there somewhere I can go to look through these?" She held up the stack, half a foot high, of typed and handwritten documents.

"Right there is fine. I've got plenty to do. I won't bother you and you won't bother me. Joanie, get me the file from last night. I want to review it."

"Right away, chief," Joanie said, and May felt like she was living an episode of *Get Smart.*

She settled into the chair and read through the sheets, arrest reports first. It was a week of drunk driving, assault, possession of weapons, drugs. The narratives were thick with physical detail. *White male subject driving 43 mph in '97 white Saturn going north on Southern Slope Drive.*

She skimmed through the rest, but there was nothing of interest in the pile of arrest records. And she thought, *Of course not. No arrest would be made in a death the police believe was accidental.*

She went on to the next stack of papers, the incident reports. There she found the report on Stacey's death, third one in the stack.

Incident: Body found floating in backyard swimming pool.

Complainant: Emily Cooper, 43 Willow Street, 585-0381

Disposition: County coroner's office called. Crime-scene team called. Detective squad called.

Narrative: *Body of white female found lying on her back on concrete pool deck in backyard of 39 Willow Street, home of the deceased. Body had been removed by Alan Bell, a neighbor of the deceased, in attempted rescue. Bell, Cooper, and UPS deliveryman Steve Roberts made positive ID. Deceased was discovered floating on her back in the pool motionless by Roberts at 12:30 p.m. when he attempted to leave package on back patio. Initial visual examination showed large contusion apparent on crown of head.*

"Find something interesting?" the chief asked, noticing that May was no longer speedily skimming through the reports but sitting stone still. "Whatcha got there?"

"Stacey Blum's death."

"Oh. Yeah. Horrible that kind of thing."

"Do you believe it was an accident, too?"

"I don't bother believing anything. I prefer to wait until I know."

"Is this case regarded as a murder or as an accidental death?" She instantly regretted the question. Her tone had changed completely, from casual and friendly to dogged, and she knew the chief picked up on it. As if he were a Doberman pinscher, his ears came to attention. He picked up the phone, but this time he didn't call his wife.

"Get Detective Smith in here." He hung up. "Why don't you ask the man in charge yourself?"

His office door opened a moment later. The man who walked in looked to be about her age, with thick, dark hair and muscular arms that showed their strength from beneath his shirt.

"Sit down, Detective Smith," the chief said. "This is Miss May Morrison. She's making a TV talk show about police, but she's particularly interested in the death of Stacey Blum. Isn't that right?"

"Yes," May said quietly.

"What exactly interests you about it?" the detective asked her, settling into the visitor's chair next to hers.

She measured her words, carefully. "I want to know if Stacey's death was as straightforward as it appeared to be—an accidental drowning, I mean. I want to know how your police officers determined it was an accident."

His eyes narrowed. "Tell me again why you want to know. Because you're writing a television show?"

"I'm a producer for the talk show *Paula Live,*" she explained. "And I'm producing a segment on local police."

"She's interested in us," the chief offered.

Detective Smith nodded. "But why did you pick Mrs. Blum's drowning to focus on?"

"Are you sure that's what it was? An accidental drowning? Are you still investigating?"

Detective Smith nodded, but May realized it wasn't in answer to her question. It was to some other question he hadn't articulated, one that she'd unwittingly answered for him.

"Do you have some information about what happened?" he asked her. He pulled a small notebook out of his shirt pocket, then put his hand over his mouth, as if he had to hold himself back from saying more. Having set the detective on her, the chief sat back now and observed.

She'd heard guests talk about this sensation, when events began to carry you away on a course you hadn't meant to chart. "No, I have no information," she admitted.

"But you know something, or you wouldn't be here," he prodded her. "Putting the talk show aside, for a moment."

He'd seen right through her. The only way out of this hole was to dig her way out with the truth. "You're right. I am a producer for *Paula Live*. But that's not why I'm asking about Stacey."

The chief stared grumpily.

She took a breath and pushed on. "She was my friend.

Something was wrong with her, right before she died. Something had scared her. She wanted to tell me about it, but she never got a chance."

Now their interest was piqued. Detective Smith scribbled a few more words in his notebook. "What do you think it was?"

"I don't know," she admitted. She considered telling them about the coincidence of Margaret Harris's death, but she didn't understand the connection yet herself, and she didn't want it to be easy for them to dismiss her as a fool.

"Who do you think would know what was going on?" he asked.

"I don't know," she said again. "Stacey's husband. Or her children. Or her nanny. I don't know. I do know that her sister, Lydia Steiner, got the same kinds of calls I did, worried, frightened calls. But she didn't connect with Stacey in time, either."

He scribbled some more. "Mrs. Morrison, I'll be honest with you. I don't believe Mrs. Blum's death is anything more than it seems."

"You're still looking into it, though, aren't you?" she asked, "Or is the case closed?"

"Nothing is closed until we get all the facts," the chief chimed in. "That's what we deal in. Facts."

"Do you have any facts you'd like to share with us?" Smith asked.

May shook her head.

"Then I recommend that you don't make any suggestions or assumptions," he told her, and stood up.

Chief Smargiassi hit his hands on his desk, startling her. "So. Let's discuss this talk show you want to do."

"I don't think she's interested in that, chief. Not really."

The chief looked at the detective and something silent was shared. The chief stood up. "I'm all out of time," he said. "If you're interested in doing a show about me, call Joanie and make an appointment. Joanie," he called, and his assistant appeared instantly. "See Miss Morrison out, please."

It was an old producer's trick, leaving her purse lying on the rug next to her chair. She got halfway down the stairs before she pretended to suddenly remember it.

Joanie followed behind her as she raced back up to the chief's office, stopping outside.

"I know it's going to be weeks, but can't you just call down to the county coroner's office and see if Lester will tell you how it's going?" she heard the chief say.

"Chief," a voice came up behind May's ear—it was Joanie, and it was angry. "Chief, she forgot her purse."

The chief walked out of his office, May's large leather bag dangling from his beefy arm like a Barbie accessory.

"Thanks," May said quickly, and went down the stairs without looking back.

Twenty-Two

THE MOBSTERS' WIVES WERE WAITING for her when she arrived at her office, twenty minutes late for their appointment. Charlotte had done the best she could, installing them on May's love seat with a bottle of Pellegrino and a platter of cookies. They'd been laughing up a storm until May walked in.

Dressed like bookends in matching tweed power suits that they'd obviously picked out without regard for the unseasonably hot day, they straightened at the sight of May and moved apart, suddenly sullen.

The blonde, Luanne, tucked her tongue into her cheek where it stuck out like a tumor.

Connie, the redhead, spoke her mind. "You think we're just a couple of bimbos, right? You think you don't have to come on time for people like us?"

"I'm terribly sorry," May apologized. "There's no excuse for being late. I've just lost a very dear friend, but that's no reason to impose on you."

"What do you mean, 'lost'?" Connie asked.

Luanne put her tongue back where it belonged. "Lost like luggage or lost like in heaven?"

May looked upward and nodded.

"Oh, I know all about that," Luanne commiserated.

"Don't we both," Connie said. "When I was a little girl, I'd come home from school, and over cookies and milk, my mother would tell me who dropped dead. Cousin Mikey, Cousin Louie, Uncle Sammy. You don't want to know."

"That would be good to talk about on the show," May said, seizing the opportunity to move the meeting along.

But the wives didn't want to be moved along quite so fast. They had another agenda. They weren't sure they wanted to come on the show at all, for starters, and not because May had been late for their appointment, either. They were nervous, they explained, tired out from being pursued by everyone in town. As a solution to their fatigue, a rival show—they wouldn't say which one—had offered day treatments at Elizabeth Arden to help them relax. Someone else suggested dinner at Windows on the World.

"I want to help you promote your book," May responded. "I know our audience would enjoy you. And if you come on with Paula, I can promise a dramatic rise in your sales figures." She ignored their unsubtle fishing for perks because she didn't have her heart in this woo.

"That's all very nice," Luanne said. "But we'd be a bunch of basket cases if we did all the shows who want us. So we have to be choosy and pick the ones we like the best."

"What are your ideas for helping us stay fresh during our publicity tour?" Connie asked, sitting at the edge of the couch. This was her favorite part, hearing what goodies were in store for them.

"We've got a very good makeup team," May told them blandly. "Although they don't do hair." She tried not to stare at Connie's hair, a Crayola shade of red that had no resemblance to her eyebrows. After a moment she realized the wives were waiting for her to offer something better. She'd had enough. She stood up. "Let me know what your plans are. If you're interested, I know Paula would be delighted to make time for you."

"That's it?" Luanne asked, dumbfounded.

May plowed on. "I know how busy you are, so I don't want to take up any more of your time. Thanks so much for stopping by."

"I can't believe this," Connie whined.

Luanne grabbed her friend's sleeve. "I can. With what I've seen in my life, I can believe anything. Come on. Let's go."

"Danny is not going to be happy," Connie warned.

"Have a nice day," May called after them, and closed her door, closing the women out of her mind.

Charlotte buzzed instantly, ready to come in with the call sheet update, but May put her off, telling her she needed five minutes alone to make a call. She dialed Scott and hoped he was home.

"Hello?" He picked up on the first ring, sounding groggy.

She checked her watch—it was almost noon—and apologized for waking him.

"What's wrong?" he asked, as if an emergency was the only excuse for calling at this hour.

"I just wanted to know how you were doing," she said, cautious because she wasn't sure what to expect after yesterday's outburst.

"I could be better," he said quietly. "How are you?"

"Not great," she admitted. "When I went to school with the girls this morning, I spoke with Mrs. Lazar, the school counselor. She told me Stacey was planning on moving."

"What?"

"She said Stacey had requested the children's records and that she needed them quickly because you were moving. Actually," she added—full disclosure—"she said *she* was moving."

He let out a long, slow breath. "Well," he said after a moment, "I suppose I can tell you."

May's body shuddered with a chill as she waited to hear what the news flash would be.

"Stacey hadn't been well over the past few weeks."

"She had the flu," May said to let him know this wasn't news.

"No. That's not what I meant. I mean," he hesitated. "Not well in her head."

May felt her stomach clench. This didn't sound right at all. "She was fine."

"She was very good at putting on a certain face to the world, that's true. But she wasn't fine," Scott said. "People who are fine don't try to pull their children out of school on the pretense that they're moving, when they're not." His voice began to rise. "They don't take their dog to their internist and demand that she be seen."

"You mean the vet."

"No. She took Rosie to see Nick. It caused quite a scene in our waiting room."

"I had no idea," May said quietly.

"She was trying awfully hard to keep it a secret. I think she wanted to keep it a secret from you most of all."

May tried to take it in, but it didn't feel right. "Keep what from me? That she wasn't well?"

"Her breakdown. People didn't know—I guess you didn't know—how fragile she was."

It was as if she was hearing about someone else, someone she'd never met.

"I'm sure that was what she wanted to talk to you about," Scott went on. "That her psychological condition was . . ." He paused, looking for the words. "Let's just say she had deteriorated beyond the power of St.-John's-wort to help her."

May struggled to find even a hint of a memory that would support Scott's words, but she couldn't. Stacey's mental health seemed like everything else about her—robust.

Then she thought of the day Hector came to shoot the video. Stacey had certainly been acting strange that day. Had there been other days like that? Many of them? Had May been totally blind, totally fooled?

"Was she getting any help, Scott? Did you take her to a shrink?"

"I tried." He sounded weary. "But she refused. She was very paranoid and depressed. Very depressed."

She chose her words carefully. She didn't want to antagonize him. "I had no idea."

"I guess she put off telling you because she knew that would make it real."

An enormous wave of sadness came over her. "Do you know yet when the funeral is going to be?"

His anger flamed. "An hour after they release the body." Then, just as suddenly, the rage drained away. "I'm sorry. You were very important to Stacey. I know that. You just have to understand, this is very hard for me. And your questions just make it . . ." his voice trailed off as he collected himself. "I've got the funeral home on full alert. We'll be ready to go as soon as the police release the body. It could be tomorrow or the day after—I don't know. I still don't see why they even had to do this."

May resisted the urge to explain it all to him. Instead, she offered help. "I can ask Paul to make a call for you. I bet he can find out where they are on this." She wanted him to feel as if she were entirely on his side here, even though she wasn't. She was on Stacey's side.

He didn't even consider it. "No. Let them finish whatever the hell it is they have to do. When they're done, they'll let me know. Thanks, though," he added, an afterthought.

"I'm so sorry for you," May said. He was in so much pain.

"Thanks."

She took a breath and pushed on, hoping she'd softened him up enough to be forthcoming. "It does make more sense to me, now." She dropped her voice. "Last night I found a message from Stacey on my machine. It was so strange, hearing her voice." She paused, then told him the rest. "She said she was scared, that she needed my help."

"She wasn't well. I didn't understand how far along her confusion had become."

Suddenly May thought of Matthew Harris and his conviction that the reports saying his aunt had killed herself were wrong. That's how she felt now. That Scott was wrong. She took a breath and pushed her luck a little further. "Do you know of a friend of Stacey's named Margaret?"

"No. Why?"

"I was just wondering if you were going to invite her to the funeral."

"I don't know her. But even if I did, I wouldn't. I don't want a circus. It's going to be small, a family thing."

"What about Stacey's friends?"

"You're invited, May, if that's what you're asking."

"I know that. But what about her other friends? Her friends from work, from the neighborhood, from the spa? I'd be happy to call her friends from the spa, if that's the problem. If you give me their numbers, I'll call them right now."

He must have picked up on something in her voice. "You're not still thinking about putting on that show about the spa, are you? This isn't about your grief at all, is it? It's about your goddamn work."

She started to defend herself, but before she got out a word, the phone went dead in her hand.

Twenty-Three

WHEN SHE HUNG UP THE PHONE and walked out of her still office, she felt like Dorothy, coming out of the black-and-white portion of her life and into the color. Frenetic motion was all around her.

Charlotte was slitting open envelopes, the phone crooked at her shoulder, the postbox on her computer screen flashing to let her know she had mail. Paula stood in the middle of the hallway—Frank three steps behind her—laughing at Margery, who was getting to the end of a story. Colleen, arms filled with folders, stood waiting, impatience painted on her face, for Paula to finish. Henry stood next to her, chuckling as he purposefully ignored Hun, who was waving, struggling to get his attention.

"And there she is," Paula said, when she noticed May. "Margery's been trying to cheer me up, but it didn't work. Now it's your turn. We've got ourselves an MIA. We've got ourselves an MIA!" she shouted in case there was someone on Mars who hadn't heard her the first time.

It was the worst possible catastrophe, worse than having a sheriff curse at Paula on air—a guest who didn't show up. May surveyed the producers, saw Henry's sweaty brow, knew the no-show guest was his.

"Viewer mail," Colleen updated her. Carl, trailing behind her, handed May a stack of letters.

"You each have ten minutes to pick out your top twenty letters," Colleen announced.

Paula's mood was blackening before their eyes. "Try Diane or Barbara," she called out to no one in particular. "It's about time they did me a favor. Or see if Katie will come on. Or Jane. Or Meredith."

No one answered. Paula was in fantasy land now. None of the powerhouse broadcasters she mentioned were close enough to her to do her this kind of favor. But there was no upside in pointing that out now.

"Okay," Colleen said, taking the only wise course, acting as if she hadn't heard Paula's suggestion. "Does everyone have at least a dozen letters?"

There was a chorus of confirmation.

"Henry, do you have at least twelve dozen?" she queried.

He quickly counted. "I have twenty-four letters."

"Okay. In ten minutes, we meet in the conference room. Henry, get someone down to the studio pronto to make sure we hold on to our audience."

The crowd dispersed. May took a detour to Henry's office. He was sitting behind a desk that suddenly looked too big for him. Today he looked less like a sniveling backstabber than a little boy playing grown-up. She resisted the urge to suggest he use phone books to sit higher in his seat, and sat across from him.

"I confirmed him," he said, as if she'd asked what happened. "Dawn confirmed him. Which means someone else must have called him and canceled. Someone," he leaned closer to confide, "who is out to get me."

She leaned forward in her seat. She didn't have to do this, but she couldn't stand to see him self-immolate.

"Henry, let me tell you the facts of life. No one here wants you to have a lot of success. Not me. Not anyone. No one wants your shows to win Emmys or do a sonic boom in the ratings. But no one—believe me—not one person here wants you to fail to the point that the show looks bad. Because that makes everyone else look bad."

He looked up at her, hope in his eyes.

"These things happen to all of us. It's a rite of passage. A certain number of guests in your life will be no-shows. A couple of others will get stage fright and clam up as if they have no tongues. You'll have a few lunatics, a couple of assholes, a fraud. One or two will get swiped by another show. It happens. The good news for you is you've gotten one of your no-shows out of the way. It probably won't happen again for a long time. But Henry, be a mensch. Thank people for their help. Offer to do the same when it happens to them. Don't start accusing them of sabotaging you."

He blinked. May said a silent prayer that no tears were coming.

"You're right," he said finally. "I can rise above whoever's done this to me."

May smiled, turned around, and rolled her eyes. She'd done her best.

As she passed Charlotte's desk on the way back to her office her assistant covered the mouthpiece of her phone with her hand and whispered to May, "It's the prince."

The only royalty May knew was the royal pain in the neck she'd just wasted a pep talk on. But when she picked up her phone and heard the voice, she realized who it was, a little-known prince she'd found when everyone was scraping the bottom of the royal barrel in the post–Diana-car-crash weeks. At the time, the prince had been interested in doing the show. But before they could wrap up the details, he got an invitation to go ballooning with a friend and because the winds were predicted to change within days, the ballooning party had to leave right away and he backed out.

Of course she'd accepted his change of heart with good grace. And now, with princely timing, here he was again.

"Can you ever forgive me," he began. "Did I leave you in a terrible jam?"

"Don't be silly," she said. "How did the ballooning go?"

She let him describe his hot-air adventure, and when he was done, she said, "It's funny how things work out sometimes. Your calling today of all days, for example. We hardly ever have last-minute holes in our schedule. Of course I'm sure you're busy this morning, anyway. But if you're not, if you have nothing planned, would you like to spend an hour talking to Paula about what it's like to be a prince?"

There were the shows she drudgingly nurtured for months, even years. And then there were these last-minute episodes put together with spit and fear.

Paula was ecstatic to hear she was trading in a show on viewer mail for a live prince. She loved, absolutely loved, royalty. In fact, she not-so-secretly aspired to marry or at least have sex with one someday. At news of the prince's imminent arrival, she rewarded May with a kiss, a hug, and to Colleen's dismay, a command that she take the rest of the week off.

Tomorrow was a work-at-home day anyway, and a Friday as well, but May knew enough to say a grateful thanks.

Good, she thought as she rode home on the bus that afternoon, after the prince had charmed Paula and the studio audience with tales of motherly cooks who let him have doughnuts for dinner and wicked tailors who because they resented him, purposely cut his clothes too tight. Now she had a three-day weekend. Three days to get to the truth behind Stacey's death.

Twenty-Four

As soon as she settled herself on the bus, May pulled out the obituary she'd gotten from Charlotte and skimmed it. It was a small-town paper and the obituary was a list of dates: when Margaret Harris was born, educated, died. A record that she existed, nothing more.

She considered calling Matthew to ask him straight out what was driving him in his search. But she quickly rejected the idea. The nephew gave her the creeps. She had to take her gut's advice and keep her distance.

Anyway, she didn't need him. Boynton, Pennsylvania, couldn't be too far away. If there was anything fun to do nearby, she could turn it into an overnight getaway with the girls. Then she could do her own snooping around.

Pleased with the plan, she opened her front door. Sabrieke was crying. Susie was standing naked in the living room. Delia was down to nothing but her socks, which she was struggling to pull off. Morgan was the last part of the picture to come into focus, sitting on the floor, folded into herself, staring at the floor.

"Mommy," the girls called out, racing over for their usual leg-gripping hugs.

She quickly assessed the situation. The girls were okay.

Sabrieke hopped out of her chair and wiped her eyes, embarrassed to be caught with tears cutting narrow rivers through her makeup.

"Don't worry, Mommy. She's just crying," Susie explained. "You know how sometimes I get sad and I don't know why?"

"We're cheering her up," Delia explained.

"Putting on a show," Susie said.

"Based on a movie," Delia added.

"The Full Monty," Susie sang out, then started to giggle.

"They saw only twenty minutes of the video," Sabrieke quickly interjected. "I made them turn it off when it got to the bed scene, so it is no problem."

It was a problem, but May wouldn't go into it in front of the children. She turned to them. "I have an idea. Go upstairs and get dressed. Then, when you come down, go look through the cabinets and pick out anything you want for dinner."

"Anything that's in the cabinets?" Susie asked. "Even Oreos?"

"Put whatever you want out on the counter and when you're done, we'll negotiate."

"Oreos?" Delia asked, incredulous. "You'd let us eat Oreos? For dinner? That's not very healthy."

"Maybe just one," May told her, smiling. "In a salad," she went on. "But you'll have to find a vegetable that goes with it. Oreo and carrots, maybe. Or Oreo and tomato with mozzarella cheese."

The girls raced each other upstairs to see who could get dressed first.

Sabrieke knew she was in trouble. "I am so very sorry," she began. "I was feeling so much to cry, and so I let them watch some video before I checked what it was. It took some time because first I put cold water on my face. Then I do my exercises. I talk to Manu. I call home to cry some more. Nothing helps. Then Morgan comes over and tells me what has happened to her now and it only gets worse."

May turned to Morgan. "What's happened to you?"

Morgan looked up to reveal that her big green eyes were watery, too. "He sent the children to Lydia's, that's first of all. And isn't she the cat who ate the canary."

"What do you mean?" May asked.

"It's always been my personal belief that Auntie Lydia thought they'd be better off with her. I think she's wanted them for a long time. She'd always say things to me, to let me know what a better mum she would make than her sister. 'Stacey is too easy,' she'd say. 'She doesn't keep control of the children like she should.' Then one day, Stacey told me the rest of it, how Lydia once wanted to borrow Scott to get herself pregnant. Did you ever hear of such a thing?"

"What did Stacey do?" May asked.

"She told her no, of course. She knew what kind of trouble that would bring. After that, she didn't invite her sister 'round as much, which is exactly what I would have done, except I'd have cut her off forever. And now, Stacey's gone less than a week, and he's sent his children to live with her. I tried to talk him out of it, but he was so agitated after the phone call, he wouldn't listen to what I had to say."

"What phone call?" May wanted to know.

"I answered the phone," Morgan explained, "which I usually do. It was a man named Matthew. I don't recall the second name. I'm not very good with second names."

May sat up a little bit straighter. "What did he want?"

"I have no bloody idea. All I know is first thing Scott did when he got off the phone was to call Lydia and ask if she would come and take the children for a little while. Then he started screaming at me,"

"For what was he angry with you?" Sabrieke asked.

Morgan shrugged. "Just another temper tantrum. He had them a lot. They both did, he and Stacey. They'd been fighting all the time."

Again, May had the feeling she was hearing about strangers, not the affectionate couple she thought she knew. "Scott and Stacey fought? About what?"

"I never could hear. Mind you, I did my best not to hear. They would go into the bedroom and then the door would slam and the yelling would begin. Sophie was the one who'd always put on the music right away, very loud, to drown them out. We wouldn't say anything; we'd just start dancing around the living room, getting wilder and wilder. They'd always forget, the children would, what made us start to dance. They'd be having fun, twirling and pretending to do Irish dancing and the tango." She smiled, remembering. Then her expression changed. "Scott says I can stay as long as I need to, until I find another job."

"Maybe you should stay with us," Sabrieke suggested. "You can sleep in my room for a few days, just until you can decide where you're going to go." She turned to May. "She can sleep with me, in my bed, no? So she doesn't have to stay with Scott alone."

"It's all right," Morgan said. "I'm fine there. I'll make my plans and make them fast, is what I'll do. I'll be all right."

May could hear the banging of cabinet doors, the girls giggling, cans being stacked, toppling over, being regrouped. She turned to Morgan. "Let me ask you something. Scott told me that over the past few weeks, Stacey had been paranoid and depressed. Do you know why?"

"Stacey? No way. Scott is the paranoid one. He must have been talking about himself."

"No. He was talking about Stacey."

"Paranoid? No. Not her. Not depressed, either, except maybe for a while after their fights. The worst she ever got was cold—you know, distant. An on-again, off-again kind of thing, if you know what I mean—one minute cozying up to you, the next, wanting you to leave her alone. But depressed and paranoid? I don't see that. I don't see that at all."

Sabrieke was crying again. "I'm sorry," she apologized. "I cannot stop. I don't know what is wrong with me. It's not about Stacey, because I felt like this already before. It makes no sense. Why should I be homesick now, one and a half years after I'm already here? I don't know what's wrong with me."

May thought back to the time in her life when she'd cried nonstop for weeks without a clue as to why, until her mother had suggested one. "Sabrieke," she said. "I hope you don't mind my asking, but is there any chance you might be pregnant?"

At that, Sabrieke stood up and raced upstairs, sobbing. The girls ran into the living room, Delia holding a box of Kix. Susie clutched a tub of Duncan Hines chocolate frosting.

"What happened?" Delia wanted to know.

"What did you do to her?" Susie demanded.

"She's homesick is all," Morgan spoke up. "She's missing her mum just as you would, if you were living thousands of miles away from her. Which I'm sure you're never wanting to do."

Delia dropped her food and came running to her mother, missing her already. Susie did the same.

"Girls," May said, accepting their affection, "Morgan is going to be staying with us for a few days."

"No. Thanks for offering, but I'm not," Morgan corrected her. "I've got calls into agencies all around the area, and I'll have a position by week's end, I've no doubt." She looked up the stairs. "Do you mind if I go up to be with her?"

"Please do," May said, and watched Morgan's sturdy legs disappear up the stairs.

May gave the children their dinner: Oreo men salads—celery-stick bodies, carrot-stick arms, and Oreo heads with raisin eyes. Pasta with red cheese sauce—cheddar melted and mixed with ketchup. And for dessert, graham crackers carefully coated with chocolate frosting. After dinner, after Sabrieke and Morgan left for the closest drugstore to buy a First Alert Home Pregnancy Test, the girls got busy sculpting bakable clay figures while May cleaned up the mess.

Susie was on her tenth snake when the phone rang. There was the usual race to see who would get there first. Susie was small, but she was fast; she won.

"Hello?" She said it so quietly May wondered whether the person on the other end could hear. "Fine." Her voice stayed barely audible. "Fine. Macaroni and bloody cheese."

The dinner report told May who it was. Susie wasn't good on the phone with anyone yet, not even her father.

"Making a clay snake," she said next, and May knew Todd was going through his usual routine. *What did you have for dinner? What are you doing now?*

"No," Susie said, then, "Yes. Okay." She turned to Delia. "Here," and as her sister took the phone, she whispered—she knew this wasn't good news—"It's Chloe."

Why the hell are you calling my children? May wanted to scream out, but she didn't. *Why do you insist on having a relationship with them?* She wished she could say it out loud, but she couldn't. She had to be big about it.

She left Delia and Susie alone until she was sure the conversation would be over.

But when she came back into the room, Delia let out a quick "Oh. Here she is," and handed the phone to her mother. May froze. How could she get out of talking to Chloe? As if sensing the problem, Delia said, "It's Daddy."

Because she knew the girls were watching carefully, she got on the phone with a cheery "Hi there."

"What the hell is going on over there? Someone is dead again? I was thirty-two years old before anyone I knew ever died."

The girls were staring. May smiled as she spoke. "You're forgetting a few people, honey. JFK, Martin Luther King Jr., John Lennon."

"They were public figures who were assassinated. I'm talking about regular people. What the hell is going on?"

"Life," she said, keeping it short as she watched Delia soak up the tension, then squash her clay dog. Susie ripped apart her snake.

"Who died, May?" he growled. "What the hell happened this time?"

She sighed. She forgot about Todd. Even long distance, he knew how to complicate things.

She turned her back to the girls and walked with the portable phone into the living room, for privacy.

"Her name was Stacey Blum. She was a friend, a new friend. You don't know her."

"Goddamn it," he said. "Why did I have to hear about this from my children? Can't you protect them from this? Do you read them the goddamn obituaries every day? How the hell did this one die?"

"I killed her," May growled into the phone.

"Mom!"

May swung around to see Delia standing there, looking angry and hurt. *Damn you, Todd,* she thought.

"I was kidding, sweetie," she said quickly, covering the mouthpiece. "You know how Daddy and I tease each other." She blinked back her tears and said to Todd, "Can you believe that Delia thought I was serious?" First she forced a laugh, then she forced herself to speak. "It was an accident. A fatal accident," she explained, pretending Todd was a normal person asking a normal question.

"What kind of accident?" His voice was thick with accusation.

"Are you finished with your sculptures?" she asked the girls, covering the mouthpiece again.

They nodded.

"You want me to bake them?"

"Finish with Daddy first," Susie instructed her.

"Drowned," she told her ex.

"At the beach?"

"In her pool."

"You don't let the girls swim unattended, do you, May?"

She practiced the deep-breathing exercises she'd learned in the yoga class she went to once and didn't have time to go to again. When the children stayed with Todd during the summer, she called them every day, and never screaming. Why couldn't Todd manage the same?

"That's nice," she said to Todd's stony silence. "Have a good time. Love to Chloe." And she smiled as she hung up the phone. "Daddy says go to sleep."

It took two extralong stories to calm the girls down. When she checked on Delia at nine, the night-light reflected off the open whites of her eyes. She'd been crying.

May knelt beside her. "I love you, sweetie." She stroked her daughter's silken hair. "And I'm sorry Daddy and I still fight, even three thousand miles away."

Delia nodded like she understood. She knew from experience that that was what she was supposed to do.

"I want to tell you something I found out about Stacey," May said, taking a chance that this, as much as anything, was contributing to Delia's wakefulness. "I didn't know, but it turns out she was very sick. She wasn't supposed to go swimming, but she did anyway."

"Like after you eat and you get a cramp?" Delia asked. Her voice was hopeful, making May feel she was on the right track.

"Yes," she said. "Exactly. She wasn't supposed to swim, but she did."

"I'd never do that," Delia assured her. "Would you?"

"Absolutely not. Never," May said. "I'm always careful, sweetie. So I guess I'll be around fighting with Daddy for a long, long time."

"Good," Delia said, and then they both laughed. Taking her cue from that, May planted a kiss on the top of Delia's head, and left. When she checked back on her ten minutes later, both girls were snoring quietly.

She closed up the house, then got ready for bed. It wasn't quite ten when she made her last call of the day, to Lydia.

Even before she could get in a word, Lydia asked, "Where were you today?"

"At work. I didn't stop by the house because I don't feel that I'm welcome," May explained.

"I'm talking about the funeral," Lydia said.

"What funeral?"

"Crap," Lydia muttered. "He didn't tell you."

May's head felt heavy. "It was today? But I spoke to him this morning and he didn't say it would be today."

"It was late this afternoon," Lydia said. "Just a few hours after the police gave her back." She was silent for a moment before going on. "There was hardly anyone there. He decided he couldn't wait for people to come in from out of town, but I thought at least he'd call her close friends, at least he'd call you."

"He should have called me," May said quietly. "Stacey would have wanted me there." She wondered how things had gotten to this point so fast. Then she shook off her disappointment. She could use this. She got back to the point of her call

"Did you and Scott work out when you're coming over to the house to go through Stacey's things? Or did I miss that, too."

"I'm going over tomorrow," Lydia said. "I was going to call you to tell you, but you beat me to it."

May didn't challenge the lie.

"I'll give you a call when I leave my house," Lydia promised, and then quickly got off the phone, leaving May to duck into the only peace she could find—sleep.

Twenty-Five

"MOMMY!" The call broke through the dead quiet of the night.

May ran to Susie's bedside so quickly she was there even before she knew she was awake.

"It's okay, sweetie," she said, stroking her daughter's sweaty forehead. "It was just a dream. Everything is okay."

"Mommy!" Susie screamed again, as if May weren't standing there staring directly into her terrified eyes.

"I'm here, Susie." She backed away and turned on the light. "You're awake, sweetie," she said, trying to draw her out of her night terror.

"Mommy!" Susie yelled, and stood up in bed, tears streaming down her face.

"Susie," May called out, sternly now. "I'm here. I'm with you. You're dreaming. Everything is fine. You're okay."

Susie stared at her mother for a moment and then plunged down under her bedcovers, pulling the blanket up over her head.

May stood over her and watched until she saw that Susie's chest began to rise and fall rhythmically, until she knew that she was back to a restful sleep. Carefully she lifted the blanket off her daughter's face and kissed her forehead. "Good night, sweetie."

Susie opened her eyes. "Good night, Mommy," she said, as if she'd been sleeping peacefully for hours. Her eyes snapped shut and she was gone, to sweeter dreams.

May returned to her room, stopping at the clock to check the time: 4:45. She climbed into bed and lay atop the blanket. Within ten minutes, she knew she was hopelessly awake. Deciding not to fight it, she got up, showered, dressed, put up a pot of coffee, and began to plan her day.

But she hadn't gotten beyond locating a pencil that actually had a point, when Sabrieke joined her. The au pair was wrapped up in a white corduroy robe, her hair pulled on top of her head in a scrunchie, her face clean and pretty without makeup.

"I got up early to do the test," she reported quietly.

May waited for Sabrieke to tell her even though she could read results on her face.

"It is positive. I am positive. Positively pregnant."

"I don't know what to say," May admitted.

"Congratulations?" Sabrieke suggested.

"Congratulations," May said, half-heartedly.

"It's good news. Manu, he wants to marry me even he does not know I am pregnant. But I told him he has to move up in his career from busboy. He has to have a future before he can have me for his wife. Do you think that is wrong?"

"No," May said, because she was the last person to give anyone advice on love and marriage.

"I will tell him tonight. But first I must call my mother."

"What are you planning on doing?" May asked, leaving out the second half of the question: *When are you leaving us?*

"I didn't sleep at all last night thinking about the answer to this question. So, here is what I have decided on. I am going to have the baby, of course. And I would like to keep working for you. I can do both. Why not?"

It seemed unkind to list all the reasons why not, so May simply scribbled down the name of her OB-GYN and handed it over. "We can figure it out later."

Sabrieke grabbed her in an uncharacteristic hug. "You are wonderful! Of course you know this, yes?"

May smiled. "Sometimes, yes," she admitted. *Sometimes no,* she added to herself.

"After I speak with my mother," Sabrieke told her, "I can get the girls ready for school and to the bus. It's best for me if I keep busy, if it's the same to you."

May accepted the offer. The girls sincerely loved Sabrieke, and why not? She was kind and patient and young and sweet. May loved her, too. She heaved a sigh. They'd work it out. She opened the refrigerator. At some weak moment, she'd promised pancakes.

The girls were up and happily engaged with Sabrieke, and the batter was beginning to bubble when Lydia called.

"Scott's working today, early hours," she reported. "I can be at your house in half an hour."

"Okay."

"Scott asked me to stop by anyway to pick up his key."

"Isn't Morgan home?"

"Apparently not. He's hoping she's deplaning in County Cork as we speak."

May got off the phone and when Sabrieke came into the kitchen, she asked her, "Is Morgan here?"

"No. Why?"

May decided not to share her worry. "I just wasn't sure if she'd decided to stay over or not."

"She went home," Sabrieke explained. "Oh, and speaking of that, I spoke to my mom. She wants me to come home. Big surprise. You know very well how a mother can be."

"Yes," May said, but she was only half listening, preoccupied with wondering, *Where else could Morgan be?*

"You will decide what you think is best," Sabrieke went on. "But for me, I'd like to stay. I do believe I can continue to do my job very well while I'm pregnant. Of course, if there's some problem, no, but I don't think there will be any problems, do you?"

On automatic pilot, May answered, "No."

"And once I have the baby I think I can watch three as easily as two."

May's attention was back. "We'll see. Did you make an appointment with the doctor yet?"

"For Monday morning," Sabrieke explained, and then said, "So, everything is good, no?"

May avoided answering and turned to the task at hand, making pancakes.

She was just hustling the girls out the door for the bus when Lydia pulled up. May ran out, dishes in the sink, to help her go through Stacey's things.

Twenty-Six

"DOES HE WANT TO KEEP ANY OF THE CLOTHES?"

"No. Nothing. He said get rid of everything in her closet and dresser except the jewelry. He's going to put the jewelry away for Sophie. She wanted to come with me, but I said, not now, not yet."

"Why not?"

"She's too raw. It would be traumatic."

May wondered if that was the only reason.

"We're just going through clothes and personal-care items. He doesn't want me going through the whole house," Lydia explained.

May's eyes went to where Stacey's painted wooden jewelry box used to sit on her bureau, but it was gone. "I guess he already put the jewelry box away," she observed. "It used to be right there." She hadn't spent a lot of time in Stacey's bedroom, but she had been up for occasional what-do-I-wear consultations. She walked over to the dresser and touched the vacant spot where dust hadn't yet had a chance to accumulate. "It used to be right there." A wave of sadness settled over her.

"Maybe he was worried I might steal something," Lydia said, but despite the words, her tone suggested she didn't much care. May vacillated between hot cheeks, sweaty palms, and sudden surges of nausea. Lydia might as well have been clearing out the refrigerator before going on vacation.

May forced herself to push on, touching the pastel suits, soft silk shirts, crocheted beach cover-ups, beaded cocktail dresses, clothes that had been so full of life on Stacey, and now hung like the rags of fabric they really were.

They worked silently, pulling the clothes off of hangers, opening drawers, lifting out neatly folded T-shirts, jeans, chinos, and socks, some pairs rolled in balls, some orphans waiting for the match that would now never come.

The worst of it was the underwear—bras, panties, intimate apparel she was never meant to touch. Finally, by the time she got to the pantyhose and slips, she felt numb; it was routine. Pull out the pantyhose, throw them on the bed; when the mountain of clothes on the bed reaches a certain height, gather it all up and fill up a plastic bag.

"What about her purses?" May asked, staring into the closet, empty now of clothes, but filled with shoes and bags. There were at least a dozen, Coach bags, Prada knockoffs, totes, backpacks, black and cream beaded evening purses from back when attending black-tie affairs was part of Stacey's job description.

"Do you want any of them?" Lydia asked.

"No," May said quickly, repulsed by the idea of walking around with her dead friend's purse hanging off her shoulder. "I guess we should empty them."

"Be my guest," Lydia said, as she began a close inspection of a brown leather briefcase she'd just pulled off a hook. "I'll keep this one," she said, and slung it over her shoulder, ready for work.

May opened the bag she recognized as Stacey's everyday one, a small black leather backpack. With a deep breath, she stuck her hand inside and began pulling out the contents. A handful of crumpled unused tissues, a lipstick, keys, a comb, a small photo album of her kids, her wallet, a checkbook, a broken crayon, a reminder card for Michael's dentist appointment, already passed. Then at the bottom, she found a pile of notes.

She glanced up to see what Lydia was doing—checking herself out in the full-length mirror to see how the briefcase looked—and quickly slipped the notes into her jeans pocket.

"Any chance Scott will come home early?" she asked, feeling like a bit of a burglar.

"He told me office hours are over at four. Why?"

May shrugged and dug her hand into the next bag, lifting out a department-store cosmetic sample of eye cream, a small change purse, a list of drugstore items titled "For Sophie," and some more crumpled papers. She quickly stuck the papers in her pocket, this time while Lydia was bent down in the closet, scooping up shoes. "I guess I don't think he'd be too happy to find me in his bedroom emptying his wife's pocketbooks," May said as she drew out several credit-card receipts and two movie ticket stubs.

"He's the one who should be avoiding running into you," Lydia said. She threw the last pair of shoes, dusty clogs that were probably twenty-five years old, into a bag and tied the top into a knot. "If I were you and he didn't tell me about the funeral of my best friend, I'd probably march right into his office and shoot him dead."

May stuck her hand into the purse, feeling for any loose change at the bottom. She came up with one dirty Tic Tac and a broken comb.

"In fact, I wish you would shoot the bastard," Lydia said. Her affect was off. She might as well have been saying, *I wish you would move your car. I wish you would get a new haircut.* "You know, legally I'm next in line to be the children's guardian. They'd be a lot better off if you'd just shoot him today."

May felt a rising sense of discomfort. She struggled to sort out whether Lydia was kidding or whether she should heed her gut's warning that danger was about.

She didn't want to leave now, not before she had a chance to look around for Stacey's phone book. But it wasn't worth risking her safety for that.

Then Lydia said, "I'll start taking these down," and May's unease vanished. She watched Lydia lift two heavy garbage bags and, with the briefcase still slung over her shoulder, slowly carry away the first load of Stacey's things.

Immediately May went to Scott's drawers, quickly sliding open one after another, feeling around inside. For what? There was nothing there.

She tried his night table next, found pills, loose photographs, loose change, birthday cards—nothing. When she heard Lydia coming back upstairs, she quickly started stuffing the purses into a garbage bag. Wordlessly, Lydia picked up another two trash bags and, like a soldier on a mission, marched downstairs.

This time, May went to the top of Scott's dresser, to a clutter of receipts and papers. Quickly she rifled through the pile, but there was nothing that told her anything. She opened his closet door next, saw clothes hanging, clothes piled neatly on the top shelf, shoes organized, carefully, along the floor. His ties hung on a rack, lined up like a rainbow, by color. She took a breath, a look behind her, and then reached inside one of Scott's jackets to feel around. Tissues, a gum wrapper, a crumpled five-dollar bill, a parking receipt. Nothing. She tried the next jacket. Nothing. But in the third suit coat, in the inside pocket, bingo: she found a thick envelope with Stacey's name on the outside. She opened it quickly, still careful to listen for Lydia.

Three plane tickets. One marked for Stacey, one for Sophie, one for Michael. They were going to San Diego. But why? Why without Scott?

Suddenly she was aware of how much time had passed. She returned the tickets to the pocket, took one last look at her friend's Ralph Lauren–decorated bedroom, then bent down to lift up the remaining two garbage bags to carry downstairs. That's when she saw it, peeking out from under what she knew was Stacey's side of the bed. The corner of a small book, an address book. Stacey's address book.

Her prize in her purse, she raced downstairs and deposited the remaining garbage bags in the center of the hall with the rest of the collection. Then she followed the sound of movement to the kitchen, where she found Lydia, filling up Stacey's briefcase with papers.

When she heard May, Lydia turned suddenly but offered no explanation for her pilfering. She put the briefcase on her shoulder and headed toward the door. "That's it. We're done. Scott said to leave the bags in the hall. He's got someone coming later to collect them."

May couldn't help but ask, although she knew she had no right. "What did you take?"

Lydia looked up blankly and lied. "Nothing."

"You just put something in the briefcase," May said, challenging her.

"No, I didn't," she said, and that was that, unless May wanted to wrestle her to the floor.

Lydia opened the door and waited for May to leave. Then she bounded outside and slid into her silver Lexus. "Good luck," she said, and drove off.

"Good riddance," May muttered under her breath and walked home. She stopped on her front steps to unfold Stacey's papers. She studied credit-card receipts, shopping lists, notes with unfamiliar names and numbers. Nothing. Nothing until she uncurled a square of paper so old or handled so much it had turned nearly tissue thin. The carefully printed words, black ink turned to gray, made her shoulder muscles quiver briefly, as if they'd gone into spasm.

Matthew Harris, it said at the top of the note, with an out-of-town number hastily scrawled next to it. Below that, written with a different pen, was a message Stacey wrote to herself: "Call Dr. Lichtman, Nirvana Spa."

May sat down on her steps and stared straight ahead,

not even noticing the woman who eyed her unpleasantly as she walked by with her Border collie because her friendly hello had gotten no response.

That was because May hadn't heard it. She sat frozen, except for her brain, which was spinning, whirring, calculating, planning. Now, more than ever, she needed to know who this Margaret Harris was. She had to confront the nephew. As for Dr. Lichtman, she had to find out if the link between them was a coincidence—a later unrelated message scratched on to the same notepaper—or whether there was a connection that went further than she figured.

Her focus on high beam, she opened her front door and marched inside to figure it out.

Twenty-Seven

SHE COULDN'T SEE ALL THE WAY into her living room, but from the foyer, she could see the trouser legs. Sabrieke heard the door and ran to head her off.

"I just called over at Stacey's to find you, but there was no answer. You have a visitor." Then she added, under her breath, "Why doesn't Morgan answer the phone?"

"She isn't there. She didn't come home last night," May told her. Although it nagged at her and the lines on Sabrieke's brow told her she wasn't alone in her worry, she had a bigger worry now. Who was her guest?

Sabrieke followed her gaze and said, "It's someone from the police."

May quickly strode into her living room. Detective Smith stood up to greet her.

"What happened?" she asked in a rush. "Are my children okay?"

"Everything's fine, Mrs. Morrison," Detective Smith said, and Sabrieke excused herself and disappeared. "I just wanted to talk."

Nervous, May sat down. Except for the one she was in love with, she didn't have a good history with cops.

Smith crossed a leg over his knee and leaned back into the couch. "Can we talk about Stacey Blum's death?"

"Yes," May said quietly.

"When you came to see the chief you told us you believed the death might not be an accident. Do you remember that?"

"Should I have a lawyer here?" she asked, because despite his relaxed stance, his tone made her feel as if she were in a courtroom again, as if he were a prosecutor, trying to tear down a witness.

He laughed, a hearty, long, and heartfelt laugh. "No, ma'am," he said. "Of course you're welcome to have one, but no. You don't need one. At least I don't think you need one," he added, the laughter clearing out of his eyes.

She counted backwards from ten, so the burning red in her cheeks would settle down. "Then why do you ask?"

"I'm interested in knowing, that's all. Why you were suspicious. I just want to know what you figure happened."

She knew she wasn't supposed to give him anything more than what he asked for, so she chose her words carefully. "I have no idea. I just don't buy the accident story."

"Because?"

"Because of a lot of things. Because she wasn't herself. Because she was scared about something. Because I heard she was planning on moving, all of a sudden, in a rush, as if she were running away."

"Moving where?"

"I don't know," she said, but didn't meet his eyes. A change in the atmosphere of the room told her that he'd noticed.

"Was she going alone?"

"No. With her children. Just her children." She let that fact sink in and then went on. "And there's another thing. It might be totally unrelated."

"I'm wide open here," the detective said, encouraging her.

She took a breath and went on. "Stacey had a friend

whose nephew has been hounding me because his aunt died recently—supposedly an accident—but he didn't think so."

Sitting up straighter on the couch, Detective Smith reached for his notebook.

"And he was hounding you because?"

"He said his aunt was supposed to be coming on a show I'm producing. Margaret Harris is her name," she added, and spelled it without being asked. "From Boynton, Pennsylvania."

"What was the show about?"

"That's the thing. I have no idea. I couldn't find any record of her."

He wrote that down, too.

"Look, maybe I'm just looking for shadows where they don't exist. Maybe Stacey died the way it seemed." She thought of the day in her friend's living room when Stacey dropped a book on May's foot and made a joke about her clumsiness. "Maybe she had the flu, it made her clumsy, and she hit her head." She laughed. "Even I don't understand why I don't believe that."

"Mrs. Morrison," Detective Smith said quietly. "We know Mrs. Blum did not die of the flu."

"I know," May said and recited the next as if she were a kindergartner giving back what she'd learned by rote. "She died because she hit her head on the wall of the pool and she drowned."

Detective Smith stared at her, hard. "I'm not saying that, either."

"What are you saying, then?"

He ignored her question. "Putting aside your gut, do you have any concrete evidence to support your suspicions that Mrs. Blum was murdered?"

She met his eyes dead on. He didn't break the stare. "No."

"Do you have any reason to believe someone might have wanted her dead?"

"No," she said. "Do you?"

"This is an ongoing investigation" was all he'd answer.

"Oh," she replied, and remembered Paul's explaining that *an accident gets an inquiry. A murder gets an investigation.* "How exactly did Stacey die, Detective?"

"That's public knowledge. Mrs. Blum died from a blow to her head." He stood up. "If you have nothing more to tell me, I'll be on my way."

She rose and followed him to her front door.

"Thank you, Mrs. Morrison," he told her and handed her his card. "If you remember anything, if you think of an incident where someone had a confrontation with Mrs. Blum, if she ever mentioned that someone made her feel uncomfortable, or fearful, call me. Will you do that? Will you call me if anything else occurs to you?"

"Yes, of course," she said. It was only after he'd walked down her front path, after he'd gotten into his squad car, after he'd driven up the street, cigarette smoke leaking out of his open window, that the weight of his words hit her.

He'd said, *Mrs. Blum died from a blow to her head,* not *She died from smashing her head into the end of the pool.* She closed the door and leaned against it, going over the words again and again until finally it was as clear and loud as if he'd shouted it out. Stacey hadn't hit her head. Stacey's head had been hit. Which meant Stacey Blum was murdered.

The doorbell rang and she swung it open, expecting the detective had come back. It was Manu, Sabrieke's blond halfback-size Belgian beau, clutching an enormous bouquet of flowers. His cheeks were flushed with excitement. "Would it be all right if I could see Sabrieke for a few moments, please?"

Without replying, her mind filled up with unanswered questions, May went off to find Sabrieke.

Twenty-Eight

STAYING IN THE KITCHEN to give Sabrieke and Manu the chance to be alone in the living room, she tried the number for Matthew Harris. When his answering machine voice greeted her, she hung up, unnerved. She wasn't ready to commit to leaving a message.

Rifling through her desk, she came upon the list she'd made of Stacey's friends and family. She studied it.

Scott. What Lydia said was true. After every evening-news shot of a grieving husband came the next day's image, the man being carted off to jail in handcuffs. It seemed inevitable. Still, she couldn't quite buy it. She'd never liked the man, but she couldn't actually imagine him harming his wife.

And what about Margaret Harris? Could her death be related to Stacey's?

She went back to studying the list, her eyes stopping at the names of Stacey's friends. Then she pulled Stacey's address book from where she'd carefully laid it, and opened it.

Her breathing slowed as she saw Stacey's careful handwriting. She ran her fingers down the page over the perfectly formed numbers and printed names. She started with *A* and found it under *R*, Risa Ricardo, with an upstate New

York area code. Using her laptop, she quickly tracked down the town on a map. Risa Ricardo lived just over two hours away. She dialed the number.

It took several rings before a male voice answered with a gruff "Hello" that held no friendliness, no invitation to say more.

"May I speak to Risa, please?" she asked.

"Risa? What number are you trying to call?"

May read back the number she'd meant to dial and the man listened. "Who did you say you want to talk to?"

"Risa Ricardo."

There was a moment of silence and then, "Oh. You must mean Theresa. I'm her husband, Joe Ricardo."

May quickly explained she was a friend of Stacey Blum's, that she was sorry to disturb him but that she needed to speak to Risa.

"Theresa can't come to the phone," he explained. "She's in bed, sick. She's resting.

"It's important," May explained.

"I'm listening," Joe said, though he didn't sound happy about it.

May knew this wasn't going to work. From years of experience soliciting guests, she could tell when a phone call needed to be upgraded to a face-to-face.

"I'd like to drive up and see you," she told him. "I have to be up that way anyway this afternoon. I can bring lunch. Please," she added. "If Risa can see me for even a few minutes, it would mean so much."

She didn't tell him the rest, didn't say what had happened to Stacey. She didn't want to scare him away.

"All right," he said finally. "If she's awake when you come, you can see her, but just for a minute. And you can't upset her. Whatever you do, you can't upset her."

She found Sabrieke in the living room nuzzling Manu as they admired, by turn, the flowers and the wonder of her flat stomach. After May confirmed that her au pair would be back on duty at 3:30 to meet the school bus, she put in a call to Paul to let him know where she was going. When he didn't answer his page, she left a message.

Her next call was to Dr. Lichtman at the Nirvana spa. Again his nurse reported the doctor was out. This time May didn't believe her. She didn't bother to leave another message.

Her final call was to Colleen—some emergency shmoozing was in order—but her boss was out, too. Before she could hang up, Margery picked up the line.

"It's your day off and you're going to spend it driving up to the country to interview a sick woman?" she asked, after May explained her plans.

"It's not my day off," May clarified. "I'm working from home. On the spa show."

"Right. Well, sugar, here's the deal on that. When you get to the part where you actually go to the spa, count me in. I want to come along. Do you think we could sell me as a coproducer on this one?"

And May thought, yes, she should do that. She should go to the spa, find out if there was a link to Margaret Harris.

"It's no fun anymore, sugar," Margery was saying. "Not with these watered-down shows Paula's been wanting me to do. Not with Colleen whimpering about how being an executive producer is a thankless job. I wish I could turn the clock back to the days when I could do shows about security guards who turned out to be cannibals, the days when Gil chewed his Bic pen tops to bits but let a person take a chance on something that might turn out to be better than good." She took a breath. "Going to the spa with you might clear my head. Or at least make me look ten years younger."

"It's a great idea," May said. "Between the two of us, we should be able to convince Colleen to let us coproduce it. And if I'm going to be poking around into a possible murder, I'm going to need a great crime-beat producer like you to watch my back."

"Then you go right ahead and interview that sick lady," Margery advised. "I'll start dropping hints with Colleen that I'm feeling restless, jittery, and in need of an emergency perk. Or a Percocet. Whichever comes first."

May got off the phone with a smile that didn't last much into the ride to Olivebridge. When worry returned—Where was Morgan? What happened to Stacey?—May found an oldies station, blasted music, and sang along out loud to get her brain to stop. Eventually, too much static put the station out of reach and she drove in silence. It was just under two hours when she turned the car off the main road and began following the winding rural routes of Dutchess County.

When she knew she was nearly there, she stopped at a rickety package store at the side of the road and ordered two sandwiches, specials of the house. Then back in the car, several farms later, she passed the bright yellow colonial with red windowboxes that Mr. Ricardo said was the landmark, one house before his own.

She drove to the two-car garage with the giant iron eagle sprawling across the front, then turned and followed the wide gravel driveway up to the house.

She wasn't prepared for such a grand house. Perched atop a high hill, it offered a sprawling view of the valley below and the Shawnagunk Mountains beyond. At one side lay a pond, lily pads floating at the shallow end, tall reeds at the other. Behind the pond was a large square vegetable plot surrounded by a tall chain fence meant to keep out deer. The deer had gotten in, though, making further mess of a garden already dense with weeds and half-gnawed oversize vegetables lying on their sides—huge zucchini, blackened tomatoes and peppers, rotting.

"Pity, what's happened there," a voice came up behind her. "Used to be my pride and joy."

She swung around to see a man she put at his early sixties, with thinning white wisps of hair, a wide jowly face, and friendly brown eyes.

"Joe Ricardo." He extended his hand.

She introduced herself. "May Morrison. It's beautiful," she said gesturing to the view.

"I don't see it anymore," he said. "When we first moved here, I would put a folding chair at that spot right there at the top of the hill." He pointed to where a single swing on a tattered rope hung from an ancient maple tree, marking the highest point on the property.

"I'd sit there and do nothing but watch the grass grow. If it's clear, you can see for miles. The colors were what always amazed me. People don't realize how many colors a mountain has."

He stared off in the distance, then looked away and shook his head. "I can't even see them anymore." He yanked up his pants and tucked in his plaid flannel shirt, probably for the tenth time that day. His pants were loose. His shirt was big and, May thought, he looked as if he'd been a robust man not so long ago.

"Come on in. I'm not much of a host, but we can sit inside and you can tell me what's on your mind."

May followed him up a slate path into a large country kitchen. Dishes were piled in the sink. He followed her eyes to the mess as if he hadn't noticed it before.

"Didn't have time to clean up for you," he said matter-of-factly.

"My house looks the same way," she said.

"This one never did. My wife is one of those clean nuts. Throws away sponges as if they were paper towels. Constantly spraying countertops against germs, washing the floor twice a day. Lot of good it did her." He shook his head. "Sit down, sit down." He motioned to some chairs set around a long wooden farm table.

She sat down and handed over the bag of sandwiches like an offering.

He took the bag reluctantly, then peered inside. He placed it on the table, making no move to remove its contents, and sat down. "What can I do for you?"

She got to the point. "My friend, Stacey Blum, met your wife at the Nirvana Spa a few years ago."

He nodded. "There was a bunch of them. I remember your friend, a wit sharp as a knife. That's what Theresa loves, a sharp wit. That and a good heart." He had nothing more to say, so he waited for the rest.

"Stacey died—recently."

The color drained from Joe's face all at once, as completely as if someone pulled the plug on him. He blinked slowly, looking to her as if he was considering the pros and cons of passing out. "How?"

"They say she drowned in her swimming pool," May told him.

He opened his eyes wide with surprise and laughed. May's face gave away her shock at the sound.

"Sorry," he said quickly. "I was just figuring you were coming to tell me something different. Something totally different. Sorry to laugh. Sorry for you. Losing a friend and all." He shook his head. "I should have known when you asked for Risa you were a friend of Stacey's. She's the only person in the world Theresa would let call her that. Risa. I didn't even know who you were talking about."

"She called me Maysie," May admitted.

"At least she knew enough not to call me Joey," he said, and as he laughed, May laughed along, for the first time all day. Then they both got quiet.

"I don't know about telling Theresa about this," he said. "It's an awful lot of friends to die, all at once. And accidents are hard to take, you know." He didn't notice May's cheeks turning scarlet. He couldn't tell her chest was beginning to constrict.

She took a breath, steadied her voice and asked, "Who else died?" But Joe didn't have to answer for her to know. Because suddenly it clicked. May was Maysie. Theresa was Risa. Margaret was Greta. Greta was dead.

"He came to visit," Joe was saying, and she brought herself back to him. "I'm very popular, you know." He chuckled but couldn't sustain it for more than a second. "Mostly it's doctors and preachers who come. Then he came. Greta's nephew. Very upset. Couldn't accept his aunt's death at all."

"Greta Harris," May stated quietly, to herself. "Matthew Harris's aunt."

"That's right," Joe said. "Matthew Harris was his name. He rambled on about Aunt Margaret for so long it took a while for me to understand what he was saying—about her accident. I didn't blame him for being upset. Run over by a train—sounds horrible to me."

May listened hard to every word. She wanted to be sure she knew the story as well as if it were her own—for later, when she went over it all in her head.

"He told me the authorities claimed she did it on purpose, suicide, but he didn't believe it. He said she wouldn't. She loved life, was a glass-half-full type of person. So I asked him what happened. Did she fall? He said he didn't believe that either. He said he'd been to the scene and there was nothing he saw that would make her stumble. So I asked, 'Do you think someone pushed her?'"

May shook off a shiver as she remembered how she'd asked Paul the same question, about Stacey and the pool.

"'Well, no,' he told me," Joe went on. "No one saw anyone push her. 'What do you think happened, then?' I asked him. He said he didn't know. He was hoping I could tell him—me, who never met his aunt. He started asking me questions, about Theresa, about her illness. After a while, I couldn't stand it anymore. I mean, why on earth would I tell some stranger the details of Theresa's illness? So I plain out asked him, 'Why do you think your aunt's being run over by a train has anything to do with me?' By then I'd had it. I was sick of it. When he said he didn't know, I suggested he get on his way."

Joe looked away, toward the door, as if he could still see Matthew standing there. "I felt bad about it afterwards. He wasn't a bad sort of fellow, just someone searching for answers. Just searching." He looked at May. "Like you."

She shifted in her seat.

"When I got the call about Toni, I decided right then and there I wasn't going to tell Theresa. You probably think that's awful. Withholding that kind of news, as if she were a child."

May's hands felt so cold she was afraid they'd gone numb. "What happened to Toni?"

His brown eyes opened wider. "You didn't know." It was a fact, not a question.

She shook her head.

Joe heaved a sigh. "Something was wrong with her for quite some time. We all knew it. She would go into these rages. Out of the blue. Rages. For a while after Theresa got sick, Toni would come here every week to visit, even though it was over an hour from where she lived. But finally I had to tell her to stop because it was so upsetting. You never knew what would set her off."

"What happened to her?" May asked again.

"I got a call about the funeral, that's all I know. I expressed my sympathy and regrets that we couldn't go. Theresa can't go anywhere, and I don't like to be out of the house for more than an hour. I don't like to be out of the house at all." His eyes looked toward the darkened hallway.

"It's a lot of dying in a short time," May said.

"Yes, indeed," he replied, and his eyes glazed over, avoiding something. Then he came back to himself. "It's your turn. What's on your mind?"

"Just this. Before she died, Stacey was trying to get in touch with your wife. I wanted to know if they ever connected."

He nodded. "She called. I put the phone to Theresa's ear and held it there while she spoke. I wouldn't exactly call it a conversation."

"I need to know what she said. You see, Stacey wanted to tell me something, too. She tried to reach me right before she died, but I never got a chance to talk to her. I'm trying to find out what was on her mind. I'm trying to find out what really happened to her. I don't think Stacey died by accident, either."

He looked toward the narrow hallway leading from the kitchen into the house and said, "I don't want you telling Theresa that Stacey's passed. She's very weak. I'm working hard to get her strength back. She's not strong enough to handle hearing that Stacey passed."

"I won't tell her," she said. "I promise I won't tell her."

He heaved another sigh. "All right. It's a long drive to come for nothing." He stood up. "Not more than a couple of minutes. She needs her rest."

May followed him down the dim hall into the living room and through another long hall to their back bedroom. The room, like everywhere else in the house except the kitchen, was dark and stuffy. It took a moment for May's eyes to adjust enough so that she could make out that the cluster of clothes on the bed was a person.

"Theresa?" May said.

"Kiddo," Joseph called, "we've got company."

The lump under the covers moved. A head appeared, sunken cheeks, a pasty face, watery eyes.

"She can't sit up today," he explained. "The doc is sending over some new medicine. Theresa," he called her name, louder now. "This here is a friend of Stacey's." He walked close to May and said quietly, "She'll hear you if you stand right next to the bed. I'll hear you, too." It was a warning, and once it was made, he backed away and sat down in an old nubby easy chair pulled up close to his wife's bedside.

"Theresa," she started, "I'm a friend of Stacey's. You remember Stacey, don't you?"

Theresa looked distracted, as if she'd heard something mildly annoying, a buzzing noise or a plane overhead. Slowly she turned her head toward where May stood. Her eyes searched the air as she strained to focus. Finally, she found the spot that was May. She opened her mouth slowly but no words came out, just a wild, frightening sound that May realized was a laugh.

The sound seemed to sail through the air and hit Joe smack in the face. He got up and left the room. May thought he might be crying. She turned back, knelt down, put her face right next to Theresa's.

"Did Stacey tell you something?" she asked right into Theresa's ear. "Did she tell you about something that was worrying her?"

Theresa's head moved toward May. May put her ear next to Theresa's mouth.

"Nirvana," she whispered. "I'm in Nirvana." And she broke out in another raucous laugh that made May jerk her head away from the sound. This time the laughter went on and on until it turned into hysteria, laughing and crying mixed together. May hurried out of the room and found Joe in the kitchen, hunched in a chair. She wondered if he realized his wife was dying.

"She needs to go to the hospital," she told him. "She's very sick." It seemed so obvious to her.

"She's not going anywhere," he said. "She's getting better. I'm taking care of her, good care of her, and she's getting better."

There was nothing more to say, so after a few more awkward moments, she turned and left him alone with his dying wife.

Twenty-Nine

SHE DROVE LEANING INTO THE WINDSHIELD, straining to see through rain that had gone from drizzle to downpour within moments.

Stacey and Greta, dead. Both supposed accidents. She thought of Theresa dying, of Toni dead. *Is all this death even possible?* But she brought people on *Paula Live* every week whose lives were stranger than truth. She felt the subtlest ignition—*Could these coincidental deaths be a show?*—and quickly extinguished it.

What is the connection? Is it Stacey? Scott? Is Nirvana—the spa—the hub? Her mind searched for a glimpse of an answer but came up blank.

With the wipers on high and her body on full alert, she pushed on, stopping twice for coffee, making her plan. She would go to Boynton, Pennsylvania, herself and find out exactly how Margaret Harris had died. Then she'd be able to confront the nephew, to insist he share everything he'd discovered so far. After that, she'd go to Nirvana, taking Margery with her. It would be a legitimate business trip, research for her show. But it would also give her a chance to find what she could about her friend.

Most of all, she had to talk to Scott. Despite Lydia's

accusations and assumptions, her instincts told her this was about something else, something different, something more.

She pulled the car off at her exit, glad to be close to home. The rain, changed now to a soft drizzle, had tired her out. She pulled into a Dunkin' Donuts, a half-mile away from her house, ordered a large cup of coffee, and then laughed at herself as she waited for it. Out of all the coffee shops that had sprung up around town as if the town she lived in were Seattle, she'd chosen this one, the Dunkin' Donuts across the street from where Scott's office sat.

She wasn't much of a believer in coincidences. She accepted that she'd driven here because it was where she wanted to be. So after getting her drink, she drove across the street to Scott's parking lot and sat in her car sipping coffee while she watched patients come and go. When she was done, she got out, threw her empty cup in the trashbin beside the door, and followed a slow-moving elderly Asian couple inside the small medical building.

She waited at the receptionist's desk for her turn and then stepped forward. A nurse, sitting behind a glass partition, spoke through a small hole not much larger than the size of a check. "Sign in, please." She had a phone stuck between her shoulder and her ear and was quickly flipping through the appointment book.

"I'm not a patient," May began, but the nurse—her small rectangular badge said Phyllis—interrupted.

"Everybody signs in," Phyllis said, covering the mouthpiece of the phone. "Reps, too."

May didn't care who the receptionist thought she was talking to as long as she got to see Scott. "I'd like to see Dr. Blum."

"He's with a patient right now. If you can wait, I'll let his nurse know you're here. It's going to be a long wait. You might want to just drop off your samples." Phyllis looked back to the phone and barked into the receiver, interrupting herself. "No," she said to the patient who'd been holding past his patience. "The next appointment I can give you is not today at five. It's tomorrow at ten."

"I'll wait," May whispered, and Phyllis acknowledged her with a quick nod and went back to her scheduling problems.

From the far wall, a painted pale gray door opened and Marcy, Scott's nurse, stepped out, clutching a folder. "Mrs. O'Grady"?" she called.

May sat stiffly, waiting to be discovered, but Marcy had perfected the art of staring straight ahead without making eye contact with anyone.

"Here," a white-haired lady said, as if she was back in school, answering roll call. Very slowly, she stood up and made her way to where Marcy stood.

"How are you today, Mrs. O'Grady?"

"I'm fine, Marcy darling, and yourself?"

"We're doing the best we can," she said as they disappeared inside.

May felt the nurse's *we* like a bee sting. Marcy looked good. Her teased tower had gone through a chemical treatment and descended into a neat bob, inches above her shoulders. Her makeup—in fact, her entire demeanor—had turned modest and subtle since May saw her last. She looked lovely, for someone just doing the best she could.

The door opened again, and another nurse—May remembered seeing her at Stacey's the other night, although they hadn't been introduced—stood in the doorway with folder in hand. "Mrs. Hecht?"

The mother of a frightened toddler picked up her son and carried him in. "He's been nauseous all morning," she explained, and the nurse quickly closed the door.

May continued waiting. Twenty minutes passed. The Asian couple sat stiffly at her side. Finally she got up and tapped on the window.

"When do you think I might be able to see Dr. Blum?"

Phyllis was on the phone again, doing an exceptional job of ignoring her. She might have ignored her forever,

May thought, if the inner door to her glassed box hadn't opened, discharging Nick.

"Phyllis, I need a mop-up in room two," Nick said. "And some air freshener." Then he caught sight of May.

"Hey there. Don't tell me you're sick."

Phyllis, unhappy with being put on cleanup duty, left to get the mop. Nick slid into her chair.

"No," May told him, "I'm here to talk to Scott."

"Does he know you're waiting?"

She shook her head. Nick's nurse returned to the receptionist's cubicle and the sick boy and his mother appeared beside May at the window. The mother clutched her checkbook in one hand and a brown paper bag, open and ready, in the other.

"Put her in room five," Nick told his nurse, pointing to May.

Moments later, the door opened and Nick's nurse called out, "May Morrison?"

May glanced back at the Asian couple to see if they were going to complain that she'd been called first, but the man's eyes were closed and the woman sat staring straight ahead, waiting. May entered the interior of the offices and followed the nurse to room five.

It was large, as exam rooms went, decorated with posters of the digestive tract, the respiratory tract, and the top ten causes of asthma. On a long table against the wall were magazines spread out in a careful fan to show their titles. There were several specializing in alternative health and herbal medicine, the rest on travel and sports.

Something about the room struck her as familiar, and then she realized the walls were painted with the same glazed golden color as Stacey's living room. Everywhere, in fact, were reminders of Stacey's taste. She had decorated the offices. May was sure of it.

"Doctor Ellman will be with you in a moment," the nurse said. "There's a robe in the changing room." She pointed to a small curtained nook.

May didn't bother explaining that she wasn't here for a checkup. She simply nodded as the nurse left. Nick came in almost immediately.

"Hi," he said, and May noticed he was speaking quietly, his voice nearly a whisper. "You should go. Scott doesn't want to talk to you."

"Did you tell him I was here?"

"There's no point. He doesn't want to talk to you."

"Why not?" She couldn't help it. Now she was whispering, too.

"You want my best guess?"

She nodded.

"You make him think about Stacey. And he doesn't want to do that. Not here. Not while the pain is still so bad."

"He's not hurting too much to work." She hadn't meant it to come out like an accusation, but there it was. "Of course, Marcy's here to help him feel better." She threw out the comment, fishing for a reaction, but got none.

"What would you have him do? At least here, he doesn't have to think about her. At least not as much."

For a moment she was silent. Then she said, "Look, Nick. There's no reason for you to do anything for me. But if you ever cared about Stacey at all, please do this. Get him to talk to me. Remind him that I'm not the enemy. I didn't steal her away. I didn't kill her."

His eyes softened, as if he was about to agree. But before he could speak, the door opened a crack. Someone was peering inside. It swung wide a moment later. Scott stood occupying the entire doorway, his pain worn all over his face.

"What do you want?" He didn't sound mad, but he took no pleasure in seeing her, that was clear.

"I want to talk to you. For five minutes. That's all."

"I'm working here. Can you understand that? Why are you hounding me?"

Nick got off the stool and put himself between Scott and May, a human wall. "Hear her out. I'll cover for you. What room were you in?"

"I don't want you to cover for me and I don't have anything to say to her." He pushed his partner aside, not gently. "You are not welcome here," he said when he had a clear view of May's troubled eyes. "Is that clear enough for you?"

For a moment, she felt like a child sitting in the doctor's office blinking back tears. Then she stood up, reclaiming her composure. "I want five minutes of your time, that's all. Five minutes of your open mind." She was careful to take deep breaths so her cheeks wouldn't turn crimson. "I've been talking to some people. I've heard some disturbing things. If you care about your wife, Scott, if you ever cared about her, you'll hear me out."

"How dare you?" he said, his voice rising as his eyebrows fell in a scowl. "How dare you question my feelings about my wife?"

"Come on, Scott," Nick said, coming closer, urging him with his voice and his body to calm down. "Give her a chance. She was Stacey's friend. She deserves a few minutes of your time."

"She deserves nothing," he whispered, concious now of where he was, that his rage had no place here. He went on, calmly now, as if she wasn't there. "I cannot have this kind of disturbance while I'm working. Under no circumstances is she to be allowed inside these offices again." The condescension in his voice made Nick look away, embarrassed.

May realized nothing productive would happen here, not now. "I'll see myself out," she said, brushing past them both.

Nick caught up with her in the parking lot.

"He's not himself," he said. "It's shock. You have to understand."

"I can understand shock," May said. "I can understand grief. But I can't understand why he seems so full of hate."

"I can't explain it," Nick admitted as she slid into her car.

"Then don't defend it," she replied. She watched as Nick walked, shoulders hunched, back inside.

Heavy with sadness, she turned her head to back out of her parking spot and saw her neighbor, Marlene, slamming the door of her car closed and running toward the building.

Quickly, May lowered her window and honked. Marlene swung around, startled to see her. May turned off her car and got out. Marlene remained frozen where she was, on the concrete steps.

"What are you doing here?" May asked.

Marlene fumbled with her purse as she tried to figure out how to answer. "I have an appointment," she said in a rush, settling on that.

It was so clearly not the truth. "Marlene. Don't lie to me."

Her neighbor let down her shoulders. "I have to talk to Scott," she admitted, then quickly looked away from May's piercing eyes. "It's nothing to do with Stacey. It's personal," she added hoping May would be satisfied with that. Still, May wouldn't look away.

It was clear there was something Marlene wanted to tell her. "What is it?" she asked, then lowered her voice and switched to her producer's head to draw Marlene out. "Is it about . . . ?" She raised her eyebrows but didn't finish the sentence, as if it didn't need to be said.

Her neighbor met her eyes, defiantly. "Well, if you know, there's no point in either of us pretending."

Bingo, May thought, careful not to blink. She counted backward from ten so her cheeks wouldn't betray that she was burning inside, hungry to find out what Marlene thought she already knew.

"What happened between Scott and me was wrong. You do know it's over, don't you?" she asked and May nodded. Marlene went on, relieved. "It wasn't something we decided with our heads, you know. It just happened. He didn't take advantage," she said quickly. "I don't want you thinking he was an ogre about it, taking advantage of a woman in his exam room just because she had nothing on but a thin paper gown. It wasn't like that."

"I know," May said.

Marlene nodded, happy May hadn't jumped to conclusions. "He was very respectful, very careful. He waited for me to make the first move. I mean, he let me know he wanted me; I'm not saying he didn't. But then he waited until I let him know I wanted him, too."

May started with fifty, and counted down from there, but still felt her temperature rise.

"Anyway, it's over, long over. And Stacey never did find out. That was important to him, to both of us, that she never find out. And she didn't. Not about me."

May took another chance. "Didn't you care that there'd been others?"

Another direct hit. Marlene's cheeks turned as red as May's. "Face it, May. Some men are like that. He loves women and he can't help it. Anyway, it's not like he cheated on me. Once it was over, it was over, and so what if he moved on to someone else? Who was I to say anything? We're still friends, you know. We still care for each other very much."

"Who else was there?" May asked, the urge to know winning over the need for restraint.

"He's very discreet." Then she thought for a moment. "Marcy. That's all I know for sure. The rest, the ones before me, that would be plain guessing."

"Morgan?" May tried.

"I hope not," Marlene said, and her cheeks flushed again.

May struggled to keep shock at bay. She knew this happened. Todd had cheated on *her,* after all. Why did the surprise of it still shock her now?

She had no more time to ponder it. Suddenly, there were two police cars pulling up, lights flashing, two patrolmen walking quickly into the office building.

"What's happened?" May asked out loud, but Marlene was already gone, getting into her car. May followed her. "What happened?" she asked again through the open window.

"It's Morgan," Marlene reported quietly, as if she feared being overheard. "They found her. Dead." And she turned on her car and sped off, leaving May dumbfounded in her wake.

A moment later, the front door of the office building opened and Scott came out, flanked by the two patrolmen. A cop opened the door to one of the cruisers and Scott slid inside. She saw him, as the car sped away, sitting with his head buried in his hands, his shoulders heaving as he wept.

Thirty

WHEN SHE GOT HOME AND FOUND the children having their snack, plates of apple and pear slices and pieces of mozzarella cheese that Sabrieke had cut into perfect cubes, she had a vague and familiar sense of being out of her body, of watching herself going through the motions of life but not really being there. She struggled to act as if this were just any other afternoon. Nothing was more important to her now than this, that she appear normal to her children. Until she knew more, Morgan's death was news she did not want to share.

Sabrieke was telling a story about when she was a young girl in Belgium and got to meet the king. *I have to tell Sabrieke,* May thought, dreading it.

It was Friday, the weekday on which the ban on TV was lifted, so Delia and Susie quickly finished their snack and raced each other to the sunroom to see who would get control of the remote. Sabrieke began cleaning up, getting ready to go off duty, putting the snack dishes away, throwing out the napkins. As usual, she looked serene, and May thought, *Not for long.*

She took a deep breath, was about to begin, when Sabrieke turned to her. "Oh, I forget to tell you. Morgan gave me something for you. I will get it from my room." May got ready to spring the bad news, but Sabrieke was off, jogging upstairs, so she waited.

The au pair's new pregnancy had taken nothing away from her spry agility. She was back in a minute and handed over an eight-by-ten manila envelope. "This is what she left for you," she said and then added, "Also, Emily Cooper called to say you should come to her house this afternoon at four-thirty." They both looked at the clock and saw that that was just five minutes from now. "There will be a policeman to answer questions and to interview people who live on the street. She said to tell you to bring the girls. Everyone is bringing their children. She said they can destroy her basement; she doesn't care." In relaying the news, Sabrieke's face had turned somber.

It was time. "I have to tell you something," May began. "Sit down."

Obediently as a child, Sabrieke sat.

"You know Morgan didn't come home last night."

"Oh no."

"This afternoon, they found her."

"What do you mean, 'found her'?"

May kept perfectly still and met Sabrieke's eyes.

"Is she alive?"

"No."

"What happened?" Sabrieke whispered.

"I don't know yet," May admitted.

Sabrieke let out a long breath, as if she'd been holding it in all day.

"I don't want the children to know," May said. "It's very important to me that they don't hear about this right now. Not until I figure out how to tell them."

"I understand." Sabrieke stood and smoothed her thin white T-shirt over her belly. It was an unconscious act. "Then I don't think right now I can be with them." Her voice was shaky and her hands trembled.

"Call Manu," May told her. "Stay with him tonight.

You can come back first thing in the morning. Maybe by then I'll know more."

"I am frightened," Sabrieke said.

"It will all be okay," May told her, and hoped she spoke the truth.

As soon as Sabrieke went upstairs to call Manu, May tore open the envelope Morgan had left for her. It was stuffed with papers of all sizes and types, some blank, some scribbled on. There were paper clips, rubber bands, small scraps of paper. It was as if Morgan had emptied an entire drawer into the envelope, one filled with Post-its, memo pads, pencils with no points. It was Stacey's kitchen desk drawer, May suddenly realized, filled with the scraps of her life.

Her hand felt something larger, another envelope. She pulled it out, then carefully unwound the string closure. Inside were several pieces of newspaper clippings. Obituaries.

She sat down to read them. The first was Margaret's, the one she'd already read. Then came Toni's and underneath that one was one more, about a woman named Darlene Altschul. *Who was that?*

Quickly scanning the obit, she learned the woman had died in a car accident. Darlene had been sick, was on her way to the doctor, had lost control of her car, and had driven her brand-new red Volkswagen Beetle into a tree.

The phone rang, making her jump.

"I heard," Paul said as soon as she picked up. "About Morgan."

"Who told you?"

He let out some air. He wasn't happy to admit this. "I put in a call last week to a detective out there where you live."

"Smith," she said, and he didn't correct her.

"I asked him to keep me in the loop. Professional courtesy. Told him I'd do the same for him if he ever had the misfortune to need it. Are you mad?"

She ignored the question. "What happened to Morgan? Did he tell you?"

"Do you know where Ridge Road is?"

"The reservoir?" The reservoir was less than a ten-minute drive away. There was a brand-new road around it, built just last winter. It was the perfect place for learning to ride a bike. It was where Delia had learned to ride in the spring—a new smooth road, generally deserted.

"Apparently Morgan had rented a car. At some point, she drove to the reservoir. Smith said she might have been ducking out somewhere private for a nap. Apparently, she locked the doors. She failed to engage the emergency brake, though. And it doesn't appear that she woke up when the car rolled into the water. There was no sign of a struggle."

May said nothing. Paul went on. "Someone was out walking their dog this morning and came on the tracks of the car. It could have gone undetected for months."

"He says it's an accident?"

"Apparently."

"I don't think so. You've got it wrong. They came for Scott. I saw them. They took him away."

"They took him to the morgue, to do an ID."

"Her car just rolled into the reservoir and they didn't even question him?"

"They questioned him long enough to know he's a lucky man with a bunch of perfect alibis that keep him off the hook."

"What do you mean?"

"When Stacey died, he was in the office with a patient. When Morgan's car went down, he was at the hospital."

"How do they know exactly when the car went down?"

"The dashboard clock stopped when the car became submerged."

"Scott—someone—could have changed the time on the clock before the car went in the water. Didn't anyone think of that?"

"There was a watch, too. Morgan was wearing a cheap

watch, the kind you buy off a guy on the sidewalk who says it's a Bulova and then you get home and see it's really a Bolivia. It wasn't waterproof. The watch died the same time the car went under, the same time she went under."

May let facts percolate in her brain but said nothing.

Paul had something else on his mind. "Tomorrow is my sister's barbecue."

"I know. We're coming."

"Don't. Take the girls out of town. Go somewhere. To your mother's. Anywhere."

"We're coming to the barbecue. The girls will be okay. I'll keep an eye on them."

"Who's going to keep an eye on you?"

"I'll be fine," she told him. "I'll be careful. And tomorrow I'll be with you."

"Bridget's worried for you, too. She asked me to tell you that. She agrees with me that it's better if you don't come, if you go away. Think about it. Will you at least think about it?"

"All right." She agreed to that. "I've got to go next door now. Detective Smith has called a meeting. Believe me," she added. "I'll do what's best."

"What's best," he told her, "is to do what's safe."

She got off the phone and made one more call.

"Joe? This is May Morrison. I'm sorry to bother you, but I'm trying to find out about another person who may have been part of Stacey and Theresa's group of friends. Her name is Darlene Altschul. Do you know her?"

"No," he said. "I never heard of her. She wasn't part of that group." He sounded bad, thick tongued and sluggish.

"Are you all right?"

"Yes," he said. "It was a quiet death. Theresa felt no pain. I'm all right." He hung up the phone.

The children appeared in the kitchen doorway complaining that they were hungry again. May took them next door.

Thirty-One

THE GIRLS WERE ALWAYS HAPPY to go to the Coopers'. May didn't know at precisely what number son Carter and Emily stopped paying attention to the details, but by now they operated in a state of triage. They still had family rules, but they were rules like Whoever knocks out the tooth pays for the dentist. Carter boasted that the You-break-it, you-pay-for-it rule was the best encouragement he'd ever come up with to keep his boys' bones intact. The rest of it—the part May bothered with, like forbidding Froot Loops for breakfast, insisting on sitting at the table to eat, putting away toys—had no place in the five-boy chaos of the Cooper home.

"Wait until middle school," Emily had told May once. "You'll think back on the days when spilling a cup of cranberry juice on your white couch was your worst nightmare and you'll laugh."

No one was laughing now, at least none of the neighbors gathered on the assorted sofas, easy chairs, dining-room chairs, and hassocks that Carter had dragged in to accommodate the crowd. As the captain of the Neighborhood Watch committee, he'd always taken his responsibility seriously, hosting yearly meetings at which Detective Sharon Burker would come and apprise them of the latest in break-ins, car thefts, and disturbances of the peace. Everyone who came enjoyed the meetings. Detective Burker was an attractive cheerleader of a cop who had a way of making everyone feel on guard and well protected at the same time.

Today, she was in the background, leaning against the wall, listening. Today, Detective Smith was in charge. He acknowledged May with a nod of his head.

She took one of the few available seats and scanned the room. The detective was making small talk with the people next to him as he waited for the last of the stragglers to come in. Marlene was sitting near him, her good-natured dumpling of a husband, Wally, at her side. As soon as she noticed May, she got up and came over, sitting next to her. Through a smile that covered clenched teeth, she whispered, "What I told you was in confidence."

"I know," May said.

Marlene kept her eyes on her husband, who was sharing a day's worth of internet jokes with a neighbor. She leaned closer. "If you tell anyone about Scott and me, I'll kill you."

The words made May sit up a little straighter. Instantly, Marlene began to babble. "I didn't mean that seriously. My god, I can't stand this. A person can't kid around anymore without getting arrested for a comment, an innocent, silly comment."

"It's all right," May said quietly, taking Marlene's hand. "Your husband won't find out."

Marlene sank into her chair. "Did you ever do something without any thought of the consequences?"

Married Todd, May thought, but she just nodded.

"I've lectured Jordan for hours about this, about acting without thinking first, about not thinking about consequences. Then I went and did the same thing." Her shoulders slumped even more.

Detective Smith stood up, ready to begin.

"Pinky-swear," Marlene hissed.

May nodded but refused to offer her a finger to hook through. Reluctantly, Marlene returned to her proper seat, next to her husband.

May watched them, a happy couple who sent out no signal that there were secrets, troubles stuffed beneath the surface of their marriage. She looked around and wondered, *Who else has secrets?*

Many of the neighbors present were strangers to her. She knew those whose school-age children were young enough to require their parents' presence at the bus stop—and that was it. She didn't have the spare time to join neighborhood organizations, the ones that planted flowers in the park, or had coffees for politicians, or formed tax-cut lobbies or school review committees. She worked, spent time with her kids, ate, and slept. And tried to solve the murder of her friend, she thought, sadly.

"I'll be happy to answer all your questions then," Detective Smith was saying, and she realized she missed his introductory comments.

Emily, who'd been in the kitchen putting the finishing touches on platters of crudités, arrived to lay the platter on the table. She slid into the empty seat beside May.

May leaned close and whispered, "Where's Scott?"

Emily shrugged. Too well mannered to speak while the detective was talking, she mouthed her question. "Jail?"

"No," May said shaking her head, and then looked back at Detective Smith.

"Your best protection," he was saying, "is to keep your eyes wide open and to keep your doors locked shut. I know sometimes people feel shy about being suspicious. But I'm asking you, for the time being, be suspicious. Be overly suspicious. Call any time you see anything or anyone that strikes you as odd. We'll have extra cars patrolling the neighborhood. If anything makes you uncomfortable, help can be here within minutes. If it turns out it was just your imagination, we won't be disappointed—we'll be relieved. Do you all understand what I'm saying?"

There was a lot of nodding, and heads leaned toward each other as neighbors quickly shared words of fear, advice, and worry.

"I've heard a lot of rumors, but you still haven't told us," Marlene interrupted the rumble. "Was Morgan murdered?"

"We don't believe she was," the detective said.

"But you don't know for sure," May called out.

"No," he admitted.

"And what about Stacey?" Marlene continued to pursue him. "Is it true you no longer believe that was an accident?"

"That's correct. We do not believe it was an accident," the detective said, remaining stingy with details.

"So what exactly are we watching out for?" Marlene went on. "Some madman hiding behind the bushes?"

"I'm afraid I can't answer that," he said blankly.

Now it was May's turn. She chose her words carefully. "Why isn't Dr. Blum here tonight?"

"As you all know, this meeting was voluntary. Dr. Blum chose not to come."

"Is he a suspect in his wife's death?" May asked. The room was now stone still.

"I'm not here to discuss who our suspects are," Smith said flatly.

"Let me ask you this." It was an old man who spoke, a stranger to May. He had thin white wisps of hair carefully combed down the lower half of his head, and he clutched a bone-colored cane with his gnarled hands. "Have you considered the possibility that this nanny person committed suicide? That maybe she felt guilty because *she* was the one who killed Mrs. Blum?"

The prune-faced woman beside him grabbed his arm with her veiny hands. "Very good thinking, Earl."

Earl nodded, happy to have figured it out, looking as if

he was waiting for a prize. The room broke out into a dozen private conversations. It was a love triangle, a real estate deal gone bad, a lovers' quarrel.

The detective was trying to speak, but he couldn't be heard over the hum of the neighbors' hypothesizing. Crowd control was not his specialty.

"Let him speak," May called out, and the room quieted.

"Detective Burker and I will be coming around to all of your houses to talk to you," he explained, and May could hear the annoyance in his voice, as if this, the chatter of busybodies, was his pet peeve. When he shot May a quick but thankful smile, she knew she had moved up in his esteem now that he knew she was the girlfriend of a cop.

"At that time, we will be more than happy to listen to all of your theories. Please, do try to limit them to those that are actually grounded in truth."

"Detective?" Carter Cooper stood behind his wife, Emily, his arms crossed over his chest. "We know you're all doing the best job you can. We just all want to know: are we safe, or is there a killer on the loose?"

Wally, Marlene's husband, spoke up next. "Or in our midst?"

"Let me answer that with another question," Smith said. "Is anyone ever safe?"

"Do you think it's someone we know?" a woman called out from the back of the room.

"I can't answer that, ma'am," he said. He stood silent, watching the crowd as they broke back down into clusters of worried conversation.

Then questions came. "Should we leave all the lights on?" "What do you think about security systems?" "Do window bars work?" These were questions from people trying to believe that being safe was all a matter of finding the right lock.

But maybe because May already knew that wasn't true, she couldn't listen to it anymore. She slipped out of the room and retrieved her children, who now bore fake tattoos on both cheeks and magnetic earrings that May insisted they remove from their noses so they didn't accidentally take a deep breath and inhale them.

She made her decision on the way home but waited until the girls were tucked into bed before calling Paul.

"I'm taking your advice. I'm going away with the girls for a few days," she told him.

"Good." The relief in his voice was clear. "Where to?"

"Pennsylvania."

"Good." There was a moment of silence, and then his relief was replaced by suspicion. "Why?" He knew no one close to her lived in Pennsylvania. He knew her mother lived in a condo in Florida, her ex-husband lived in a glass box in Malibu, and Margery and her other work friends lived in doormen buildings in New York.

"I learned a lot last year," she said. She didn't need to refer to the episode any more than that for him to know what she meant. "Sending the girls to the country for a few days was the best thing I ever did." It was while the girls were away that the episode finally came to its terrifying head. She didn't need to remind him of that, either.

"So where in Pennsylvania are you going?" he asked, refusing to be diverted by her flattery.

"Boynton. Have you ever seen the Liberty Bell? I can't believe I've never seen it."

"Boynton, Pennsylvania? The Liberty Bell was in Philadelphia, last time I checked." He was silent for a moment and then he said, "Oh. Margaret Harris is from Boynton. What is it, a fifteen-minute drive from there to the Liberty Bell?"

It didn't surprise her that he knew Margaret was from Boynton. She knew he collected facts for a living and that he had a memory that provided for their instant retrieval.

"I wonder if she ever got a chance to see it," May said, ducking him again. "I know people around here who've never been to the Statue of Liberty. Have you ever been there?"

"I live on Staten Island, remember?" he said as if that

explained anything. Still, he wouldn't be diverted. "What are you going to do in Boynton?"

"See the Liberty Bell. And the Franklin Institute. And the Boynton Public Library. Want to come?"

"I wish I could," he said. "But I'll be lucky if I get to stay at Bridget's barbecue long enough to have a hot dog."

"Something going on?"

"Nothing good. You'll see tonight if you tune in to any of the local news programs. It's too gruesome for Paula to be interested in but I guarantee some bottom feeders will be sniffing around the perimeter of the crime-scene tape by this time tomorrow. Sorry," he said, realizing May might take insult at the expression.

"No problem. I know I'm not a bottom feeder," she said quietly. I don't take offense when you talk about slimy producers any more than you do when I talk about corrupt cops." He didn't comment, so she went on. "What's the bad news?"

"I've got three naked corpses, kids, with needles stuck in their arms and private-school IDs stuffed in the smiley face–patched back pockets of their fifty-dollar fringed bell-bottoms. The parents don't believe their little children stripped and stuck themselves, and neither do I. So I'm not going anywhere for the next few days. And I wish you would go somewhere else."

"I know you do," she said, because she knew how much he worried for her.

"But you won't," he said, because he knew her as well. "If I can get out of here for a while, I'll come by. My kids are over at Bridgets'. With the hours I'll be putting in, they'll probably stay there all week."

"Come any time," she told him.

It was ten o'clock. She had checked that all the doors and windows were locked, had the phone within reach, and had even brought Delia's baseball bat to bed, when the doorbell rang.

She peered out her window, saw the familiar car parked

at the foot of her driveway, ran downstairs, and opened the door.

"You don't want this," Paul said as soon as he walked inside. "But take it anyway." He handed her a steel container that looked like the petty-cash box she had at work, except it was longer and the metal padlock on it looked more serious, not like it could be broken with a few twists. "Here's the key."

She stared at the key, and then at the box. "What is it?"

"It's your gun box. Put it on the top shelf of your bedroom closet. I've got a poison sticker for you. That's what I keep on mine. Kids are more afraid of poison than they are of guns. Even so, you have to keep it locked at all times. And always, no matter where you go, you've got to take the key with you whenever you leave the house."

"Come on, Paul. What do I need a gun box for? I don't own a gun."

He shook the box and she heard the sound of metal clanking against metal.

"You don't have to use it," he said. "But I want you to have it." He handed it to her.

"I don't want it," she said, refusing delivery. "I don't know how to shoot a gun. It's crazy." She stepped back, as if even accidentally touching the box might cause the gun to go off.

"Come on," he said, and with the box under his arm, he walked briskly through the house and out the back door to the backyard. He stopped under one of the outdoor spots that flicked on whenever it detected motion.

He reclaimed the key, put the box on her weathered wooden picnic table, and opened it. The gun inside was barely visible in the shadow of the box, but she could still make out its dark, threatening shape. He took it out, emptied the bullets from the chamber, put it in her hand, ignoring her recoil. "You saw me take the bullets out, right? It's empty, right?"

She nodded.

"It doesn't matter. You're still never going to point it at someone unless you mean to shoot. Even if you swear you knew it was empty, you don't point unless you're willing and ready to shoot."

She stared without speaking. He curled her finger around the trigger.

"That tree, you see it?"

Even in the semidark she could see the outline of the giant maple tree. She nodded.

"That's a bad guy out to murder your children. He's got a gun. He's told you your children are about to be killed. He's standing there smiling because he knows you can't do anything about it." He took her hand, her finger still curled around the trigger as if he'd glued it there, and pulled it, straightening her arm until it pointed at the tree.

"Squeeze and your children are safe," he said.

It was surprisingly simple to do.

One by one, he put the bullets in the chamber, then put the gun back in the box. He took a poison sticker out of his pocket, closed the box, locked it, and smacked the sticker on the outside.

"Top of the closet in your bedroom. Key stays with you at all times. Okay?" His voice was steady, but she heard the urgency. His arms were outstretched; he held the gift before her.

"No," she said quietly.

"I'm worried about you. Take it."

She shook her head. "I can't. I appreciate your worry, but I can't. I wouldn't be able to sleep with that in the house. I know you just want me to be safe, but I can't." She stopped herself from saying more and waited for the inevitable. This was it, the impasse. She was—she knew it without his saying so—the first person he'd ever met who'd refuse the offer of a free gun.

But when he put the box down on the table, it was with resignation but not surprise, as if he'd expected that would be her response all along.

"I swear I don't compare you two," he said, with a tone that gripped her attention because it was new. "But Eileen didn't want one in the house either. Of course if you marry me, you get no choice." He shook his head. "I didn't mean it like that. I'm not proposing. Not that I don't want to propose," he added quickly. "I might propose sometime, someday. I just didn't mean to do it now. I didn't do it now. I don't think." He let out a long whistle.

She laughed but let him go on.

"What I'm saying is I'm a cop and I come with a gun."

"And I'm not and I don't."

"Right," he said.

"So what did you give Eileen to use for protection?"

He smiled and pulled a thin canister out of his pocket, the size of a lipstick.

"What's that? Napalm?"

"Plastique," he said, and when he saw her widened eyes he laughed. "Pepper spray. That's all. Two little sprays into the eye and you've got time to run away. If I had napalm or plastique, I would have brought it, but this is it, the end of my portable arsenal. If you won't take the gun, take the pepper spray. If you won't take the pepper spray, don't go to Boynton. Please," he added, because he couldn't tell her what to do.

She closed his hand around it. "I feel sneezy at the thought of using it. Guaranteed, I'd spray myself. Some people are just not meant to carry weapons."

His pager cut through the quiet of the backyard like a siren.

"I wish you could stay," she said, but she knew he couldn't, so instead they came together for a kiss that went on until they had to part, shaking.

"Lock up," he said, as he jogged to his car to return to the scene of the day's earlier crime. He didn't feel good about that one. And he didn't feel good about this.

Thirty-Two

NORMALLY, SHE WOULD HAVE CHOSEN a historic inn, something built in the 1700s, thirty rooms all furnished in period, breakfast and afternoon tea included. The girls generally saved their spitball fights and wrestling matches for the confines of their home. When they were traveling, although they got tired and needed frequent snacks, they also found hidden sources of flexibility and remained surprisingly good-natured and well-behaved.

But this time May didn't want charm. She wanted a hotel that was part of a chain, that had twenty-four-hour front-desk service, and porters lingering in the lobby. There was no particular sense to it, she thought as she drove down the turnpike, checking once again in her mirror to make sure no one was following her. Because she was driving just under the speed limit, there was little chance of anyone following her. Cars zoomed by like rockets on both sides of her.

There wasn't even anyone in particular she imagined would be following her to Philadelphia. She didn't expect Scott had left a patient in the waiting room so he could lurk until dark outside her hotel. Nor did she really believe the aged porter who took her bags or the teenage valet who took her car would be much help if she did find herself in trouble. There was no good reason that staying somewhere with an 800 number should make her feel safe, but it did.

The girls were thrilled with the plain accommodations. The room was large, the king-size bed placed perfectly in front of a huge TV, which the bellman had explained came with remote control video call-up.

In the car, they'd expressed delight at each suggested activity: the Please Touch Museum, the Franklin Institute, the Liberty Bell, Betsy Ross's house, an old-fashioned library. Each attraction was received with an "ooh, cool, wow"—even the last, which they didn't know was the reason they were here on this spontaneously planned vacation. But now they were happy to do nothing more than lie on the big bed and dial up for the remake of *The Parent Trap.* While they watched, May took advantage of the respite and hit the phones.

Charlotte was first. That generated a half-dozen other must-return calls. Then she dialed Matthew Harris.

"No one answers in that room," the receptionist at the La Guardia Airport Hotel told her. May left her hotel room number, then regretting it, engaged the extrasecurity deadbolt on her hotel room door.

When the *Parent Trap* parents were reunited and the girls were told no, that does not usually happen in real life, there was still time for a swim in the hotel's overchlorinated indoor pool and then a quick shower before grazing at the hotel buffet lunch. While the girls gorged on dessert, May went over the after-lunch schedule. They'd do the Liberty Bell first, then Betsy Ross's house, then the library, and finally the Please Touch Museum. She saved the Please Touch—the most fun—for last, when the girls would be tired and need a lift.

But by the time they got to the Liberty Bell, Delia was already tired, and at Betsy Ross's house, Susie was peeved that every one of the many chairs was cordoned off with thick maroon rope and guarded by people in uniform to make sure no one, like her, sat down. Luckily they passed The Olde Fudge Shoppe shortly thereafter and Susie settled down, happily eating her brick of fudge as May drove across rolling hills to the town of Boynton.

Following the directions she'd hastily scrawled on a page from the hotel scratch pad, she crossed the railroad tracks and arrived in downtown Boynton, two blocks of stores and the library.

"This is it?" Delia asked, gazing at the plain square structure.

"Do they have chairs?" was all Susie asked.

"Let's go in and see," May advised, escorting her tired children down a flight of stairs to a basement door that led to the children's entrance of the Boynton Public Library.

The heavy door slammed shut behind them as they entered. May took it in quickly: the woman sitting in a cozy corner on a denim couch reading an oversize picture book to a young boy, the heavyset matronly librarian behind a desk cluttered with paper and magazines.

"Where are the chapter books? How many can we get?" Delia asked, surveying the scene.

The librarian, who wore a badge announcing her name as Mrs. Gordon, looked up over her half-glasses and smiled. "Chapter books are over there," she said, pointing. "And you can take out five."

May hustled over to Delia and said quietly, "We can't take out any. This isn't our library."

"What's the point of coming if we can't take out any books?"

May couldn't honestly answer the question, so she stalled. "Find what you like. I'm going to talk to the librarian." She knew Delia assumed the subject of the conversation would be their lending policy for out-of-towners and she allowed the mistaken impression to stand.

"Do you have a moment?" she asked Mrs. Gordon, after she'd gotten the girls settled in a far corner of the room.

"Surely. What are you looking for?"

"I need to find out some information."

"That's what we're here for." Mrs. Gordon's soft fleshy face turned into deep folds as she smiled.

"About Margaret Harris."

"Oh." The smile fell off instantly, the folds of her face evening out to smooth skin. "I can't help you with that. I have no information about that."

"You see, there's been some concern that her death was not what it appeared to be. I hate to pry and I'm sorry to bring it up, but I've been asked to look into the matter for the family."

"I can't help you," Mrs. Gordon repeated quietly, her brown eyes flashing bigger behind her thin lenses. "Mr. James, the manager, might know. He's upstairs. If he's here today, he's upstairs."

"May I leave my children alone here for a moment?"

"I'd rather you didn't," the librarian said.

"I'll be right back," May replied, since the librarian hadn't actually said no. She stopped off where Delia sat with a stack of books beside her and Susie played with the puppets she'd found in a plastic bucket.

"Girls," May whispered. "I have to go up to the grown-up part of the library for a minute. Will you be okay here alone?"

Both nodded, delighted at being left unattended, ignorant of Mrs. Gordon's irritated eyes on them.

May hurried upstairs in search of Mr. James but found instead a bespectacled reference librarian who offered to check in the back. He returned moments later to report that Mr. James would meet her downstairs.

The children hadn't moved from where she left them, but even so, Mrs. Gordon seemed incredibly relieved from the bondage of watching them. When May explained that Mr. James was on his way down, Mrs. Gordon nodded indifferently and went back to her work, shuffling papers, careful to remain listening distance away.

Finally May heard the clack of heavy steps down the stairs. A narrow, tall man appeared.

"I can't help you" were his first words, even before May explained what she wanted to know. "It was a terrible accident. Mrs. Harris worked here for many years. We were very sad when she left."

"Did she seem depressed or unwell?" May asked, refusing to be diverted.

"I can't help you," he said again. "I'm not a doctor. I wouldn't know."

May tried many different ways to get him to add details, to admit what she was sure he was hiding. But it was as if she were interviewing a wall. Behind her, she could feel the children getting restless.

"I really can't help you," he insisted for the last time.

"Thanks anyway," she told him, because she knew enough not to burn bridges. She might want to come back and try again. "It's time to go," she said to the children without turning.

She felt someone standing behind her, assumed it was Delia about to throw a fit, and was surprised when she turned around to find herself face-to-face with the young mother who'd been reading to her restless son on the couch.

"You want to find out about Mrs. Harris?" the woman asked.

May nodded.

"I can tell you about her," the woman said quietly. Her son pulled at her pants leg. "Go sit with the little girl for a minute."

Delia greeted the boy with a roll of her eyes, but Susie welcomed a new playmate.

The two women moved far away from the large ears of their children.

"I come here every day. Benjamin loves to look at books." She glanced at her son, who was watching Susie arrange the puppets into an audience. "I was here the day she died," the woman said.

"Can you tell me what happened?"

The woman whispered. "We didn't come back for days afterward. It was horrible."

"How so?"

"She was yelling at the children, at Benjamin. She said horrible things." The woman leaned closer. "She wasn't well. She hadn't been well for a while."

"Did you know her?"

"Just from coming every day. She didn't know my name or anything. When I first met her, she was very nice and helpful, very friendly. Then she changed. Over the past year, she changed."

"How?" May asked, keeping her voice low.

"I don't know how to explain it exactly. She got forgetful. And she'd laugh at things that weren't funny. And she became very short-tempered. But the last weeks were the worst. She was acting strange. She would go into rages, for no reason."

Rages, May thought. Joe Ricardo had used that word about Toni.

"I think she was drinking," the woman went on. "Her speech was slurry. She was wobbly. Once, she even fell down. I'll tell you, I think she drunk herself sick." The woman moved closer to confide this. "When I heard she killed herself, the first thing I thought was *So would I.* If I drank myself out of my mind, so would I."

"Mommy," Susie called out. "He took all the puppets."

May turned to see the little boy lying on top of a mountain of matted fake fur.

"Benjamin, that isn't nice. Get up."

But Benjamin wouldn't get up, and when Mr. James came back to see what the ruckus was about, May quickly told the girls the museum would be closing soon. They left, leaving Benjamin wailing, his mother yelling, and Mr. James watching, his hands on his hips, his forehead collapsed into worry.

Thirty-Three

SHE MADE THE DECISION that night, lying in the hotel king-size bed, her children snoring quietly beside her. Details remained to be worked out, but the basic plan was this: the coming Thursday and Friday were statewide teachers' conference days. Schools were closed. If she could get the girls a Monday-evening flight to Florida, they could spend a week with her mother and end up missing only two days of school. With luck, Sabrieke would agree to go along, too.

May would fly to the spa. She'd make sure Margery would come along. She couldn't be positive there was something to find out there, but it seemed ever clearer that it was where the connection began. Maybe she would even be able to find out more about Darlene Altschul, Stacey's mystery friend. At worst, if she was wrong and found nothing, she'd still get work done, grooving up the spa show. She was ready to be done with it.

She woke sometime before seven to the sound of Susie whispering to Delia that today they shouldn't wake Mommy up before eight. The TV went on, low, then gradually got louder, as they tired of straining to hear. Fred was fighting with Wilma about Barney's noisy new lawnmower when May got back on the phone.

Her first call was to her mother, who agreed to the plan with delight. She called Lydia next to fill her in on what she knew so far, but Lydia quickly cut her off.

"Don't get me involved in this," she said. "I want to keep the children here for a while. I don't want to antagonize Scott. Call me if you find out he's a killer." And she hung up the phone.

Finally May tried Matthew Harris. She was about to hang up after the fourth ring—she didn't want to leave another message with reception—when a voice answered.

"Hello?"

She didn't know Matthew very well, but she knew this voice, pure Brooklyn tough, wasn't his.

"Is Matthew there?" she asked

"Who's speaking?"

She wasn't saying. "May I speak to Matthew Harris, please?"

"He's not here. Who's this?"

"Is this Matthew Harris's room?"

"Can I have your name, please, ma'am?"

The "ma'am" made her spine straighten. She recognized it as a cop's courtesy. "Do you know when he'll be back?"

"If you give me your name, I'll be glad to tell you."

She wondered what Paul would say when she told him about this, how she slammed down the phone as if it might bite her, then moved far away from it, and joined the girls on the bed, pretending to watch the TV.

When the phone rang seconds later, she didn't answer it, even though it was more likely to be Paul than the man she'd just hung up on. The girls didn't notice the ringing. They were too busy laughing as Dino stuffed Fred's bowling bowl down the garbage-disposal dinosaur. Nor did they notice when it rang again, several minutes later. Still, she ignored it, just as she ignored the message light that began to flash and continued flashing even when she picked up the receiver to order their room-service breakfast.

When Delia finally noticed the light, May simply said, "It means I ordered room service." Delia nodded disinterestedly, then went back to watching her show.

If it had been thc cops, May reasoned silently as she ate rubbery scrambled eggs and an overtoasted English muffin, there was no way they could get from the La Guardia Airport Hotel to this one in half an hour. But still, she ate fast, as if they might come knocking at the door at any minute. She couldn't explain why she feared them even though she had done nothing wrong. Then she realized it wasn't them she feared. It was the news she feared they'd bring.

After breakfast she agreed to the girls' pleas for a morning in the hotel pool and to a family dunk in the poolside Jacuzzi, despite the sign next to it prohibiting guests under eighteen from entering. *Live dangerously,* she thought, as they all plunged into the warm bubbling water.

They checked out after lunch and spent the car ride discussing the things they missed most about home, as if they'd been traveling for months.

May felt a heaviness hit her the moment she turned the car down their block, which turned into sadness as they passed Stacey's house. She saw the single light flick on in what she knew was Stacey's bedroom window. She wondered, if Scott was innocent, how he could bear to live there.

When she got home, she managed to put Scott, Stacey, Matthew, all of it, out of her mind. She was organizing the laundry, getting the girls in and out of the shower, feeling accomplished and in control of the chaos, when Susie announced, "The stuffed animals don't work anymore."

"Last night she dreamed she was snatched," Delia explained. "She woke me up to tell me. It was three-o-five or three-o-two," she said, and then explained she couldn't exactly be sure of the numbers on the hotel digital clock. "I told her to wake you up, but she wouldn't."

"Because when I wake you up, you get mad," Susie admitted, "so I don't like to."

May sighed, then tousled Susie's hair. "You can always wake me up if you've had a bad dream."

"But what if you get mad at me?"

"Then you can get mad right back."

"Told you so," Delia said.

"So, pumpkin, what do you think we should do to scare away those dreams tonight?"

"Sleep with you?" Susie asked, even though she knew it was a school night and the answer would be no. "Sleep with her?" she suggested hopefully, pointing to her sister, then laughing at that one, too.

May put her hand lightly over Delia's mouth because she could see Delia was about to start petitioning on her sister's behalf. "Any other ideas?"

"I know." Susie marched down the hall, heading up the stairs to the third floor.

With Delia right behind her, May followed, noticing how little Susie looked from the back, skinny arms sticking out of her short, tiny kitten-print pajama sleeves. Her hair was in its usual thick, unmanageable tangle. *Just like mine,* May thought. Susie's tiny fingers, so busy all the time, tapped their way up the banister. May found it a constant surprise: because Susie and Delia took up so much space in her mind, she often forgot how small they really were.

Susie stopped at the door between May's small office and Sabrieke's room, the one to the large storage closet.

"What do you want from in there?" Delia asked.

"Something." Susie opened the closet door and walked inside. Although May had to bend down when she poked around in the closet looking for suitcases or sleeping bags, Susie easily fit. She got on the tips of her toes to pull the string that lit up the room. It took her less than a minute of poking around before she found what she wanted, a carton she dragged into the hall.

May recognized it at once, the box filled with the photographs Todd took all the time—before he left. May had insisted on keeping them, fought for them, telling Todd she needed them so she could make photo albums for the kids. At first he fought back, but he was feeling so guilty at the time that he gave in without too much of a struggle.

May hadn't made the albums yet, though she intended to the minute she squeezed out some spare time. Susie's interest in them only confirmed that she was right to fight to keep them. She wondered now how often they snuck upstairs to look at them.

After rummaging through several inches of loose pictures, as if she knew exactly what she wanted and where to find it, Susie stood up, a photograph hidden behind her back. "Okay. We can go down now."

"What did you pick?" Delia asked.

Susie kept it out of sight. "Something to sleep with."

"Let me see," her sister demanded.

Reluctantly, Susie passed over an eight-by-ten color photograph of May and Todd on their wedding day. "Don't show Mommy," she whispered, even though she knew it was too late; Mommy had already seen.

"Susie," Delia hissed.

"It's okay," May said, even though her heart was breaking. "I used to sleep with a picture of my grandpa under my pillow when I was your age."

"I have a better idea for you," Delia said, and suddenly the three of them were carting the box downstairs, laying it on May's bed, three sprawling bodies in a sea of pictures. There were birthday party pictures, Halloween celebration pictures, school play pictures, a series of Thanksgiving pictures, all occasions May knew the children viewed as from a happier time, when their family was whole.

It was 9:00 when May glanced at the clock. Susie lay beside her, sleepy-eyed, clutching the wallet-size photo her sister had convinced her to sleep with, Delia's first-grade school picture. The picture reminded Delia of the time in first grade when she was unfairly sent to the bench for a time out at recess. They had all heard the story many times before, but Delia wouldn't be diverted.

Susie was the first to close her eyes and drift. May must have followed shortly thereafter. The next time she opened her eyes, she saw it was 11.

She carried one and then the other of her sleeping girls off to bed, more convinced now than before that sending them away for a week was a good idea.

She'd meant to call Paul, but it was too late—she didn't want to wake up his sons. It wasn't too late to phone Margery, though.

"What days are you taping this week?" she asked her.

"I've got back-to-back shows on Thursday. How's that for rotten scheduling? I'm telling you, sugar, Colleen is in way over her head. I don't much mind if she shoots herself in the foot, but I don't want to end up lame, too."

"Come with me, then. I'm flying to Arizona tomorrow, to the spa."

"How can I come? I have to be back on Thursday."

"I'm planning on coming back Wednesday."

"Twenty-four hours? Can I have everything done in twenty-four hours?"

"Everything short of a face-lift."

Margery was game to come along, so May left a message at the travel desk at work, relaying their plans. Then she waited up for Sabrieke to come home, sipping tea and reading the trades, *Variety* and *Hollywood Reporter.*

Her baby-sitter came in at 1:00, frightened to find May waiting for her, worried that there was more bad news, that someone else had died. May thought, *Someone else* has *died,* thinking of Matthew Harris, but she didn't share the thought.

When Sabrieke heard May's reason for staying up—the plan to go to Florida—she broke down in tears of relief. Manu had been pressuring her all night to move out, she explained. He was afraid for her, afraid for his unborn child. It wasn't safe here, he said, and she couldn't completely disagree. Now she could make everybody, including herself, happy. She kissed May once on each cheek and, teary-eyed, went up to sleep.

May packed a bag for herself, and then a bigger bag for the children. When they woke they were delighted to hear the news of another surprise vacation. Now all she had to do was get them through the day without hearing what had happened to Morgan. She waited until the last possible moment to go to the bus stop. With no more than a second to spare, they ran to the corner, and the girls hurried onto the bus, happily waving their good-byes.

"What's going on?" Marlene asked her, still not sure if May was going to turn her in with her juicy gossip.

"Can't talk. Got to get to work." Then May ran off, making her own bus with only seconds to spare. She settled in a seat, pulled a pile of papers out of her bag, and disappeared into other peoples' lives.

Thirty-Four

SHE BLEW IN TO WORK LIKE A HIGH WIND, a blur racing past colleagues offering the muffled hellos of a lazy Monday morning.

Charlotte stood up at her desk as May passed, holding out the morning call sheet. May grabbed it but didn't bother to look at it as she closed her door and made her first call of the day, to Paul.

It was a lucky break. The assistant D.A. with whom he was waiting to meet was late, so he answered his page right away. Still, he didn't have much time. She got straight to the point, telling him she was sending the girls to her mother and going to the spa with Margery for two days.

"Can't you stay longer than that?" he asked. "Two days isn't much time to figure things out."

"I'm pretty quick," she boasted. "You'd be surprised."

"I didn't mean you," he said. "I meant Detective Smith." She heard a voice bark at him.

"One more thing," she added quickly. "I think that Matthew Harris just turned up dead."

"You think or you know?"

"I think," she said. "He was staying at a hotel out near

La Guardia Airport. Do you know anyone there who might tell you for sure?"

She heard the voice call him again, the sound of it harsher now. She instantly regretted her request. He had enough to do.

"I'll call you later," he said quickly, then added, "Stay longer." He disconnected, too hurried—or was it too worried?—to risk a good-bye.

As soon as May hung up, Charlotte poked her head in, holding up her copy of May's call sheet. "Ready to start returning?"

"After I talk to Colleen." She sprinted down the hall to her executive producer's scented office.

Curry was the smell of the morning. May briefly wondered what its power was supposed to be. All she knew, as she sat down on one of the guest chairs was that she was suddenly hungry for Indian food.

She waited while Colleen took a succession of phone calls as if she were alone. A rival producer, Paula, her therapist, an editor, her personal trainer, a journalist. The calls were quick and to the point, none lasting more than hi-how-are-you-when-can-I-see-you. It was about ten minutes later when she put down the receiver.

May didn't waste any time. "I want to do my spa story up next. On Friday morning, I've got the old man reunited with the boy he saved fifty years ago. I've got the smart-ass kid who out-witted the SAT next Tuesday."

Colleen let loose an exaggerated yawn.

"He's good. He's a natural stand-up comic. A fifteen-year-old Seinfeld."

Unconvinced, Colleen shrugged. May went on. "I want to get the spa story grooved up by Thursday."

"Suddenly it's a rush. Why? I don't feel any heat on this." It was a fair question. She added another. "This is a personal thing with you, isn't it? Because of what happened to your friend."

"It's partly personal," May admitted. "But that's not

necessarily a bad thing." She reminded Colleen that the recent miniseries on drugs, the one everyone was talking up as a definite Emmy, had been inspired by the host's own family experience.

Colleen sighed on the truth as she yanked out the roster for next week's shows. "I don't have any spots open. Unless I bump something. What can I bump? Everything we've got looks good."

May read the roster upside down. "What about that?" she pointed. "We're not actually doing a show on mother-daughter strippers *again.*"

"Get off your high horse, May. People liked that show. And I think our audience will like another show about strippers a lot better than a show about some spa they'll never be able to afford to go to." She sighed again. "I hate my job."

In the olden days—last week—May would have pursued the throwaway complaint, but she didn't have time to commiserate now. "You want me to dump the spa story?"

"No. Well, yes, but you can't. Paula loves it. She loves it, loves it, loves it and I cannot talk her out of it. I hate my job."

"So then I'll fly out tonight, groove it up tomorrow, and be back here by Thursday morning. Margery's coming with me. We're going to coproduce it."

"What? Carl could handle this one. Why do I need to commit two top producers to a job the mail clerk could handle? I swear I should just commit myself."

"Because Margery's got back-to-back shows on Thursday and she's not happy about your scheduling, that's why."

"She's not?" Colleen asked. She sounded worried, but it was hard to tell. Her recent Botox treatment had given her forehead a permanently blank and frozen look.

But May was playing to one of her weak spots, the fear that the entire *Paula Live* operation would fall apart the first year it was under her watch. Mass resignations had happened on the show before. They were an executive producer's nightmare.

"Margery is not happy at all. It's been months since Paula decided she doesn't want any unpleasant true-crime stories. Let me tell you, Margery is running out of happy crime ideas."

"I hate my job," Colleen repeated.

"Trust me. Coproducing this show with me, one Paula loves even before we've done it, would really perk Margery up. You have to let her do it. Unless you want to lose her."

"Okay, okay. All right. Good idea. Go ahead. But if you don't come back with a show in your pocket, I'm considering this a vacation and you're paying for it." Colleen swiveled around and picked a small bottle off her credenza. She opened it, put her finger at the top, turned it upside down, dabbed a few drops on either side of her neck and in the space between her upper lip and her nose. "Ocean," she explained. "Soothing. Want some?"

"No," May shook her head. "I don't have time to be soothed right now. Do you have any double-time smell?"

Colleen nodded. "Espresso," she said, and picked up another dark small bottle. "Sorry. I'm all out of it." She slid open the top drawer of her desk, fished around inside, and came up with a small packet of dark brown leaves. "I have this." She passed the packet over to May. "Try it."

"What is it?"

"It's a tonic Dr. Wu gave me last year. For energy."

Dr. Wu was the same Chinatown herbalist Margery visited annually. Some days it seemed to May she was the only producer in the business who didn't make a yearly pilgrimage to Dr. Wu.

"I should go get some more, but who the hell has the time?" She dabbed a few more drops of ocean, this time on the inside of her wrists. "Steep it in hot water and drink it like tea," she said, pointing to the packet of herbs. "It's a great energy booster. I used to use it for jet lag, too. I don't need it for that anymore, now that I don't go anywhere."

May couldn't continue to ignore the comments. "Is everything okay?"

Colleen looked relieved at the invitation to spill her guts, but she had to swallow them instead because Paula walked in, ending the conversation.

"How's the spa?" she asked May, taking the empty seat beside her. "When do I start my rejuvenation?"

"She's flying this afternoon," Colleen jumped in. "She's leaving now."

"Terrific," Paula said. "You won't come back looking younger than me, will you?"

"Not a chance," May reassured her.

As she got up to leave, Paula turned to Colleen and announced, "I am not a happy camper."

May hurried out and went straight to the booker's office to finalize her travel plans. When she got back to her own office, Charlotte reported that she'd just missed Detective O'Donnell's call.

"He said to tell you you were right."

"About what?"

Charlotte checked her note pad. "About Matthew Harris. He also said to tell you to stay for a week." She looked up at May. "Are you going to be gone for a week?"

"No," May said. "Three days." She glanced up at the TV. Two of Jerry Springer's guests were threatening to punch each other out. She switched channels. A woman complained her boyfriend said he liked her better when she was fat. May jumped channels again. A commercial. She pulled out her daily diary. Good. All the meetings scheduled for the next three days were meetings Charlotte could handle alone. No senior publicists, no best-table-in-the-house agents, no shining-star editors who would object to pitching to her second-in-command. They were the usual motley crew: women taller than their husbands, rescue pets, miraculous recoveries. May advised Charlotte to introduce herself as a producer and, if asked, to explain that May was away on assignment.

"Look," Charlotte interrupted. May glanced at the TV to see their friend the binge eater covering her mouth. The camera switched to a close-up of Montel's surprised face. The audience howled with delight.

"She may actually be the world's first professional projectile vomiter." May switched the channel again and began returning calls.

At 1:00, she joined Margery in a car headed toward New Jersey. Miraculously, the travel department had been able to find a flight to Florida that departed only one hour before May's flight to Arizona. She picked up the girls from school, then went on to the house to gather Sabrieke and the bags. The five of them plus their luggage squeezed back into the town car and made it to the airport with no traffic.

May spent a small fortune in the gift shop on Beanie Babies, mini M&M's, puzzle books, and a T-shirt, extra large, for Sabrieke. As the girls' flight took off, May stayed at the giant picture window, waving long after the plane was gone.

"Come on, sugar," Margery said, pulling her away toward their gate. Their plane was delayed for half an hour, but both women had brought along one carry-on suitcase each, just filled with work. After May had skimmed eighteen magazines, they were in the air.

Thirty-Five

"I KNOW THEY SAY YOU SHOULD DRINK only water when you fly," Margery said, slurring the words, a pitcher's worth of cocktails into the flight. "But what I don't know is who the hell *they* are."

"*They* are the people from Poland Spring," May said, and then went back to the increasingly difficult task of getting Margery to focus her Bloody Mary brain on their plan. "We'll get into their files and find the names of every single person who was at the spa the last time Stacey came. We know Margaret was there. We know Toni was there. And I bet anything we'll find a record that says someone named Darlene Altschul was there."

"When was the last time Stacey visited this place?"

"I don't know. That's what I'll have to find out."

Margery laughed. "In twenty-four hours? Ooh—you have a lot to do. Well, when you find what you need, let me know. I'll be in the massage room."

"Great. Request Rolando. Stacey raved about Rolando, said she got wonderful massages from him every day she was there. Maybe Rolando will remember when he saw her last."

"Your every wish is my command, your highness. I will spend as much time with Rolando as I can."

"There was a facialist she talked about, too. Inge or Onga, something like that. She said the woman's hands were like butterflies."

"You can have Onga," Margery said, her eyes closing as the plane dipped, readying to land. "I'll be with"—she imagined a tango and rolled her tongue—"Rolando. I'm going to leave with such a glow," Margery said, gripping the sides of her seat tighter as the plane's wheels hit the tarmac. "A post-Rolando glow."

"You'd better also leave with a show," May remarked as she reached for her carry-on in the overhead compartment. "Colleen told me if we don't come back with a good solid hour for Paula, she's going to consider this a vacation and make us pay for it out of our own piggy banks."

That snapped Margery out of her stupor. "Don't kid with me, sugar. I don't own a piggy bank, so I sure as hell hope yours is big enough for the two of us." She said it like she meant it, but she didn't meet May's eyes. She knew the only piggy bank in May's house belonged to Susie.

They were met at the baggage carousel by a tan, blond muscular man who identified himself as their driver. He then introduced them to their fellow van passengers, two women in their sixties, returning for their second Nirvana visit.

Margery, the Bloody Marys beginning to wear off, instinctively turned them into sources. "Oh you look divine," she cooed to the one named Beady. "Tell me exactly what you do at the spa, because I want to do exactly the same thing. Who should I see? What treatments do you get?"

Minnie, Beady's companion, quietly confided the good news that there was absolutely no one to avoid. Everyone was wonderful. Beady cheerfully concurred.

Margery wasn't quite ready to give up. She leaned closer to

Minnie, who recoiled slightly at the boozy smell of her breath. "What about Rolando?" she whispered. "I hear Rolando has hands of fire."

"Everyone is wonderful," Minnie admitted, "but Rolando is unbelievably wonderful."

While Margery continued her fact-finding mission, May drifted, gazing into the distance as the van raced along, cutting through the desert mountains. After half an hour, it slowed and turned onto a winding road that led through the stone gates of the Nirvana Spa.

The resort unfolded in a confusing labyrinth of pink adobe buildings partially hidden behind sculpted bushes, flowering cactuses, large plantings of multicolored snapdragons, and stone fountains that dribbled, spurted, and sprayed soothing cascades of water.

When the van stopped, the door swung open and May stepped out into heat so dense it felt like a wall. A symphony of soothing sounds—rushing water, cooing doves—surrounded her, none of whose sources were visible. There were footsteps, too, of unseen people crunching along camouflaged paths. Through it all came the steadying sound of a flute played into the air from hidden speakers, as if a Navajo were sitting in the treetops, playing to the sky.

The driver told them he was taking their bags to their rooms. The other passengers, because they were returning guests, got to go straight to their quarters.

May and Margery stepped inside the reception center, into a large square room decorated in calming shades of peach. A woman in white appeared from nowhere—a door May noticed was painted the same shade of peach as the walls, rendering it nearly invisible.

"We've been expecting you," the woman said, and while May tried to determine if she was a nurse or their tennis pro, the woman introduced herself.

"My name is Candace and I'm here to help you today." She passed over two Lucite clipboards each holding a folder thick with papers. "Have a seat, please, and answer the questions as completely as you can."

With a sweet smile she was gone, disappearing as quickly as she came, leaving them alone with piped in flute music and wafting scents of potpourri whose source, like everything else, was nowhere visible.

Margery yawned and opened her folder. "'How many naps a day do you normally take?'" she read, and turned to May. "Okay. What's the deal? Do I lie a lot or a little?"

"You take one nap every day," May told her, keeping her voice low because she had the distinct feeling that even though they appeared to be in a self-contained room with only one door and no windows, she felt as if somewhere, Candace was watching them.

Sure enough, as soon as they put down their folders, the door opened and Candace was back, the same smile plastered on her face. "I'll take that," she said, and briskly whisked away their paperwork.

"What will do you do with it?" May asked.

"The doctor will look at it before your consultation later today, and then we'll input all the information into our computers so we can follow your progress from visit to visit."

"Where are your computers?" May asked, trying to seem just another curious guest, nothing more. "A big old ugly white box could really ruin this decor."

"Don't you worry. They are completely and discreetly out of sight."

Before May could explain that she wasn't worried at all, Candace was ushering them outside and onto a small golf cart–like vehicle, which she drove to their room.

"Have a pleasant rest," Candace said, opening the door to their personal adobe home. "After you've had time to refresh yourselves, just walk right down this path to Medical Center B, where you'll meet the doctor. If you need anything before then," she said as she backed out of the room, "just pick up the phone and I'll be there."

"We don't want to rest," Margery told her. "We're here

on the rush plan, twenty-four hours to sample all your delights. So what's first?"

"There is always time to rest," Candace said, pleasantly. "Instructions are in your room." And with a flick of a button, her golf-cart transporter disappeared with her into the lush desert bloom.

Margery followed May into their room, slamming shut the door behind them. "Do you think she got the full or half-lobe lobotomy package?"

"She's just being pleasant," May said, defending Candace. "We're just not used to people being pleasant." She heaved her suitcase onto her bed and picked up a small welcome card. "'Nap instructions,'" she read. "'Welcome to Nirvana. We recommend beginning your stay with a guided nap. Turn the cassette player to Nap.'"

Margery found the player on the dresser and pressed a button.

"Good afternoon," a soothing woman's voice greeted them. "I am your nap guide. Are you ready to relax?"

As a joke—their shoes were still on and their suitcases were not yet opened—they both lay down on their beds. Within minutes, they were fast asleep.

May was in the studio, facing a packed audience. Paula was nowhere to be found. The guests hadn't arrived. People were shouting, asking when the show would start. A loud noise was causing rumbles of discontent; people were holding their ears. "It's just the dinner bell," May told them. "We have to have dinner now."

"Damn," Margery shouted, sitting up in her bed.

Startled out of her sleep, May sat up, too, her eyes snapping open. They were both silent, trying to figure out what had shocked them awake.

Then their nap guide spoke up. "Welcome to the wakeful world. Before you get up, take a few moments to feel how relaxed you are, how loose your limbs have become, how the muscles of your face have lost all tension. Now, open your eyes. Enjoy this feeling, this peace of mind."

Margery's shoe, flung with perfect aim, hit the tape player, sending it backward into the wall.

"I don't think we have the right attitude for this place," May suggested, and they both laughed, then went to their personal sinks to wash up.

At 3:30, frighteningly on time, according to the schedule they discovered lying beside the nap machine on their dresser, they followed the marked path to Medical Center B, where they each had appointments to see a doctor for their evaluations.

Another nurse–tennis pro greeted them. "I'm Kimberly," she said, as she led May to a small white cubicle to work out her schedule. "All righty, are you ready?" She hit a few keys on her small computer.

"All righty, you bet I am," May echoed. Then, choosing a tone she hoped Kimberly would relate to, she said, "That computer is adorable. Is it really big enough to hold all the names of all the people who've had the good fortune to come here?"

"I don't know much about computers," Kimberly admitted. "So what treatments would you like?" She handed over a laminated menu of massages and wraps.

Scratch talking technology with Kimberly. "I'd like a facial first. Do you have a facialist named Inge or Onga?"

"We have Helga," Kimberly came up with. "She's wonderful and . . ."—she clicked three buttons—"good news. She's free this afternoon at five-thirty."

Within fifteen minutes, May was fully booked and being escorted back to the waiting room, where she found Margery, sulking.

"I feel like I've been transported to the land of the living Barbies," she complained, just as a door opened and another nurselike person emerged.

"Good afternoon, ladies," the perky blonde said. "My name is Barbie. Follow me."

Margery mouthed, "Where's Ken?"

Barbie swung around. "Pardon?"

"I didn't say anything, sugar," Margery said, smiling pleasantly. "I am so overcome by the hospitality of this place I have been rendered positively speechless."

"Isn't that nice," Barbie said, and then turned to lead them to their small dressing rooms. "There are magazines and personal CD players," she pointed out, gesturing inside. "And the doctors will see you both shortly."

"Is he blond, too?" Margery asked.

"Pardon?"

"She said, 'Will he be long, too?'" May piped up.

"No," Barbie said, and then closed them each into her own room. "How about a glass of iced tea or lemonade?" she asked through the door.

"That would be lovely," Margery replied. As soon as the receding footsteps disappeared, she hustled out of her room, dressed in her thin pink robe. When May emerged from her room moments later, she asked her, "Was Stacey eerily calm when she came home from visiting this place? Was she a robot right before she died? Is this going to be a Stepford wife experience? Because, sugar, I'm not married. There would be absolutely no upside whatsoever to my becoming a Stepford wife without a Stepford husband to keep me."

"She wasn't like them," May said quietly. "Scott said she was paranoid, but to me she seemed more scared than anything."

Thinking about it quieted them both. They waited in silence until finally Barbie came back, refreshing drinks in hand, and told them the doctors would see them now.

Thirty-Six

As she sat across from Dr. Lichtman and looked into his friendly eyes, perfect ovals not much smaller than the lenses of his glasses, she wondered if the trip was an expensive mistake. The eyes meeting hers now didn't look malevolent or threatening. They were open, friendly, alive. The doctor was almost childlike in his enthusiasm for his work.

Was she wrong about the spa's being the hub connecting it all together? Could the deaths of so many women be unrelated?

And what about Darlene Altschul? May couldn't connect her to the spa, not yet. Morgan and Matthew didn't fit in here, either. How could she ignore the possibility that she'd made a wrong turn somewhere, or missed something obvious, something right in front of her eyes. *What?*

"Do you tune out a lot?" Dr. Lichtman asked her, as he stuck a tongue depressor in her mouth. "I can see you haven't heard a word I've said."

"It's a terrible habit," she managed to mumble.

"Hmmm," the doctor replied as he removed the depressor, tossed it in the trash, then took a small steel hammer from the neat row of tools Barbie had carefully placed on a thick paper towel on the countertop.

He hit each of her knees and then her arms. "Are you under a lot of stress?" he asked.

"Yes," she admitted, and then seized the opportunity to expand. "A friend of mine died recently," she said, then laughed nervously, which wasn't an act. "Several friends have died recently, as a matter of fact."

"I'm sorry to hear that," Dr. Lichtman said. He kept his eyes on her and didn't glance away, making her feel as if he was sincerely sorry for her pain.

"It's the damnedest thing," she went on. "My friend Stacey Blum—" She stopped. She couldn't be positively sure of it, but wasn't that a flicker of surprise—or was it fear?—that flashed across the doctor's face.

"Do you know her?" she asked, even though she already knew Scott had friends at the spa.

"I believe we've met," he said, and sat back down in his chair, swiveling slowly from side to side. He didn't seem to be aware he was doing it, but Barbie was. Standing back against the wall, a silent observer, her eyes followed his knees swiveling to the right, to the left, to the right. She looked worried. This wasn't a normal piece of business.

"I heard the news. Devastating news." He shook his head, but his eyes remained locked on to May's.

May continued. "What's even sadder is that a bunch of friends she met here at the spa have also died recently."

"I didn't know that," he said. "How sad. How sad for you. What happened to them?"

"Different things," May said, feeling a rise in the tension in the room. Now she needed to move on to the next, to the pitch. "You know the one thing—the only thing—those women had in common was that they loved your spa. They planned on coming back every year. Now, of course, they never will."

"Mrs. Morrison, in addition to the hormone cocktail

that I'll prescribe when I get your blood work back tomorrow, I'm also going to give you something for light depression."

She stiffened slightly. "I'm not depressed. I'm sad that my friend died. That's normal."

"Of course. And I'm not talking about any kind of serious medication. But we do have several herbal treatments we use around here whenever life throws us a curve ball. You'll take it for a few weeks, that's all, to get past the crisis. It won't make your feelings disappear. It will just keep you feeling centered, so you don't end up spiraling further down. Wouldn't you like that?"

"I suppose," she said, trying to sound grateful.

"All right then." He got up, scribbling on the paper on his clipboard as he left.

She thought, *I should have done it the other way around—hit him up for the show first and then, once he'd bit, broached the subject of the deaths.* But no sense looking back. She'd pitch it straight to his ego. She would get him. She was sure of it.

Barbie interrupted her thoughts. "You can change now."

"Isn't Dr. Lichtman coming back?"

"Tomorrow. Nine o'clock. To go over your blood work."

"But he must be coming back. He didn't even say good-bye."

Barbie laughed. "Doctor never says good-bye. He knows he'll run into you later, either at the dining room or in the pool. You'll see," she said, and opened the door to the changing room that was beginning to feel to May like a small tomb.

Margery had already run off to her first afternoon treatment, so May quickly dressed and hurried off to see Helga. She wasn't much help, either.

"My memory for skin is unbelievable," the facialist

said, her fiery red hair pulled back in a neat French twist. "I'll never forget yours now that I've met you. Skin is unforgettable, honey. Names are another story."

May pushed on. "I have a photograph of her in my room. Maybe tomorrow I can see you again and show it to you."

"That would be nice, honey," Helga said, mildly. "But you must wait a few days between facials, to let your fine skin rest." She readied a soft compress. "This will feel cool," she said, as she placed it over May's eyes. "This will feel warm," she said moments later, as she set a steaming container of scented water before her.

Rose-scented steam began heating May's face. She could hear Helga rubbing lotion over her hands, then felt the firm, strong strokes of confident fingers on her neck, chin, cheeks.

"You're lucky to have such good skin, honey," Helga said. "I recommend products to my clients all day long so they can have skin like yours. You're a lucky, lucky lady, honey."

"Thanks," she said. "My friend Stacey told me your hands were like butterflies."

"That's nice," Helga said. And then her fingers turned into wings, gently beating along May's cheeks.

"She said you were the best. The very best."

"That's nice. We get so many nice women here. From all over the world."

May felt her forehead stretched, massaged, stroked. "My friend, Stacey Blum, died several weeks ago."

"Ach," Helga replied, one hand lifting off May's forehead, her strong fingers moving down to her neck. "The things that happen these days. Now don't speak for a while. I'm putting on your tightening mask. Think calming thoughts and sink into the chair. Calming," she said again, almost a reproach.

May fell into an easy silence. Between the rose-scented

mist, the apricot mask, and the gentle massage Helga had begun on the palms of her hands, for a while she forgot the sadness that had brought her here.

She remembered at dinner. When she got to the dining room, she found Margery already seated and finishing her salad.

"Rolando was wonderful," her friend reported dreamily. "I've got him again tonight for some kind of hydro experience. It's in ten minutes," she said as the rest of her dinner arrived. "Which is why I didn't wait for you." She began devouring her grilled salmon and anorectic asparagus. "This is no way to unwind," she said between bites and then narrowed her eyes. "How's the show coming? I make a damn good living, but I think Rolando makes an even better one, and I want Colleen to be the one to pay him."

"When I meet with Dr. Lichtman tomorrow morning, I'll pitch the show. I promise. Once I get his okay, we can put it together fast. Basically all we need is a list of names." She leaned forward. "I mentioned Stacey's death and he went pale as a ghost."

"I'm not sure that was wise. Shouldn't you have waited to bring up your friend's demise until after you got him pinned to the floor about the show?" She didn't wait around for an answer. "Want the rest of my salmon?" She slid over her plate of half-eaten food, said, "See you after I'm water-therapized," and rushed to her next appointment.

May had kept her evening free, but not to take part in the evening's offerings of spiritual healing discussions, art therapy classes, or getting-in-touch workshops. Instead, she wandered the spa, looking for some central administrative building where she might make friends, snoop around, steal the files. She never found one.

She was back in the room by 9:00, the time Paul said he'd call. The phone rang exactly on time.

"He was found floating in the bathtub," he said as soon

as they got past their hellos. He didn't bother saying who was found floating. She knew—Matthew Harris.

"Murdered," she said.

He answered as if it were a question. "Unconfirmed but likely. Are you doing okay?"

"I haven't found out anything yet, if that's what you mean," she said. "Today I learned the lay of the land. Tomorrow I'll go looking for answers."

"Don't come home so fast," he urged her. "Enjoy yourself and wait. Until it's safe."

She didn't want to argue with him, but she had no intention of extending her stay. "I promise I'll call you before I take off," she told him. "I'll call you again when I land. But I can't just hang around here waiting for someone to figure it all out. I can't," she said again, hoping he could understand.

"You can," he pointed out, "but you won't."

They got off the phone, both feeling empty and sad. She called Florida next, and her children's happy, effusive young voices worked to temporarily drown out her worry. They were enjoying the novelty of being on vacation without a parent and said, almost as an afterthought, that they missed her as if they needed to say it for her sake, so she wouldn't feel bad.

By the time she hung up, she was exhausted, despite the afternoon guided nap. She fell asleep fast, as if diving to safety. She didn't rouse when Margery came in or when she left again at dawn for her organized two-hour mountain hike.

When she finally snapped awake, it was eight and sunlight was peeking through the drapes, hitting her between the eyes. She dressed quickly, postponing her shower for later, at the gym. She ate alone, a quick breakfast of hot cereal and helpings from a large fresh-fruit buffet, and arrived ten minutes early for her scheduled follow-up visit to Medical Office B.

Her intention was to locate the doctor's files, but once

again she found that filing cabinets and computers had been edited out of the decorating scheme, as if the sight of anything so mundane would ruin the experience. She had no time to dwell on it. At precisely 9:00, the nurse appeared to usher her into Dr. Lichtman's office. He greeted her warmly.

"You're in excellent, excellent health," he told her. "And I must say you've come exactly at the right time. At the very beginning of perimenopause. This is why you're experiencing fatigue."

She couldn't remember mentioning fatigue and wondered if it was just assumed.

"There are some areas you should keep a close eye on, though," he continued. "Your skin, in excellent condition for a woman your age, will be changing shortly. You may begin to notice symptoms such as new hair growth in places you don't want it. We will try to prevent these symptoms as best we can, but as soon as they arise, you should schedule another visit. If new symptoms occur, anything unusual, unpleasant, distasteful, let us know right away."

"Okay," May said. She was half listening, half readying herself to jump in and change the subject as soon as an opening arose.

"Of course any doctor would tell you this: you need to start calcium supplements as well as a free weights program. But we'll also be adding a mixture of hormones that will begin to resupply what your body has just started to lose. You'll be surprised how quickly this will translate into increased energy for you." He closed the folder. "And I've added a mild blues-lifting supplement as well. This afternoon when you meet with our nutritionist, she'll go through the regimen pill by pill."

"It sounds so simple," she said. "I thought there would be a lot of mumbo jumbo, but it's very straightforward."

"That's right. No hocus-pocus here at all, just plain common sense, finding what your body is missing and replacing it, fine-tuning anything that's off-kilter. That's all we do. Simple as that."

"I have a question, but it's not about my health."

His face tightened. "About your friend. Thank you for bringing it up again. I made a note here to ask you: have you considered meeting with one of our therapists for grief counseling? They're very, very good."

"It's nothing about that. I'm a TV producer for a daytime talk show, *Paula Live.* Do you know it?"

He shrugged and smiled, as if the question amused him. "No."

"I'd like to change that. I'd like you to meet Paula."

"Send her here and I promise we'll take very good care of her."

"That's what I want to do. Well, not exactly that. What I really want to do is get you to come to her, to talk to her on the show. About your spa. About life changes and the health enhancement that you do here."

His smile widened. His eyes sparkled. The effect was not at all friendly. "I am so popular these days. Why is that?"

"What do you mean?"

"You're not the first to approach me. Of course, you already know that."

"I'm not?"

"You don't have to pretend. I respect people who are willing to clean up other people's messes."

"I don't know what you're talking about."

"You don't? Well, then I'll tell you. I got an invitation, a most unpleasant invitation, I might add, from someone on your show."

She stared blankly.

"What was his name?" He began fumbling inside his desk looking for a piece of paper.

But there was only one choice, one man on the show. "Henry?" It made no sense. Why would Henry try to steal this show?

"Ah, here it is," he said. "No. Not Henry. Harris. Matthew Harris. Yes, my note here says Matthew Harris, producer from the *Paula Live* show." He looked away, remembering. "Very unpleasant conversation. Accusatory, actually." He looked at her. "Is that why you're here? Are you following up in the same vein? Do you believe that this is some nefarious death trap?"

"No," May said, trying to keep her voice steady. "Dr. Lichtman, Matthew Harris does not work for *Paula Live.*"

"No? What is he? A stringer—is that what you'd call him?"

She thought, *I'd call him dead,* but all she said was "He never had anything to do with our show. His aunt was a guest here. A friend of my friend Stacey's. She died as well."

The doctor lurched to a stand, several papers sliding to the floor. He made no move to retrieve them. "This conversation is over." He pressed a button on his phone. His hand was trembling.

"Matthew Harris has nothing to do with me. He misrepresented himself."

"Yes, well, I have people waiting."

Barbie opened the door.

"Show Ms. Morrison out, will you?" he snapped, and then stormed out into the hall.

May hurried after him, but he was gone, vanished into another well-concealed doorway.

"We have to set you up with a nutritionist," Barbie called out as May ran out through the lobby and into the hot Arizona air.

She walked through the gym, past the instruction rooms, into the steam room and Jacuzzi complex, but Margery was nowhere to be found. At the treatment suite, despite her best efforts, the receptionist stonewalled her. Finally she went back to her room.

As soon as she got to her building, she saw the door was ajar. She quickly scanned the walkways for a cleaning cart, but there were none around. Pushing her door open, she called out, "Hello?" and slowly entered, wishing she had taken up Paul's offer for pepper spray. "Hello?"

There was no one in the room. She saw that right away. She also saw that her bureau drawers were open and empty and that her small suitcase had been laid out on her bed, her clothes neatly folded and fully packed.

She called Paul to tell him her revised flight plans.

"Wherever I go, I'm just one step behind him," she said.

"That's too bad," Paul observed. "Considering that he's dead."

Thirty-Seven

"WHAT A WASTE. WHAT A TOTAL WASTE," May muttered. She'd been repeating this like a mantra, roughly on the quarter hour, every hour of their homebound flight.

"I swear I will strangle you with this," Margery growled, holding up her set of airplane headphones, "if you say that—if you even think that—one more time."

"I didn't make a dent in figuring out what happened there. I've totally let Stacey down. Not to mention that I've also got nothing to bring back for the show. We're going to have to pay for this trip, you know."

"That's not going to happen, sugar."

"It will. I blew it."

"Slow down. Let's take this one step at a time. What precisely were you hoping to find? A recipe for a slow-acting poison tucked away in Stacey's file?"

"What file? I couldn't find that. I've got nothing. Not even a single vitamin."

"Here." Margery reached under the seat in front of her and pulled out her oversize purse. Digging inside, she came up with a small leather case embossed with the word *Nirvana.* "When I went to the nutritionist to get mine, I picked up yours as well." Before May could thank her, she went on. "As for the show, I was going to wait to surprise you with this, but here." She shoved several sheets of paper in May's hand, then watched, looking smug, as May unfolded them.

"How did you get this?" she asked, as she stared at an alphabetized list of all registered guests who checked into the spa the week of June 18, the week of Stacey's last visit, with Stacey's own name heading the list.

"Did you know," Margery said, leaning close to May so she wouldn't be overheard, "that in the massage rooms, some of the doors have internal locks? And did you know that every single table is built to handle a weight of up to three hundred and fifty pounds without uttering a creak? I didn't test them all, mind you, but I was told. Every one of them."

"What are you talking about? How did you get this?"

"I am in love, sugar. Completely, achingly, exhaustedly in love."

"With whom?"

"Rolando, of course. He is a god. A Latin god. The god of desire. Did you see him?"

"No."

"Well, he knows all about you. And he's very impressed."

"Why?"

"Because you're willing to risk personal safety for the sake of a friend. In fact, he made me promise to bring you along to lunch next week when he comes to New York."

"He's coming to New York?"

"To meet with Paula."

"Our Paula?"

"Yes. For the show we're pitching to save your neck. On the latest massage techniques being used for preventive medicine. Your job is to find a couple of great-looking charismatic insurance reps—good luck—who'll discuss whether health plans that cover therapies like massage and meditation are on the cutting edge or committing fraud."

"I love you," May said.

"I'm working on him to come sooner. I told him if he can get here by Thursday, I'll take him to the Rainbow Room bash."

"What Rainbow Room bash?"

"Oh, sugar, as sure as I'm alive, Colleen is out to get you. You don't know anything about the party she's throwing herself?"

May shook her head.

"If you don't start watching yourself, you're going to be phoning in your pitches from the unemployment office. Tell you what: you take Rolando in to Paula."

"No. He's your catch. You take him."

"Why? So I can end up the only producer on the show over the age of twenty-five? No thank you."

May leaned over and gave her friend a hard kiss on the cheek. "That's for getting me the names of the spa guests. You go ahead and pitch Rolando yourself. I'm a grown-up. I can handle Colleen."

"All right," Margery said. "But I'm worried about you."

"Don't worry about me," May said quickly. "I'm fine." She held up the list of spa guests. "Worry about them." She studied the list in silence, noting the names she recognized, four of them dead. She looked for one more, Darlene Altschul, but didn't find her. She was still thinking about it, about the one person who didn't fit anywhere, when the plane bumped its way to a landing.

May and Margery made their way off the plane, through the terminal, to the baggage carousel where they'd arranged to meet their drivers.

May spotted hers first, standing at the bottom of the escalator clutching a bouquet of yellow mums.

Margery saw him, too. "You'll notice my driver," she said, pointing to a man in a black suit standing close to the exit, "brought me nothing." They all stared at the man holding up a small sign on which Margery's name was scrawled, childlike, in large letters.

"I should have brought you flowers, too," Paul said to Margery, as he received May with a tight hug and a kiss that didn't want to stop.

"That's enough," Margery shouted out. "I am leaving this very minute. There is nothing more revolting than viewing someone else's romantic encounters. Oh, and by the way, sugar. I'm not going in to work tomorrow. Colleen thinks we're out until Thursday. It's a get-out-of-work-free day. You going to turn us in?"

May shook her head. "Thanks again," she called as Margery made her way to her driver, who she immediately began lecturing about going the extra distance and saying it with flowers.

"Success?" Paul asked May, as he escorted her to his car.

"Not complete," she explained. "But not a disaster either. Margery managed to get a list of former guests. So tonight's activity is calling them all. The live ones, that is."

Paul pulled the car onto the highway. "I was hoping tonight's activity would be me making you some of my famous spaghetti and meatballs. After you make your calls?" he added, because he was practical and could tell her mind was set.

"It's a date," she said, and settled back into her seat. "How about you? Catch any bad guys today?"

"Actually," he said, "today was a pretty bad day to be a bad guy in my part of town. A damn bad day." He smiled broadly, then turned to share the brilliance of his good feelings.

She didn't ask for details. She knew by now that Paul worked with complete focus, giving one hundred percent of his attention, but when he was done, when he was off duty, he didn't like to give the ugly mess of the day another thought.

They rode home in silence. When they got to May's house, there was no discussion of how the evening would unfold. They walked in. She set her suitcase on the floor and put the flowers on the kitchen counter. He took off his jacket. She shed her linen duster. They came together.

She couldn't say who led whom up the stairs, who moved whom towards the bed. There was no reason to reason to rush. But when they got to her room, they hurried nonetheless, urgently removing each other's clothes, as if to strip away the day, the week, their lives, until they collapsed, one atop the other, naked, sweating, hungry.

Thirty-Eight

Later, in the kitchen, showered but still flushed, May showed Paul her new stash of multicolored soft-gels.

"What are those?"

"Hormones and vitamins," she told him.

"For who? The entire Third World?"

"It's my three-month starter kit."

"Wow," Paul said and picked up a handful. He let them fall through his slender fingers. "They expect you to take all of these pills in three months?"

May nodded.

"You haven't taken any yet, have you?"

"Yes," she lied. "But don't worry. I feel fine except that—" She made a gagging sound, then dropped her head hard onto the table. "I'm dead," she said a moment later

"Don't joke about this, May."

"Sorry. Here." She pushed the pills towards him. A few rolled off the table. She got down on her knees to gather them up. "Send these to the lab, will you? Then we can find out once and for all exactly what's in them." It was a joke. Paul didn't get it.

"That's a great idea," he said.

"I was kidding."

"I'm serious. I know a guy at a lab who owes me a favor."

Sometimes it seemed to her that half the world owed Paul a favor. She didn't ask for details, though. She just leaned over and began sifting through the pile, picking out several pills of each color and size, a sample for the lab.

"I'll call him tomorrow," Paul told her. It was a challenge for him, helping May figure this out without taking the whole thing over, but he was trying. "What's your next move?"

She pulled out the purloined list from her purse. "Phone tag. Let's see if any of these people are it."

"Okay. While you make your calls, I'll make us dinner."

"You're on," she said, and then picked up the phone, took a breath, and began.

"May I speak to Ellie Crowell?" she said, as soon as someone answered. She tried to lift her voice and lighten it, to sound younger. She wondered if there was a way she could make herself sound blond.

"Hello, Mrs. Crowell," she said when the woman got on the line. "I'm Taylor, from the Nirvana Spa. We're following up on your visit. Yes, it's a new service we've instituted. I just have a few questions about how you've been feeling since you've left us. Do you have a moment? Terrific." She waved her papers in the air. "Here we go, then. Have you been sleeping well? How about your appetite?" She laughed sympathetically and said, "Mine, too." She paused to pretend she was writing it all down.

After several more questions, she knew Mrs. Crowell was feeling healthy and fit. "Will we be seeing you back here anytime soon? Really? That's great. I wish I could, but I can't take reservations. Would you like me to transfer you? Can you hold? Thanks."

May put the phone against her chest and silently counted to five. Paul, chopping onions on a wooden cutting board, shook his head and looked at her, sharing his amusement. She didn't want to laugh, so she struggled to ignore him as she put the phone back to her ear.

"I'm afraid all the reservationists are busy right now. Would it be too much trouble for you try again later? Thank you so much. Oh, one more thing. I have a hello for you from another Nirvana guest, Stacey Blum. You don't? She certainly knew you. Oh, sure. I understand. I don't like to make friends when I'm in my robe, either." She laughed at something else the woman said and then wrapped it up. "Thank you so much for your help. There will be a small gift in your bag the next time you visit us. I'll see you soon, then."

She hung up and put a small check mark next to Ellie Crowell's name. "She's certainly perky."

"How many of those calls are you planning on making?" Paul asked her.

She held up the list. "All of them."

He reached for the pack of Zantac in his pocket and took one. "Do you have a plan? Do you know what you're trying to find out?"

"No," she admitted. "When you're checking out a lead, do you know?"

"Usually," he said, using his sleeve to wipe away his onion tears.

"Me, too," she told him. "But not always. Sometimes when I'm going after a story, I jump in blind and just feel my way around as fast as I can until I figure it out." She watched him look around the countertops, searching for something.

"The garlic is in that stoneware jar," she told him, pointing to the countertop.

He found the jar, reached in, and pulled out a head. Then he started opening drawers.

"The garlic press is in there," she said, and directed him to the second drawer from the top.

He had barely opened the cupboard door to peer inside when she called out, "Oil is over there."

He stopped and turned toward her. "Okay. I get your point. I won't offer any help to you unless you ask for it, either."

She smiled, picked up the phone receiver, and dialed again.

"Is Julia Dean there? Oh. All right. Yes, I understand. Thank you. I will." She looked over at Paul, who wasn't moving. "What's wrong? Am I all out of tomato paste?"

Coming over, he pointed to the list. "How is that person?"

"I thought we weren't paying attention to each other."

"Is she okay?"

She smiled at his worry. He was good at so much, but a failure at this, hiding his worry.

"Julia is at the gym right now, in an aerobics class. Then she's going cycling. If she doesn't go back to the gym to swim, she should be home in two hours."

Paul tried not to look so relieved at the news, but instead of returning to the stove, he sat down at the table across from her. "We haven't talked about Matthew Harris yet."

It was true. She'd diligently avoided the subject and hoped he'd continue to do the same. She met his hard gaze, afraid to know what she would hear.

"I spoke to a friend who covers the neighborhood around the airport to make sure he knows that this death might not be isolated. I told him there might be out-of-states in involved."

"What did he say?"

"He grunted. Which I understand. Once you got out-of-states, you have to start considering the FBI and no one wants to do that."

"Why not?"

"Because suddenly you've got a dozen guys coming in who don't know the territory, who aren't connected to the community. You get some good guys, don't get me wrong. But you also always get a couple of cowboys, the kind who put themselves in charge of what they don't know the first thing about. It's not particularly productive and it's hardly ever worth it. If you let a cop do his job, give him whatever backup he needs, whatever resources, he'll get the job done just fine.

"But in this case, I don't think it would be half bad. There are dead people—quite a number of dead people—scattered around quite a few divergent locales."

"Do you think the FBI will come in?"

"It's not my call. But if they do, believe me, you'll be among the first to know. They'll be ringing your doorbell. That's for sure."

"So I'd better get busy and finish," she said, moving to pick up the phone.

"Look, I'm not telling you to give up what you're doing," Paul said. "But I am saying I think this is bigger than what you first thought when you started. And at some point, you're going to have to step back. You're going to have to give up being the hero who solves the murders of the world."

"I'm not trying to solve the murders of the world," she told him quietly. "I just want to find out what happened to Stacey. Then I'll stop, okay?"

"Okay," he said, and leaned over to kiss her. But this time it was a kiss without heat. This was a kiss of worry.

Paul went back to his sauce. May went back to her phone list. It was slow going. Excluding the ones she already knew were dead—Stacey, Margaret, Toni, Theresa—she made contact with every spa guest on the list or at least contacted a family member who was happy to report on their health and well-being. Everyone was fine. And no one, not one person she called, had any recollection of meeting a woman named Stacey Blum or Darlene Altschul. More than ever, May wanted to locate Darlene Altschul.

When she had called her way through to the end of the list she leaned back in her chair and let out a sigh. "That's one bunch of fit and happy customers," she reported.

Paul came up behind her and laid his long fingers on

her tight shoulder muscles. Slowly he pressed, digging deep into her tension.

"It's better this way," he said quietly. "You wouldn't have wanted to uncover any more dead people." He pressed his fingers even deeper, at the portal of pain. "It's like this with all footwork. It's tedious. Unproductive. Then one day you get something and—bam—the whole thing comes together."

She turned to him. "Do you think that will happen to me?"

"If you get lucky," he told her straight. "Usually right before it comes together, I try to eat an incredible meal. Spaghetti and meatballs, garlic bread, and wine. It's uncanny how much that helps."

She smiled and followed him into the dining room, where she saw how hard he'd worked to get ready. Somehow he'd found a tablecloth. He'd gathered the assorted candlesticks she kept around the house but never used. He even found the few pieces of good china that she stuck in the back of the dining-room corner cabinet. She hadn't even noticed him looking. He pulled out her chair, and when she was seated, he lit the candles and poured the wine.

"To the truth," Paul toasted her.

"To the chef," she toasted back. "I didn't know you liked to cook."

"I've been holding out on you. I wanted to make sure you didn't love me just for my sauce."

The sauce was delicious and they both ate dinner too quickly. When they had sopped up the last of the sweet sauce with their warmed garlic bread, May sent Paul to relax in front of the TV while she cleaned up in the kitchen. When she was done, she found him there, fast asleep, his head tipped back, his mouth slightly open, snoring. She woke him gently. He checked his watch and lurched to attention.

"Bridget is going to kill me," he said as he gathered his stuff. He grabbed May for a good-night kiss. When they pulled apart several minutes later, he looked dazed. "Who did I say is going to kill me?"

"Bridget, your sister," she reminded him, and they both laughed as May pushed him toward the door.

"Triple locks," he told her as she started to close it. "And keep Delia's baseball bat at your beside."

"I'll be fine," she reassured him, and then gave him one more quick kiss on the lips. She closed the door and hoped she'd kissed on the truth.

Thirty-Nine

IN HER DREAM, THE PHONE RANG, but when she picked it up, the ringing got louder, so loud she woke herself up to escape it.

She found herself holding her bedside phone to her ear. Apparently she had already said hello.

"Mommy?" It was Susie's voice.

"Hi, pumpkin." May sat up and forced herself to come fully awake. "How's Florida?"

"We went to Disney World yesterday," she reported, "and I'm not forty inches yet, so I couldn't go on all of the scary rides. I did too want to," she yelled to someone. To her mother, she explained, "I just didn't whine or cry about it. I've got to go," she said. "It's Delia's turn."

Delia's voice came on, loud. "Guess what? Grandma let us stay up to see the light show and the fireworks."

"That's lucky," May said.

"Is everything okay there?" Delia's voice dropped. "I heard Grandma tell someone that a lot of people got killed near us. Are a lot of people getting killed near us? Is that why you sent us to Florida?"

The question made May's entire body sag. "No, honey.

I sent you to Florida so you could spend some time with Grandma. She's lonely, you know."

"She doesn't look lonely." She lowered her voice for the second time. "She and Grandpa kiss all the time. Yuk."

May shuddered at the image of her mother and her new stepfather—Todd's father—nuzzling. "Put Grandma on, pumpkin."

"How are you, dolly?" came Grandma Shirley's voice. "Anybody else croak?"

"Shh. I don't want to scare the girls."

"Who's scaring the girls? Girls, the roof is falling down. You'd better leave. Nothing. They're back to watching cartoons. If I told them I was leaving on a spaceship to Jupiter, maybe—maybe—they'd look up and say, 'Okay, good-bye.' But they wouldn't take their eyes off the screen. We just got a big-screen TV is why," Shirley confided. "Your father . . . your father-in-law—what do I call him?"

"Mr. Morrison," May suggested.

Her mother ignored her. "He loves to watch ball games on the big TV. Too bad you couldn't come down here, too."

"Maybe next time. Listen, could you please try not to talk about people dying anymore?"

"All right. But in Florida, that eliminates the major part of daily conservation."

As soon as her mother let her off the phone, May called in to work.

"I need to get scheduled in with Colleen," she told Charlotte. "Anytime tomorrow." It was time to confront her boss with her second-city status.

She heard the phone ring while she was in the shower. It was ringing again when she got out.

"I remembered something," Lydia told her when she picked up. "I thought you'd want to know. It came to me while I was sitting on the can. Stacey's friend, the one I told you she talked to me about? Her name is Lena."

Lena, May silently repeated. "Lena," she said again out

loud. Then it clicked. "Could Lena be Darlene? Darlene Altschul?"

"Oh. You already know her."

"Just by the name," May said, and then suffered through Lydia's update on how happy Sophie and Michael were, how she'd just dropped them back at the house to visit their dad, how she hoped they were safe and that this didn't cause them to backslide into despair.

May did nothing to extend the conversation. As soon as she could, she got off the phone and headed for the envelope of obituaries Morgan had given her. *There it is.* How had she missed it? Darlene and Stacey worked for the same company. This changed things.

May struggled to think, but her mind felt as clogged as a stale bottle of Elmer's glue. *Darlene wasn't part of the spa group. But Darlene is dead. Why did Stacey save the obituary?* She came up blank.

After sitting produced no results, she decided to try thinking things through on a walk. That's when she saw the FOR SALE sign staked into the Blums' front lawn.

Good, she thought. For days, it had been bothering her. How could Scott choose to remain living in a house where his wife had turned up dead? Now this seemed another sign that Lydia was wrong about him. That maybe all of his short-tempered outbursts, his unreasonable behavior, his displaced anger was easily explained by the simple fact that he was in mourning, heartsick, broken-hearted.

She climbed the steps and rang his bell. It was foolish, she knew. He probably wouldn't talk to her. She rang again.

But no one answered. Even Rosie was too disinterested to bark. She faced the empty house, searching for an answer, as if the house could give it. Then she walked to the side and, without meaning to, around back.

It was as if she'd been heading here all along but hadn't known it. For the first time since Stacey's demise, she was there, staring at the scene, at the pool.

No sign of the tragedy remained. Prospective owners

who strolled through the backyard now would never know what had happened here. They might note that it seemed untidy, but if they hadn't seen it before, in the days when Stacey pulled up migrant grass even before it had a chance to firmly root, it probably wouldn't even strike them as particularly neglected.

The pool hadn't been cleaned in a while. The surface was coated with debris. Stacey had been meticulous about keeping it clean. She claimed it relaxed her, running the small net across the top of the water, skimming off dead bees and leaves. Now, the water rippled as whirligigs landed, floated, then sank.

May stared at the leaf-covered concrete, at where she imagined Stacey's body had lain. At first she thought she could still see its outline but when she looked up, shivering, she noticed it was just a cloud passing overhead, making shadows as it went. She scanned the yard, wondering if anyone came back here at all anymore. Then her eyes caught something unfamiliar, out of place. She moved closer to where several feet of lawn had been dug up, the sod hastily replaced, now brown, like hay. She shook off the thought like a chill—it looked like a grave.

But when she got right up to it, she saw that was exactly what it was. A primitive sign had been stuck in the ground. She kneeled to read it.

"Here lies Rosie," she read out loud. "We loved her well."

A voice called out, "What are you doing?"

She swung around, saw Michael.

"You're back," she said. "It's great to see you."

"My dad doesn't want you here."

"I'll leave, Michael," she said, not wanting to disturb the boy. Then she glanced again at the grave. "What happened to Rosie?"

He was only ten, too young to keep a firm hold on the conversational reins. "She died," he said, and sounded mad about it.

"I'm so sorry."

"Yeah, well, she was just a dog."

His toughness was so hollow it made May's eyes swell with tears. "How did she die?"

"Sophie said it was a broken heart, but Dad says it was just some dog flu."

In a flash, she pictured Rosie and Stacey sitting side by side, shaking off a chill, both stumbling as they walked, both sick and sleeping too much. Suddenly May felt dizzy, too, as if she might pass out. She didn't want to do that. Not here, in front of Michael.

"I'm sorry about your dog," she got out.

It seemed to soften him. "You don't look so good, Mrs. Morrison. Are you okay?"

"I'm fine, Mikey. I'm sad, but fine."

But she wasn't fine. She hurried down the driveway, her stomach roiling. When she reached the street, she held on to the nearest lamp post for support. There. She caught her breath and steadied herself. Again she flicked on the image of Rosie, shivering, losing traction, following Stacey around the house like the sick dog she was. *She said dogs don't catch things from humans,* Stacey had said to May about the vet, and then she had added, *but I guess no one told Rosie that.*

May hurried back to the yard. Michael hadn't budged.

"Mikey, honey," she called quietly. She didn't want to startle him. "What's the name of your vet? I need to call your vet. Do you know his name?"

"Mike," came a booming voice, and May swung around to see Scott standing at the back door, legs wide on the slate patio as if he was preparing himself for a fight. "I want you in the house, now."

Michael immediately disappeared inside.

"What are you doing here?" his father demanded to know.

"What happened to Rosie, Scott?"

"Nothing that concerns you."

"Stacey and Rosie were sick with the same symptoms. Why?"

"Why won't you leave me in peace?" He sounded wounded.

"I will," she said. "All you have to do is tell me what you know about Rosie's and Stacey's deaths."

"How dare you? How dare you tell me what I have to do?"

"I'm going to find out what happened, Scott. I'm incredibly tenacious, you know. I do this for a living."

"Goddamn your living," he replied. "I want to be left alone. Are you deaf or just dumb? Get out of my life."

"Why? I'm not your enemy, Scott," May pleaded as she came toward him, her hands outstretched. "Why don't you want—"

He cut her off. "May you don't speak English. Let's try this: I've purchased a gun."

She froze.

"It would be understandable, don't you think? I don't feel safe anymore. If I were to find an intruder in my backyard, if I were to shoot before asking questions, who could blame me?"

"Have you lost your mind?" she asked him. "Are you threatening me?"

"No," he said quietly. "I'm just saying it like it is. I lost my wife and I can't have her back. But I want my life back. Which means I want you, and all the other people like you, to get your nose out of my business and leave me alone. I don't want to be your research project. For the last time, leave me alone, or I'll call the police."

"I thought we were friends," May said quietly.

"There's a show idea for you. People May Morrison mistakenly thought were her friends. I bet the list is a long one."

She might be determined, but she also knew when to retreat. As she swung around the front of the house, she saw Michael sitting on the steps.

"Are you okay here?" she asked him.

He nodded, then glanced toward the backyard. "Call Dr. Ackerman," he said.

"What?"

"Our vet. Call Dr. Ackerman." He said it quietly, just loud enough for her to hear.

She didn't risk a reply, nodding her thank-you instead, just as Scott came out from the backyard. He glanced at Michael to see what he was doing, but all he saw was his son crushing ants with a stone.

"Get inside," he barked at him, and May assumed, though she didn't turn to look, that the boy obeyed.

Forty

"AND THE NAME IS?" the veterinarian's nurse asked.

"May Morrison."

"And what's wrong with May?"

"Nothing's wrong with me. I'm May."

"And you're calling about?"

"Rosie Blum."

"Oh," the nurse said.

"She's dead," May explained.

"Yes, I know."

"I need to talk to Dr. Ackerman."

"I see," she said, though she clearly didn't. "I'll let the doctor know you're calling, but she has a very busy schedule today." She waited a moment, putting her words together so as not to offend. "Don't get me wrong. I'm very sad about what happened to Rosie. But there's nothing we can do for her now." She was used to dealing with pet owners, ones who were anxious, overprotective, grateful, sad, but this was always the hardest, people who had trouble accepting their favorite dog was really gone.

"Actually I'm investigating the death of Rosie's owner, Stacey Blum. That's what I need to talk to Dr. Ackerman about."

"Oh," she said, and then, "Investigating. Oh. That was so tragic. Those poor children, losing their mother and then their dog. Hold on. Let me see what I can do."

A chorus of kids singing "How Much Is That Doggie in the Window?" began playing into May's ear. They were on to "The Cat Came Back" when the nurse picked up.

"Can you come now? We've just gotten a cancellation. Dr. Ackerman is very busy, but she can give you a couple of minutes if you come right now."

"I'm on my way," May told her. "And thanks."

She starting planning how to explain herself even as she pulled the car out of the driveway. But every time she got to "I'm investigating Stacey's death," she stopped, hung up on the obvious question: For whom? Could she admit the truth to the vet—that it was for herself?

Halfway down her block, she slowed the car and pulled it to a stop across the street. Who were those people in front of Stacey's house—two women and a man? At first she thought they were arguing, but then one of them laughed.

She opened her glove compartment and took out a map, unfolding it over the steering wheel so that if they happened to glance her way, she would look as if she were studying it. She hoped no one could tell from all the way across the street that the map she was perusing was of the mountains of New Hampshire. She lowered the passenger window half an inch to better hear what they were saying.

"Lovely swimming pool," the woman in the suit declared. "And so unusual to find in a house of this kind on a real family block."

A realtor, May thought.

"It's a death trap," a voice called out.

The realtor and her prospective clients turned as one to see a boy—Michael—sitting on the front steps of his house. "Very dangerous," he said seriously. "I would never get a house with a pool like that."

The realtor made a joke May couldn't hear. Her clients nervously laughed along.

Scott, hearing visitors and sensing trouble, opened the front door and stepped outside. Michael immediately disappeared into the house, running past his father and up the stairs.

"Hello," Scott said, striding down the path to greet his potential buyers.

"This is Dr. Blum," the realtor explained.

Scott extended his arm to greet the couple standing before him, but as he did, he noticed May's car idling across the street. He let his arm drop to his side as he squinted, trying to see who it was. May could almost feel the chill when his eyes locked on hers. "Excuse me a moment," he told the assembled group, and started toward the car.

He walked like a man on a mission, and it wasn't one of goodwill. Quickly, she dropped the map on the seat beside her, threw the car into drive, and pulled away—was that her tires squealing?—avoiding looking in her rearview mirror until she'd made the turn off the block.

Her guess, though she couldn't be sure, was that these particular buyers wouldn't be making an offer on the Blum house, at least not anytime soon.

Forty-One

THE BELL WAS BROKEN, but when she tried the knob, it turned. She opened the old wooden door and let herself in.

The receptionist's desk was unattended, but May signed in on the clipboard set out on the ledge. Where it said "Patient," she wrote "Rosie Blum."

She found a spot on the brown vinyl couch and sat down. The short yellow hairs lying all around her jumped onto her pants as if she were a giant magnet. She noticed the stone floor was hairy, too, and in need of a good washing.

An American Kennel Association poster hung on the wall displaying tiny snapshots of dozens of breeds of dogs. A poster next to it showed the five basic steps in cat care. A third depicted a pair of parrots in a jungle setting with the caption DOES YOUR BIRD HAVE ENOUGH ROOM? The strong smell of disinfectant permeated the air, along with the faded smell of dog.

An interior door opened and a woman walked out smiling.

May introduced herself. "I just spoke with you on the phone."

"Yes?" The woman's blond hair was clipped short. Her glasses sat low on her nose. Her brown eyes looked tired, her skin parched from too much sun. "Becky will be right with you." She reached into the goldfish bowl that sat on the front desk and took a handful of sourballs.

"Help yourself," she told May. Then she leaned over and peered into a second bowl, filled with small Milk-Bones, and sniffed. Coughing, she disappeared back through the door. Moments later, it opened again.

"Because they're stale." May heard someone shout, and then another voice answered, "I said I'll change it."

A needle-thin woman with eyes so deep set it was hard to see their color came out, shaking her head in annoyance. "Ms. Morrison?"

May stood up.

"Right this way." She led May down a narrow hall and then stepped aside before the doorway. "Right in there."

May walked into the small room and found the blond woman sitting on a stool beside a stainless-steel table. Her head stuck in a chart, she sucked noisily on a sourball. When she heard May come in, she looked up over her glasses.

"I'm Dr. Ackerman," she said, and extended her arm.

May returned the firm shake. "Thanks so much for taking the time to see me."

"No problem. How can I help?"

"I'm a friend of Stacey Blum's."

"I'm so sorry about what happened."

"Thanks." Already it was getting easier to hold back the tears. "I've been doing some research," she chose her words carefully, "for the family. I'm sure you know there are some unanswered questions about Stacey's death."

"Don't assume anything. The only reason I know she died at all is that her daughter called to tell me about the dog. She wanted to know if a dog could get depressed. I told her yes. She asked if a dog could get depressed to the point of illness. I figured the daughter was the one who was really depressed but I told her to bring Rosie in anyway, so I could take a look. She never did. When I realized I hadn't seen the dog, I called back to see how they both were, but she wasn't home. By then, she was staying with a relative, I think."

"Her aunt," May explained, as if that mattered.

Dr. Ackerman nodded, then waited.

"Before Stacey's death," May explained, "she and Rosie didn't feel well. They both had similar symptoms. We wonder if there might be some connection."

"What kind of connection?"

"That's what I don't know. That's why I need to find out why Rosie died."

Dr. Ackerman looked startled by the question. "Well, I wouldn't know. I mean, I didn't see the dog. It could have been anything. A heart attack. Poison."

"Poison?"

"We're not talking Ingrid Bergman in *Notorious* here. I don't mean someone was putting poison in her Alpo. But we lose a lot of animals to household poisons—glugging down cherry-flavored cough medicine, gobbling lemon-scented furniture polish. Sometimes they eat something off the street. I can't tell you what happened to Rosie because I don't know. I went over her chart. I see she was ill for several weeks. Stacey had called, concerned. But she never brought her in. I wish she had."

"She probably didn't bring her in because she was sick herself," May explained.

"That's right," Dr. Ackerman said. "She did call me to ask about that. She wanted to know if they both might have the same thing. I told her dogs and humans don't like to share germs. Fleas, yes. Germs, no."

"They had exactly the same symptoms, Dr. Ackerman."

"I don't doubt it. Many infections, viral and bacterial, look the same. What was the presentation?"

"It was like a flu. They had the shivers. And Stacey complained of being clumsy. Sound like anything?"

"Sounds like many things. But I never got to examine the dog," the vet repeated, "so I can't say. I wouldn't even begin to guess."

"What about if you examine her now?"

"You'd want an academic research facility for that." Her voice changed. "What exactly are you looking for?"

"An answer," May said quietly. "Several of Stacey's friends, as well as Stacey and her dog, all died within a very short time."

"It sounds like instead of talking to me you should be talking to the Centers for Disease Control. Or to the police."

Becky, the nurse, stuck her head in the office. "Peanut and Desiree are here."

"At the same time? What kind of scheduling is that?" The vet stood up. The meeting was over.

"Dr. Ackerman, Stacey was my best friend. I want to find out what happened to her. And that means finding out what happened to her dog."

The vet stepped over to the counter, opened a stainless-steel drawer, pulled out a pad, and scribbled a number. "Call here. It's a top-notch research center. One of the best in the country. I don't know if they'll have the time to help you, but they have the expertise. I have neither."

May took the note and thanked her, and the doctor quickly ushered her out of the room, glad to be done with it.

When May got to the waiting room, a large Rottweiler stopped nuzzling the rear end of a disinterested poodle and both animals began barking at her.

Becky came out from behind her desk and looked at May harshly, as if she'd done something to incite them. Then she turned her attention to the dogs. "What's the problem, ladies?"

May quickly let herself out.

Forty-Two

WHEN SHE GOT HOME, May ran straight up the stairs to her bedroom, where she'd left her computer. Finding the number for the institute was easy. They had their own home page on the internet. Finding someone who would help her was the challenge.

She started with a woman named Miss List, who made it clear from the start that she didn't think May sounded like much of a dog owner.

"How much did your dog weigh?"

May hadn't the vaguest idea, so she gave Susie's weight, figuring it would be close. "Thirty-five pounds."

"Oh, that's so sad. Had she stopped eating?"

"Did I say thirty-five?" May quickly corrected herself. "I meant eighty-five."

"Whoah. Big girl," Miss List remarked, and May left it at that.

Miss List asked how long the symptoms had persisted.

May took a guess. "Two weeks."

"Had she been sleeping more than normal?"

Another educated guess. "Yes."

"How did her elimination go?"

"That's what I'm trying to find out," May snapped, feeling as if she were playing a befuddled Lou in an old Abbott and Costello routine.

"How many times a day did she poop?" Miss List tried again, putting it more plainly.

"Twice a day." That seemed reasonable.

"Normal consistency?"

"I'm not sure," she said, and when she heard the sigh of Miss List's frustration at her limited knowledge, she changed her answer to "Yes."

"Would you like to hold or shall I have one of our scientists call you back? It might take a while," she explained.

"I'll hold," May said. In less than five minutes, a male voice came on the phone.

"Adler."

"Hi," May began all over again. "I'm trying to find out what happened to my dog."

"Miss List gave me some information, but I need a bit more before I can tell if I'll take her."

"You can't take her," May said, disappointed to discover that Miss List hadn't even gotten that much right. "The dog is dead."

"That's a load off my mind. I don't like dissecting live animals."

She managed a quiet. "Oh."

"Your vet's name?"

"Dr. Ackerman."

"Address?"

"I don't have it in front of me."

Adler laughed. "I know. You can drive there blindfolded but you can't tell me the address. You and the rest of the world. Does he have the remains?"

"The dog is buried in the backyard."

Adler groaned. "Oh. Too bad. What was the time of death?"

Another question May didn't know. "I'm so bad with time."

He groaned again. "Okay, what was the day of death, then?"

When she didn't answer that one he asked, "Was it today? Yesterday? The day before that?"

"It was this week," she offered, the best she could do.

"You don't know what day your dog died?"

"Two days ago. I'm almost positive."

Adler was silent for a moment. "Mrs. Morrison, is there someone more familiar with the animal with whom I could talk?"

There was no point in lying. "I'm not the owner."

"No kidding."

"I'm a friend of the family. The owner is dead."

"Is this *Candid Camera* or something?"

"I'm not joking. The owner is dead."

He pulled himself together. "Sorry to hear it."

"The owner, who died shortly before the dog died, had come down with the flu. The dog had the same symptoms. Several of the owner's friends had been ill, too. Every one of them is now dead."

"They all died of the flu?"

"No. Several of them died in peculiar accidents. Except I don't think they really were accidents."

His voice went up an octave. "Oh."

Her shoulders sank. "Look, I don't know what really happened. I'm just following my gut. And my gut tells me there's a connection between how the dog died and how those people died."

"Sounds awfully intriguing, but without the animal I don't know any more than you do. And since it's not your animal, you can't release it to me."

"Mr. Adler—"

He corrected her. "Dr. Adler."

"Dr. Adler, could the dog have been sick with the same thing my friend had? Are there viruses people can catch from their dogs?"

"There're parasites, like fleas."

"I mean something more like the flu."

"Your friend and the dog, they didn't just move here from England, did they?"

"Why do you ask?"

"It was a joke, a bad joke. Okay—it's extremely rare, hardly ever happens, for a disease to move across species. Bovine spongiform encephalopathy—BSE—is one of the few that does. You know it as mad cow disease. If you were to tell me your friend just got back from a trip to London where she shared her hamburger with her dog, I'd say it was time for a quick call to the Centers for Disease Control. Is that the case?"

"No."

"Or if she lived in Kentucky and ate squirrel brain for dinner, you might have something to worry about. Was your friend a big fan of squirrel brain?"

"No."

"Good. BSE goes right to the brain. I personally advise against eating brains of any kind."

"The dog chased squirrels. Could she have gotten this disease from biting a squirrel?"

He considered this. "Maybe you should work on getting someone from the family to deliver the dog to me. Can you manage that?"

"I can try," she said.

"If you succeed, call me back."

"Thanks," May said, and feeling vaguely nauseous, hung up the phone.

She sat perfectly still for several moments, considering her options. They did not include calling up Scott and asking him to dig up his dead dog. Asking Michael or Sophie was equally out of the question. She turned off her PowerBook and carried it downstairs, still thinking. She was in the kitchen, visualizing herself digging up the Blum backyard in the middle of the night, when a gust of wind blew her hair, drawing her out of her fugue.

Her eyes darted to the sliding door leading to the backyard. It was wide open. Tiny hairs on the back of her neck stood up.

Slowly she walked to the door and peered outside. Nothing was moving, except for decaying leaves fluttering on the branches of autumn trees and whirligigs spinning to the ground.

And she asked herself if she had gone out to the backyard this morning? Had she left the door open when she went to the vet? It seemed so completely unlike her, and yet she'd been so distracted, she knew it was possible. She tried to remember if it had been open when she came home from the vet.

But she didn't remember going out to the backyard. Could she have forgotten that, too?

As she stared through the doorway, she suddenly noticed the screen door was open, too. Closing the screen door was something she did on automatic pilot. The girls always forgot, but they weren't home. So who left it open like that?

"Hello?" she called, her voice small, like Susie's. She opened the basement door, peered down into the dark cavern below. "Hello?" Only this time, she knew Delia and Susie weren't hiding out, playing a joke on her. Paul wasn't due back any minute with Chinese food.

"Hello?" she called again. Her voice was quiet, low. She didn't really want to hear an answer.

She removed the largest knife, a chef's knife, from the butcher block holder and slowly walked through the first-floor rooms. Was that a creak she heard?

Slowly, she moved to the phone. Her fingers clumsily pressed Paul's number. His instructions were terse.

"Dial 911 and get out of the house."

With the knife in one hand and the portable phone in the other, she stealthily crept to the front door, dialing as she raced outside, where she waited for help to come.

Forty-Three

SHE'D LEARNED IT during last year's episode—that cops liked to be heroes. They had little patience for people playing at being detectives, so she didn't mention to these officers that she was looking into her neighbor's death, that she was close on the trail of something she couldn't yet explain or understand. She simply said that she'd been out and that when she returned, she found her sliding back door open.

"No," she told them, trying to sound sure of herself. She hadn't left it open. She was sure of it. She was diligent, obsessive about locking up her house. "No," she added, there was no one else home to leave it ajar. Her baby-sitter, who might well have left it open, was in Florida, with her children, visiting her mother.

One uniformed cop interviewed her while his partner did the walk-through. She could hear him, the floor above her creaking with his heavy steps.

When he returned, he reported that everything looked secure.

"Did you check under the beds? In the closets? Behind the shower curtain in the top floor bathroom?" He looked too young to drive, not responsible enough to be trusted in the kitchen, certainly not seasoned enough to check her house thoroughly, the way she would have. "Did you look in the furnace room? In every closet?"

"Your house is secure," he repeated. "Who else has a key?"

And then, because it hadn't occurred to her that it could have been a neighbor, she said, "Oh."

"You didn't think of that, did you?" the cop who interviewed her asked. "It's easy to let your imagination go to the worst, but I find it's usually something really simple. Don't get me wrong. It's good to call us. 'Specially with what's been going on. We're very happy when it turns out to be nothing."

The other cop piped up. "Like maybe someone found a package on your front steps and decided to bring it in the house for you, to keep it safe—something like that."

She didn't bother explaining why that was unlikely, that the delivery man always put her packages on her side porch. That she didn't have neighbors who would just let themselves in without telling her in advance.

"How many people have your key?" the cop asked, and while she thought about it he went on. "Do yourself a favor and call around. See if I'm right, if any of them came in. Maybe someone was trying to reach you and couldn't and got worried. The way things have been around here, friends might have thought something happened to you." He cocked his head as if to say, *Could have happened, right?*

Finally, he'd come up with a reason she could believe. But who would worry about her? Who had a key to her house who would worry about her? Emily Cooper has a key. And Stacey. Immediately, she realized, *No, Stacey doesn't have my key. Not anymore. It's Scott who has my key now.*

"You going to call your neighbors?" the cop persisted. "I'm sure that's what happened. Either a neighbor dropped in to do you a favor or someone worried about you so bad they had to check on you, or else you left the door open and forgot. It happens." He leaned in to confide, "My mother does it all the time."

May swallowed a groan. She couldn't stand that he was comparing her to his mother.

"I'm not big on leaving the key with neighbors anyway," his partner added. "Do you know about our Friendly Key program? You drop a key with us, and in an emergency, you always have a place to go. You should try us out. Lots of people do."

"Thanks," May said, as they walked down her front path toward their squad car.

"Make sure you lock up now," one of them said, but she wasn't listening. She was thinking, *Who let themselves in? Who has a key?*

Forty-Four

SHE WAS STILL PONDERING the question when the phone jogged her out of her thoughts. She got to it on the second ring.

"Mom?" came Delia's happy voice. "Guess what?"

"What?" May could hear in her voice that it was good news.

"Susie went on Tower of Terror. She stood on her tippy-toes when they measured her and they didn't even notice."

"Really?"

"And she threw up!"

"That's great."

Delia's enthusiasm vanished. "Mom, you're not listening."

It was true. She'd heard the words, but they'd failed to register. She recaptured them and quickly played them back in her brain. "I meant it was great that she got to go on Tower of Terror. I know she really wanted to."

"Well, it wasn't great for Sabrieke. She ended up with a lapful of puke and then she threw up, too."

"Was she mad?"

"Sabrieke doesn't get mad, Mom . . . Stop!" Delia yelled at someone. "I'll ask her."

"Ask me what?" May said, to prove she was listening now.

"I know the answer is going to be no, but can we stay until Tuesday? There's a rocket ship launching at the Kennedy Space Center on Tuesday and Grandpa has a friend who works there who can get us in to watch it. It's science," she added giving it her best try.

May couldn't help but grimace at Delia's use of the word *Grandpa.* But she pushed her foul expression off her face and concentrated on the offer put before her. It was a hard one to refuse. She hated to bring them back now, to this, a house she felt scared in, an unsolved murder, intruders real or imagined.

"Mama?" Susie claimed the phone. "I have to put the phone down on the table because otherwise I won't be able to do this." May heard a clunk that told her the phone had been put down. Then Susie's voice came on. "Please," she begged. "Pretty please with sugar on top. Please, say yes."

May could picture her there, crouched on her knees, hands clasped close to her chest. "Put Grandma on," she told her daughter, and Susie did.

"Dolly." Grandma Shirley spoke too loud into the phone. "They are so good. How come you complain about them? They're little angels. They remind me so much of myself as a child."

"I guess that kind of thing skips a generation."

Her mother didn't disagree. "What do you say? Will Delia get thrown out of second grade if she stays to watch a spaceship launching?"

"Please," Delia and Susie were calling out in the background.

"You hear this? I'm going to get a notice from the management if they keep it up. What do you say, dolly?"

May tried to sound like she was struggling. "I guess so," she said finally, and heard the children cheer. "It's okay with me if it's okay with you and . . ."—her voice choked on the word, but she pushed it out—"Dad."

"You said it. I don't believe it. I told him you'd never say it, but you said it. Your father will be so happy. Both fathers. You know, dolly, your real father, he only wanted me to be happy." She paused, thinking about it, then remembered she was still on the phone. "Is everything okay there?"

"I'm in the middle of something, that's all," May ducked the question. "I have to make a call."

Leaving her mother miffed, she hung up and quickly called her next-door neighbor.

"Of course I didn't let myself into your house," Emily said when May explained the situation. "Why would I do that?"

"I don't know. I just know the door was open when I got home," May explained.

"What did the police say?"

"They asked me which neighbors have a key. They said someone probably let herself in to do me a favor."

"Well, it wasn't me. I would never do that. Who else has a key? Uh-oh. Stacey had one, didn't she?"

"Yes," May admitted.

"So now Scott has it. But he wouldn't use it. Would he?" Emily hated to think ill of someone, so she changed the subject. "Try Marlene. I bet it was her."

May couldn't remember if she'd ever given a spare key to Marlene. "I'll call her and see."

As she dialed Marlene's number, she thought about Scott, about how he did have her key, how she wanted it back. She'd changed the locks once already, last year, to keep Todd away. She didn't want to have to do it again.

When Marlene got on the phone, May skipped the background and went straight to the point. "Did I ever give you a spare key?"

"As a matter of fact, you never did," Marlene said. "Which hurt me, now that you bring it up. When Jordan felt left out of the soccer game at recess last week, I told him I knew how it felt to be left out of a clique. I was thinking of you and Stacey." She paused and then asked, "Are you locked out?"

"No," May said. "I was just checking to see what I did with my spares."

"Well, you never left one here." She hung up the phone sounding hurt.

As May sat in the calm quiet of her kitchen reflecting on the morning, she decided it was entirely possible she'd left the door open after all. The way she'd been feeling lately, distracted all the time, there was no telling what kinds of things she'd forgotten.

She needed to stop, take a time out, unwind, recharge. She put a call in to Paul, left a message that everything was okay, and then went upstairs. A bath would be a start. She opened her medicine cabinet.

Inside was a full complement of bath oils, beads, and gels, pretty bottles people insisted on giving to her as birthday presents, even though taking a bath was something she rarely did, opting instead for the time-saving speed showers that set her off on her day. She reviewed the choices and picked Respite, a bath oil Paula had brought back for her from France last year, guaranteed to eliminate stress.

She poured the peach-colored liquid into the tub, watched the foam begin and the water rise. Then she undressed, got in, submerged, and lay there for half an hour, not moving, all thoughts finally silenced.

When she got out, she felt revived, better than she had in days. She slipped into a pair of black sweats and a T-shirt and went downstairs, stopping in the kitchen to stare out her now locked back door.

Is it Scott? she wondered. *Is it Scott trying to scare me?* She peered out, looking for answers, slid the screen door open, closed, open, closed, hoping some memory would emerge, but none did. She stepped outside.

She looked up and asked the sky to tell her: *What happened to Stacey?* When she looked back down, she saw it.

Had the container been there forever? She had one just like it, a huge bright bucket, but hers was red, not purple.

Hers was in the garage, filled with roller skates, tennis balls, and baseball mitts.

Where had this one come from? Had she seen it somewhere before? Didn't Stacey have a purple container just like this one in her garage?

She walked over and looked inside.

"Awwh," she cried out and jumped back a foot. She couldn't say exactly what it was she'd seen, but she knew what it wasn't: baseball bats and Nerf ball sets. It was something gooey and wet—something that smelled bad. *What?*

The odor coming from the container was strong enough so that her stomach reeled. With her lips pressed closed, not breathing, she forced herself to take a closer look.

The first thing she made out was the clump of matted fur. Then something moved. She jumped back, her sweat glands fully engaged, her face hot, her body sticky. Again she forced herself to look. She peeked again and saw that what was moving was a small garden snake. She recoiled—not at the sight of the snake—but at the realization that the hole it had just poked through was a pale brown snout.

"Oh my God," she called out when she realized she was staring at the decomposing head of Rosie Blum.

She ran back into the house, into the bathroom, put her head over the toilet bowl and waited as her temples pounded. She waited some more, but her churning stomach wasn't giving, and after a while, her legs began to cramp. She stood up slowly, grabbing the wall to steady herself. Then she went back outside to face what lay ahead.

Forty-Five

SHE DOUBLE-BAGGED two leaf collection–size trash bags and put on a pair of heavy-duty latex gloves. Then, averting her eyes, she dumped the head in the bag. She didn't breathe until she'd tied on several twist ties, until there was nothing to see but a lump lying at the bottom like a rock—and even then, she had to look away.

Tentatively, she took a breath. It seemed okay, now, the stench contained within the bags. She carried the package inside the house, forcing her mind to go blank as she headed down to the basement, to the spare refrigerator in the laundry room. At one time she had had great plans for using it, plans to store carefully packaged stews, roasts, and lasagnas that she imagined she would cook ahead in big batches, a time-saving economy that never happened. She'd have to call someone to cart it away now. There was no way she'd ever store food there again, after this.

Good, she thought as she closed the refrigerator door. Now her prize would stay chilled. That was how she'd begun to think about it, as her prize. It had come to her even as she held her head over the toilet bowl. She knew the terrifying remains of the dog's head were meant to scare her away from her search. But she viewed it as a gift, one she would pass along to the pathologist, Dr. Adler.

But first she needed to confirm her suspicion—her conviction—that it was Scott who'd left her the present. She had an idea how to find out, too. All she had to do was get into his garage. If the purple container was there, stuffed, as usual, with hockey sticks and skateboards, she'd have to consider alternative ideas. But if it was gone, if the one that now sat in her yard, smelly and contaminated with death, belonged to the Blums, she would know for sure. The purple can would tell her.

As usual, all the flashlights she had, the one in the kitchen, the one in the furnace room, the skinny one in the overstuffed kitchen gadget drawer, were missing, all sacrificed to let's pretend games of *Harriet the Spy.* But the Fisher-Price supersize flashlight, too babyish to be used in a game of make-believe, was in its usual dusty spot on the top of Susie's dresser. May grabbed it and took off with it, outside into the gray day. It would have been better to wait for the cloak of night, but that would take patience, and patience was something she no longer had.

She tried to look like she was simply out for a walk. She tried not to seem directed or in a hurry. It wasn't easy to keep her pace from sliding into a slow run. Luckily, no one was out. She didn't have to stop, make small talk about the weather, explain away the toy she clutched in her hand.

The problem was going to be if Scott was home. But surely he'd be at work today. That was where he went to feel better. Nick had said so.

Stealthily, she crept up his driveway, no signs of life outside. The house looked dark, but in the daytime, it was hard to tell. She listened for noises of life or movement—radio, television, voices talking on the telephone—but heard nothing. She listened for Rosie's barking, and then remembered she wouldn't be hearing that anymore. The memory drove her on, working against the other memory playing in her mind, the one of Scott's threats. She hung back, keeping to the shadows beneath the eaves of the house.

She reached the garage windows and peered inside. There was nothing to see but the dark. She lifted up the large flashlight, turned it on, shined it in.

Scott froze in the light, froze in the act of loading cartons onto a dolly. The box he was holding dropped to the ground.

"Shit," he called out. "Who's that? Who the hell is that?"

But May was already gone, racing across his lawn, faster than she'd ever run before, flying down the block, ducking down a neighbor's driveway. She ran to the back of Marlene's house and knocked on her kitchen door.

"Hi there," Marlene said, opening it, then added, "What's wrong?" when she saw how disheveled May was, how her cheeks were flaming red. "Come on in."

Jordan was home, either sick or suspended—May didn't bother to find out which. He lay sprawled out in their living room, watching cartoons.

"Say hello to Mrs. Morrison, Jordan," Marlene said. The boy mumbled something. Marlene quickly led the way into the kitchen. Without asking if May wanted tea, she put up a pot of water. "Sit down," she said and placed two mugs on the table. May sat down, putting the flashlight on her lap, wishing she had dumped it somewhere first. Marlene didn't seem to notice it.

"What in the world is going on?" Marlene asked her. "You look like you're going to ignite." But before May could come up with a good answer the sound of sirens racing down the block interrupted her. They waited silently, to see if the sirens would fade out of range or stop nearby. The sound cut off abruptly as if the car had stopped right outside Marlene's house.

The women walked quickly to the dining-room window, which faced out front. Jordan was already standing there, watching two police officers step out of the their car and into Scott's house.

"What now?" Marlene muttered. She looked at May, suspicion, mixed with fear, in her eyes.

"Let's go see," Jordan pleaded. "Come on, Mom. Please?"

"What do you say, May? Should we see what the police are doing?" The question was a dare.

"Why not," May replied, and, holding her empty mug, followed Marlene outside.

It wasn't long before a couple of other neighbors joined them. As they watched the Blum house, they discussed among themselves the events of the past few weeks. The facts traded were jumbled or wrong, but May didn't bother to correct them. She just stood in the middle of the crowd, another nosy neighbor, and was still standing there when the police officers came out of Scott's house, flashlights in hand, pointing them under bushes and behind the trees on Scott's front lawn, looking, she knew, for her.

When the police were done, about to get back into their car, Marlene told the neighbors that someone had to find out what happened. She boldly walked over to do the job herself. Several minutes later, she returned to make her report.

"An alarm went off by accident," she said, and amidst a chorus of "Oh!" and "Is that all?" and "What a relief!" the crowd dispersed. Marlene immediately turned to May. "I didn't hear any alarm go off, did you?"

May shook her head and said, "No. I didn't." Then she handed back her mug. "I wish I could stay, but I've got some things to do."

Marlene wasn't surprised. May always had something else to do. "Did you find what you were looking for?"

Confused by the question, May didn't reply.

"Jordan," Marlene called out, "Go in the house and get Mrs. Morrison's flashlight for her."

May considered explaining herself, but she'd have to go so far back for any of it to make sense that instead she just stood, accepting Marlene's inquisitive glare, and waited.

"Nice flashlight, Mrs. Morrison," Jordan said as he handed it back to her.

"Thanks," she replied and turned to leave, mother and son watching her with arms crossed over their chests as if they had something to hide.

Forty-Six

SHE WAS RELIEVED to find Dr. Adler in.

"I have partial remains of the dog," she told him on the phone. "They dropped it off at my house," she said, and hoped he wouldn't press for details.

"Good work," he said. "You know, I've been thinking about our conversation all day. I'm very intrigued. When are you coming up?"

"As soon as I can."

"It will take you a couple of hours."

"Then I'd better leave now."

She retrieved the trash bag and stuck it in a large plastic cooler. Then she emptied all her ice trays inside. She wasn't sure if it mattered, keeping the head cold, as if it might spoil, but she did it anyway, just in case.

She tried Paul again, waiting fifteen minutes for him to call back, but he didn't. If he was in the middle of a crime scene, it could be hours before he could get away to call. She couldn't afford the wait.

The drive upstate was an easy one except for those moments when she remembered her macabre passenger, twice causing her to nervously swerve off the road. By the time she arrived at the doctor's laboratory, the sun was low in the sky and her energy was drained. Fending off sleep, she waited in a small room for the doctor to come out. When he did, she was struck by how ordinary he looked. He didn't have the air of a scientist. There was nothing rumpled or distracted about him. He had a pleasant face, neat black hair, and small oval glasses. He wore an unremarkable striped shirt, khaki pants, and a cheap plastic watch. But when he began to speak, when he started talking science, he came on fire and woke May up.

"One day it's something no one can pronounce, the next day it's one of the hottest research fields in medicine. And it's me, the low guy on the medical food chain, the animal doctor, who they're all coming to." He laughed at this.

"If you called me with your story five years ago, I'd have directed you to our behavioral sciences building for counseling. But today because of what we now know about this disease, if we can even call it a disease, your story is fascinating."

"What disease?" she asked, still baffled.

"Used to be your average family physician could be born and die without ever hearing of BSE or Creutzfeldt-Jakob. But no more. Even, say, three years ago, if a doc at a medical convention in Florida presented a paper on scrapie, ninety percent of the audience would be swimming in the hotel pool before he got to the end of his opening paragraph. But not now. We're still in nursery school with these diseases, but we're working hard to get smart fast."

The cooler sat on his desk right between them. She tried to ignore it, focus her eyes on something else so it would go blurry. She tried looking over it, around it; tried to trick herself into believing it was filled with beer, soda, ice. Finally she was able to concentrate on the notebook on her lap, in which she was hastily scribbling notes, trying hard not to let her mind wander, not even for a moment. If she wandered, she'd lose the confusing thread of Dr. Adler's words.

"Slow down. I'm not quite with you here," she confessed.

He changed gears, moving away from the science for a moment. "It's the Oprah problem. Mad cow."

"You think my friend might have gotten this from contaminated hamburgers?"

"Forget hamburgers. Listen. Imagine we find a viruslike thing in a cow we own that's been sick and acting funny. It's our worst nightmare: bovine spongiform encephalopathy—BSE. We now know, even if we don't understand every part of how it happens, that humans can catch this virus, if it even is a virus. In humans, the disease is called Creutzfeldt-Jakob. Now, we're not stupid and we're not evil. So we're not going to take a chance on making people sick by selling our contaminated cow's meat. So we destroy the cow. End of story, right?"

She nodded.

"Wrong. Because let's say between the slaughterhouse and here, some guy somewhere says, 'Hold on. Why have this be a total waste? We don't want anyone to die or to get sick, so we won't use the animal's meat for food. But this person—and he's not a bad person, he's an uninformed person—he says, 'Let's not get hysterical. At least let's use the bones. We can strip and clean and boil and disinfect the bones. Bones are bones.' End of story, right?"

This time she didn't answer.

"So the bones are sent off somewhere for processing. And they're put through all kinds of procedures to make them clean and safe. Now, these procedures will actually reduce infectious material, but they cannot absolutely eliminate it. Do you know what the current thinking is on how much of this stuff needs to be present in order for the disease to be transmitted?"

"No," May admitted.

"One."

"One cow?"

"One molecule."

"I'm never eating hamburgers again," May said.

"See? That's your mistake. That's exactly what Oprah said and looked what happened to her."

She felt thick. "Do you think the dog died from some kind of contaminated meat?"

"I told you, don't worry about meat. This is bigger than meat." He looked at her fingers. "Ever use nail polish?"

She closed her hands into a fist. "Yes."

"What do you use to take it off?"

"Nail polish remover," she said.

"There you go. Right there. No good. Check the ingredients on the bottle next time. See if it's got gelatin in it. Gelatin is what gives it the right consistency. It's added to everything. I just found out they put it in apple juice, even organic apple juice. No one thinks, 'Where does the gelatin come from?' And speaking of organic, what about organic fertilizer? Organic material from where is what I want to know. Where do you think bone meal comes from? Same place as where gelatin comes from." He stood up. "Don't get me started. Anyway, we don't even know if this has anything to do with your dog's demise. So let me get to work and find out."

"What are you going to do?"

"An autopsy on this brain for starters. I'd like to have some spinal fluid, too."

She felt dizzy with information.

"Where's the rest of the animal? If it turns out it's contaminated, we'll have to ship off the whole animal and deal with the soil. Otherwise, imagine this: it's happily decomposing in the dirt, and in a couple of years, someone plants a vegetable garden. Now that would be a bunch of beans that could repeat on you for years."

"I only have the head," she said.

"Considering that this disease goes straight for the brain," he told her, "getting the head makes it my lucky day."

"Should I wait while you do your thing?" she asked him.

"Only if you rented an apartment in town. I won't know anything for at least two weeks, maybe three."

She felt her shoulders sink. "Does it have to take that long?"

"At least."

He lifted the cooler. May averted her eyes.

"Go home, Ms. Morrison. I'll call you as soon as I know what we're dealing with." He smiled. "It always amazes me, people like you, calling out of the blue, with a possibility like this." He got up. "Can you find your way out?"

"Sure," May said. "Thanks."

"Don't mention it," the doctor told her, then disappeared through a steel door leading somewhere May was sure she wouldn't want to go.

Forty-Seven

SHE DROVE FOR AN HOUR with her mind spinning with questions. Did the dog die from mad cow disease? If she had, how did she get it? And what did that have to do with Stacey's murder? Or the deaths of Stacey's friends? What about Matthew Harris and Morgan?

The questions circled one after another and then back to the first until May felt her eyelids begin to droop. She pulled in at the next rest stop, her car looking tiny alongside the semis lined up for their breaks. She locked her door and closed her eyes, but the questions began spinning again. She was about to give up and get back on the road, but then she was dreaming, dreaming that she was running, that a dog was right behind her, chasing her. He was so close she could hear his panting, the sound mixing with her own labored breathing. Her lungs were aching, her cheeks so red she worried they might explode, but she had to go on because if she stopped, he would get her.

Ahead, safety, her house waited for her. She pushed herself to go faster, so fast that the trees whizzed by, a blur.

Where are my neighbors? she wondered. *Where are their houses?* It wasn't supposed to be like this, just her house, sitting alone in the middle of an empty plot as if it were marking a grave.

Finally she was there. With the heat of the dog behind her, she quickly dug her hand in her pocket to get her key. When she yanked it out, she found that she held a hypodermic instead.

She threw it to the ground and pushed open the door, which hadn't been locked at all. Then, suddenly, the house began to crumble. With horror, she realized it had rotted, turned to bone meal raining down on her.

She screamed and woke herself up. She looked around, reminding herself where she was and why.

She started up the car and drove the rest of the way alert and ill at ease. When she pulled the car off the highway at her exit, she checked the clock on her dashboard for the hundredth time. It was just after one in the morning. The streets were deserted. The town was locked up, fast asleep. She was passing Scott's office when, without any forethought, she turned into the empty parking lot.

Why did I come? she whispered to no one.

She had no answer, just a vague feeling driving her, the need to know more and the hope that this was a place where she might find it. Something was missing. In the pile of disconnected fragments she'd collected, she was missing the largest piece of all. She just didn't know what it was.

She got out of the car, stepped into the cool, clear night, and stood for a moment, thinking. What would Scott do, she wondered, if he heard from Dr. Adler that his wife and her friends and his dog had ingested or come into contact with something so tainted it could prove fatal? Would he be horrified? Surprised? Or did he already know?

Slowly, she walked toward the two story building. *Think things through,* she told herself. *Think outside the box.*

She looked around. There'd been some landscaping done recently, just enough to soften the building's square cement shape. *There's nothing to find here,* she thought, but continued to walk on.

It was a beautiful night, perfectly still except for the humming of the spotlights set up like guards around the building. *Guarding it from what?* she wondered. *From me?*

As she walked closer to the building, she moved more slowly, as if she needed to sneak up on it. The narrow blinds were drawn and the lights were out. No one was inside.

Of course not. It was the middle of the night. She climbed the four steps to the door, let her hand go to the brass knob, found it locked, the rectangular electronic security fingerpad alongside it proof that their alarm system was in place.

She stared at the pad for a moment. Something about it struck her as odd. She looked away and then looked back, hoping a fresh glance would tell her what her mind had noticed but couldn't name. *What?*

She stared some more. She had an alarm pad like this at her own side door, but hers looked different. *Why?*

Then she saw it. On her pad, all the numbers were bright and clear, easy to read. Her pad looked good as new because she hardly ever used it, her fingers rarely touched the pad. The numbers on this fingerpad weren't like hers, crisp and clear. These were blurry and worn out. This pad was well used, dutifully put on and off every morning and every night.

There it was, what had struck her without knowing it. Not all of the numbers were faded equally. In fact, when she looked closer she saw that only three of the numbers were worn out. The numbers that made up the code, the numbers that were pressed so many times a month they were nearly worn off: two, four, eight. She laughed at the silliness of it, that Scott and his staffers felt protected by this alarm, yet anyone who stopped by and glanced at this security fingerpad for more than an instant could figure out the numbers that made up their code.

She laughed again, out loud, and thought, *If I press the right combination of two, four, and eight, that little red light will turn green and I can go inside.* She laughed a third time, but this time the sound served as a way to distract herself from the sweeping motion of her arm as she hastily reached and pressed the three numbers. Nothing happened.

For a moment she thought, *This isn't what I came to do.* Then her curiosity flared again. Could she actually break in? She hadn't come with this in mind, but could she? She tried, casually at first, two-four-eight, then four-eight-two, then several more combinations before suddenly noticing that the number two was more worn out than the rest. In fact, when she really studied it, she could see—it was so obvious now—the number was completely rubbed off. Her brain had read it as two but the actual key was blank. A blank key sitting between the numbers one and three. And she knew: *I have to press two twice.*

It was that easy. She tried several combinations and then two, two, eight, four and the light turned green.

She'd done it. Without setting out to, she'd cracked their code. The green light was on. Would she still need a key? She tried the door—no key needed. The alarm had released the lock. The door was open. She could go in now, if she wanted to. She laughed at the thought of a person like her breaking in. She'd never imagined herself as someone who would break in somewhere.

It had been so easy. *Beginner's luck,* she thought, and she stepped inside.

Forty-Eight

THE FOYER WAS PITCH BLACK, so she used her hands to feel her way, stumbling at the small step leading to the reception area. She caught herself, arms to the wall. It was too dark here, dangerously dark. She thought of the flashlight in her glove compartment, and carefully propping open the front door of the office so it wouldn't close behind her, she ran out to the car to get it.

She rifled through the nest of papers, maps, and old directions that clogged the glove compartment until she found it, the flashlight. It was skinny, the kind doctors use to check sore throats, powerful when it worked—which wasn't now. Now the batteries were nearly dead, the flashlight as weak as headlights in a thick fog—useless. She threw it on the seat and softly closed the car door.

It was better not to use it, she told herself as she walked back into the building. If a police officer happened by on an early-morning drive and saw the flickering strobe of a flashlight inside the medical building, there would be no chance she could talk her way out of it. It wouldn't matter that her intention wasn't to steal. Breaking into a medical office was a crime, and Scott would celebrate her capture.

At least she had the light of a full moon. She walked around the perimeter of the reception room, twisting the plastic wands on the narrow blinds. With the blinds fully opened, moonlight shining in, there was enough of a glow that at least she could find her way.

The room came into focus, the couches, chairs, side tables, magazines, posted articles. Slowly she made her way to the receptionist's cubicle and walked inside. Standing behind the desk, she turned in a circle, a human scanning device, checking, checking, checking. *For what?*

She turned on a small desk lamp, figuring that wouldn't attract attention from the street. People in offices frequently left a light on at night. *They want to scare away intruders like me,* she thought.

There were several phones, one computer, and an appointment book on the main desk. Behind that was a wall of floor-to-ceiling files, folders color coded with narrow tags to protect against misfiling. She went to them, moving her finger along the row marked *B,* searching until she found the one she'd hoped was there. She slid into the receptionist's swivel chair and read Stacey's file.

As she knew, Nick was her doctor. The visits had been few. Flu shots, strep cultures, a suspicious mole on her back. Nothing to show that she'd sought treatment for rages, dizziness, clumsiness. Stacey was impressively healthy for a dead woman.

May returned the folder to its spot and continued down a narrow hallway. She came to a door and opened it. It was the bathroom. She turned on that light, too. With the bathroom door slightly ajar, she could see fairly well down the hall now.

There were several other doors along the hallway. She opened one—found a closet hiding nothing more than a forgotten raincoat and a cornflower-blue sweater whose wide weave let the white plastic hanger show through at the shoulders.

The next led to another closet, this one storing boxes,

one piled atop the other, each with a label identifying its owner: Dr. Blum, Dr. Ellman, Dr. Ellman, Dr. Blum. She lifted the lid of the one on the top—Ellman—and found stacks of old invoices and bills. She closed it, shut the door, moved along.

The four examination rooms were nearly identical, drawers filled with neatly laid out instruments, pill samples, latex gloves. On the countertops sat models of parts and systems of the human body, waiting to facilitate discussions. There were the changing booths with lemon-yellow curtains as doors, blue plastic gowns piled neatly in stacks on painted white benches, magazines racks filled with last year's news. Nothing.

When she got to Scott's office, she was stopped by an eight-by-ten photograph of Stacey that sat prominently on his desk in a polished silver frame. Her friend's face smiled at her. May felt a wave of sadness and looked away.

Scott's office was neat, pristine, a place where a doctor met with patients to discuss a program, a future, a diagnosis. Diplomas were displayed in eye-catching frames so no one could miss the names of the schools—Johns Hopkins, Columbia—where he had studied.

She moved to the wall that held his library, shelves thick with scientific manuals, encyclopedias, directories. She ran her fingers along volumes titled with unpronounceable skin diseases, respiratory ailments, oncology. But their dusty bindings told her Scott's practice was not dedicated to the seriously ill. It was easy to tell which books he looked at most, the ones missing a thick coating of dust, the ones hastily returned to the shelves askew. These, she saw, were books on herbal preparations, Chinese medicine, Indian cures.

Her eyes jumped to the thick spine of a volume—she tilted her head to read it—*Diseases of the Brain*. She wondered why this one had caught her attention. Were the letters especially bold? Was the color brighter than the rest?

She ran her finger down the spine, dust free, and pulled

the heavy book off the shelf. Immediately she thought, *I shouldn't have touched it.* She pictured Paul in her place. He would have stood and looked, listening to his gut before he moved, looking everywhere, carefully, for signs of something he might not yet understand. He wouldn't have pulled the book off the shelf without first eyeballing every inch of it, maybe even photographing it with the camera he'd taken to carrying in his pocket. If he thought it might be something, even if he couldn't say what or why, he might have borrowed it, placed it in a plastic bag, made a call to a fingerprint technician to see what he could get.

No, she thought, *he wouldn't do that.* Paul wouldn't have come at all, not yet. He wouldn't have broken in. Not without a warrant, or unless he thought someone inside was in danger.

She opened the heavy cover of the book and ran her finger down the indexes list of diseases until she came to Creutzfeldt-Jakob.

She turned to the page indicated and skimmed it, plowing past information she didn't understand. Then she got to the symptoms, clear as day. *Mental deterioration. Slurred speech. Difficulty in walking.*

I'm the queen of the klutzes, Stacey had said, dropping a book on May's foot. Was this why? But it wasn't why she died. It didn't explain who killed her.

She took a Kleenex out of a box that sat inside a fine brown leather dispenser on Scott's desk and, using it like a glove, pulled open his top desk drawer. There were pens, his prescription pads, notepads, a small calendar, a calculator, an eyeglass case, a leather business card holder with a pharmaceutical company logo on it. Nothing.

Reluctantly, she moved on to Nick's office, where it looked like work actually got done. Books were piled on chairs, charts laid out on a table along the back wall, stacks of physician referral reports piled next to them. Along the opposite wall, his computer was set up at a large workstation. Next to the printer was a pile of correspondence from their web site, "Ask Dr. Curewell." She skimmed the first page of the Dear Dr. Abby–style complaints. A man who couldn't shake a cold, a woman with thinning hair, a man with acne, a man with fatigue, a woman with tremors. Nothing.

His desk was the neatest place in the room, just a large blotter and on top of it a stack of invoice orders marked "Return." Nothing.

What do I expect to find? she asked out loud, and couldn't answer.

She went back to Scott's office one more time, again searched through his drawers. But even when she found a small tape recorder he used for dictation, all she discovered was that Helen Gross was suffering from swollen glands and got antibiotics. Arthur Lovell complained of malaise and got testosterone. Keith Conway was short of breath and got a referral to a cardiologist. She heard a noise and froze.

She turned the small tape recorder off and stiffened as she listened, then heard it again.

Quickly she raced around the offices until she found a window that looked out on the parking lot. Keeping to the shadows, she peered out through the open blinds, then jumped back when she saw there was another car parked next to her own. It took her a moment to place it—Nick's blue Isuzu Trooper—before she heard Nick's footsteps on the path.

There was a back way out. Stacey had told her about it, that Scott used it when he was running late. His patients, sitting in the waiting room out front, would assume he was stuck in an exam room giving some other patient too much time. He used the back door so they wouldn't have to see, after sitting for twenty, thirty, forty minutes, waiting, that he strolled in, take-out coffee cup in hand.

She raced down the hall toward the back, heard another noise, the front door opening. Then she saw it, the back door blocked by a pile of boxes that stood as high as her waist. She pushed them aside, her hands turning black with their dust. As quietly as she could manage, she shoved them against the wall.

"Hello?" Nick called out. His voice was full with suspicion, on the edge of anger. "Hello?"

Carefully, she turned the knob. It was locked.

Light streaked down the hallway as Nick turned on the lights to the reception room.

Damn, she thought, and turned the knob again. *Why do you have to be locked?*

"Hello? Is someone here?" More light flooded the hall as he entered the receptionist's area, flicking on the rest of the lights from some central switchplate.

That's when May saw a key ring hanging from a brass hook on the wall. *Please work,* she thought, as she took the key. With a shaky hand, she placed it in the lock.

"Hello?" He was following the same path she had. He was peering in the bathroom now.

The key turned. She slipped outside, had nearly closed the door when she remembered she'd left the key in the lock. Her hands trembling now, she slipped back inside, pulled the key out of the keyhole, hung it back on the wall, softly closed the door behind her. She could hear Nick making the turn down the hall—"Hello?"—so close he might have seen the door shut, the doorknob turn.

She got into her car, left the headlights off, started the engine, and pulled the car out quickly onto the dark street. She struggled to think clearly as she drove. *He parked next to my car. Does he know my car? No,* she assured herself. *If he knew it was my car, he would have called my name. So he doesn't know it was me. Good.*

Not good, she thought a moment later, when she realized that of course he would tell Scott. He would describe the make and color of the car in the lot and Scott would know.

She was five blocks from her house when she impulsively pulled the car to the curb. She rotated her house key off her key chain, pocketed it, and threw rest on the floor.

She opened the glove compartment, scooped out the contents, and dumped them on the floor, too. Then she got out and fled, leaving the two front car doors ajar.

She hurried, glancing around to be sure no one was out, or peering from a window. She couldn't risk being seen. If she was seen by anyone, the story wouldn't work. She had to get home, go to bed, and wake at a reasonable hour before she called the police to report her car was stolen.

It was just after two when she let herself into the house, climbed up the stairs, and got into bed. She wanted to get out of her stale, smelly clothes. She meant to get up and wash. But the exhaustion that had been strangely absent all night arrived now with undeniable power. Before she could protest its assault, she was asleep and dreaming.

Forty-Nine

SHE HADN'T SET THE ALARM CLOCK but she was up at five, wired awake. She busied herself, straightening, cleaning, household chores that required no thinking. She ate a light breakfast, a vanilla yogurt and black coffee. She dressed for work and left the house at seven, as if walking to the bus. She looked at the driveway, where her car should have been. Saying a quiet "Oh my god—the car is gone," as if there was anyone to hear, she went back inside and called the police.

It took about five minutes before a patrol car pulled up outside her house. A cop she had never seen before got out. She opened the door for him and tried not to look too panic stricken when another car pulled up behind his and Detective Smith emerged, stopping for a few words with the cop on her front walk. He followed behind him to her door.

"Come on in," she said to them both, and they did.

The detective motioned for the uniform, who introduced himself as Tomkins, to go ahead and speak. Tomkins knew the basics, that her car was stolen. Now he wanted the details. Make, color, condition, license plate number, contents, distinguishing marks, place it was last seen.

"Did you hear any unusual noises last night?" he asked

her. "Sometimes people hear the break-in but don't put it together at the time."

She shook her head. "I don't think they had to break in. I think I left the keys in the car."

"Oh," the cop said, and made a note. "Do you do that often?"

Again she shook her head. "I guess I deserve getting my car stolen for being so dumb."

The cop was generous. "Come on. Everyone leaves their keys in their car at least once. It doesn't mean it gives the right for someone to just drive off with it. It does make it easy for them, though. Coming across a car with the keys inside, it's like giving a thief a birthday present."

She smiled weakly.

"Was it running?" he asked.

"No. I'm sure I turned it off," she said, and he wrote that down, too.

She thought she was through with it—she had nothing more to report—when Detective Smith spoke up.

"How did you get in your house, then?"

"Pardon me?"

"If you left your keys in the car, how did you get in the house? Someone let you in? Was the door open? What?"

"My house key is on a separate ring." She had thought of this beforehand. She had taken a key ring, the miniature Etch-A-Sketch one, off of Delia's old backpack, and then put her key on it.

"That's unusual. Most people keep their keys together. Why do you do that?" Smith asked.

"My older daughter wanted to practice opening the door and she had trouble doing it with all the other keys dangling in the way. So I took the house key off. I guess that was a mistake."

"Appears so," Tomkins said.

"What are my chances of getting the car back?" she asked.

Detective Smith was studying her. She breathed deeply to keep her cheeks from flaming red.

"Sixty-forty," Tomkins said. "In what condition is another story." He stood up. May stood up. Detective Smith remained seated.

"I'd like a few minutes with you, too," he said. "After you're done with this."

She nodded, and tried to smile as she walked the patrolman to the door.

"Good luck, Mrs. Morrison," Tomkins said.

Even as she thanked him, she wondered what he meant.

When she got to the living room, Detective Smith was on his cell phone, but he finished his business quickly.

"We got a call last night from Dr. Blum," he said, wasting no time. "When his partner," he checked his notebook, "Dr. Ellman, passed by the office on the way back from the hospital last night, he saw a car in the parking lot. He stopped to investigate, found the door to his office open but no one inside. Nothing appeared to be missing," he added.

"What does that have to do with me?"

"Dr. Blum says it was your car in his lot. He thinks you broke into his office last night."

She needed to be careful. "Maybe it was. I don't know where the hell my car has been. Is it still there now?" She let some of her nervousness mutate to anger and seep into her voice.

Smith wasn't happy. "No, it's not." Something was bugging him but he wasn't sharing it. "It's quite a coincidence, isn't it," he said, his eyes stuck on hers, searching.

"There have been a lot of coincidences lately," she replied. "Obviously I didn't break into their office," she added. "I'd appreciate it if you'd explain that to Dr. Blum."

"I don't get involved in people's personal business," he explained. "Unless it includes homicide."

The detective stood up. He was done. May saw him out. Then she called Scott's office.

The receptionist put her through immediately, to

Marcy. "Why don't you leave the poor man alone?" the nurse said, and hung up.

May called back. This time she insisted on speaking to Nick.

From his first words she could tell that his friendliness and warmth were gone. His voice was cold, filled with anger. "What can I do for you?"

"You think I broke in to your office, don't you?"

"I don't have any idea who broke in," he admitted. "I saw a car in the lot and Scott recognized by my description that it was yours."

"You can tell him from me that my car was stolen out of my driveway last night. I don't know whose car you saw but even if it was mine, it wasn't me who drove it there." She nearly believed herself now, even caught herself wondering who it might have been.

"Your car was stolen?"

"Yes," she repeated, glad he couldn't see her cheeks flushing.

"I'm so sorry. You can understand the mistake. Scott's very upset, distraught, really. And he's decided you're the cause of it."

"Why? Does he think I killed Stacey? Or Morgan?

"He thinks you're after him, and for no good reason."

"I have a perfectly good reason," she said. "He's acting like a guilty man."

"He's not guilty, he's devastated. Cut him some slack. Leave him alone."

"I'll leave him alone when I'm done," she snapped, and hung up the phone.

She tried Paul, but he was still stuck at work, deep in something that wasn't good. She left a detailed message on his home machine about her visit with Dr. Adler, then made her next call to Florida. She got her stepfather, the first time they'd spoken on the phone.

"The kids are out," he reported. "And what a couple of

cuties they are. You know, the little one looks exactly like Toddy did when he was a boy."

Satisfied the girls were fine, she quickly disengaged and raced out of the house to the bus, where she worked feverishly, going through her folders, making lists of what she had to do to catch up on her upcoming shows. She wasn't close to being grooved up to her normal speed. If she didn't put this thing with Stacey to rest soon, something was going to have to give.

Fifty

When she stepped into her office she saw yellow Post-its everywhere, stuck on her phone, on the back of her seat, on her window.

"See me," "Call me," "E-mail me," they said, all in the flowery handwriting Margery had learned at the now-defunct Saint Agnes's Elementary School for Girls.

May skipped the electronic highway and walked five steps to Margery's office. Her friend was on the phone but waved her in.

"Listen to me," she was saying. "At *Paula Live,* we do not embarrass our guests or try to catch them off guard or make them look stupid." She motioned for May to sit down, then went on. "I understand, sugar, but that would never ever happen here." She flicked her remote and May watched as first Sally Jesse then Montel then a CNBC news reader flashed by in quick succession. Margery stuck her finger in her throat to let May know that the competition made her gag.

She lowered her voice to a soft massaging tone. "My most recent female prisoner ended up with five offers of marriage after doing our show. Now, I'm not saying that's what your sister is looking for. I'm just saying on *Tell*

Tonya, she was humiliated. On *Paula Live,* she will be celebrated."

She winked at May, then cooed into the receiver. "Wonderful, sugar. I am so thrilled. I'm talking about next Wednesday. Will that work for you? Wonderful. Annie will call to take care of all the arrangements. And don't worry about that warden. I've known her for years. All right. That's great. Yes. 'Bye, now."

She crumpled the paper in her hands, threw it in the garbage, and looked up at May.

"Good news. Paula decided true crime can be gritty again. Hallelujah!" she screamed out, then narrowed her eyes. "Now the only problem left in my life is you."

"What's wrong with me?" May asked, though she didn't really want to know.

"Nothing yet. But Colleen is gunning for you—and I mean big torpedo-size guns that possibly have nuclear warheads. Bottom line, she's decided Paula wants to replace her and that it's your fault."

"What? How do you know this?"

"It doesn't matter how I know it. I know it. So you've got a problem. Now, her first line of attack is going to be the goddamn spa story, the failed spa story."

"What about Rolando and the therapeutic massage show?"

"I'm ashamed to admit my research on Rolando was not up to its usual thorough standards. It turns out before he went to Nirvana, he worked at that day spa around the corner. Colleen knows him. Intimately. And their time together did not end happily for her."

"That's not good."

"Right. She's just looking for excuses now, ways to build her case against you. Failing to get that Nirvana story is reason number one. But admit it, sugar, you've been out a lot more than you've been in."

May gazed at Margery's wall, where framed certificates proclaimed her an honorary member of police departments across the country. Something was nagging at her, something just beyond the fringes of her consciousness. What?

"See what I mean?" Margery was saying. "You're not even here when you're here."

May blinked hard and focused back on her friend. Margery was right. She had to get her head back into work.

"I'll do my mea culpas with Colleen," she said. "She'll understand. We all follow leads that turn into dead ends. She's been there. She couldn't have forgotten that."

"Want to bet on it?"

"I'll pay for the visit to the spa." She tried not to gag on the words.

Margery grabbed her arm. "Now don't get hysterical. What you do sets precedents for us all."

The intercom sounded and the voice of Margery's assistant, Annie, announced the booker's meeting had just convened.

"You said it was at ten," Margery snapped.

"It was," Annie's disembodied voice announced. "But Colleen changed her mind a second ago and now it's now."

"Knowing you is turning out to be dangerous to my health," Margery told May as they hustled toward the conference room. "But I'm going to save you anyway."

"I don't need to be saved," May protested, as they rounded the corner to the hallway that led to their meeting.

"Oh yes you do," Margery insisted. "Because if you offer to pay for that spa trip, I'm going to have to kill you. Now get in there and let me do the talking."

May laughed her friend off, and led them into the meeting.

"How nice of you to decide to join us," Colleen said. "I hope we didn't get you out of a"—her eyes went to May's naked nails—"manicure appointment."

May opened her mouth to speak, but Margery interrupted. "Calendar confusion. May told me you rescheduled, but I insisted she was wrong. Sorry."

May sat down next to her friend and smiled pleasantly.

Colleen wasn't sure how to react, so she moved on to the business at hand: item one, hanging May.

"Let's catch up fast so we can move on. First on my agenda is you, May. We've been waiting days, weeks—I feel like it's been months—for your spa story. Paula's been hounding me to death. I wish she was here to hound you yourself. What did you get?"

"Well—" May started, but again Margery jumped in.

"To tell you the truth, it wasn't so much of a spa as a very top-of-the-line herbal clinic. So May and I—you know how flexible we have to be—have decided to shift our focus. This afternoon we're meeting downtown with Dr. Wu."

Colleen's face brightened a shade. "Dr. Wu? My Dr. Wu?" Then her crankiness came back. "Why the hell are you going there on my time?"

"To groove up a show, a good show, contrasting Nirvana, a fancy herbal clinic, with Dr. Wu and his plain Chinatown storefront."

"Forget it. Don't waste your time or mine. I've tried to get Dr. Wu to come on the show a hundred times. Number one, he doesn't own a TV. Number two, he thinks TV is dangerous for your health. And C, he can barely speak English, so what's the point?"

"Besides, that's health," Henry piped up, their personal Greek chorus of complaints. "And I'm health."

Margery plowed on. "You're right about Dr. Wu on every point, Colleen. But I have discovered that Dr. Wu has a son. A Western-educated, tall, good-looking, single, photogenic doctor son who loves television."

"A son." Colleen was intrigued, which annoyed her. She didn't want this show to work out.

"A son who very badly wants to come on our show."

Colleen thought about it. Even though she wanted to kill the idea, she could see its potential. "All right. If the father agrees, all right. If not, it's dead. Done. Over. Understood? I don't want any more of our collective time wasted on this no-brainer."

May and Margery nodded quickly.

"While you're there, would you ask him to refill my tonic preparation?" Colleen asked.

"What do you take?" May asked, eager to be helpful.

"I have no idea. It's on the recipe card, it smells bad, and it works. That's all I know. Now let's move on. Henry, you're up. Tell everybody about what you got on that female fishing-boat captain."

Henry turned to May. "Don't worry. It's not human interest. It's health."

"Really? What's the health angle, Henry?" May asked. "Did she survive because of the nutrient value of whale blubber?"

"You have been going through my things," Henry said. "I knew it. There's no other way you could have found out about the whale blubber. I have an exclusive."

"With whom, sugar?" Margery chimed in. "The whale?"

Colleen pushed the meeting along, and when she announced it was over, she asked May to stay behind. The rest of the producers and associate producers scattered, eager to avoid getting hit in the cross fire of an argument. Margery waited in the doorway. Colleen closed the door, closing Margery out.

"I don't like how your schedule is working out," she began right away.

"I know you don't," May said, holding off on her defense until she knew the charge.

"I need you five days a week. The job can't be done in three."

"I don't do it in three," May explained. "I just don't always do it here, so you don't always see me doing it."

"What I see is that things aren't getting done. You go out of town to catch a story, you spend thousands of dollars, and you come back empty-handed. That's not like you." And she added, "Gil wouldn't have stood for it."

"I'm not empty-handed," she said. "Margery and I are still on it. We're just grooving it up a bit. Giving it a tighter spin." She didn't respond to the comment about Gil, even though she knew it wasn't true.

Colleen drummed her French-nail fingertips on the burl of the conference-room table. "You're making me look bad. Like I don't have a tight rein."

"You don't need a tight rein. I'm not a horse. All you need is to let me do my job."

Colleen's assistant knocked and called through the door, "Paula's on the phone for you. She needs you now." She paused, trying to think of any other way to say it, but she couldn't, so she went with her first impression. "She's pissed as hell."

"We'll continue this later," Colleen said to May, as she headed out the door. "I need some more honeydew oil," she called to her assistant. "I'm all out of honeydew oil."

Margery caught up with May as she raced back to her office.

"Don't worry, sugar. When we go to Dr. Wu's, we'll get some more of Colleen's tonic, and we'll have him add a little kava to it. They say it works wonders for anxiety. It will take the edge right off her."

May wondered if that was the kind of thing you could drop into the water cooler. It seemed as if everyone, herself included, could use the edge taken off.

Fifty-One

TIME TO GO INTO HIGH GEAR, she thought as she stopped in the small kitchen and poured herself two mugs of black coffee, which she carried back to her desk. As soon as they cooled, she chugged them, one after another, as if she were a college student trying to get a quick buzz from a couple of beers. Then she called Charlotte on the intercom.

"I've got to wow Colleen this morning," she explained when Charlotte came in. "I've got to groove up four stories within the next hour. Four magnificent three-hankie stories. Four Emmy stories." She handed her assistant the folder of clippings that had been sitting for too long on her desk. "Put both our phones on voice mail. If anyone manages to get through, tell them I can't be disturbed."

Charlotte nodded eagerly, ready to follow her leader into battle.

May went on. "I want you to put together folders for each of these articles and find me contact numbers—I don't care who I have to talk to—on every one of them. Got it?"

"Got it," Charlotte replied, and grinned widely, happy to see May back to form.

"Shut the door," May called after her, and Charlotte did.

Merciless, she turned to the pile of papers that had grown helter skelter, a compost pile of ideas, on her desk.

"No. No. No. No," she said, tossing papers, press releases, and letter after letter into her wastebasket. At one time in her career, she might have spent weeks massaging some of these ideas into shows. But that was when she was just starting out, ambitious and young, with time on her hands. But she had no extra time now.

She flipped through one after another of the small-town papers, some of them, appallingly, a week old. She skimmed—looked up at the TV screen—and tore out an article, a headline, a paragraph—switched to another channel—tossing the refuse under her desk, her trash can already filled past its limit.

Two hours later, she was just finished organizing the third of three solid leads, all stories with a good chance of turning into something special, when there was a knock at the door. Charlotte, sheepish, peeked in.

"I'm so sorry," she apologized. "Linda called from the front desk. She's got Detective O'Donnell on the line. He says it's urgent that he speak with you."

"Thanks," May said. "Put him through."

A moment later, her phone rang. She picked it up. "Is everything okay?"

"Are you okay?" His voice had an edge to it she hadn't heard before.

"Yes. Why?"

"I've been working straight through for over twenty-four hours. This is the first time I've had a chance to call you."

"Are you okay?"

He ignored the question. "You shouldn't have driven alone to that lab last night. You have to watch out, May. You have to be smart. Going alone wasn't smart."

She felt her back stiffen. "It worked out fine," she told him.

He heard the hurt. "I worry, that's all. I didn't mean you weren't smart."

"It's okay. I know I'm smart."

He sighed. "Let's start again."

"Okay."

"Hi, May. I just got the lab results from my friend. On the pills you brought home from the spa."

"And?" She braced herself for the news.

"They can't check for everything in the world, you know that, right? They check for what's most likely."

"And?"

"The results say that everything's fine. The pills are excellent quality with no surprises."

"Which means nothing from the spa was tainted," she said, thinking out loud.

"It means nothing you brought home from the spa was tainted with anything they checked for. You've still got the results from the pathology on Rosie to wait for. I wish you'd give it up. You've gotten so much done. It's enough." He got quiet again, even quieter than usual.

"What's wrong?" May asked, because it wasn't like him to be this remote, not with her.

He let out a heaving sigh. "Today, I was at a crime scene. The deceased was sprawled on the floor on her belly, legs spread apart. Nothing unusual. I've seen hundreds of corpses in the same position. But this one shook me up. I couldn't see her face, but I saw right away she had good clothes, a gray suit that matched her shoes exactly, and hair just like yours, thick and wavy. And all I could think was, it was you."

"I never wear gray," she joked, to take the edge off the tone of the conversation, but he ignored the comment, and she regretted it.

"I knew it wasn't really you. I was in her apartment. I had her name in my notebook. But the thing was, I knew it could have been you. I don't want you to get in trouble, May. And if you do, I want to be there so I can help you."

She smiled. "I promise not to need saving. I promise not to end up belly-down on the floor."

"Take the gun back."

"No."

Voices yelled in the background. "Shit. The press. I've got to go." And he was gone, leaving her holding the phone with a hand that had begun to tremble.

Was that what he meant to do, to scare me? It had worked, except the fear did a funny thing. It galvanized her, made her even more intent on getting this done. She just had to be careful, to use her head.

She called her old au pair coordinator, Carol.

"How is Sabrieke?" the coordinator asked as soon as she heard May's voice. "Is she going home soon? Is that why I have the pleasure of your call?"

"No. Sabrieke is still going strong. Although it probably won't be too long before I call you on official business. She's pregnant," May explained. "She says she wants to stay on, but I'm not sure."

"Oh," Carol said. "That would be a trip. An au pair with a baby. Well, don't worry. We've got some dynamite girls. You know, things have changed a lot over the past year, ever since that incident in Boston. The girls have a lot more training."

Skipping the Alice in Wonderland discussion over how you can have more if you haven't had any, she got to the point. "Listen, I'm trying to track down a couple of au pairs who I think are in your program. They were friends with Morgan. Did you hear about Morgan?"

"Oh yes. I got a lot of calls after that. She wasn't one of ours, you know. She came over from Ireland on her own. Illegal. That's the problem—"

May cut her off because experience told her Carol would pontificate for hours, if left unchecked.

"I'm looking into the circumstances of her death for a friend. The other day, I overheard two au pairs speaking outside my kids' school. I'm trying to track them down. They were either English or Irish. One had spiky hair with green tips. One was really tall. Do you know them?"

There was a moment of silence. Then, "Yes."

"Can you give me their names and numbers?"

More silence. "I have to think about this."

"I'm not trying to hire them away or anything."

"I know. But I'm responsible for them. And I don't think I can just give out their families' numbers without permission."

"Then why don't you call them and ask them to phone me? It's very important." She could tell Carol wasn't ready to commit, so she changed her tack. "The au pairs I overheard made it sound like Morgan was having an affair with her host father. Do you know anything about that?"

"Unfortunately, I know more about most of those girls' sex lives than they do themselves. But Morgan wasn't in my program. I can't help you there."

"Yes, you can. You can ask those two girls to call me."

As soon as Carol agreed, May hurried her off the phone. Then she got Charlotte back into her office and they focused on the work at hand.

A dozen phone calls later, they'd grooved up three new shows they both thought would be great. At noon, when Margery came to get her, May felt as if she'd begun to get back on track at work. But like a rubber band snapping back to its original shape, on the cab ride downtown her focus returned to Stacey.

"You're very quiet, sugar," Margery observed after telling the driver to stop at the curb next to the statue of Confucius that sat watching over the busy streets of Chinatown. Traffic wasn't moving. It would be quicker to walk.

"I was just thinking about the Siamese twins they had on *Simon Says* yesterday," May said.

"Now that was one even I think was in terrible taste," Margery opined. "Obviously the ratings will be through the roof."

"So will the ratings on this one," May countered, unconvincingly.

They hurried along the crowded streets, maneuvering

their way between women doing lunchtime marketing at sidewalk stalls, small children being dragged along by impatient mothers, men in suits discussing business in loud voices, and kitchen workers in aprons and black shiny pants, rushing, late, to their next job.

They bypassed the tourist streets, the ones crowded with dim sum restaurants and souvenir shops that had kissing dolls, paper fans, parasols, and battery-operated weasels stacked up outside on pressboard shelves.

"Here we are." Margery stopped in front of a dingy storefront.

May looked up and tried to read the scripted sign that hung above the doorway, but it was in Chinese. She gazed into the window at a dusty display of jars, bottles, boxes, and a pile of what was either antlers or bones. It wasn't a window designed to draw people in off the street. Rather, it looked meant to drive the uninvited away.

"How did you find out that Doctor Wu had this westernized son?" May asked, hesitating at the door.

"I'll tell you my little secret," Margery shared, "if you promise you won't tell another living soul."

"Cross my heart."

Margery lowered her voice and looked around to see if any of the passers-by might be spies from rival shows. "I read about it in a source of mine. A great source. The best. I don't know if you've ever heard of it."

Intrigued, May leaned closer. An obscure magazine, an off-beat newspaper, anything no rival producer was reading was a valuable tool in their hypercompetitive business. "What is it?"

Margery bent her head so she could whisper directly into May's ear. "Promise you won't tell?"

May nodded.

"*Time* magazine."

"Really, what's it called?" May asked, and then took another look at Margery's face. "*Time* magazine? You read it in *Time*?"

"Yup. They did a whole piece on intergenerational struggles, assimilation, that kind of stuff. Wu and his son were featured as an example of how different generations who carry on in the same professions are sometimes informed by the impact of their peers, blah, blah, blah. What do you think? Is that a show we should be doing?"

"It's a show," May told her. "A nice dull show. Unless of course father and son start screaming at each other."

"Or throwing things."

"Sesame noodles. Or green tea," May suggested.

"Only if it's hot," Margery added, and laughing, they pushed open the door to the shop. An orchestra of chimes, hung for the purpose of announcing visitors, jingled wildly, silencing them.

A woman sitting behind a counter at the front counter stood up from her stool and met May's stare but didn't greet her. She waited, calmly, not moving. Either the visitors would announce what they wanted or they would turn around and leave. Either way was fine with her.

"We're here to see Dr. Wu," Margery said.

"Name?" the woman asked, her voice so clipped and quick May couldn't quite understand.

"Margery Riegle and May Morrison."

Without comment, the woman stepped out from behind her counter and walked with tiny steps to the back of the store, disappearing behind a multicolored beaded curtain.

"Look at this stuff," Margery said, pointing to the jars on the walls. Some were filled with what looked like twigs, others with powders. Many had leaves and a few contained things that looked as if they might be stewed organs.

The woman stepped out from the curtain. "Come," she said brusquely, as if they'd been keeping her waiting for hours.

"Come," Margery repeated, hustling to the door.

"Will he beat us if we're late?" May asked, breathless from keeping up with Margery's sprint, but her friend didn't answer, she just kept on moving, pushing through the beaded curtain with a swipe of her hand. Beyond it was a small dark room lit by a naked bulb. A man, May assumed it was Dr. Wu, sat on a wooden straight-backed chair, studying something on his desk. Watching the old man staring down, not moving, May's first impression was that he was dead. Then he spoke. His voice was a surprise—very loud and strong. The rest of him, thinning white hair and wrinkled skin, looked fragile.

"What is the problem?" he barked.

May tensed, worried suddenly that he'd been warned about them; that he'd been told they were coming, and meant to scare them away.

Unfazed, Margery listed her ailments. "Fatigue, wrinkles, constipation, and stress."

"What medicine do you take? What conditions do you have?"

Margery rattled off, "Synthroid for hypothyroidism, a daily vitamin, a calcium pill, and vitamin E. That's all. And coffee. I drink three cups of coffee a day."

"Don't stop Synthroid. You need calcium but I'll give you something better. What kind of E do you take? Pill?"

"Yes."

"Soft?"

Margery thought about it and said, "Yes."

"Okay. Listen closely. Synthroid, yes. Keep taking the hard pill. Calcium, I'll give you that. Vitamin E pill, forget it. Make my tea instead. Much better for your body. You understand? No more gobbling up the soft pill." And he made a noise like a dog scarfing down food.

Although May was aware that Margery was speaking, she didn't hear the words. She was busy thinking, *That's what Rosie did—gobbled Stacey's soft-gels.* There was one in particular the dog liked. Stacey had told her.

She dug her hand into her large oversize purse and felt around. Did she still have it? Yes, she'd never taken it out of her bag. She pulled out the bottle. Valerian. Was that the one Rosie liked?

She untwisted the top and poured a few into her hand. The doctor had been speaking, but he stopped to watch what May was doing, let his glasses slide down his nose, and peered over them. She reached out, holding the pills in her open palm, the way she might offer food to an animal she didn't completely trust.

"What's that there?" he asked.

"Valerian," she told him. "Do you know what valerian is?"

He took one of the opaque pills from her hand, held it up to the light, then he placed it carefully on his desk. The desk was old. The wooden drawer, slightly warped, stuck hard. He yelled at it in Chinese. With the next yank, it moved, and he opened it to draw out a tiny knife. Carefully, he split the pill in half. Then, with a spoon not much bigger than the silverware in Delia's dollhouse, he scraped out its oily contents. She watched carefully as he smeared the tiny spoon on a tissue, then threw the tissue in a wicker wastebasket under the desk.

"What did you do that for?" May asked.

"That? That's just inside stuff. That's nothing. Useless garbage. But this." He held up the pill's soft casing, squashing it further between his fingers. "This I don't like."

The beaded curtain rattled and a tall young man with round wire-rim glasses and an easy stride walked in. He touched the old man's shoulder, and when the old man turned around, he greeted him in Chinese.

The old man grunted but didn't look up. "I don't like this," he said again to May.

"Hello, I'm Tony," the young man said.

"I'm Margery Riegle." Margery offered her hand.

Tony turned to Dr. Wu. "Dad," he said. "These are the women I told you about. Miss Riegle is a patient of yours who works for the TV show that's interested in our coming on."

The father looked at his son for several moments, his face blank, his gaze unwavering. He nodded, clearly unimpressed, then went back to his work, rolling the soft-gel casing around on his fingertips.

"This one is no good."

"Here he goes," Tony said with a roll of his eyes. "It's his latest gripe. He doesn't mind that Western medicine is going herbal, or so he says. But he insists that Western doctors are messing it up, getting it wrong."

He spoke as if his father wasn't there, and in fact his father barely seemed to notice his son speaking at all, which made May wonder whether Dr. Wu had some hearing defect she'd failed to notice until now.

"Dad," the son said, tapping his father on the shoulder again to get his attention, confirming May's suspicion. He spoke quickly in Chinese and then turned to the women. "I keep telling him the casing is just the envelope. It doesn't much matter what it's made from so long as it's easily digestible and safe. I keep telling him that people like it, that they find it more convenient." He went back to Chinese to address his father, then switched to English. "Boiling leaves into essences takes a lot of time, which is something most people don't have much of these days. Plus, let's be honest, most of this stuff smells really bad. I keep telling him Asians will boil the tea and hold their nose, but if he wants to go beyond the neighborhood, he has to offer alternatives."

"Tea is by far best," Dr. Wu insisted. "What is in this?" He held up the squished soft-gel. "Do you know?"

"Valerian," May told him again.

"No," the man yelled. "What is *in* this? In *this?*" He pointed to the casing. "This," he hissed. "Do you know?"

May shook her head.

"Do you know?" he asked Margery, who simply shrugged her shoulders. She wasn't following this at all.

"How about you, big shot?" he asked his son.

"Think of it as a tea bag, that's all," his son tried, first in Chinese, then English. "A different kind of a tea bag."

"Ahhh," his father yelled. "You don't know. It could be ground-up cat hair. It makes no difference to you." Dr. Wu's voice was a growl now.

"They didn't test that," May said quietly, a piece of the puzzle falling into place as lightly as rain. She turned to Margery, who had no idea what she was talking about. "Paul told me, but I didn't hear him. They don't test for everything. They never tested the casing."

"You think it's made of cat hair?" Margery asked in disbelief.

"Yes," the old man was nodding vigorously.

"It's not made of cat hair," the son insisted.

May touched the old man's bony arm. "Can I have that back?"

He followed her eyes to the squashed gel cap he held in his hand, and gave it to her. "You understand?" he said quietly, so only she would hear. "You will throw it away?" he asked, louder.

"Yes, I will. Thanks." She stood, walked to the curtain, pushed aside the beads and strode through the store.

"Sugar," Margery called after her racing to catch up. "Where the hell are you going?"

The woman sitting on her stool behind the counter watched but said nothing. May pushed open the door, sending the wind chimes into their dizzying tangle.

By the time Margery caught up with her, May was climbing into a taxi. Margery called from the doorway of the Chinese apothecary, demanding that she come back inside, that their work wasn't done. But May pretended that the noises of the busy street were drowning her out.

"Hurry," she told the cabby, and he made his way, weaving around people and double-parked cars, back past Confucius, who watched with his unflinching gaze.

Fifty-Two

SHE TOOK THE TAXI ALL THE WAY HOME, using the backseat as her office, working her cell phone like a sales rep. The first call was to Dr. Adler, but he was working in the lab and no amount of bullying could convince the young man who answered the phone to disturb him.

She tried Paul's pager next, then checked her home machine, where she heard Delia report that Susie was homesick and Margery yell in to the phone that she'd better have a damn good explanation for running away. There was a message from the police, too, telling her they'd found her car. The last message was a tentative young British voice, an au pair returning her call.

"I heard you want to talk to me," the girl said. "Carol explained what you want. It's not what you think." She hesitated, as if she wasn't sure how much of a message to leave, then said, "I'll call back," and quickly hung up.

May immediately called Carol.

"I told you I can't give out anyone's number," the au pair coordinator explained.

"She called me. She just forgot to leave her number on my machine. Come on, Carol. This is important. It might be a matter of life and death."

"You sound exactly like one of the girls. If you knew how many au pairs call me every night telling me it's a matter of life and death. The family won't let them use a car and it's a matter of life and death. They need to borrow a hundred dollars, it's a matter of life and death. They must change families immediately, it's a matter of life and death. What it's a matter of is you want her number. And when she calls back you'll get it." The conversation ended with a click, and then a beep as the low-battery light came on on May's phone.

The cabbie pulled up at her front door. She paid him his exorbitant fare, then headed straight inside and to her kitchen desk. She knew exactly what she was looking for. She had scribbled the information on the front page of the spa guest list she'd been using when Paul first mentioned his friend at the lab. There—underneath several days' worth of mail she hadn't even glanced at—there it was, Almar Laboratory. Thankful that she was a compulsive doodler who mindlessly scribbled down anything anyone ever said, she picked up the receiver and began her search.

It took a while before she got the right borough, Staten Island, and then was misdirected twice until she reached the lab. Finally she found him—Paul's friend, Stu.

"No," Stu admitted easily, "I don't ever check the casings. Not unless there's a suspicion of tampering. Paul said only that you were interested in the contents. That's what we normally check."

She told him, "That's true. We were interested in the contents. But now I'm wondering if maybe the casings themselves might be contaminated."

"With what?"

"I'm not sure." She didn't want to tell him about her BSE suspicions over the phone. She was afraid he'd just laugh.

"I can't check for everything, but if you bring over some more samples, I'll check for your best guess." He gave her the address and directions to the lab.

She rummaged through the medicine cabinets, gathering a dozen more bottles that Stacey had given her throughout the year. She dumped them in her satchel and then set out for the short walk to the police station.

When she got there, it was a comedy of errors that wasn't the least bit funny to her. No one could find her car. She planted herself on an old green chair, the cracked vinyl seat splitting further beneath her as she restlessly shifted, and waited for over an hour. Finally, the cop who parked the car returned from his shift, laughing when he heard the dilemma. He jogged off to the street behind the police station, where no one had thought to look, and retrieved her vehicle.

She tried to speed to the lab, but it was rush hour and the traffic held her to a crawl. It was ten after five when she pulled into the parking lot of the squat redbrick building. She hurried to the front door and found it locked. The hours posted gave her the bad news: they closed at 4:30. She rang the night bell three times, but no one answered.

Damn, she said, and got back in the car.

Fifty-Three

SHE WAS MINUTES FROM HER HOUSE, still thinking about Stacey when it clicked. Like a newsreel she pictured it, Stacey handing out Scott's pills as if they were Life Savers, Tic Tacs, bubblegum. Melatonin gel caps, valerian capsules, kava. Stacey hadn't known that what she had was contaminated or that one by one her friends—and her dog—would get sick. *Not all of her friends,* May thought, thinking of Marlene. She shivered at the memory of the bottles pressed into her own hand, in friendship.

It was another warm night, and as she turned down her street, she saw lots of people were out lingering in the last light of the day, chatting on the sidewalks, playing with dogs on their front lawns, rocking cranky babies in strollers, back and forth. As she passed Stacey's house, she saw all the lights were on inside. Nick's Trooper was in the driveway. She made a hasty decision and pulled the car over. She got out, went to the door, rang the bell, and waited. She didn't know how much Scott knew, but she was determined finally to find out.

When he opened the door, he didn't look at all surprised to see her.

"We have to talk," she said quietly.

He moved aside to let her in.

"No," she said. "Out here."

Surprising her, Scott stepped outside.

"I think I know what happened," she said.

"Who asked you?" Scott replied. "Do you get bored when things are going well? Do you have some need to feel unsafe?"

She checked her surroundings. Half a dozen neighbors were outside, all within earshot. She shook off her fear and looked Scott in the eye.

"Actually, I want to live happily ever after. And so did Stacey."

"Goddamn it!" he raged, and then noticed people a few houses down looking his way. He dropped his voice. "Don't tell me about Stacey. She was my wife. Mine." He narrowed his eyes and walked closer until May could see the pores of his skin, the day's new growth of beard sprouting from his cheeks. "No matter what I do or what I say, you just won't go away. You're like a mosquito, buzzing, buzzing, buzzing, buzzing in my ears."

"I'll go away once I find the truth. That's all. Look, if something went wrong, if something out of your control went wrong, no one will blame you. There are good people who can help you. Let me help you." She reached out her hand.

He laughed, some spit spraying her. "What kind of help are you going to get me? Not what I need. What I need isn't possible for you to give me. No one, not even you, my dear, can bring back my wife."

"It's not too late for you."

"Too late for what? It's an interesting number you do. You want to do good. You want to help. All in the name of the truth. But do you even know the truth?"

"I think so," she said quietly.

Scott sat down on the steps and spat out like a dare, "I'm listening."

She sat beside him. "There was a bad batch of pills. The

ones in the garage," she said, suddenly remembering the night she saw Scott organizing cartons in the dark. She remembered now how Stacey said the old ones were in the garage, on hold for a lawsuit.

"The ones from our first plant, in Los Cuervos," Scott said.

May thought of the plane tickets she'd found to San Diego. She'd bet anything that that's where Stacey had been going, to Los Cuervos via San Diego, to find out more.

May pushed on. "No one knew the pills from Los Cuervos were corrupted. And Stacey gave them out to her friends, like prizes of her affection."

"Did she give any to you?"

"Yes," May said, "but I never took them."

Scott shook his head. "Not bad. Not bad at all." He was loosening up a little, as if he couldn't resist this, a chance to do a bit of bragging. "The factory that produced those pills did it for so little money that Nick and I used to joke about it. I said it must be a cover-up, money laundering for a cocaine operation. Nick guessed amphetamines. We were kidding. But we didn't really want to know. What we did know was that the deal we got from those guys was too good to be true."

He went on. "Don't think it didn't bug me. But it took a long time before we finally found out what was going on there."

"It was the gel caps, wasn't it? The gelatin was contaminated."

He blew out a long whistle. "The bastards had gotten a real bargain on the raw material. They never asked why. Like us, they didn't want to know. They just rendered the bones until they got their product." He sighed. "The important thing is that once we did find out, we did the right thing. We collected all the pills. We called every single patient and said there's something wrong with them. We said, 'Don't take those pills,' and then we replaced them for free with twice as many. Every person we called brought them back. Except the ones we didn't know about. The ones that were dispensed by my wife without my knowledge. I couldn't find out who she gave them to without telling her why I needed to know. And I couldn't tell her that, could I?"

"Why not?"

He just shook his head. "It's not a sure thing, contracting this disease. It's not like salmonella—you ingest it, you get it. It was a gamble, with out-of-sight odds. Like getting hit by lightning. Only I figured the odds out wrong. Stacey's friend Toni was the first to go, but I didn't make the connection. Even when the rest of them started presenting symptoms, I didn't get it. But Stacey did."

He got quiet for a moment, then like a battery recharging, his energy returned. "I didn't kill her, do you understand that?" His voice was urgent. "I would rather have killed myself."

In the silence that followed, May thought about the others, the ones he hadn't mentioned—Morgan, Matthew Harris. He hadn't bothered to deny killing them.

"Where's Nick?" she asked, suddenly aware that though his car was present there was no sign of him.

"I don't know." He looked at her and smiled. "You think I killed him, too? You think I killed Stacey and now I'm going to kill you? Maybe I should, to put you out of your misery. You know," he told her, "'There are good people who can help you.'" Laughing at his own mimicry, he got up and went back in the house, leaving her stunned and alone.

Fifty-Four

THE PHONE WAS RINGING when she got into the house. It was Paul.

"Where have you been? Stu told me you were going out there with more samples and you never showed." He didn't need to add that he'd been scared for her. His anger told her that.

"I called you," she explained. "I left messages."

"I know," his voice softened. "I'm hard to reach." Then he admitted, "I thought for sure you were in trouble."

"I'm not. I'm fine. I just came back from Scott's." She let a little boast into her voice. "I finally got him to talk." She went on to repeat what she'd learned. "You know, he really didn't set out to hurt anybody. He's not an evil man. Things just kind of snowballed on him."

"That's good. That means he doesn't have to worry about murder in the first degree."

"We don't know for sure that he murdered anybody."

"And we don't know for sure that he didn't. Look, there's a couple of things we have to do right away. We have to notify the CDC about those pills. And we have to get the police back in on this fast. Some of those deaths may have been because people swallowed a big mistake, but the rest are homicides. The question is, have you primed our star witness for a confession?"

"You think I might have gotten Scott ready to say he murdered his wife?" There was a hint of pride in her question, and Paul heard it like a scream.

"It's time to stop, May. Promise me you'll back off. Don't go running over to Scott's and try to tie up all the loose ends—because some of those loose ends could kill you. Do you understand what I'm saying?"

"Yes," she said quietly. He was scaring her, and she didn't like it.

"All right. I'm leaving here now. I'll be at your house in less than half an hour. Promise me you won't do anything more until I get there."

She agreed, but he could tell by her clipped reply that she resented his authoritative tone.

She sat on her couch, doing nothing, nothing more than waiting. The minutes went faster than she'd have predicted. By the time the doorbell rang, her annoyance was gone, washed away by a surge of relief. She swung open the door. As soon as she did it, she knew she should have checked through the peephole first. Instead of Paul, she found Nick.

"We have to talk," he said.

She started outside, to be safe, but then Nick told her, "I just called the police on Scott. I told them I'd wait for them here."

A voice of caution sounded in her mind—it was Paul's—but it was so constant now it had become a boring drumbeat, easy to override and ignore. She stepped aside to let Nick in.

He followed her into the kitchen. "I don't believe his story of what was in those pills. But I do believe one thing for sure. Scott killed his wife." He let out a breath as heavy as a groan, then rested his forehead in his hands. He looked bereft.

"How do you know?"

"He told me straight out, like he was proud of it."

"But why?" She wasn't sure of much, but she knew Scott had loved his wife. At least she thought she was sure of it.

"He said he did it to save our necks. Because after Greta died, and then Toni and Risa got sick, Stacey became suspicious. When her friend Bonnie had that weird accident, she started digging around for a connection. I guess she didn't find one, so she came up with that cock-and-bull story about the pills. She had no proof," Nick said. "And I didn't buy it."

"How come Scott did?"

"Don't ask me to explain his mind. It's an ugly place."

"But something was wrong with those pills," May told him, her senses on high alert. "Scott said you recalled them. Or are you saying he made that up, too?"

"No, that part's true. We did recall them all. But not for why you think. We just didn't like the quality control at the plant in Los Cuervos. We stopped those shipments because of the quality issue. Stacey didn't believe that," he went on. "She decided she had to go down there and see for herself. I still don't know what she thought she'd find."

May said nothing. She didn't know either.

"Before she went, Scott came to me. He said, 'If she tells people this story, I'll lose her and I'll lose everything I ever had.' I told him to chill out, that there was nothing for her to find there, nothing for her to reveal. I thought that would be the end of it. If he was a sane man, it would have been. I didn't know until after that he wasn't."

"Until after what?"

"Until after he got in the pool with her. Until after he caught her and held on to her torso. Until after he drove her head into the tiles as if she were a battering ram."

The image of it took May's breath away. A few moments later, she was able to ask, "Did he kill Matthew Harris, too?"

Nick nodded. "He told me today that after the first one, it got easy."

"And Morgan?"

"That was just a lovers' quarrel."

The phone rang. Nick gestured *Go ahead, pick it up.* She lifted the receiver distractedly. "Hello?"

"This is Fiona. You wanted to speak to me."

It took her a few seconds before she realized it was the spike-haired au pair. "Yes. Hi," she said, and was about to ask for a number to call her back when Fiona interrupted.

"I can't talk long," Fiona said, her voice low and whispery. "My host family doesn't want me involved in this. I think they're scared something might happen to one of them. So what exactly do you want to know?"

May covered the mouthpiece of the phone and told Nick she'd be a moment. Then she walked into the living room, for privacy. "The message you left said I had it all wrong. What did you mean?"

"Oh, well, Carol told me you thought Scott was making the running with Morgan. You know—having relations with her. That's what I meant. You're wrong about that. She wasn't involved with him in that way. She did have a boyfriend. Very possessive. He wouldn't let her go out with us anymore, even if we were just going for coffee. But it wasn't Scott."

"Did you know him?"

"He was awful. He stopped taking her out altogether. Just had her over to his flat for sex all the time."

"Who is he?" May asked, and when Fiona hesitated, she added, "He may have murdered her. If you know who he is, you have to tell me his name."

"I'm quite sure he didn't murder her. He wasn't that kind of a bloke. I didn't like him. And why should I? He didn't want to meet any of us. He thought we were beneath him. But he wasn't a murderer. He was a doctor."

"Was his name Nick?" she whispered into the phone. "Was it Nick Ellman?"

"Yes. That's it. That's right. So you do know him? What's this about?"

Nick came into the room and smiled—a warm, open smile.

"'Bye," May said. "Thanks for calling." She disconnected and tried to unfreeze.

"Everything okay?"

"Yes," she said quickly.

"You're upset," he told her. "I can see it."

"No, I'm not."

"Yes, you are. It's understandable. Anyone would be. Come with me a second." He led her back to the kitchen. His medical bag sat on the table. She didn't remember him holding it when he came in.

"Here," he said. "Take these." He handed over two small yellow pills. "It's just a mild sedative. It will take the edge off, calm you down."

"I'm okay," she said quietly. "I've lost my taste for taking pills, if you know what I mean."

He laughed. "They're not gel caps."

"I'm okay," she said again, and offered them back. "I don't need them."

"Please, I insist." He made no move to reclaim them. "I insist," he said, and this time, May heard a new tone that frightened her.

He got up and filled a glass with water. Her eyes followed him. Her limbs felt numb, asleep, like dead weight. She worried that as in a bad dream, she might not be able to move if she needed to.

She concentrated her focus, thought of her children. She needed to stay safe for her children. Almost instantly, the room seemed to brighten, objects became more crisp and clear. Her heartbeat felt strong and quick. She flexed her hands. They were hot and sweaty. Her body was ready to lunge or run.

"Here," he said, passing her the glass. When she made no move to accept it, he leaned toward her. "Take the pills, May. They're just tranquilizers." The tendons in his neck strained.

"Why did you kill Stacey?" she asked plainly.

"I had no choice. She was about to ruin my life."

"Does Scott know?"

He laughed, a hollow, humorless grunt of a laugh. "There are two kinds of knowing—the kind where you go to the police and the kind where you have nightmares for the rest of your life. He's been complaining a lot of nightmares lately."

"What did you do to Matthew Harris?"

"He was a pit bull, concentrated trouble. The world's a better place without him."

"And Morgan?"

He looked away for a millisecond, then met her eyes. "That was just a lovers' quarrel." He put the glass down on the table. "You havc to take those pills."

"What will happen to me if I do?"

"They're not going to kill you. They'll just make you relax. And then I'll have time to think."

"And if I refuse?"

"I'll do what I have to, quick and messy." He stared at her. "You hate me, don't you? I never wanted you to hate me."

"I don't hate you. I know none of this was your fault. You got sucked into something awful. You didn't have a choice."

She breathed a quick rush of air as Nick lifted a syringe out of his bag.

"That's a fairy tale," he said. "You don't believe it." He filled the syringe, slowly, so slowly she felt as if time had crawled to a stop. "If you won't take the pills, I'll use this. You'll just feel a pinch," he explained. "You'll be fast asleep before the needle's out of your arm."

"Oh, Nick," she called out, hoping there was some humanity left in him.

He smiled. "I have no tolerance for your pity and compassion, so don't pretend to care about me, May. Because you know what? Even if you did, what difference would it make to me at this point? You'd be the only one."

"You're wrong," May said, her voice finding a new tone, one of strength. "You just don't realize what a compelling story you make. You can't imagine the numbers we could get on a show about you."

"About me? Why? Because I screwed up and killed a friend to save myself?"

"You didn't screw up. You were screwed. Big difference there. Screwed and desperate," she said. "It's a winning combination." She felt the adrenaline rush of the hunt. "As far as I'm concerned—and I'm speaking for every producer in daytime talk—you are the ultimate get. In fact, if I didn't know you, you'd probably be too hot for me to get close to."

"What do you mean?"

"Oprah would grab you in a second. Whoever Oprah wants, she gets. Unless you went the Larry King route. Look," she moved closer to him. "No matter what happens to you after today, can I tell you something?"

He was listening now, standing perfectly still and listening.

"If you want it, you've got an incredible future ahead of you. You think it's the end of the line and you're trapped? You're not. I can get you on any talk show you want. I can get you a book contract. And my guess is we can wangle a movie deal here. At the least, TV. I'm telling you Nick, you've got a story people should hear. You could have let those pills filter through the entire country. Thousands of people would have gotten sick. But you didn't. I think you're a hero. You shouldn't go down in the history books as a creep. You want people to know you're a hero, don't you?"

"Why? So I can feel proud in my nine-by-twelve cell?"

She sidled even closer and lowered her voice as if she might be overheard. "One of our producers is like this"—

she crossed her fingers—"with every goddamn prison warden in the country. She can wangle anyone she wants a get-out-of-jail-free pass to come on our show. And then . . ." she lifted her eyebrows, fetchingly.

She could feel him aching to know more.

"If you get locked up," she whispered, "I can get you out."

In the second he took to think about this offer, he relaxed his grip on the syringe and May lunged and grabbed for it. Before he knew it was gone, she had plunged it in the beefy part of his upper arm.

For a moment, they stood staring at each other in total silence. It was as if she'd turned them both into stone. Then all at once, he fell, a heap of clothes on the floor.

"May," a voice called out, and she turned to see Paul. The room went into a spin and everything cut to black.

Fifty-Five

"I'M DEFINITELY GOING TO BE AN ASTRONAUT," Susie announced.

"I thought you wanted to work at Disney World," Delia said. "You're going to stand at the entrance to Space Mountain and let in all the kids who are too short."

"I changed my mind," Susie told her. "I want to be an astronaut now." She turned to her mother. "Did you know rockets go even faster than the Tower of Terror?"

"What about you?" Paul asked Delia who brightened now that they were talking about something more interesting. "What are you going to be?"

She smiled, showing off two holes where teeth had been just a week ago. "Guess."

"Hmm." He stroked his chin. "Let's see. A doctor? A teacher? A tooth fairy?"

She beat him over the head with her napkin.

May started clearing the leftovers, dumping half-filled Chinese food containers into plastic bowls, snapping on the lids.

"I want to be just like my mom," her daughter answered, then smiled sweetly because she knew the answer was a winner. She scrunched up her forehead and added, "Except married. For the whole time of my life, not just a few years."

May put a huge mound of uneaten rice down the garbage disposal, turned on the water, and let it grind for much longer than necessary. When the rice was flushed away and the flush on her cheeks had faded, she turned around.

"Okay. No more daydreaming. Tomorrow is school. So you,"—she returned to the table and kissed Susie's head—"Miss Astronaut, have to wash your face and brush your teeth, and you,"—she kissed Delia's head—"Miss TV Producer, you have to take a shower. And you," she kissed Paul on the lips, "have to go home to your children."

"Do I have to take a shower?" Delia, worn out from the trip home, couldn't keep the whine out of her voice.

"Do I have to wash my face?" Susie asked, echoing her sister's weary tone.

"Can't the boys just drive over here and camp out with me in the basement?" Paul joined along.

"Please," the girls cheered.

"No," the mother yelled.

"Mean," Delia muttered, then started giggling, because even she knew the complaint was ridiculous.

"Can we at least take a shower together?" Susie pushed on to the next possible win.

"I'm not dirty," Paul teased.

"Me and Delia," she corrected him.

May agreed. The girls cheered. She started the water, set up washcloths in opposite corners, made the no-tear shampoo and conditioner reachable and the water temperature moderately hot. Then she left them to lather.

In the kitchen, Paul and May caught up quickly, acutely aware that the delighted screams coming from the upstairs bathroom wouldn't last long.

Having spent the night at the police station, Paul had the latest update. "No bail," he told her. "They don't even know how big the case is going to be yet, how many people have been affected. The FBI is coming in. I don't know what will happen to Scott. No one is talking about him, yet. But he's not off the hook."

"He doesn't want to be off the hook," she said. Scott had been by to see her the night before. She'd just roused from a deep recuperative sleep when Emily walked into her room to tell her he was waiting.

"He said he'd understand if you don't want to see him," Emily had explained.

She found him in the front hall looking worn out and profoundly tired.

"Whatever I get, I deserve," he'd told her, as if they had been in the middle of discussing it. She'd simply nodded.

"I didn't know," he whispered. "I didn't know what Nick had done."

May still didn't know if she believed him.

"Mom?" Delia called, bringing her back. "We need more shampoo."

May went upstairs to minister to the dirty. "I just opened that bottle. What happened to it?"

"I don't know," Susie innocently reported, ignoring the huge pool of bubbles at her feet.

When May got back to the kitchen, Paul was putting things away. "I've got to go pick up the boys at Bridget's."

She watched him finish loading the dishwasher, wiping the counter and thought, *He looks so much like he belongs.*

He felt her stare and swung around, put down the sponge, put his hand in his pocket. "Close your eyes," he told her.

She did, and waited to be kissed. Instead, she felt him take her hand, put something in it.

"Okay. You can open them now."

She uncurled her fist and stared at her palm, at the ring that sat there, white gold with a square-shaped diamond in an antique setting.

"Mom," Delia called. "Can we get out now?"

"It was my mother's," he told her, "and then it was my

wife's. My first wife's," he added, trying out the sound of it.

May blinked and stared at the ring.

"Mom!" Susie yelled as loud as she could because her sister told her to. "We want to get out."

"They don't like to get out by themselves," she explained to Paul, who didn't know. "It's beautiful," she added, as she started up the stairs and called, "Coming."

"You're not going to do this to me," Paul said from the foyer. "Let me stand here without an answer."

She thought it unkind to point out that he hadn't actually asked a question. A thousand other responses flooded her brain. *I need more time. I'm just not sure. I want to wait. I need to talk to my children, my ex-husband, to my mother, to Margery, to Paula, to Stacey. Not Stacey,* she thought sadly. For a moment she let herself imagine how it would be. Paul and his three boys. Her two girls. Sabrieke rocking the baby stroller. Manu out front mowing the lawn. Bridget cooking a dinner of stew for the usual number, eleven. She laughed at the insanity of it. Then she looked at Paul. His gray eyes looked prepared for sadness, but his eyebrows rose with hope.

"It would be ludicrous," he said, as if reading her mind.

She slipped the ring on her finger. He must have had it resized. It fit her perfectly. "But it would never be dull."

She walked back down the stairs and they came together in an a long kiss that was ended by a chorus of giggles as Susie and Delia, naked, dripping wet, and proud that they'd finally figured out how to turn off the water all by themselves, laughed at the sight of two grown-ups caught in what they thought of as *the act.*

Fifty-Six

As she walked down the halls of her office, she was greeted by enthusiastic applause. She smiled but didn't stop to chat as she headed for Colleen's office, ignoring the protestations of her executive producer's protective assistant.

She knocked once, opened Colleen's door, and stepped inside.

"Hey there," Paula greeted her. She sat in Colleen's chair, her long legs resting atop the desk, the soles of her shoes perfectly clean, as if when she walked she glided inches above the ground. A man sat in the leather guest chair across from her, but his closely cropped, nearly shaved head didn't move or turn.

"I was looking for you all morning," Paula told May, as she played with her thick honey hair. "Charlotte said you were chasing a hot story. Did you catch it?"

May nodded. "I caught it and I threw it back. It was bad news."

"Good. Let it go," Paula said, sounding oddly calm.

"Not so fast. Is it depressing bad news, annoying bad news, or cutting, biting, investigatory Emmy-winning bad news?" With his question, the man swung around. Between his buzz cut and his leathery, tanned skin, it took May a moment to place him. Then he started chewing hard on a plastic nib.

"Gil!" she exclaimed. He stood up to receive her embrace. "When did you get back?"

"This morning. Why is everyone so surprised? I said I was taking a sabbatical. I wasn't fired. All along, I said I was coming back."

"I'm not surprised," she explained, "I'm happy."

"That's what Colleen told me, too. Then she fainted and had to be taken away in an ambulance."

"Really?"

Paula nodded, her eyes harboring a devilish glint. "But first they fought over me. Over who loves me more. That was great," she told Gil. "I really enjoyed it."

He nodded and beamed.

"Why don't I leave you two alone for a while," Paula said, hopping out of Colleen's chair. "I know you have a lot to catch up on. Oh, Gil, I forgot to tell you. May almost got killed again."

Gil chewed harder. He didn't like being reminded of the "episode." That was fine with May. Neither did she.

"How's it going here for you?" he asked when they were alone. Before she could answer, he added, "I don't want you to worry about anything anymore. And if you have any problems, I want you to come to me. I owe you," he added quietly. "I owe you my life."

She rose to the offer. "I want to work three days a week and that's it."

"I did that already. Two days you work from home."

"No. I want three days total. None of this at-home stuff. Three days. That's it."

"Okay," Gil said. "What else?"

"I want Charlotte to be promoted to a producer."

"Is she good?"

"Very."

"Done."

She kept going. "I want you to get rid of Henry."

"No can do. Colleen gave him a five-year contract. Tell you what, though. How about he's your direct report? That way you can train him."

"He's untrainable."

"If I can train a horse, you can train Henry. What else?"

"Make this place fun again. It's been hell with you gone."

She spent a few hours with Gil catching up on the past year. They spent a lot of the time laughing.

"Go home," he told her when Paula buzzed him for a meeting. "Give yourself a break." She didn't argue.

But when she got home, with the girls still at school and Sabrieke off with Manu, she found she wasn't quite ready to take off her shoes and kick back. She had cleaning to do, a ransacking, really.

Starting at the top shelf of the pantry, she worked her way through all the cupboards and drawers searching for products she no longer believed were safe. When she was done, her trash cans were full and her cabinets nearly empty.

She stopped and examined the two small boxes she held in her hands, one orange Jell-O, the other chocolate pudding. She reread the ingredients. Then she thought about her conversation with the pathologist from the CDC. When he had called to set up their appointment, she'd tried to debrief him. He finally told her what she wanted to hear: be safe but don't be crazy. The presentation of the disease contracted by Stacey and her friends was a new variant of Creutzfeldt-Jakob, one no one had ever seen before. There was no way to predict exactly how widespread or virulent this strain would be. It was possible they'd contained it in time, that it killed itself off before spreading.

He told her, "Look, I don't walk around all day scared to eat anything or touch anything. But I'm not stupid about it, either. I know people die from car crashes, but I still ride in a car. I just always wear my seat belt."

It would have made a hell of a show, she thought, and then put it out of her mind. Not yet. Not now. Not when she had a wedding to plan.

She put the Jell-O and chocolate pudding boxes back in the cabinet and then dug into the trash and starting pulling out the rest of the items, returning them to her closet. There would be no organ meats for dinner served any time soon, though. And squirrel stew was permanently off the menu.

"We'll be fine," she said out loud to no one, and then, laughing at herself, quickly knocked on wood.